In Search of
Livi Starling

The *Livi Starling* series

In Search of
Livi Starling

Karen Rosario Ingerslev

PURE&FIRE

In Search of Livi Starling
First published in the UK by Pure & Fire in 2016
Pure & Fire, England
www.pureandfire.com

ISBN: 978-0-9934327-0-5
eBook ISBN: 978-0-9934327-1-2

'You will know the truth, and the truth will set you free.'
— John 8:32

The greatest story ever told

Our new bathroom has a patch of mould on the ceiling that looks a bit like Jesus. When I first spotted it, I wondered if we could make it into a pilgrimage site and charge people to come and see it, but my sister Jill said she couldn't imagine anything worse than a mass of mad fanatics descending on our home.

"I'll ask the landlord to sort it out," she said, adding it to the long list of things that are wrong with the house.

"Can't we keep it?" I asked.

"It's mould, Livi! Do you want to get ill?"

"Surely we won't get ill unless we eat it?"

Jill gave a screech and made me promise not to spend too long in the bathroom until the mould was gone.

"I'm serious," she warned when I giggled. "You can catch all kinds of things from mould."

My sister can be somewhat theatrical when it comes to sickness. She's the sort of person who keeps hand sanitizer in her purse and has the doctor on speed dial. We used to live in the countryside in Suffolk[1] and I lost count of the number of times Jill took herself to A&E with the fear that she had caught bird flu.

I have heard that you're a piece of everybody you've ever known. Every relative, friend or enemy has shaped you into who you are today. So, if you want to be a better person, you need to avoid all the people who are bad for you.

Of course, it's not that simple. You can't choose your family, your neighbours or your classmates, and sometimes you're just in the wrong place at the wrong time.

---

[1] In a tiny village called Little Milking, famous for its miniature cows.

Today, for example, we accidentally became acquainted with a tramp. He was sitting in a doorway in Leeds city centre, asking everyone for 37p.

Jill took pity on him and gave him £1.

As we went sauntering down the street, feeling like we'd done our bit for the homeless, a lady caught up with us and muttered, "He'll spend that on drink, you know."

"Pardon?" Jill looked at the busybody in confusion.

"Drink," the lady repeated. "He's an alcoholic. You're not helping him by funding his addiction."

"Who are you to assume he's an alcoholic?" Jill shot back, affronted at being spoken to so abruptly by a complete stranger. Strangers aren't meant to speak their minds. They're meant to just blend into the background like extras padding out a scene in a movie.

"Ask him."

Jill marched back to the tramp. "What will you spend that pound on?"

"Jusss my bus fare," the tramp slurred. He hiccupped and added, "Definitely *not* my whissssky."

The stranger gave my sister a pitying smile and strolled off.

Jill breathed sharply out of her nose. "Give me my money back."

The tramp opened his mouth and roared with laughter. His teeth were all yellow.

"Give it back," Jill repeated. She put her hand out.

People at a nearby bus stop started to stare.

"Stop it, Jill," I whispered. Wild visions filled my mind. I imagined us on the news: *'Crazed woman murders tramp over one pound coin.'*

The tramp stopped laughing, tucked Jill's pound coin into his pocket and trotted away.

We saw him later in another doorway and I wondered whether he was stalking us. I felt a little sick as he looked up and nodded, as if we were friends or something. I don't want him to be part of who I am.

I am not a tramp and I'm not strange.

I once knew a boy called Toby who ate his scabs. I'm definitely not him either.

Five facts about Livi Teeson Starling
1. _I like writing my name over and over again._
2. _I'm reasonably skilled at imitating animal sounds._[2]
3. _The biggest lie I've ever told is that I'm a famous writer in Japan._
4. _In a crowded room, I often count how many people there are and guess who's going to die first._
5. _Although I have no memory of her, my mother is my most favourite person ever._

Not far from the tramp, we passed a girl singing country songs in a pretty red dress. A big crowd had gathered and her guitar case was full of shiny coins. _Now that's the kind of person I would like to be._ I'm so sure I'd be a better person if my sister was a singer. I tried to squeeze to the front of the crowd, thinking that maybe the girl might look up and catch my eye and somehow cancel out the tramp's mark on my life. But she didn't notice me.

When we got home, Jill discovered a rash on her arm and rang the doctor to ask if tramps carry diseases. In order to ensure that I never become as anxious as my sister, I try to take as many risks as possible[3] and I'm proud to say that I've rarely been ill, although I did once catch fleas from our Aunt Claudia's cats.

Aunt Claudia is another person who, through no fault of my own, is part of who I am. Being more than fifteen years older than our mother would have been, she's almost an aunt and a grandmother rolled into one. Unfortunately, she lacks any of the charm or tenderness that one would hope for in such a diverse family member. She's the only person I know who hates cake and responds to a smile by saying, _"Don't be rude."_ But, since she is our only living relative, I do a good job of tolerating her. She lives in an old farmhouse crammed full of cats of all shapes, smells and sizes. Every time we visit, she has several more. After the flea incident, I tried to tell her that I was allergic but she told me to stop being cruel. She also keeps a field of sheep and frequently sends parcels of frozen lamb in the post. She says it's a brilliant timesaver because by the time it arrives it's defrosted and ready to cook.

Jill used to work in a farm shop close to Aunt Claudia's house and she would often spot our aunt spying on her through

---

[2] I'm particularly proud of my _Tired Meerkat_ and _Hungry Chicken_.
[3] Such as eating crisps after their best before date and only changing my bed sheets once a term.

binoculars from across the field. I sometimes wonder if this contributed to Jill's decision to leave Little Milking.

Until this year, the most adventurous thing my sister had ever done was let me paint her toenails pink. Even then, she kept her feet covered for weeks so that nobody ever saw them. So I was more than a little alarmed when she announced that we would be moving to Leeds.

"Where's Leeds?"

"You know, near London."

"London! Can we live near Buckingham Palace?"

"Don't be silly."

Nothing more was said on the matter and, a few weeks later, we were packed up and ready to go. By then, I had written a long list of all the things I would do with my new life in London and my head was spinning with excitement. I'd had the idea that London was the centre of everything glamorous and that the closer I lived to it, the greater my life would be.

It was at this point that Jill dropped the bombshell. "Oh, by the way, I got it wrong. Leeds isn't near London. It's in Yorkshire."

"Oh! Where's that?"

"About three hours north."

My heart almost shattered into pieces. *Three hours north?*

"Maybe four."

Of course I protested, with as much kicking and screaming as could be considered reasonable. But Jill would not relent. And so we spent the entire summer crawling up and down the motorway as we carted our belongings a million miles away from everything we have ever known. Jill was too nervous to hire a van so we did the whole journey eight times in our tiny tin of a car. The worst moment was when my bed fell off the roof-rack.

~*~

From my assessment today of the city centre, it is fair to say that Leeds is nowhere near as grand as I imagine London would be. It is, however, worlds apart from Little Milking.

Where we used to live, an exciting day was one where a family of ducks was spotted crossing the road. There were more animals than people and the postman only came three times a week. There was a lot of inspiration for stories (like the time I saw a cow fall over and I wrote a poem about a cow who never learned how to walk) but, ultimately, we had to move because everyone in our village was inbred and Jill was worried she would never find a husband.[4] Leeds, on the other hand, is noisy and busy and without a single duck in sight. To my utter delight, not only does the postman come *every* day but we also get all manner of flyers and leaflets arriving unexpectedly through the door. We've been here three days and already we've received thirteen pieces of junk mail including menus for *Filthy Pizzas* and *Wok on the Wild Side*, and a brochure from a local photography studio emblazoned with the words, *'The Greatest Story Ever Told— Yours!'*

The brochure was plastered with images of beautiful models who were quoted to have said things like, *'What a fantastic way to capture the best days of our lives!'* I expect they were trying to entice people to spend lots of money preserving their pretty faces on big canvases. But I don't have lots of money. Or a pretty face. So I just flicked through the brochure, mourning my old life as I wondered how great *my* story really is.

At my old school we had a teacher who tried to make us feel special by hanging a sign on the wall which read, *'You are unique!'* One day, somebody wrote beneath it, *'...just like everybody.'*

With seven billion people in this world, I wonder how special anybody can *truly* be. I don't suppose a teenage girl with an aptitude for animal noises has ever made the history books. We study kings and queens and revolutionists who changed the world. Somebody like me would never get on the news— unless it was because I'd been killed. And, even then, I would have to be killed under newsworthy circumstances. Whenever I catch sight of myself on a CCTV screen, I perfect my *'Tragic Innocent Victim'* face just in case by the evening that image is all that is left of me. Sometimes I turn my head and walk past the cameras a few times in order to give the police the best possible chance of identifying me. Once, a security guard came over and told me to stop messing about. I was aghast at his insensitivity.

"But what if I die today?" I said.

He snatched my shopping basket off me and snapped, "Then you won't need all these sweets." Then he ushered me out as though I was nobody at all.

---

[4] This is a lie but I think it's what I'll tell the students at my new school. The boring and unfair truth is that Jill made me leave because she didn't earn much at the farm shop and decided to get some fancy city job in sales.

Short of being killed dramatically, I'm unlikely to make a very big mark on this world. My life story will only ever be known to me because I am what Jill calls *'a drop in the ocean.'* In other words, I am *ordinary, one-of-many* and *insignificant.* So, after flicking miserably through the photography brochure, I drew moustaches over the models and tossed it aside. And, if it wasn't for the mouldy Jesus on the bathroom ceiling, my story would have ended right there.

But, whilst sitting in the bath tonight, I stared at the ceiling and began to wonder whether we had received the brochure for a reason. *Perhaps I'm not actually destined to be unknown. Perhaps greatness is attainable for anybody who wants it enough. Perhaps our whole move to Leeds is the beginning of something grand...*

I felt my stomach lurch and, although it could've been the evening's takeaway from *Filthy Pizzas*, I was pretty sure it was a divine sign. So I grinned at the mouldy Jesus and decided that, as of today, I would make something of my life. I would no longer be a mere drop in the ocean. Somehow, I would change the world. One day, all mankind would applaud *The Greatest Story Ever Told—Mine.*

I lay blowing bubbles under the water as I contemplated how to begin. I could travel to the moon, or invent something useful, or adopt lots of starving children. I could be a spy and infiltrate some foreign government. I could take a photo of myself every day and gain a million anonymous online followers. Or I could lead many to enlightenment through the art of animal noises. People would come from all over the world to hear me bark and, when asked how I'd got so famous, I would humbly say, *'It all began when I saw Jesus in a patch of mould.'*

I shot another grin at the ceiling, wondering whether the bathroom might become a place of deep revelation. Maybe, if I waited long enough, the mould would even speak to me.

But, before I could indulge for too long, I heard Jill yelling from downstairs, "Get out of the bath, Livi! The mould will make you sick and I've just found a dead mouse in the kitchen!"

I was about to ask for five more minutes but then she started screaming because the mouse wasn't dead after all.

So I got out with a sigh and conceded that I don't have the slightest idea how to be great. I'm just a girl in a mouldy bathroom living with a paranoid sister in a home that is far from holy.

~ 2 ~

Crashing into life

Some people say that everybody has a double and, if you meet, one of you will drop down dead. To begin with, I didn't like Leeds. The city centre was far too busy and I was worried that my double might be lurking somewhere, waiting to pounce. But, after a while, I discovered there are some things that a big city has over the countryside: *'Glorious opportunities!'* as our new neighbour, Belinda Rico, would say.

"You can swim, take ballet classes, or go ten pin bowling," Belinda exclaimed on the first day we met her. "We have an ice rink in winter and a cycle path along the canal. You can even go and visit the sheep at the petting zoo!"

"Great," Jill said dryly. "Because we didn't have sheep in Suffolk."

"In fact," Belinda continued. "I think I have a leaflet for the petting zoo. Come inside and I'll find it for you."

We followed her in, Jill rather reluctantly and me somewhat curious as to whether the houses on their side of the street were as big as ours.[5]

"Darling, we have visitors!" Belinda sang, beckoning us into the kitchen where a tall, ginger man was stirring a pan on the stove.

"Gooseberry jam," he said, giving his concoction a delicate poke. "Or *Stachelbeermarmelade* as the Germans would say."

"Oh," Jill said politely. "Are you German?"

---

[5] Actually, they're slightly bigger. Our house is a back-to-back terraced house which means we share our back wall with another house. Such houses were popular in the Victorian era but they were deemed unhealthy due to limited ventilation so there aren't many left in England now. I haven't yet decided whether this fact makes me feel special or poor.

13

"No. I'm Stanley." He held out a sticky hand and then reconsidered and bobbed his head instead.

Belinda laughed and gave a little snort.

I suppressed a giggle as Jill looked at them in confusion.

"Jill and Livi have just moved into Mr Denby's old place," Belinda informed her husband. When Stanley gave a blank look, she added, "You know; the elderly chap who fell down the stairs and died."

I crossed my fingers and hoped that Jill had his bedroom and not me.

Stanley nodded. "Nice to meet you. How are you settling in?"

"Fine, thank you." Jill forced one of the smiles that she gives when she can't be bothered to make small talk. We had only spoken to Belinda in the first place because we'd lost our bearings on the way home from the corner shop and absentmindedly tried to open the wrong door.

Stanley scooped up some jam on a spoon. He offered it first to Jill who shook her head in horror and then to Belinda who slurped it up like a fruit bat.[6]

"Delicious!" Belinda simpered. Then she turned to us and asked the dreaded question: "So, Jill, do you have any other children?"

Jill forced another smile. "We're sisters, actually. Our mother died when Livi was a baby. It's been the two of us ever since."

"Oh!" Belinda clutched her heart and almost fell over. Then she took Jill's face in her hands and cooed over her as if she were some small furry creature. "You poor, poor thing! Bringing up that girl all by yourself. What a hero!"

Jill looked like she was tempted to bite off Belinda's fingers but she pulled away and said calmly, "Well, it was lovely to meet you. We really should go and unpack a little more—"

"Not so fast!" Belinda held up her hand like Aunt Claudia training a kitten. "I promised you this leaflet. Come with me!"

Jill tried not to grimace as she was dragged into the sitting room. I followed at a distance and watched curiously as Belinda opened a large brown bureau causing a plethora of leaflets, take away menus and church bulletins to flutter to the floor. I noted that Belinda wasn't taking quite as much care over her junk mail as I was over ours. I was still keeping everything that came though our

---

[6] It was quite a good noise. I practised it when I got home.

14

door and by now I had a pretty sizeable pile. I made a mental note to ask Jill for a bureau to keep them in.

"Now then, where oh where..?" Belinda sifted through the mountain of leaflets before reconsidering and scooping up the whole lot. "Oh, have them all!" she said, thrusting the bundle into our arms.

"Thank you." Jill gave a stiff smile and carefully sneaked a church bulletin back onto the floor.

Suddenly, there was a shriek. The bulletin had bounced off the carpet and hit a small child in the face.

"I'm so sorry!" my sister exclaimed, turning red as Belinda swept over to console the crying infant.

"My precious pumpkin, are you alright? Did you get a paper cut? Are you bleeding? Stanley, come in quickly! Oscar's got something in his eye!"

Mr Rico came rushing in to tip the child upside down and check it wasn't broken. The whole time, Jill apologised profusely and offered her assistance while I pored over the leaflets in my hands. I saw one about water sports and wondered whether Leeds had a beach. Perhaps I could take up surfing. I imagined myself as *'Livi Starfish— the greatest surfer ever known...'*

Five minutes later, we'd learnt that the child was called Oscar Stanley Rico. He was three years old, he liked sleeping on the rug in the sitting room like a dog, he had an IQ that qualified him as a gifted child[7] and his first word had been *'Crucify.'* Despite the fact that Jill had just thrown a church bulletin at his head, Oscar seemed rather taken with my sister. He clutched her skirt with a snotty hand and asked if she wanted to see his room.

Jill wrenched her skirt away and began, "Not today—" but then Oscar's lip started to quiver so she said instead, "Well, alright. Quickly."

"Good boy, Oscar," Belinda simpered as Jill and I followed the chubby boy up the stairs. "Show Auntie Jill your astronauts."

Jill chuckled but, as soon as we were out of earshot, she hissed, "Never *ever* call me Auntie Jill!"

Oscar gave a toothy grin and led us to his bedroom where he introduced us to a squad of seven spacemen[8] and proceeded to

---

[7] "What kind of gifted child cries when a piece of paper lands on their head?" Jill snapped later when I teased her for maiming an infant.

[8] A bunch of dolls with chopped-off hair, painted beards and toilet paper spacesuits.

recite the planets in order. I didn't think you could learn much from a three year old, but I found his lecture on 'The Bodies of the Solar System' mildly fascinating. I didn't know, for example, that Pluto used to be considered a planet but is now only a dwarf planet.

Jill took great offence at such claims. "Of course it's a planet," she said irritably. "I dressed up as Pluto for my school science show."

Oscar let out a squeal. "Silly! You can't leave my house until you say that Pluto isn't a planet!"

I raised an eyebrow and glanced at Jill.

She pursed her lips as she told Oscar, "Pluto is a planet."

"No it isn't!"

"Yes it is."

"No it isn't!"

"Yes it—"

"Jill!" I hissed. "Just say it's not a planet."

Jill glared at me. I think it made her feel old to realise that science has evolved since she was at school. She turned back to Oscar. "Yes it is."

"We're never going to leave," I moaned.

Jill sucked in her breath and stared at Oscar.

He beamed and said, "No it isn't."

After a painful stand-off that seemed to last hours, we finally realised that a three year old, however gifted, had no power to take us hostage.

Jill said one last, "Yes it is," before grabbing my arm and dragging me down the stairs. "Let's go," she muttered.

We were halfway through the door when we heard Belinda calling from the kitchen, "Girls! I've made something for you!"

Jill gave a silent groan before reapplying her smile and wandering back into the kitchen. "We really ought to—"

"Gooseberry tarts!" Belinda held up a freshly-baked tray of heart-shaped tarts and beckoned us to come and sit down. Then she sat, looking incredibly proud of herself, as we forced the entire batch into our mouths and gave her overgenerous noises of approval. "They like the jam, Stanley!"

He nodded shyly. "I'll give you some to take home."

"It's fine," Jill insisted.

But Stanley was already in the basement hunting for jars. We had to wait fifteen minutes while he disinfected some old milk bottles and filled them with jam.

Then, just as we were *finally* about to get away, Belinda pulled out a diary teeming with various engagements and stood blocking the doorway until we'd set a dinner date for the following evening. "Come round at seven," she trilled as she scrawled our names across her diary. "You don't need to bring anything."

My sister nodded and inched closer to the doorway.

Belinda seemed to mistake Jill's move towards her for an attempt at a hug. "Oh, come here!" she exclaimed as she gathered the two of us into her bosom. "You're so welcome!"

Jill gave a thin smile and pulled away. She lunged out of the house with such force that she almost twisted her ankle on the doorstep.

"Goodness, Jill! Are you alright?"

"Yes, yes! It's just a little windy out here. You'll want to keep the heat in." Before Belinda could reply, Jill leant over and pulled the front door shut.

"Do you think everybody in Leeds will be like them?" I asked as we sprinted across the street.

"Don't be daft," Jill replied through gritted teeth. "Most people wouldn't be that friendly." She said this as though being friendly was a bad thing. My sister is quite antisocial. I wouldn't call her embarrassing as such, but I'm certainly the cool one. If I could have any superpower, I would like to be able to fly. Jill would just like to be invisible.

My sister had every intention of getting us out of our dinner date with the Ricos but, just as she was about to pop across the street to say that I was bedridden with the flu, Belinda came over unannounced and said in a sing-song voice, "Hope you girlies haven't forgotten about our dinner arrangements tonight!" Then she waltzed into the kitchen, had a nosy peek into our empty fridge and raised an eyebrow at the plate of sausage rolls left over from lunch. "Jill, dear... I have a whole shelf of cooking books that I can lend you. Don't ever feel that you and Livi have to go without." She took my face in her hands. "We'll have to feed you up, won't we!"

After that, Jill was worried that if we didn't attend dinner then Belinda might accuse her of trying to starve me, so we had no other option but to go.

Oscar the gifted child was ready for us when we arrived. "Auntie Jill," he said in an annoying whine. "Do you remember what happened to Pluto?"

"Yes, Oscar," my sister replied. "And do *you* remember what I said would happen if you called me Auntie Jill?"

"You didn't say. You just told me not to do it. But I want to." He started chanting really loudly, "Auntie Jill! Auntie Jill! Auntie Jill!"

I waited to see what Jill would do. Perhaps she would throw something heavier at him this time. But, before anything exciting could happen, Belinda appeared and proclaimed with all the splendour of a fairy godmother, "Livi, meet your new best friend!"

A girl with wavy red hair peeked out from behind Belinda's curvy frame. She stared at me but didn't say anything. She wore a baggy black t-shirt bearing the words, 'Nietzsche is dead,' and she looked incredibly solemn, like she wished *she* was dead, and I wondered if the t-shirt was out of mourning or something.

Nobody spoke for a moment so I took the initiative. "Hello."

She nodded and kept staring.

"This is Ruby!" said Belinda. "The two of you can walk to school together and sit in class together and do your homework together!" *Never has the word 'together' sounded so disturbing.*

I forced a smile but said nothing.

"Dinner's almost ready," Belinda continued, ushering us towards the sitting room. "Why don't you and Ruby get to know each other while I check on the swede."

"Would you like some help, Belinda?" Jill asked, clearly torn between meeting the strange girl and spending more time with Belinda.

"Oh, not at all!" Belinda chuckled. "It only needs one person to check on the swede."[9]

When we entered the sitting room, we were met by the peculiar sight of five black balloons tied to a red umbrella surrounded by a mountain of red books, red shoes, red toilet roll tubes and enough feathers to fly a cow to the moon. In the middle of it all sat a skinny girl with wavy red hair— an older and far more vibrant version of

---

[9] I would have to disagree with Belinda. Before now, we had only had swede once. It was at Aunt Claudia's and Jill and I had no idea how to cook it, whether or not to peel it, or how to tell when it was done. Of course, I didn't repeat this to Belinda. Neither did Jill. She just fixed a smile onto her face and followed me and Ruby down the hall.

Ruby— covered in red paint and bits of sticky back plastic. She looked like she'd just massacred a field of chickens.

"Hello," she said, as if it was the most normal thing in the world.

Ruby said nothing and Oscar went over to the rug to sleep like a dog.

"I'm Violet," the girl continued to me and Jill. "And, in case you were wondering, this is a butterfly." She flapped a feathery arm.

Neither Ruby nor Oscar made as if to mock their sister but I felt that somebody ought to so I said gallantly, "Really? Looks more like a dead chicken."

"Does it?" Violet tipped her head to one side and considered her monstrous creation. "Yes, I see that." She dabbed a little more paint onto her nose and grinned.

"It wasn't a compliment!" I spluttered. Jill elbowed me so I added, "I'm Livi, by the way."

"I know," Violet replied. "And you're Jill and you're sisters and she brought you up because your mother died."

"Nicely put," Jill muttered. She pretended to study the bookshelves.

I rolled my eyes and perched awkwardly on the sofa next to Ruby. Ruby stared at me and said nothing. She kept fiddling with the rim of her 'Nietzsche is dead' t-shirt and I was so close that I could see right into her eyes and it was like staring into an empty void. I started to feel anxious. Maybe she wanted revenge for whoever killed Nietzsche. Or maybe *she* had killed Nietzsche and was proud of this and was, in fact, about to kill *me*. I wondered if maybe her entire family were cannibals and maybe Oscar the gifted child was their leader and he was only pretending to be asleep on the rug. Perhaps, when Belinda said she was checking on the swede, she meant an actual Swedish person and they needed me and Jill for variety because we're a bit Welsh.

Ruby coughed and I almost screamed.

"So..." I began uneasily. "I suppose we could be friends..." I didn't mean this. I had no desire to be her friend. I was just looking for a way to stall for time before she killed me.

Ruby nodded and gave a small smile.

In the silence that followed, I glanced around the room in a bid to pretend that Ruby wasn't staring at me. Other than a handful of fresh flyers poking out from the brown bureau and the monstrosity that was Violet's *butterfly,* the entire room was very neat and ordered. The cushions were perfectly plumped, the shelves were dust-free, and the photos on the wall looked as though they had been captured at the *Greatest Story Ever Told* photography studio, although nobody was as beautiful as the models in the pamphlet. On another wall was a large tapestry emblazoned with the words *'Rico Family Tree'* above a web of complex squiggles joining hundreds of names together. Part of me wanted to get up and have a closer look but a stronger part of me insisted on remaining cool and aloof.

I turned back to Violet who was panting wildly as she blew up another black balloon. "The butterfly's spots," she explained, waving the balloon in the air. "And this plastic is the cocoon." When I didn't answer, she continued in a superior voice, "If you don't understand, it's because it's modern art." When I still said nothing, she added, "That's why I didn't mind when you called it a dead chicken. It meant I'd succeeded in creating a piece that works on many levels."

I brushed a feather off my foot. "Good..."

"What do *you* think it looks like, Jill?" Violet turned eagerly to my sister.

"Yeah, Jill," I said sweetly. "What do *you* think it looks like?"

Jill gave me a funny look. "I don't know... A car crash..."

"A car crash?" Violet's face fell.

"I didn't mean it in a bad way!" my sister said quickly. "It's a... very *beautiful* car crash..."

"Really?" Violet glanced at Jill before saying rather pompously, "My Art teacher said I'm one of the most ambitious students she's ever taught."

Jill raised her eyebrows but said nothing.

"I won a painting contest when I was nine."

Jill smiled politely. I caught her eye and smirked.

Violet gave an airy sigh. "I've had an idea. Ruby, can I borrow your bike lights?" Before Ruby could reply, Violet leapt off the floor, red paint dripping everywhere, and exclaimed, "I'm going to call it *'Crashing into Life!'*"

Oscar awoke at that moment and fell into hysterics as he pointed at the toilet roll on the end of Violet's chin.

Then Belinda came in and said quite innocently, "Dinner's ready— Oh, Violet! You have a tiny smudge of paint on your face."

Jill and I exchanged a quick look, trying not to laugh as we followed Belinda into the dining room. Mr Rico had just finished setting the table and was now lighting a candle and straightening a dark red tablecloth. It clashed horribly with his hair. I wondered why they were making such a special effort, just for us, but later I found out that this was how they had dinner *every* night. I didn't know whether to envy them or pity them. It looked like far too much work.

Once we'd taken our seats, Belinda dished out the meal[10] and then everybody except me and Jill held hands and shut their eyes.

Violet began to speak. "Thank you, Lord, for—"

"Shut your eyes!" Oscar roared suddenly. He grabbed his cutlery and pointed his knife at me and his fork at Jill.

I shifted in my seat and wondered whether to make a dash for the door.

"Oh, sorry girls!" Belinda opened her eyes and gave us a pitying smile. "Is this strange for you?"

It was very strange for me because I'd gone back to thinking that maybe they really were cannibals and that Violet was calling Oscar 'Lord' and, if he wasn't their leader, then how did he know that we didn't have our eyes closed? And I'm sure it must have been strange for Jill because we never *ever* shut our eyes when we eat, but she just said calmly, "No. It's not strange..."

Belinda beamed and said, "Marvellous!"

Violet concluded her speech, "Thank you, Lord, for our food and for Mum cooking it and for the lovely sunrise we had this morning. And thank you for Jill and Livi moving to Leeds and being our new neighbours. Amen."

And that's when I realised she wasn't praising Oscar. She was talking to God.

The Ricos started devouring their pie and Jill began slowly cutting up her carrots, but I sat for a moment in shock. Did Violet really thank *God* for Jill and me moving to Leeds and being their new neighbours? Surely she should have thanked Jill's new boss for giving her a job. Or Mr Denby for falling down his stairs and dying. I felt like Violet had just issued God with a formal introduction to our existence and I wondered what he thought of that. Then I became aware of Ruby staring at me again and I didn't want her to think that I didn't know who God was or something, so I mashed up some swede and stuffed it into my mouth.

"So, Jill," Belinda said, a piece of carrot hanging off her lip. "Tell us about your new job!"

---

[10] Some kind of pie with white sauce and vegetables. Belinda had arranged the carrots to look like a face. This terrified me.

Jill wiped her own mouth, probably worried that she too had food hanging off her face, and said, "I'm going to be one of the sales managers for *Undone Media.*"

"I understand," said Belinda, with the tone of someone who clearly didn't. "And what will you be selling?"

"Advertising space."

"Advertising space?"

"Yes. Advertising space."

Belinda chewed her pie and eyed Jill thoughtfully. Finally, she asked, "How does one go about selling advertising space?"

Jill took a deep breath and explained how her job would involve ringing up various companies in an attempt to cajole them into paying large sums of money to advertise in one of the many magazines produced by *Undone Media.* "All the advertising in *'Busty Week,'* for example, I'll arrange that."

Belinda and Stanley nodded politely. They obviously didn't read *'Busty Week.'*

"When do you start?" Belinda asked.

"Wednesday."

"What time?"

"Er..." Jill shrugged, clearly embarrassed by the onslaught of questions.

"Because if you need to leave early, Livi can always come for breakfast."

"Oh, she won't need to—"

"Or, if you're working late, she can come here after school. What time do you finish?"

"Er..." Jill looked incredibly flustered.

I would have felt sorry for her except that I was using all my brain power to send telepathic messages warning her not to agree to Belinda's hideous plan.

When Belinda had exhausted all the questions regarding Jill's new job and where it was and what it involved and whether or not she would have her own office, she moved on to more personal matters. "How did your mother die?"

"Pneumonia," Jill mumbled.

"Grandma died of that!" Violet piped up. "It was the worst day of my life."

Jill forced a smile and looked down, concentrating hard on her pie.

"How old were you?" Violet continued.

"Seventeen." Jill said this very quickly and then asked Ruby to pass her the water.

I shot Violet an angry glare as she exclaimed, "My age! Wow!"

In an attempt to change the subject, Belinda asked, "And where's your father?"

Jill took a long time over her mouthful before muttering, "I never met my father. Livi's is in London."

Belinda didn't even try to hide her surprise. "Oh! You have different fathers?"

I gave a careless sniff, as if daring her to judge us.

Belinda composed herself and turned to me. "So, Livi, where in London does your father live?"

Before I could answer, Jill jumped in with, "The centre."

"I see," said Belinda. "Westminster?"

"Somewhere near there," Jill said tersely.[11]

Belinda pressed on. "What does your father do, Livi?"

Jill opened her mouth to speak for me but I said loudly, "He's an actor."

"An actor?"

"Yes. He's playing Hamlet at the moment."

Jill raised an eyebrow but I ignored her. If she was going to tell tales about my father then I could too.

"Oh really?" Belinda looked suitably impressed.

"That's so cool," Violet agreed.

Ruby gave half a smile.

It seemed I had redeemed us. I grinned before adding, "And, before she died, our mother was a famous ballerina." Jill gave me a sharp look but I ignored her. "Her stage name was *Precious Starling* and—"

I stopped with a yelp as Jill kicked me under the table. "Our mother worked at a bar," she said curtly.

"She was the lead singer of a cabaret act," I insisted. "*Superb Starling and the Chicks—*"

"She pulled pints and served snacks," Jill snapped.

I sniffed and turned back to my food.

"*'Livi'* is an interesting name," Stanley said suddenly. "Is it short for anything?"

---

[11] This was a complete lie. We have no idea where my father is. He used to live in Upper Sulking, the village next to Little Milking, and we saw him quite a bit. Then, one day, just after my seventh birthday, he suddenly vanished. We've not heard from him since.

"Living Creature," I lied.[12]

"How wonderful!" gushed Belinda as Jill rolled her eyes.

Dinner was followed by apple crumble. I didn't want to like it. I wanted to be able to tell Jill later that I'd hated it and that I much prefer dessert when we have half a chocolate bar each. But I'm ashamed to say it was delicious. Their company almost seemed worth the ordeal if we could have such a tasty treat at the end of it.[13]

"Do you know how to make crumble, Jill?" Belinda asked as she offered us seconds.

Jill shook her head.

"I'll teach you."

"Even *I* know how to make crumble!" Oscar exclaimed. "She also didn't know that Pluto's not a planet!"

This made Belinda toss her head back and laugh at her witty little genius offspring. "Ah, yes Oscar," she cooed. "I expect you could teach Auntie Jill a lot!"

"I hate that woman. I HATE her!" Jill yelled as soon as we got home. She slammed the front door so hard that a piece of the doorframe splintered and fell off.[14] *"'Where's your father?' 'Can you make crumble?'* Who does she think she is?"

"What about Ruby!" I protested. "She didn't say a word all evening. She just *stared* at me! I don't want to be her friend."

Normally, Jill would've jumped in with a reproach such as, *'Don't be mean,'* or, *'Give her a chance,'* but, on this occasion, she just sniffed and said, "You'll make new friends in a week or two and then you can ditch her."

Well, it's been a month and Ruby is still my only friend. She's not too bad once you get over the creepy intenseness.

---

[12] Actually, it isn't short for anything. My mother was called Livi and she passed it on to me. According to Aunt Claudia, my grandparents got the name off a packet of biscuits whilst on holiday in Barcelona.

[13] I still pretended to Jill that I hadn't liked it. I think she knew I was lying because I was kind of salivating when I said it, but hopefully it made her feel better anyway.

[14] Another thing to tell the landlord. When Jill phoned him with her list, he said he'd be *'right on it.'* Judging from the fact that he's not called back, that seems to be code for *'not my problem.'*

~ 3 ~

Violet's every flavour Bible Dip

Getting to know Ruby was a bit like getting to know a pet fish. Not as rewarding as training a puppy, but remarkably satisfying when she began to swim my way.

"Do you like reading?" I asked during our first week together.

No answer.

"Can you ice skate?"

Blank look.

"Would you like to go to the petting zoo with me?"

Nothing.

I asked about school, about Leeds (which, to my dismay, does not have a beach), and about her crazy family.[15] I even asked where she got her *'Nietzsche is dead'* t-shirt and whether there were others in the same range; perhaps *'Shakespeare is dead,'* or, *'Long Live Bigfoot.'* But she just stared at me and chewed her fingernails.

A breakthrough finally came one lunchtime. We'd just had double Maths with a man who is fast becoming my least favourite person in the world. His name is Mr Lester but I heard a sixth former refer to him as *'Fester'* which I think suits him better. He is as tall as a door and twice as dull and he behaves as though his ability to perform complicated mathematics makes him a better person than us. He uses such phrases as, *'Show me your eyes so I know that you're listening,' 'It's your own time you're wasting,'* and, *'Stop disrupting the learning environment,'* he repeatedly calls me *'Libby'* despite the fact that he has my name in writing on the register, and I think he only has two shirts. During this particular lesson, he'd made me stand in front of the entire class because I'd forgotten to bring a calculator.

"In my old school we didn't need calculators," I had lied.

---

[15] I didn't call them crazy to her face.

"In that case, perhaps you can calculate the following angle in your head!" Fester replied as he drew a sloppy triangle across the white board and labelled two of its sides.

"Can *you* do it, Sir?" I asked.

"Without a calculator? Of course not!"

"Well, my old Maths teacher could. She was really brainy."

At this, some of the class laughed. I smiled a bit and stole a glance at Kitty Warrington.

Kitty Warrington is popular and funny. I wish Jill and I had moved to *her* street instead of Ruby's. I imagine her mother saying, *'Livi, meet your new best friend!'* and Kitty appearing and saying, *'Wow, just this morning I was hoping a new girl would arrive. We can walk to school together and sit in class together and do our homework together!'* Everyone would like me because Kitty Warrington would like me. When students passed me in the corridor, they'd call things like, *'Hey Livi! How's it going?'* instead of shouting at Ruby, *'Oi Weirdo! Who's the new girl?'* Kitty and I would spend our weekends at the petting zoo and she would teach me how to do a northern accent. I would read her my life story and she would say, *'That's the greatest story I've ever heard! I have an uncle who can get you published!'* Or we'd hang around outside the chip shop and sometimes her older brother, Jason, would come too. And, even though I don't fancy him, *he* would fancy *me* and all the girls in my year would say, *'Wow, that new girl Livi is so cool.'*

But Kitty wasn't laughing. She was busy texting someone on her bright pink phone. I don't think she'd even noticed I was standing.

Fester wasn't impressed with what he called my *'smart remark'* and gave me extra homework as a punishment. I was halfway through bemoaning the incident to a mute Ruby when I got up with my banana peel and aimed for the bin.

"Wait!" Ruby squeaked. "Are you throwing that away?"

I gave her a funny look. "I've eaten the banana, so... yeah."

She blushed. "Can I have the sticker?"

I turned the banana skin over and peeled off the sticker. "This?"

"Yes please. If you don't want it."

I looked at her in surprise. A week of silence and now this. "I don't want it..."

Ruby took the sticker from me. "Thanks."

I watched open-mouthed as she dug into her bag and pulled out a large black portfolio. She flicked through pages and pages of colourful stickers until she came to a half-filled sheet. Then she stuck the sticker in, shut the book and lapsed back into silence.

I stared at her for a moment. "How many have you got?"

"682."

"That's quite a lot."

She blushed again.

I think she expected me to laugh or maybe ask why she had such a ridiculous hobby. But I had been eating bananas all week and this was the first time she'd found the courage to speak to me. I was afraid of scaring her. Instead I said, "Can I see them again?"

Ruby opened her book and I gasped as I took it all in. Don't get me wrong, it was weird, *definitely weird*, but I was taken aback by the sheer variety of colours, cartoon characters and brand names.

"These are my favourite..." Ruby flicked to a page filled with jolly-looking monkeys.

"Nice."

"Do you think it's silly?"

I thought about Kitty Warrington and her bright pink phone and was pretty sure that she and her brother Jason didn't collect banana stickers. "It's not silly," I said. "It's... cool."

Ruby gave a shy smile and put her book away.

Keen to capitalise on this breakthrough and not wishing for Ruby to become mute again, I said quickly, "Can you help me with the extra homework from Fester? I mean, will you talk me through it, nice and loud?" I rummaged around for my Maths book.

Ruby took it from me and frowned. "I don't know. Do you want me to ask Violet?" She indicated her sister who had just wandered into the canteen. "She's good at maths."

I made a great show of considering this, careful not to hurt Ruby's feelings, but, in truth, I would rather run round school naked than ask a favour from Violet Rico. Violet may look like a normal teenager (except for her bright red hair which makes her look like she's on fire) but, underneath it all, she's a zealous little shrew who listens to every word you say and writes it all down in a navy blue journal so that she can remind you of it later. She keeps a tiny Bible in her back pocket and whips it out smugly at the faintest whiff of bad behaviour, which no doubt makes her very unpopular with her classmates. She and Ruby share a bedroom so, if I plan to spend any time round their house, it will be hard to escape her. Their bedroom is full of Violet's art, all of it as complex and experimental as the dead-chicken-butterfly she was making on the day we first met. Across one of their walls is a colossal painting of Jesus Christ hanging on a cross.[16]

When I first saw it, I said to Ruby, "A bit morbid, isn't it—having a picture of a dying man on your wall?"

Ruby, being mute at the time, had simply stared at me.

Violet, however, jumped up and exclaimed, "I can't believe you just said that!" She grabbed her journal and started scribbling furiously, muttering to herself the whole time. I heard her say my name and '*God*' several times in the same sentence which made me feel uneasy. I've made an effort to avoid her ever since.

I watched over Ruby's shoulder as Violet waltzed over to an empty table and sat down. She made a big show of covering the chair beside her with a grotesque paper mâché lion. Its mane was so huge that it clipped the backs of the heads of the girls at the table behind her. The girls turned and called Violet a freak.

Violet gave a conceited sneer and replied, "I'd rather be a freak than a child of the devil."

I shuddered. She may as well have been wearing a sign bearing the words, '*I hate you all. Feel free to kick me.*'

"No, don't ask Violet," I said. "She looks busy."

Ruby nodded solemnly. "His name is Paul."

"Who?"

She cocked her head towards her sister. "The lion." This was said without the faintest flicker of emotion so I had no idea what response, if any, she was expecting.

"Okay..." I muttered.

As Ruby lapsed back into silence, I stole another glance at her wacky sister.

Violet had her Bible in her hands and was whizzing through it at lightning speed. I sucked in my cheeks as I watched her. I'd encountered this frenzied behaviour before and knew exactly what she was doing. It was Violet's strange way of making decisions.

I'd first witnessed this on my second day at school. I was lost on my way to Geography and stumbled upon Violet sitting in the middle of the corridor, muttering to herself as irritated fellow students climbed over her.

"Oh, hello Livi!" she said as I approached.

I forced a smile and asked why she was blocking the corridor.

---

[16] Underneath, in Violet's curly scrawl, is written, '*God loved the people of this world so much that he gave his only Son, so that everyone who has faith in him will have eternal life and never really die. —John 3:16*'

"Just asking God something."

"Excuse me?"

She patted her Bible. "I have a free period and couldn't decide whether to go to the Art studio and work on my printing project or to the library to do some research for my Sociology coursework."

"Well, what do you *want* to do?"

"Don't know." She shut her eyes and flicked through her Bible, whispering, "Yeah, God. Show me the way..." Then she stuck her finger in the Bible, opened her eyes and read, "'*Of making many books there is no end, and much study wearies the body...*' Art studio it is!" She stood up, picked up her bag and wandered off, leaving me gaping after her.

She calls this method a *'Bible Dip'* and she swears by it (except she doesn't swear). "He never fails me!" she said snootily when I questioned her about it later. "Anything I ask, he answers!"

I find it strange that she's so sure that God is listening. Surely God, if he's real at all, has better things to do than to answer all the pointless questions she throws at him. If I was God, I would tell her to get a life.

On this particular occasion, it looked as though Violet was using her Bible to help her choose between a chocolate muffin and a pot of carrot sticks.[17]

"She calls it a Bible Dip," Ruby whispered as I continued to stare.

I turned back to Ruby and tried to smile. "Yeah, I know." I paused before adding, "Do *you* do that?"

Ruby blushed and shook her head.

I breathed a sigh of relief, hopeful that Ruby might not be too crazy after all. Then, before the silence could descend, I asked, "Can I see your stickers again?"

My old school was so small that everybody knew each other and news travelled so fast that sometimes the teachers knew things before they even happened— like the time Jill crashed the car on the way to the market.

---

[17] The muffin won.

I was in Science when Mrs Andrews approached my desk and said, "Livi, I hope Jill is alright?"

Seconds later the school secretary came in with the message that Jill had broken her wrist and I would need to walk home.

Mrs Andrews raised her eyebrows as if to say, *'I thought as much.'*

This new school is different. Some of my teachers still don't know my name. They say things like, "Did your mother receive the bulletin for new students?" and I reply, "Yes, thank you. She enjoyed it hugely."

In my History class I even said, "My mum took me to visit Auschwitz last year," and nobody questioned me.

And in French I said, "Ma mère est dans l'Alcatraz et ma soeur est enceinte,"[18] which was a lot more exciting than saying, *'My mother is dead and I live with my sister.'* Madame Maurel nodded absently and the rest of the class were asleep.

When I got into it, it was just too tempting to be a different person in every lesson. So our form tutor, Miss Fairway, thinks I'm part of a travelling circus; our History teacher thinks I'm Winston Churchill's great great granddaughter and that I live with my unemployed mother who keeps bees; our English teacher thinks I have a rare condition that prevents me from being able to read; and our Religious Studies teacher thinks I'm Jewish. I tried to tell Fester that I was allergic to maths. I wasn't completely lying as I often feel itchy in his lessons.[19] But unfortunately he didn't believe me. When he found out that I hadn't done my extra homework he made me stand up in front of the whole class again.

"Well, Libby," he said in an annoying drawl. "I expect you're about to tell me that you didn't have to do homework at your old school?"

I rolled my eyes. "My name is *Livi* and of course we had to do our homework— but only if our parents could understand it."

"Excuse me?"

"I showed it to my sister and she couldn't do any of it."[20]

My classmates shifted in their seats as Fester folded his arms.

---

[18] *"My mother is in Alcatraz and my sister is pregnant."*
[19] Perhaps he owns lots of cats. I can imagine him as a younger, male version of Aunt Claudia; a social recluse sending lumps of maths in the post.
[20] Jill's exact words were, "What is that rubbish? What have triangles got to do with real life?"

"My sister's very clever," I continued. "But she said this didn't make any sense." I pointed to my Maths book. "Therefore I assumed that I didn't have to do it. I'm sorry if I was mistaken."

A few people laughed. Kitty Warrington was looking at me oddly. I saw her whisper something to Molly Masterson, the plump girl beside her. Next to me, Ruby was cowering in her chair, as if petrified that Fester might blame her for my cheek. I took the opportunity to gaze around the room and wonder who would be the first of us to die and what I would do if it happened right now.

Fester looked at me for a long time. Then he said, "You were indeed mistaken. Do it now."

"Yes, Sir."

I sat down and started drawing flowers. I wondered what a detention would be like. I'd been a model student at my old school. I had to be— our form groups were tiny, many of the teachers were parents of my friends and the head teacher lived on my street. This school is different. It's massive. So is Leeds. If I wanted to become a wild child or rebel this would be the perfect time to reinvent myself...

"Libby Starling!" Fester's roar brought me back to reality. "Are you working or would you like to come back and do it at lunchtime?"

"I'm doing it," I said, quickly scribbling over my doodles.

On the way home from school, Ruby and I saw a squashed hedgehog by the side of a busy road. Other than its face which was a mess, it looked rather handsome.

"Oh, poor thing!" Ruby said when she saw it.

I frowned and poked it with my foot.

"You silly animal." Ruby peered closer. "You shouldn't have tried to cross such a busy road."

"Maybe it didn't know it was only a hedgehog," I suggested. Having grown up in the countryside, I generally don't feel any sentiment upon seeing a dead animal in the street.

"Poor thing," Ruby repeated, shaking her head as she moved away. "I wonder where it was going?"

I tried to come up with a clever quip but couldn't think of anything. "Dunno."

We continued walking in silence.

After a few minutes, I coughed and asked, "How do you want to die?"

Ruby stopped in shock. "I don't know! Why?"

"Everybody has to die. Don't you ever wonder how you'll go?"
She blushed and shook her head.

We walked a little further before Ruby gave me a curious look.
"What about you? How do *you* want to die?"

"I'm not sure," I admitted. "I can't decide between quietly in my sleep when I'm old... or something spectacular like falling out of a plane."

Ruby gave a splutter. "That would hurt!"

"It would make a great story though."

"But you wouldn't be around to hear it."

I shrugged and we lapsed back into silence. I debated initiating some chit-chat about school or Fester or Violet's latest art project. But nothing came to mind that could follow the sight of a mangled hedgehog.

A short while later, we reached our street. Violet was sitting on the curb, mending the nose of Paul, the paper mâché lion.

"Hey, Violet!" I called. "I have a question for your Bible."

She raised an eyebrow.

"Why did the hedgehog cross the road?"

"What?" Violet eyed us suspiciously.

Ruby squirmed. "We saw a dead hedgehog on the way home."

"Oh." Violet gave me an odd look and pulled out her Bible. As she waved it, she cautioned, "It's not a game, you know."

"I know," I said, in the most serious voice I could muster. "I just want to see what it says."

Violet sighed and murmured, "Dear God, we want to know why the hedgehog crossed the road..."

I tried not to smirk as she flicked through the pages and opened it at a random passage.

"How sweet are your words to my taste, sweeter than honey to my mouth," she read sombrely.

I blinked at her. "What's that meant to mean?"

Violet thought for a moment. "It means the hedgehog was hungry."

I let out a snigger. "That's stupid."

Violet snatched up her paper mâché lion and stood up with a grunt. "I told you it wasn't a game!" she scolded. Then she went indoors, muttering something to God as she left.

I gave Ruby a shrug. "Bye then."

"Bye," she said shyly. "See you tomorrow."

I smiled and let myself into my house, noting that since Jill's car wasn't on the street she must still be at work. She works late most days and, when she's not actually *at* work, she's moaning because there's a whole mountain of work that she *should* be doing. It all sounds incredibly tedious to me. I don't know what was wrong with her old job. But, when I suggested we pack up and move back to Little Milking, Jill snorted and said, "Do you realise how little I got paid at that farm?"

"You liked it though."

"I couldn't do *anything* on that income!"

Apparently, it makes better sense to work endless hours at a job you hate so that you can save up for the life you'd like.

I dumped my school bag in the hallway and ran upstairs to use the bathroom. As I sat on the toilet, I hummed to myself and looked up at the mouldy Jesus. The landlord still hasn't done anything about it. The last time Jill tried to phone him I suggested that we also ask for some money off the rent on account of the fact that somebody died here. But Jill told me not to be daft.

I considered the mouldy Jesus as I asked, "Why did the hedgehog die?"

Of course, the mould didn't answer.

"Was it a horrible accident or was it just the right time for it to go? Did it have a nice life?" I kept my eyes on the mould as I washed my hands. Then I tried one last question. "If the landlord doesn't get rid of you, will I die of pneumonia like my mum?" I wondered whether I would rather be hit by a car or die from a mouldy Jesus.

The mould stayed silent so I went downstairs and switched on the television, savouring the freedom of Jill not being there to tell me to do my homework. But I found myself unable to concentrate. I kept thinking about the poor hedgehog and how unfortunate it was to have had its life snuffed out so abruptly. Life suddenly felt quite precarious. What if the television blew up in my face? What if our school got targeted by terrorists? What if someone fell out of a plane and landed on my head? Without really thinking about what I was doing, I went outside, walked halfway back to school and took a good long look at the dead hedgehog.

I felt my insides churning as I whispered, "I want to be great before I die." Then I glanced behind me before taking a quick photo on my phone.

~ 4 ~

Picking the right friends

Ny birthday is on Saturday. I hope Jill gets me a new phone but I doubt she will. I think she's got me a thesaurus and some pyjamas.[21] I expect she thinks a thesaurus would come in handy for writing my life story. She doesn't realise that I can find all the words I need on the internet.

Aunt Claudia sent my birthday card a few days ago and said she wanted to give me one of the lambs from her field. *'You can have it dead or alive,'* she wrote. *'Just let me know and I will arrange it.'*

I thought this had to be the stupidest gift anyone had ever offered me but, as my birthday drew nearer, the idea of a pet lamb started to grow on me. I'd always wanted a puppy and perhaps I could train a lamb to perform like one. *'Livi's Little Lamb'* certainly had a great ring to it.

When I suggested it to Jill, however, she scolded me, "How many times do I have to tell you? A pet would set off my eczema."

"I could keep it in my room."

"No, Livi."

"We could tie it up outside the front door."

She shook her head.

"But I'd clean its mess every day and I'd wash my hands after stroking it!"

Jill shuddered. "Please, Livi. I feel like I might faint."

So I phoned Aunt Claudia and told her that I would like the lamb alive but could she please keep it in her field as the idea of getting a pet was setting off Jill's hypochondria. I added that I would like her to call it *'Stanley.'*

---

21 If they're not for me, she's hiding her own things under her bed.

"You don't want me to send it then?" my aunt said in disappointment. "I've already bought the bubble wrap."

I gave a splutter at the idea of Aunt Claudia sending a live lamb in the post.

"Well, why not?" she snapped, as though reading my mind. "It's not illegal."

"Er, actually, it is."

I knew this because in a recent episode of *Freaky Human* [22] there had been a feature about strange things people send in the mail. Apparently, when the postal service began, there were a number of instances of parents attaching stamps to their children and sending them by post. A special law had to be passed to stop such ignorant behaviour.

"Oh well. Suit yourself," my aunt replied. "I'll keep it here for you."

"And call it Stanley," I reminded her.

She gave an irritated sniff and hung up.

I wandered into the kitchen, half wishing I hadn't rung Aunt Claudia. It would have been quite exciting to have a live lamb turn up on the doorstep and I was pretty sure Jill wouldn't have had the guts to send it back.

Jill was eating a banana at the kitchen table. I pulled some homework off the work surface and sat beside her. Then I watched as she finished her banana and discarded the peel, a shiny sticker glistening from one of its yellow wings.

"Ruby collects banana stickers," I said nonchalantly. [23]

Jill rolled her eyes. "What a nut."

For some reason, I got kind of defensive. "At least I'm not hanging around outside the chip shop!"

Jill just laughed when I said this. My sister never takes me seriously. I often wonder if my mother would've done.

"Maybe I will then!" I threatened.

She ignored me. "Do you want a birthday party?"

I shrugged.

"You don't have to."

I shrugged again.

---

[22] My favourite television show.

[23] Thanks to me, Ruby now has over 700 banana stickers in her portfolio. I found out that her collection is even more remarkable because Oscar is allergic to bananas so Ruby and her family never eat them. I've been eating a couple every day to help her out.

"Well let me know, won't you?"

"Hmmm."

I doodled over my Maths homework as I pondered who I would invite if I had a party. I used to think I was fun until I joined this new school and made absolutely no friends. Perhaps I tried too hard. On my first day, I handed out sweets. I thought it would make me seem quirky but, instead, it probably made me look a bit desperate.

"What are you giving out sweets for?" a girl had asked.

"Oh, just, you know, to say hi!"

"To get us to be your friends?" someone else accused.

"No, I—"

"That's so weird!"

Some of them started throwing my sweets at the walls.

"I think it's cool." That was Kitty Warrington and that's when I set my sights on being her friend.

"Thanks!" I said. "By the way, I like your bag."

"It's from *Tizzi Berry*." Kitty sniffed. "Don't copy me though."

"I won't!"[24]

"So, you're new?"

"Yeah, I moved to Leeds this summer."

"I thought you didn't look, you know... local."

I shifted uncomfortably and asked what she meant.

"I can tell," she said simply. "It's a special sense that I have." Then she added, "Most people don't wear their jumpers. Just a tip, you know, to be friendly."

"Oh!" I looked around. It was true that the only other people wearing their jumpers were Ruby and some geeky-looking boy who was in the middle of receiving a wedgie. I took my jumper off. Immediately I felt cold.

Kitty smiled. "These are nice. Can I have some more?"

"Yeah, of course! Here, take them all..."

The next day, Molly Masterson approached me at break and said, "Got any more sweets?"

"Er..." I saw Kitty waiting across the corridor and debated giving Molly my pocket money.

But then Ruby came wandering over and Molly shot her a dirty look and said to me, "Don't bother."

---

[24] I had never even heard of *Tizzi Berry*. Later, when I researched them, I found out they were an elite fashion label. They sell handkerchiefs for £30.

And Kitty called out, "Another tip: pick the right friends!" Then she and Molly locked arms and went sauntering out of the building. I'd wanted to run after them and explain that Ruby wasn't actually my friend; she was just a girl who lived on my street. But it was raining outside and I was freezing without my jumper. So, instead, I glared at Ruby and marched off down the corridor. Bear in mind that this was before Ruby spoke to me. I had several more days of silence to endure first.

With hindsight, I'm glad that I didn't ditch Ruby. Aunt Claudia says that everybody is somebody's weirdo and I guess I don't mind Ruby being mine. But that doesn't mean I don't secretly wish that I had a few *normal* friends as well. Perhaps I did the whole thing wrong. Maybe, if I'd planned things better, I could've been friends with everyone.

I peered at my sister. "Jill, when you started your job, did you give out sweets?"

She gave me a funny look. "Why on earth would I do that?"

"No reason." I sighed and pulled out my calculator. I noticed that some of the triangles Fester had drawn had slightly wonky sides so I attempted a couple of questions before writing, *'Apparently, there are no straight lines in the universe. If this is true, perhaps mathematics is just another form of philosophy. I've recently turned Jewish so it might go against my religion.'* Then I flung my work across the table and went to see Ruby.

Violet was in the street collecting leaves. "Look, Livi!" She held up a bright red leaf. "I might make some earrings!"

I nodded. "Is Ruby in?"

"Or a patchwork quilt..." she continued vacantly.

"It'd be a bit scratchy."

But Violet couldn't hear me. She was lost in thought, doing what she calls *'artistically connecting with the universe.'* "Funny, isn't it?" she said suddenly. "The very moment the trees need to keep warm they undress themselves!"

I shrugged and went through the front door where I almost collided with Belinda who was covered from the neck up in mashed fruit. I was so startled that I screamed and turned to run.

"Good evening, Livi!"

I turned back and forced a smile, eyeing what appeared to be a blueberry on the end of her nose.

"I see you've spotted my homemade face pack. My natural remedy for aging skin."

I gulped. "Looks good."

"I'll put some in a jar for you to give Jill."

"It's alright," I said quickly. "Jill doesn't like fruit."

Belinda chuckled and called up the stairs, "Ruby, my little carrot! Livi's here!"

Ruby's ginger head appeared at the top of the banister. She gave a shy smile and beckoned for me to come up. Out of the corner of my eye, I saw some kiwi slide down Belinda's face as I sprinted up the stairs.

"Look at this," Ruby said with quiet enthusiasm as she closed her bedroom door behind me. She held up her banana book.

"You got another one?"

"Yes, but look!"

I looked closer. "Another monkey one?"

Ruby rolled her eyes. "I haven't got this one before!"

"Oh right!" I feigned excitement. "Great!"

Ruby grinned and admired her new addition.

Neither of us spoke for a moment.

Eventually I said, "It's my birthday on Saturday."

Ruby looked at me.

"I might have a party."

She nodded. "Are you going to invite Kitty Warrington?"

"Er... Maybe. Why?"

"Because I heard her tell Molly Masterson that you probably got expelled from your old school for being weird. So I thought I should warn you, you know, in case it helps your decision..."

"Oh." I stared at the floor and let this revelation sink in. "Thanks."

Ruby started chewing her fingernails.

I forced a smile. "When's your birthday?"

"It was yesterday."

I gaped at her. "Why didn't you say anything?"

"It didn't come up, I guess."

I laughed incredulously. "But still... You could've *said*."

She shrugged.

Before I could say anything else, Violet came rushing in and tossed an armful of wet leaves onto my lap. "Ta-da!" she sang.

I glared at her and shoved the leaves onto the floor.

She didn't notice and just giggled as she fell backwards onto her bed. "I feel all connected now... I just can't decide between making them into jewellery or patchwork..."

"Why don't you ask the Bible?" I sneered.

Violet turned and sighed. Then she slid dreamily off her bed and sauntered out of the room.

I rolled my eyes and turned back to Ruby. "You know my party... It could be a joint party to celebrate *your* birthday too."

She stared at me.

"If you want," I added.

"Who else is coming?"

I shifted uncomfortably. "Just you."

Ruby looked surprised. "Alright... Maybe we could go to the petting zoo?"

"Yeah!"

Neither of us spoke for a while.

I hummed and pretended to be interested in the rug on the floor. It was red with blue spots. It made me think painfully of my best friend, Clara, back in Little Milking. She had a similar rug which was blue with red spots. I wondered if they were from the same shop. "Where did you get your rug?"

Ruby shrugged. "I think it was from *Rug World.*"

I nodded blankly. I realised I didn't know where Clara's was from.

In the silence that followed, I made a mental note to check my emails to see whether Clara had written recently. We'd exchanged several teary messages when I first moved away but, in recent weeks, I hadn't heard from her. Jill had warned that people often drift apart when they don't see each other anymore but I'd scoffed and said that would never happen to me and Clara. We'd been through a lot together: I'd held her hand when her rabbit had to be put down and she'd stood up for me when some of the boys in our class made fun of my animal impressions. She was bubbly and confident and nothing like Ruby. Her mother used to call us 'Noisy One' and 'Noisy Two' on account of the fact that she couldn't hear herself think when we were around. The only thing loud about Ruby is her bright yellow lunchbox.

I bit my lip and twiddled the edge of Violet's duvet. "I'd rather sleep in the bath than share a room with *my* sister!" I said, forcing a laugh.

Ruby just smiled stupidly.

I felt a surge of irritation. According to Aunt Claudia, picking the right friends is like choosing the best fruit. They need to be sweet, ripe and without blemish. That is all very well if you're fortunate enough to have the first pick of the crop. But what if you arrive late to the market when the good stock is gone and the only thing left is a skinny carrot who doesn't say anything?

"I'd better go home now," I said finally.

"Alright."

I went down the stairs, cursing my bad luck that my only friend in Leeds is a sticker-collecting loner. But then I tripped over a pile of soggy leaves and conceded that it could've been worse. It could've been Violet.

Before I went to bed, I sent Clara an email.

'Hi Clara! Just checking you got my last message cos it's been ages since I heard from you! Bet school's really boring without me LOL! P.S. Where did you get your rug from cos one of my new friends has got the same one but opposite colours? xxx'

I sat by the screen for half an hour, hoping that she might reply. But she didn't. She didn't respond for another two days and, when she did, it was just a quick message because she was *'off to a party.'* She said that she didn't have her rug anymore because Shannon Hobbs had thrown up on it during a sleepover but that she was begging her mother for a sheepskin rug. At the end of her short message, she added, *'Oh, by the way, happy birthday for Saturday! I was gonna send you a present but I ran out of pocket money. Soz!!'*

I was a bit miffed that Clara had had a sleepover with Shannon Hobbs. Shannon had been our nemesis ever since she accidentally-on-purpose laughed at Jill winning the Mums' Sack Race one Sports Day. I couldn't help but feel betrayed that Clara had dropped her into correspondence so thoughtlessly. I was also a little disappointed at her casual birthday greetings. When I'd left, we'd vowed to write every day and Clara had promised she would *'definitely, definitely'* save up her pocket money so that she could visit on my birthday. But now, the thought of her coming to stay seemed as peculiar as the idea of having a sleepover with Aunt Claudia. It had been less than two months and already we were as good as strangers.

I wrote back and said that I hoped she and Shannon had had a nice sleepover. I added that I was enjoying my new school and that my new best friend, Ruby, lived across the street. *'She has a sheepskin rug,'* I wrote. *'It still has its head on.'* I pressed *'Send,'* resigned to the fact that Clara would probably never write again.

~*~

After much thought, Violet decided to turn her collection of leaves into hats for the homeless. She gave me one of the practise ones for my birthday and was so excited about it that she came knocking at seven in the morning, completely oblivious to the fact that I was still half asleep when I answered the door.

"It's delicate," she warned as I examined the bizarre creation. "Treat it carefully."

I told her that I would treat it so carefully that I might not even wear it.

Jill came down the stairs and said in a bemused voice, "That's nice, you should wear it today."

I narrowed my eyes at her.

"I can make one for you, Jill, if you'd like?" Violet offered.

"That's very kind. But I don't really wear hats."

"Oh." Violet looked a little deflated. "What about earrings?"

Jill pursed her lips. "You're here rather early, Violet."

"I've been awake for ages! I read three chapters of the Bible before I came."

Jill and I exchanged looks.

"Well, seeing as we're up, happy birthday!" Jill gave me a tired hug and handed me my presents.

I opened the thesaurus first. I feigned surprise, said thank you, and then unwrapped the pyjamas. They're quite nice actually, and they have pockets so that you don't have to carry things when you're sleeping.

"And..." Jill pulled out a small black box from her pocket. "One that you won't have seen under the bed." She shot me a knowing smile.

I grinned and opened the box. Inside was a silver locket in the shape of a bird, inscribed with the name 'Livi.'

"It was Mum's," Jill explained. "I found it when we were moving. I'm sure she would have loved for you to have it."

A lump formed in my throat. "Thanks," I whispered.

"That will go with the hat!" Violet said, coming over to stare as Jill fixed the locket round my neck.

I forced a smile. "Maybe..."

"I'll make you some birthday toast," Violet continued. She started busying herself around our kitchen, humming and tidying and generally behaving like a mini version of her mother. "How often do you change your tea towels?" she asked, much to my sister's annoyance. And then, "Ooh! Is that a mouse?"

Jill screamed and almost leapt into my arms. "Where?"

"Only joking!" Violet grinned.

My sister quickly composed herself. "Oh. Very funny."

"That was hilarious!" Violet roared. "You should have seen the look on your face!"

My sister rolled her eyes and insisted she was only playing along.

"No you weren't. You were scared!"

"I was not! I know we don't have mice."

Right on cue, the mouse that had been evading capture ever since we moved in poked its nose out to see what all the fuss was about.

"We do have mice," I said, pointing.

The two of them took one look and ran screaming down the hall.

Ruby came over a couple of hours later. She handed me a funny shaped present wrapped in lilac tissue paper. The homemade card on top said, *'Happy Joint Birthday!'*

I hadn't even thought to buy her a present but, without thinking, I said, "Oh thanks! Yours is upstairs, I'll just go and get it!"

I ran up to my room and hunted for something I could give her. I eyed a clay koala that I'd made in primary school but I felt that Ruby probably had enough grotesque artwork in her life, what with sharing a room with Violet. I debated giving her my new thesaurus but wasn't sure I could get away with that. Then, face-down in my pile of dirty laundry, I spotted a free red Bible which had been handed out at the start of term. Some visitors had given a talk about how this book was the most important book they'd ever read. They said we should take one and put it somewhere safe because we never knew when we might need it. Most people scoffed at the offer. I only took one to be polite. I'd not yet found *'somewhere safe'* for it, although I'd debated burying it. I picked it up and turned it over in my hands. Then I hastily wrapped it in some paper reasoning that, since Ruby's family go to church, she'll probably need it more than me.

I ran back down the stairs. "Happy joint birthday!" I sang.

We exchanged presents. I tore the tissue paper off Ruby's gift and held up a large wooden box. There was a hole in one side and a hook on the other.

"It's a starling box," Ruby said shyly. "For birds. But also because your surname is Starling so I thought you could use it for, well, whatever..." She trailed off.

I peered inside the hole. Ruby had filled it with paper birds. I didn't know what to say. I wanted to yank the badly-wrapped free Bible out of her hands and fling it through the window. I watched in disgraced silence as Ruby unwrapped it and gave me a bashful smile.

The silence was broken by Violet proclaiming, "You should have kept that for yourself, Livi. Ruby already has one."

"I thought she'd like it," I muttered.

"Come on then!" Jill plonked Violet's leaf hat on my head and led the way to the front door. "The petting zoo awaits."

Violet ran ahead and secured the front passenger seat. "We can continue our discussion about humane mouse traps!" she said to my sister.

I saw Jill grimace but she just said, "Great."

Ruby and I squeezed into the back. I felt really guilty about not getting her a proper present and hoped she didn't think it meant I wasn't a real friend.

"I love the starling box," I whispered.

She smiled.

I wanted to apologise about my gift but how could I do that without admitting I'd forgotten to get her anything in the first place? I didn't know what else to do so I pulled Violet's leaf hat over my eyes and said, "Hey, Ruby, what am I?"

I peeked under the hat. Ruby was looking at me curiously.

"Come on!" I said, swinging my head backwards and forwards and grunting softly.

"I don't know..."

"I'm an armadillo!"

"Are you?" Ruby giggled.

"Yes!" I thrust the hat at her. "You try it."

Ruby hesitated before putting the hat over her face. One of the stalks stuck out where her nose should have been.

I started laughing.

Ruby pulled the hat off and beamed.

"Hey, watch this..." I poked a couple of eye holes through the hat and wore it like a mask.

43

Ruby laughed so hard that she started choking.

Violet piped up from the front of the car, "Excuse me, Ruby and Livi. It's not a toy!"

This made us laugh even more. By the time we got to the petting zoo the hat was in several crumpled pieces over the back seat of the car.

Violet took one look and said in a withering voice, "I will make you one more, Livi Starling, just one. But, after that, you'll have to be cold."

I nodded solemnly. "I appreciate your patience, Violet."

Ruby caught my eye and grinned.

The petting zoo was a bit of a let down. The word 'zoo' had led me to expect, rather foolishly, that there might be lions and tigers, or at the very least some small monkeys. But it was mostly just sheep and goats. And we couldn't even pet them because they ran away from us. We had our photo taken with a couple of piglets and then went home.

"What do those pigs think about all day?" I wondered aloud on the drive back.

"Eating and sleeping," said Jill.

"Do you think they wonder if people might eat them?"

"I might become a vegetarian," Violet announced suddenly. She had made this decision whilst attempting to feed one of the runaway sheep. "I think those sheep perceived me as an enemy because I eat meat."

"Maybe they want to be eaten," Jill said wickedly.

"Nobody wants to be eaten!" Violet exclaimed.

"Oh, I don't know," Jill retorted. "Perhaps they would if someone explained the concept to them."

"Jill, how can you say that?" Violet looked utterly horrified, oblivious to the fact that my sister was winding her up. "I wasn't sure about being a vegetarian because my Bible Dip was inconclusive.[25] But now, I'm totally one hundred percent never eating meat again! Who's with me?" She turned in her seat and gave me and Ruby menacing stares.

Ruby shook her head. "Mum's cooking roast chicken tonight."

"Livi?" Violet stared at me.

---

[25] She had opened it on a page featuring Jesus cooking fish.

I could see Jill smiling at me in her rear view mirror. I knew her smile meant that if I became a vegetarian I'd have to make all my own meals.

"I'll do it part of the time," I said.[26]

Violet gave a loud, "Harrumph!" pulled out her journal, and turned away.

When we got home, Belinda was waiting with a plate of ham sandwiches for lunch. Violet made a show of picking out all of the ham slices and arranging them into the shape of a pig on our kitchen table. Beside it, she left a note bearing the words, 'Please don't eat me.'

I think this was supposed to make Jill feel guilty but she took one look and yelled, "Livi, don't play with your food!"

"It was Violet!"

And Belinda looked over and said, "It's modern art, isn't it, darling?"

The rest of our party consisted of me and Ruby playing cards while Violet stood at the kitchen sink frantically scrubbing the pig smell off her hands.

When everyone left, I opened my starling box and admired the paper birds. Ruby had named them all. The Ruby bird was orange and the Jill bird was decorated in blue glitter. I picked up mine. It was yellow with purple feathers and big brown eyes. A lump caught in my throat as I turned it over in my hands. On one wing was written, 'Living Creature.' The other simply said, 'Fly.' As I put it carefully back into the box I made a mental note to get up early one of these days, visit all the supermarkets in Leeds, and steal every last banana sticker for Ruby.

---

[26] By this, I meant *between meals.*

~ 5 ~

Oh, to be struck by lightning!

One night, in the middle of the week, there was a really big thunderstorm across the whole of Yorkshire. I peered in fright through my bedroom window and saw Violet across the street waving and looking terribly excited. I couldn't get back to sleep so I woke Jill and told her I was scared. She told me not to be silly but, the next morning, it was on the news that a man from Harrogate had got struck by lightning whilst lying asleep in his bed. He survived but his pyjamas exploded.

That day at school I asked Fester how likely it is for the average person to be struck by lightning. I assumed he should know because we've done statistics in Maths, but he laughed and said, "Why? Did last night's thunderstorm scare you?"

"No! I just thought you might know."

He gave a smarmy grin. "Contrary to popular belief, teachers don't know everything!"

I rolled my eyes as he came and perched on the edge of our desk, denting my pencil case with his fat bottom. Ruby went red and covered her work with her hands. I started to feel itchy.

"How are you getting on?" Fester pointed to the board which was covered in sums involving negative numbers.

I shrugged. "I don't get it."

"What don't you get?"

I held out my empty hand. "How many pencils am I holding?"

"None..."

"Not minus one?"

He gave me a baffled stare.

"Or minus two? Or minus fifty?" He said nothing so I continued, "And if I *was* holding *minus fifty* pencils in my hand and I tried to pick *plus one* up, would it vanish?"

"Are you trying to be funny?"

I frowned. "No. I just don't understand how anything can be less than zero."

He looked at me as though I was an idiot, which made me dislike him even more and wish I'd just pretended to do the work. "It's a perfectly simple concept," he insisted.

"You mean it's an imaginary number?"

"No! That's a whole other thing!"

"Oh."

Fester took my exercise book and scrawled illegibly across the page. "Do you understand now?"

"I think so..." I lied. Then I asked with a grin, "Is having zero pencils the same as having zero puppies?"

Fester groaned and put his head in his hands. "Libby Starling, you are the thorn in my side!"

Ruby caught my eye and grinned. I grinned back. Perhaps next lesson I would ask him about infinity.[27]

Our English teacher, Mrs Tilly, was suitably dressed for a thunderstorm. When we arrived at her classroom after Maths, she was perched on her desk decked out in wellies and a long black coat. She looked a little like the grim reaper. Mrs Tilly is fixated with horror. Every lesson we are bombarded with a brand new slice of death to dissect. During my first week I was asked to stand and read a passage from a story entitled, 'I Sold My Mother's Hair.' It made me think about my own mother and what might have become of her hair. That's how I ended up telling Mrs Tilly that I couldn't read.

"I saw a murder in the summer," I'd explained. "A man on our street mowed down his wife with his lawn mower. That's why we had to move and I haven't been able to read ever since."

I went into detail about how the man dragged his wife's body all the way to the market to sell as fertiliser and eventually drove himself into a train. Mrs Tilly seemed to appreciate the gore. And she hasn't asked me to read since. She just gives me pitying smiles now and then.

Today's story was called, 'The Vendetta.' It was about a woman's secret plot to kill her best friend.

"Well!" Mrs Tilly trilled after Ruby finished reading it aloud. "Wasn't that exciting?"

---

[27] Make that *negative* infinity.

47

Our class said nothing. I wondered if they were as terrified as me.

"I would like you to write your own vendetta stories," Mrs Tilly continued. "And, just like in *this* story where poor Vera didn't suspect her best friend's motives, make sure you build up the suspense so that we are kept guessing right till the very end!" She gave an excited cackle as she swept round the class like a frenzied vulture.

I chewed my pen and wrote nothing for about fifteen minutes. I felt it was important to whisper to Ruby, "I would never kill you."

Her eyes widened. "I wouldn't kill you either!"

It crossed my mind that she could be a highly skilled liar so I peered at her work just to be sure. Her story was titled, *'The Revenge of the Ripe Banana.'* I smiled and started to write.

'The Vengeance of the Vexed Arithmetic... This is the true story of Formidable Fester, who was eaten alive by the number seven.[28] Fester couldn't do maths in his head and always counted his numbers out loud. "One," he would shout, and the number one would come running. "Two, three, four," and those too would arrive...'

I chuckled to myself, fairly confident that I was one of the best young writers in Leeds. Unless, of course, my double writes stories that are as good as mine.

As the lesson ended, Mrs Tilly watched us pack our books away and said in a chilling whisper, "I wonder how the story will end?" A bolt of lightning flashed when she said this and Mrs Tilly rubbed her hands together as half the class screamed.

Maybe she's crazy and our stories are fuelling her own twisted plans of destruction. Or perhaps she hates us and is secretly taking note of the obscene things we write so that she can have us all locked up. Maybe the staffroom walls are plastered with our stories and the other teachers read them and laugh. I changed the name *'Fester'* to *'Frank,'* just in case. And I added onto the end, *'This is a fictional account.'*

Worse than a teacher fixated with horror, however, is a teacher who has favourites. After English, we had Drama with Miss Waddle

---

[28] This is perhaps my favourite joke of all time: *Why is 6 afraid of 7? Because 7 8 9.*

who is *The Queen of Favouritism* at Hare Valley High. Her favourites are all the popular people like Kitty Warrington and Molly Masterson. Miss Waddle makes jokes with them and invites them round her house for brownies. And, round her house, they're allowed to call her *'Vicky.'* I don't think she likes me and Ruby because we're what she calls *'weak actors.'* What she means by this is that we're weak *people* because we're not cool.

For the Christmas show, Miss Waddle is writing her own adaptation of *'Romeo and Juliet.'* It's going to start with everyone in a freeze-frame of a house. I am part of the back door. After the opening song, we break off into two houses— the Capulet house and the Montague house— and Ritchie Jones pops up in the middle dressed as Father Christmas, the narrator of the story.

I had wanted to audition for the role of Juliet but, when I went to sign up, Miss Waddle said, "Oh! Trying your luck, are you? Well, you never know!"

No, *I* didn't know. But *she,* being the one to cast us, did. So I asked tentatively, "Do you think I should?"

She just laughed and said, "Kitty is a strong actor. You should watch her."

To prove I wasn't *weak*, I was going to go to the audition and I was going to sing *'Big Spender.'* But the audition clashed with the First Aid Club and Ruby begged me to come with her because that week was all about burns and stings and, for some reason, she thought we would learn how to escape from a burning building. But we didn't. We just spent the session rolling each other around in a towel. So I'll have to settle for watching Kitty Warrington play the role of Juliet while I entertain myself in private with the secret knowledge of knowing all her lines off by heart.

During today's rehearsal Miss Waddle chastised us because we didn't look like a proper house.

I wanted to say, *'That's because we're people and you can't cut a hole through Ruby to turn her into a window.'*

But I couldn't say that to Miss Waddle because she's cool so I tried harder to look like a door and, later, Ruby commented, "You're a good actor, Livi. You must get it from your dad!"

I grinned and hoped that Miss Waddle was listening.

'That's right!' I would say if I was braver. *'You may teach acting, but my dad does it for real. He's playing Hamlet at this very moment!'*

But she wasn't listening. Or maybe she *was* but was pretending not to be. I imagined her at home googling my famous actor dad and thinking to herself, *'I must be nicer to Livi.'*

There was another thunderstorm in the afternoon and, throughout the whole of Science, I clung to my clothes to stop them exploding.

Our Science teacher has been away all term. A rumour is going round that she died by jumping into an active volcano whilst on holiday in Italy,[29] but the head teacher has yet to confirm this. Every lesson we have someone different. This time, we had a young pretty supply teacher who said, *'Erm,'* forty seven times and kept biting her lip. She handed out some worksheets on natural selection and asked if we had any questions.

"I was just wondering," I said, raising my hand. "What will humans evolve into in a million years time?"

"Erm, I don't know," she mumbled. "But, erm, your usual teacher might be able to help when she gets back."

I nodded and passed my worksheet to Ruby. "Can you show me how to make a paper bird?"

She took it from me and folded it several times. Then she unfolded it, turned it round in her hand, and carried on folding. Within seconds, the piece of paper resembled a bird.

"Do you reckon a piece of paper is a negative bird?" I whispered.

Ruby giggled. Then we spent the rest of the lesson trying to fold a piece of paper in half more than eight times.[30] At one point, we thought we'd done it. But it turned out we had miscounted.

That evening, Jill and I went to the Ricos' house for dinner.[31] On our arrival, we were treated to a lecture by Oscar who had just memorised the names of every known moon in our solar system. He recited them in one garbled tirade, refusing to stop for air until

---

[29] A particularly painful and foolhardy way to die, if you ask me.

[30] A feat deemed *'impossible'* on *'Freaky Human.'*

[31] This is the sixth time we've eaten at theirs. I really think Jill ought to invite them round ours soon, just to be polite, but when I suggest it she says, "Me going round their awful house and putting up with their awful company *is* me being polite."

he'd finished. Then he took a bow and ran over to hug Jill. She eyed his snotty fists and patted him tentatively on the head before reaching into her bag for her hand sanitizer.

Moments later, Belinda came sauntering in and announced that dinner was ready. As we followed her into the dining room she gave me an uninvited hug and I caught a whiff of freshly strangled flowers. Then she put a hand on my sister's shoulder, cocked her head to one side, and whispered, "And how is Jill?"

"Jill is fine," my sister said stiffly. "How's Belinda?"

"Oh, I'm delightful! Has my little pumpkin been enlightening you?" She ruffled Oscar's orange hair.

Jill and I nodded and thanked Stanley as he filled our plates with beef casserole.[32]

"He's so clever! I don't know where he gets it from!" Belinda gave us a beseeching stare, as if she expected us to exclaim that Oscar's genius was surely inherited from *her*. When neither of us said anything, she tittered and turned to Ruby. "Ruby, my little carrot, will you and Livi remind me to take the *shoo-fly pie* out of the oven in a few minutes?" She said the words *'shoo-fly pie'* really loudly and gave me and Jill another earnest stare.

Jill smiled at her, refusing to take the bait.

"Right then..." Belinda sat down and glanced at Stanley.

On cue, the Rico family held hands and closed their eyes.

I gingerly accepted Ruby's outstretched hand and nudged Jill until she took my other one.

Suddenly, Belinda looked up and said, as though it were a great honour, "Would *you* like to say grace today, Jill?"

Jill shifted uncomfortably. "No, I don't think so, thank you."

Belinda smiled politely and was about to do it herself when Violet opened her eyes and asked, "Why not?"

Jill gave her an awkward stare and said nothing.

"Oh pleeeeease Auntie Jill." Oscar banged his cutlery together.

"She doesn't want to," Ruby whispered.

"She doesn't have to!" Stanley insisted.

"Why not?" Oscar looked utterly perplexed.

"I'll do it—" Ruby attempted.

"No! It's got to be Auntie Jill!" Oscar started to cry.

Violet was shaking her head and had whipped out her journal.

Ruby bit her lip and looked at me.

---

[32] Violet, who is still a vegetarian, had her own personal stew made from veggie mince. I saw her eyeing ours a little enviously a number of times.

"Why *won't* she?" Oscar exclaimed.

Belinda leant over and wiped his snotty nose.

"Just do it, Jill!" I hissed.

Jill scowled at me. "Alright, fine!"

The Ricos beamed, closed their eyes and resumed holding hands.

Jill shot me another icy glare before muttering, "Thank you, Belinda, for the food."

Stanley opened his eyes and gave her a friendly smile. Belinda nodded thoughtfully but said nothing. Violet looked confused and opened her mouth to speak, then thought better of it and started eating instead.

Eventually, Oscar said, "That wasn't right."

"Oscar, eat your food," Stanley said quietly.

"But she did it wrong!" Oscar insisted, pointing his fork at Jill.

I tried to change the subject. "Hey, a man got struck by lightning today!"

"She did it wrong!" Oscar repeated. "She should do it again."

"Eat your food, Oscar."

"Not till it's been done right!"

"It was on the news. His pyjamas exploded."

"Come on, Oscar..."

"But she did it WRONG!" Oscar bellowed.

"HE COULD HAVE DIED!" I roared.

Everybody turned and stared at me.

"Jill, dear..." Belinda began tentatively. "Maybe you could do it again and, this time, thank *God* for the food..."

Jill exhaled loudly and snapped, "Fine! Thank you, *God,* for the food." She began furiously stabbing her casserole.

Oscar shot her a triumphant grin and started to eat.

After a moment's silence Belinda said, "Did anyone else hear about that man from Harrogate? He got struck by lightning and, would you believe it, his pyjamas exploded!"

Stanley chuckled and made some remark about how it was a good job the man was at home and not at work at the time.

"But he wouldn't be wearing his pyjamas at work!" Violet said.

"No, I know that, Violet! But I meant if he was at work and his *clothes* exploded..."

"Oh... Unless he worked in a clothes shop and he could just grab some more."

"I doubt he'd be able to get up and carry on as normal!" Stanley laughed.

"How do you know?" Violet countered. "He might have more energy than ever. Lightning is energy, isn't it?"

She turned to Oscar for the answer to this and the pint-sized scientist began a spirited but irrelevant lecture about the main differences between kinetic and potential energy. He mainly directed his ranting at Jill but she kept her head down and refused to acknowledge him.

Over all this, I detected the faint smell of burning coming from the kitchen. I was torn between an overwhelming desire to savour Belinda's unknown shoo-fly pie and a sense of loyalty towards Jill which seemed to suggest that the pie should burn and die.

Several minutes later, Belinda sniffed, cupped a hand to her mouth and ran frantically to the kitchen.

"The pie!" exclaimed Ruby. "I forgot!"

"Me too," I insisted, shifting uneasily as Belinda returned in tears.

"I'm so sorry," she blubbered. "The shoo-fly pie is ruined!"

"We don't mind," I said quickly. I chewed my thumb and tried not to stare. It's not every day you see a grown woman crying over a pie.

"But I've ruined it!" Belinda sobbed. "Ruined, ruined, ruined!"

Stanley gave me and my sister an awkward smile as he got up to console his quivering wife.

"Oh, Stanley!" she moaned into his armpit.

"It's fine, Belinda." Jill stood up and patted her cautiously on the shoulder. "I'm full now anyway."[33]

"Really?" Belinda snivelled.

"Yes. Besides, we couldn't have stayed much longer as I have a whole load of work to do. Come on, Livi!"

I put down my cutlery and got up from the table.

"You're not going because of *me,* are you?" Belinda wailed.

"Of course not!" Jill said. "We've had a lovely time."

"Oh good!" Belinda looked relieved. "We'll have you round again soon, I promise."

If Jill had smiled any wider, her whole face would've snapped in half. "We'd love that," she said, hurrying me out of the room.

As we left, we heard Belinda tell Stanley, "It's the weather. All this thunder and lightning. It makes me feel so peculiar..."

---

[33] This wasn't true because she'd barely touched her casserole and when we got home she ordered a take away.

At this, Violet said, "I wonder if I could catch some lightning in a bottle and sell it as art..."

I started the day feeling very sorry for the man in Harrogate. But then he was on the evening news sharing his *'remarkable story'* and his wife was fussing over him and he looked rather pleased with himself. As I went to bed, I decided that I would quite like to be struck by lightning after all.[34] I would feel kind of special and unique. If anyone should ask me to tell an interesting fact about myself, I could shrug and say, *'Well... There was the time I got struck by lightning...'* I think it would do an awful lot for my quest for greatness.

So I climbed out of bed and went to do some research on the internet. I concluded that to improve my chances of being struck I would need to become a man, stand under a tree, wait on a golf course, or venture deep into the mountains of the Congo. It would also help to wear metal shoes. I discovered that lightning hits the earth 100 times every single second and that, at any given moment, there are probably about 1800 lightning storms raging. I looked out of the window, full of excitement, but it was a clear, dry night.

---

[34] Only if I survived completely unharmed and fully clothed of course.

~ 6 ~

Anything but average

My collection of junk mail has now become unsustainable. Jill refused to get me a bureau to keep it all in so I started storing everything under my bed. I now have so many flyers that they spill out across the floor causing me to slip over every time I get up in the night. Originally, I spent my Sunday mornings laying them all out as I marvelled at the abundant opportunities at my fingertips. But now, the whole thing has become a somewhat painstaking chore. New flyers arrive every day and it takes ages to sift through them all to work out which ones I've already got and whether the menus which cater for Chinese *and* Italian belong with the Oriental pile or the pizzas. I have an endless array of business cards from local gardeners (but no actual garden to invite them to), at least thirty thousand pounds in fake cheques and a catalogue bigger than all my schoolbooks put together from the Polish supermarket down the road. To top it all off, the once exciting act of choosing an evening's take away has become a nightmare as I have to consider more than fifty five menus before I make my choice.

"Just stop hoarding them!" Jill exclaimed when I said I didn't know what to do.

"I can't help it..." I insisted, my eyes straying to the doormat where a political leaflet beckoned.

My sister gave me a despairing look and said, "What's wrong with you?" Then she took me upstairs with a bin liner and started hauling the flyers out from under my bed. "For goodness sake, Livi!" She grabbed a handful of leaflets and threw them into the bin liner as if they were meaningless trash, which I suppose much of it was.

"Wait," I said weakly. "Let me keep a few." I picked up a menu plastered with cartoon chickens and the brochure from the photography studio.

"Don't be daft." Jill snatched them out of my hands and flung them into the bin liner.

"Fine! But don't come crawling to me when you don't know what to have for dinner."

Jill snorted and pointed to a pile of letters addressed to *Ms Joll Sterling*. I wrinkled up my nose and grudgingly threw them in.

There was a sudden knock at the door. We looked at one another and groaned.

"Church," I said with a snigger.

Every Sunday, Belinda comes over to ask if we want to join her family in going to church. Every week, Jill politely refuses.

"I need to put a sign in the window," my sister muttered as she traipsed down the stairs. *"No flyers, no salesmen, and please leave us to rest on Sundays."* She fixed a smile onto her face and opened the door.

"Hello!" Belinda sang. "How's Jill?"

"Fine." Jill gritted her teeth. "How's Belinda?"

"Very well, thank you. Hello Livi!" Belinda smiled at me as I came sliding down the banister, swinging my bin liner. Then she gave a small cough and said on cue, "Jill, I just wondered whether you and Livi would like to come to church with us this morning?"

"We're quite busy actually," Jill replied.

"We're clearing out junk mail," I added.

"Oh." Belinda looked disappointed. She cocked her head to one side and said, "I can sense a great void in your life, Jill."

Jill forced a laugh. "I'm fine, thanks."

"I'm always here for you."

Jill said nothing.

"Jesus loves you very much—"

Jill closed the door on her.

I'm sure if we'd had a cat-flap Belinda would have poked her head through and carried on speaking but, instead, she had to make do with sticking her fingers through our letter box. "I'll pray for you!" she warbled as my sister stormed off down the hall.

I followed Jill into the kitchen. "Can we make a bonfire with my junk mail?"

"No."

"Can we make cookies?"

"You can, if you want." Jill sat down and pulled out a folder of work. "I've got to do this by tomorrow."

"Oh." I sat watching her for a while.

"Livi, I can't concentrate with you staring at me. I thought you were going to make cookies?"

"Nah." I didn't really want to make cookies. I just wanted to eat them.

"Go and do some homework then."

"Done it," I lied, pulling half a Geography essay off the work surface. "Shall I read you what I've done so far?" When Jill didn't reply, I continued, "It's about sedimentary rocks. It's only rough so say if something sounds strange and I'll explain—"

"Livi!" Jill slammed her work on the table. "I've just wasted ten minutes helping you clear out your junk mail. If you're bored you can go and change your bed sheets."

"I changed them when we moved in."

"Livi! You'll get scabies! Do it now."

I gave a growl and stomped up to my room. So much for resting on Sundays.

~*~

I have an *above average* number of arms. I discovered this when attempting a worksheet on averages whilst watching a documentary about a woman with only one arm.

Fester had written, *'If five people have three apples, three have two, and two have only one, what is the average (mean) number of apples?'*

In response, I drew a one-armed woman holding an apple and wrote, *'If most people have two arms, but a lady on the television has only one, then the average (mean) number of arms is 1.9.'*

Following this revelation, I decided to spend a day without an arm to see what it was like to be average.[35] I couldn't decide between keeping my right arm or my left arm. On the one hand, I would get through the day easier if I could use my right arm. But, on the other, I've always wanted to be left handed and today would be a good day to begin.

Ruby met me on the pavement and offered me half a blueberry muffin. I was already using my hand to hold my P.E kit and wondered if I ought to tell her I was going to be one-armed today.

---

[35] Initially, I was going to do it without *any* arms but I had to upgrade to one when I couldn't get out of the front door.

"I'm not hungry," I said in the end.

Ruby smiled and shoved it into her lunchbox.

We walked to school and made idle chit-chat about the weather and muffins and how hard our French homework had been. All the while, my right arm dangled limply as I savoured the delight of being secretly one-armed. I wondered if that was what it felt like to be a spy.

I got through the day with moderate success. At one point, I sneezed and accidentally raised both hands and, during P.E, I got told off for what our teacher called *'a ridiculous method of serving a shuttlecock.'* I also had trouble getting my trainers on. But, in actual fact, running around one-armed in badminton was a breeze compared to the awkwardness of sitting still that afternoon in History.

Our teacher posed a seemingly innocent question. "If you could spend a whole day with anybody from history, who would it be?" When nobody put their hand up, Mr Holborn caught my eye and said, "Let's start with you, Livi."

Without thinking, I said, "My mum."

I heard somebody behind me snigger.

Mr Holborn looked vaguely surprised. "You must be very close to her."

I felt myself blushing. I'd forgotten that he thought my mum was alive and well and a budding beekeeper. "Yeah," I mumbled.

Mr Holborn turned to the girl behind me. "What about you, Melody?"

"Probably Marilyn Monroe."

"Are you sure you wouldn't pick your mum?" Molly Masterson said with a smirk.

A few people laughed.

The next person said Mozart. Someone else said William the Conqueror. I saw Ruby write something in tiny writing. It looked like it said *'Jesus,'* although Mr Holborn didn't ask her and she didn't put her hand up.

Kitty Warrington waved her arm wildly before exclaiming, "How about *Mother* Teresa?"

At the mention of *'mother'* everyone laughed again.

"Are you alright?" Ruby whispered.

"Yeah," I said coolly. I pulled out some paper and pretended to be concentrating on something. I spent the rest of the lesson writing my name over and over with my left hand.

Finally the bell rang and our class ran cheerfully to the door.

As I picked up my bag, I proclaimed to Ruby, "I just did a whole day with only one arm!"

She gave me a funny look. "I wondered why you kept turning the pages of the French dictionary with your mouth."

I shrugged. "I bet *you* couldn't do it."

We had walked halfway across the playground when Ruby stopped to check if she still had her locker key. There has been a recent spate of locker robberies and, even though the only thing Ruby keeps in her locker is her bright yellow lunchbox, she's become a little paranoid.

As Ruby dug around in her bag, I glanced absentmindedly at a nearby patch of grass and saw what appeared to be a rabbit's paw. It looked as though it were waving hello. *Or, more appropriately, goodbye.* It looked quite beautiful just lying there and it seemed somehow wrong to ignore it. Although it was no more alive than a lost shoe or abandoned crisp packet, there was something about it that compelled me to stare. I wondered where its head was and whether its soul was wherever my mum was. Ruby was busy attaching her locker key to her skirt so I carefully took my phone out and took a quick photo.

I'd just put my phone away when Ruby noticed the paw. "Ew! What's that?"

"What?" I asked casually. "Oh, that? I think it's a rabbit's paw."

Her face wrinkled up in disgust. "That's horrible."

"Yeah. Let's go."

Jill was still at work when we got to my house so I followed Ruby to hers. Violet was in the sitting room looking incredibly pleased with herself.

"My latest art project," she said, waving an old book of fairy tales under our noses.

I flicked through the book. It seemed Violet had simply scribbled over half of the content.

"It's called '*All My Own Words.*'"

"This is *art?*" I muttered.

Violet shot me a disparaging look. "*Yes.* It's modern art."

I was about to protest but was interrupted by the sound of something whacking into the window.

"What was that?" asked Violet.

Ruby ran to the window and gasped. "It's a bird."

I sprinted to join her. A little brown bird was lying motionless on the pavement in front of the window.

"I think it's dead," Ruby continued sadly.

I couldn't believe our luck. Two dead animals in one day! "Let's go and check," I suggested.

The three of us ran outside and huddled round the fallen creature.

"It's definitely dead," Violet said, poking its wing.

"Silly thing!" Ruby scolded. "Why did you fly into the window?"

The bird lay lifeless before us, its beady eyes locked in a silent farewell. One of its feathers stirred lightly in the breeze. My fingers itched for my phone.

"Oh well," Violet said, standing up. "That's life."

I stared at the bird and wondered where it had been flying to and whether anything would miss it. When I looked up, Violet and Ruby were lingering at their front door.

"Are you coming back in?" Violet demanded.

"Er..." I tried to stall for time. "I'll come in a bit."

Ruby eyed me curiously. "It's dead, Livi."

"I know... It's just so sad." I pretended to wipe my eyes, feeling like a spy on a brand new mission.

Ruby came and put a hand on my shoulder. "Take as long as you need."

I took a deep breath. "It's alright. You don't have to wait with me."

"Of course we'll wait with you!" she exclaimed.

Violet nodded and echoed, "Of course."

I opened my mouth to argue and then closed it again. If only I was a real spy I would know exactly what to say to get them off my case. When it became clear that they weren't going to leave me with the bird, I forced a smile and said, "I'm just going to take a quick picture."

They looked at me in confusion.

"Why?" Ruby asked eventually.

"Er... I want to show Jill."

Ruby paused for a moment and then repeated, *"Why?"*

"She needs it for work," I said in my best undercover spy voice. I held my phone above the bird and took a hasty snap, humming as I did so. "Okay, done!" I said cheerily, ushering Ruby and Violet back into their house.

Ruby shot me a quizzical look but said nothing.

Violet opened her mouth and closed it again.

"Anyway," I said, after a moment's pause. "What's this all about?" I shuffled towards the tapestry labelled *'Rico Family Tree'* and pretended to study it.

Violet came over and started to tell me about their web of relatives, their tenuous links with various celebrities, and about how their ancestors were thrown off a Scottish island for stealing sheep. "And this lady..." Violet pointed to some woman's name dated in the late sixteenth century. "She ran a secret underground theatre when theatre was banned in London..."

"How do you know?" I cut in.

Violet gave an irritating grin. "It's our family history. It's been compiled over centuries and handed down through generations." She patted the tapestry greedily. "One day, this will be mine!"

I found myself feeling somewhat peeved. I wished I had a tapestry of family history. I don't even know what all of my grandparents were called. "Interesting," I muttered. "Anyway, I'd better go now."

Violet looked a little taken aback.

"Don't you want to stay till Jill gets home?" Ruby asked.

"I've got a headache," I lied. "I think I'll just go and lie down."

"Oh alright." Ruby walked me to the door. "I hope you feel better soon."

"I will."

When I got home, I flicked through the three photos on my phone. *Dead hedgehog. Dead paw. Dead bird.*

I wondered whether I ought to start a collection. It would be somewhat more mysterious than collecting junk mail. But then I grimaced as I imagined what Jill would say if I started keeping photos of dead animals under my bed.

~ 7 ~

The greatest comedy of the year

This time last week, the most astonishing thing that had happened to me since moving to Leeds was seeing a small boy pee against the wall in the bus station. But, this weekend, something happened that makes the sight of a small peeing boy seem mundane, dull, commonplace, ordinary, routine, normal, unexciting, expected and humdrum.[36]

Jill was celebrating a minor success at work and decided we should go to the cinema. We opted to watch 'Miss You, Hyena Face' which was tipped to be the funniest animated film of the year. I wondered if it was going to be so funny that someone would die laughing. I considered that might be a good way to go.

The film's release coincided with that of a horror movie called 'Death and the Swan.' All the cool kids at school had bragged about going and sitting on the front row. There was quite a queue inside the cinema and I saw Kitty Warrington and Molly Masterson waiting impatiently as an attendant inspected their fake IDs.

Jill kept checking her watch, paranoid that we were going to miss the start of the film. She's the kind of person who feels short-changed if they miss the adverts at the beginning.

When we finally got our tickets, Kitty and Molly were lurking by the pick and mix. The attendant had refused to sell them tickets and they were swearing loudly and threatening to call Kitty's brother.

I sauntered past, hoping they would see me and possibly think that I'd been allowed entry to watch the horror film, but the moment was ruined by Jill yelling, "Livi, the hyena cartoon is this way!"

I scowled and ran to join her. "Can we get popcorn?"

---

[36] The thesaurus has its uses after all.

"Fine, but let's be quick!"

Usually, the only challenging thing about going to the cinema is the choice between sweet or salted popcorn. Not so today. We arrived at the popcorn counter and got the shock of our lives: MY DAD.

My dad who we haven't seen since I was seven was standing there serving popcorn. I had to grab Jill's hand to keep from falling over. I nudged her and mouthed, *"Look!"* and she went bright red and held my hand tighter. He didn't notice us to begin with and, for a moment, it seemed as though Jill was going to drag me away and pretend we hadn't seen him. But then he turned and stared at us.

"Jill... Livi..?"

I didn't know what to do so I just gave a silly grin.

Jill cleared her throat, pointed to the popcorn and said, "Sugared, please."

Dad looked at her for a long time before saying, "Oh but you're sweet enough!"

Jill glared at him.

Dad forced a laugh. "Livi, how are you?"

"Fine, thank you," I whispered.

"You look... older."

"I am."

He nodded slowly. "What are you watching?"

I held up the ticket.

"Ah, yes! That's a great film. You should have told me you were coming. I could've got you in for free!"

"Oh really," Jill said coldly. "So, despite the fact that we've not seen you for seven years, we should have rung up the cinema on the off chance that you might work here?"

Dad chuckled nervously. "My shift is nearly over. I'll come and watch it with you."

I gulped as he handed me an extra large box of salted popcorn.

Jill pursed her lips, looking like she didn't quite have the audacity to turn him down.

So, ignoring the large queue that had grown behind us, my dad abandoned the popcorn counter and followed us into the auditorium. The adverts had already begun and our entrance was met with the flashing lights and cheery jingle of the new *'Mr Tooth'* toothpaste commercial. *'Tooth white, tooth bright! This is your moment to shine!'* My stomach churned as the sparkle from Mr Tooth's pearly smile followed the three of us like a spotlight all the way down the aisle.

With every step I took, I expected to awake from a dream. The whole of eternity stood still as we slid into the middle of a row and sat like dumbstruck monkeys. My hands felt like clammy chicken skin and my heart was beating so fast that I thought it might explode at any moment. The seats around us filled up quickly and a couple excused themselves as they squeezed past, nodding at us as though we were any ordinary family. I tried to nod in return but I was sure that if they got too close they would hear every cell inside me screaming, *'My dad is sitting next to me!'*

Having no idea how to conduct myself, I pretended to be engaged in the trailers before the film, but I couldn't take anything in. My brain was buzzing as I fretted over whether I looked ugly or lanky compared to when he'd last seen me. I kicked myself for wearing my old yellow jumper instead of my smart blue one.

Suddenly, Dad leant across and grabbed some popcorn. "Did you know, popcorn is a member of the grass family?"

I gave a dopey giggle and made a mental note of this, in case I am ever on a game show and it comes up as the winning question. I tried to think of an interesting reply but my mind was totally blank.

In the silence that followed, a stickman with ears like a hyena popped up on the screen and the film— the greatest comedy of the year— began. As far as I could work out, it was about a man who looked a little like a hyena travelling to the big city to find himself, getting lost, and somehow acquiring a pet sloth.

Jill did not laugh once.

Dad, who it transpired had seen the film six times already, laughed non-stop. "Ooh, wait for this! This is a good bit!" he said every few minutes. "This is the part where the sloth falls over!" He even knew some of the punchlines and said them before the characters did. It kind of ruined the film. And he ate all the popcorn.

But I didn't care. I sat watching him out of the corner of my eye, totally in awe of him— the way he flared his nostrils when he laughed, the way he tossed the popcorn down his throat and choked on it slightly, how his smell brought back a million unnamed memories, the crazy stubble on his chin and the fact that his hair was somewhat thinner than in all my photos of him. It was like beholding a king, or the prime minister, or some other elusive superstar. My elbow was touching his arm. I wanted to crawl into his lap and have a hug. But I also wanted to run and hide. I wondered what he would do if I leant over and bit him. Would he laugh or cry or swear or bite me back?

The end credits had barely begun when Jill got up and walked out of the auditorium. Dad and I followed her out.

"We'd better go," Jill said to me. "Parking will cost a bomb."

I looked at my dad and he smiled and asked, "Where do you live?"

I fumbled around in my pockets for a pen before writing our address and phone number on the back of my movie ticket.

"I'll call you," he said.

"Alright." I gulped and wondered whether I could hug him yet. Instead, I gave a dumb wave.

Jill was already out the door. I turned to follow her but, before I left, I asked my dad quickly, "How long have you worked here?"

"About three years."

"Has anyone ever come in who looks like me?"

He looked confused. "No..."

"Good." I could finally put to bed my fears of bumping into my double.

"It was nice to see you, Livi..."

I shot him an awkward smile and ran out.

Jill barely said a word the whole way home. I could tell she was shocked at seeing my dad after so many years. She never talks about him except to moan about what a bad father he is for leaving and never contacting me. I figured I had time to ask questions later. For now, I was so excited that I couldn't stop shaking. I was *sure* my dad's sudden appearance was evidence that my great life story was truly beginning. I wound down my window, imagining my name in lights as I belted out show tunes for 'Livi Starling the Musical'— Act One: The Grand Reunion.

Jill kept glancing at me and then looking away. She waited for my rendition of 'Tomorrow' to reach its climax before asking, "Are you okay?"

I sat back in my chair and exhaled. "Yeah. Are you?"

She nodded slowly. "Yes."

Later, Ruby called and asked how the film was.

I tried to play it cool as I said, "Unbelievable."

"Was it funny?"

"Hilarious."

"I might go and watch it."

"I'll come."

"Was it that good?"

"Yeah."

I didn't tell Ruby about seeing my father but I went with her the next day and watched the film again. I didn't want my dad to see me so I kept out of sight and wore a hat but, from behind a pillar by the ticket desk, I stood for ten minutes and watched him serving popcorn. He scooped it up like a pro and I imagined him on a stage. Once or twice, he sneezed and covered his mouth with his arm. He was wearing a red shirt which was clearly too big for him— a mere costume as he played the intricate role of *'Popcorn Assistant Number One.'*

At one point, Ruby waved a hand in front of my face. "Livi? Are you alright?"

I looked up and grinned.

"I said: *Do you want to get some popcorn?*"

"No," I said quickly. "It's made of grass."

Ruby shot me a quizzical look as I grabbed her arm and ushered her out of the foyer.

"Screen six," I said, turning to steal one last glance at my father.

I imagined the popcorn scooper was a skull and I imagined him proclaiming, *'Alas, poor Yorick! I knew him!'*

I imagined the applause.

~ 8 ~

A very no-nonsense teacher

When I was little, I had a story about a stegosaurus named Bangbo who ran away from the jungle because he had no friends. His quest led him all the way to England where he met a lonely girl called Lillian. My dad used to read it to me whenever he came over until, one day, I couldn't find it. I don't know whether I lost it or whether my dad grew so sick of reading it that he secretly disposed of it. I remember thinking that 'Bangbo' was such a wonderful name for a dinosaur that it was a travesty nobody liked him. For a competition in primary school I plagiarised the story, exchanging the name 'Lillian' for 'Livi,' and won a bottle of shoe polish. Around this time we went on a school trip to London Zoo. There was a horned lizard sitting on its own on a log in a big glass tank and I was certain that it was Bangbo.

I shouted, "Bangbo! BANGBO!"

But nobody else knew who he was.

"BANGBO!" I could have sworn I saw his beady little eyes twinkle. I started to bang on the glass. "Bangbo, I'll be your friend!"

My teacher, Mrs Bailey, put an arm round me and said, "Livi, are you alright?"

"It's Bangbo!" I squealed.

"What's Bangbo?"

"Bangbo the stegosaurus! He's here. I found him!"

Mrs Bailey gave a kind chortle. "Dinosaurs are extinct, Livi! You'll never find a stegosaurus in a zoo!"

"But Bangbo—"

"That's a lizard."

I felt tears welling up and took one last look at Bangbo as he fell off his log and slipped out of sight. Mrs Bailey led me away and offered me one of her special toffees which I took eagerly because she didn't present them very often.

"Feel better now?" she asked as I unwrapped the special toffee and popped it into my mouth.

I nodded because that was the only grateful response to a toffee from Mrs Bailey. But, all the way home, I sat in guilty silence, ashamed that I couldn't save Bangbo. Was that really how his story had ended, I wondered, with him trapped in a glass tank masquerading as a lizard?

I thought about Bangbo many times after that encounter. Even when I grew old enough to know that dinosaurs are dead and gone and that it truly was only a lizard, I still wondered about him secretly.

After the cinema trip, I was thinking about Bangbo[37] and began to feel rather wistful. I waited by the phone all weekend but my dad didn't call. I assured myself that he was probably rehearsing what to say.

At one point, Jill caught me sitting in the hallway and gave me a little look of pity. "Are you alright?"

"Just waiting for my dad to call!" I told her brightly.

"Hmmm..." She went to say something then changed her mind and wandered off into the kitchen, sighing as though I was setting myself up for a fall.

I knew better. That isn't how great stories end.

~ * ~

On Wednesday afternoons, we have a pointless lesson called Personal and Social Development. As far as I can fathom, we're supposed to be learning how to become responsible and conscientious citizens. However, our teacher, Mr Jakes, doesn't seem to be a particularly responsible or conscientious citizen himself. Apparently, he's dating a sixth former and goes drinking every Friday. I'm not sure how much he *truly* cares about our personal and social development. Last week, for example, we designed posters on how to cross the road. The class is such a non-event that I'd had little intention of including it in my life story. But then, this week, something happened: Mr Jakes was dismissed.

---

[37] Or rather, I was thinking about my father and the few poignant memories I have of him.

Instead, we had a brand new teacher who came swooping into the room with a very determined look on her face, shooting a loud, "*Ahem!*" at Wayne Purdy who was breakdancing on her desk.

Wayne giggled as he scampered to his seat and the new teacher kept on staring at him until he stopped giggling and started to look quite uncomfortable.

I exchanged a glance with Ruby and whispered, "Who's that?"

"No idea," Ruby whispered back.

Right on cue, the new teacher looked across and said in a glamorous accent,[38] "I'm Ms Sorenson and I shall be your Personal and Social Development teacher from now on."

A hush fell over the whole class as she took off her grey jacket and swept her auburn hair behind her ears. She wrote her name on the board before continuing, "Right then, 9.1,[39] you have thirty seconds to find a partner. Pick wisely because you will be working together for the rest of the term."

There was a momentary pause and then the whole class erupted in commotion as people clamoured for their best friends, grabbing hold of their absolute favourites and casting lots in the event of a tie. I tried to look pleased that Ruby and I were able to choose one another so quickly although, admittedly, it would've been nice to have had a choice.

Ms Sorenson watched us all with the same firm gaze. When we'd settled down, she said, "Thank you. At the end of term, you will give a presentation in your pairs." She smiled and went to sit behind her desk.

A worried mumble rippled through the class and some were so audacious as to protest.

"What sort of presentation?"

"Are we getting marked on it?"

"Where's Mr Jakes gone?"

Ms Sorenson silenced us with a hand. "You can do the presentation on anything you like. Yes, of course you will be marked. Mr Jakes was dismissed for inappropriate behaviour."

There was an uncomfortable silence and then Kitty Warrington put her hand up. "Excuse me, Miss," she said in her most sickening sucking-up voice. "When will the presentations be... because I've got the main part in the Christmas show...?"

---

[38] Quite possibly the nicest one I've heard since moving to Leeds.
[39] At this point, we could tell she was going to be a very no-nonsense teacher. Only the strict ones call us by our form name.

To my delight, Ms Sorenson saw right through her. "Don't you think I will use my intellect in the way that I schedule my classes?"

Kitty blushed and put her hand down.

"Any more questions?" Ms Sorenson demanded.

Nobody dared speak.

"Good. I want you to pick your topic by the end of this lesson."

There was a gasp, followed by frenzied chatter, as we broke away in our pairs. Ruby and I sat speechless for several minutes. Every now and then we looked at each other and grimaced. I felt that whatever we chose had to be the *absolute best project idea ever*. But it appears that when you start trying to come up with good ideas, everything seems stupid. Suddenly the entire world was empty and devoid of inspiration.

Finally, Ruby whispered, "What do you think, Livi?"

I chewed my bottom lip and glanced across the room. Ms Sorenson was busy sticking up posters. The ones nearest us read, *'Fail to prepare and you prepare to fail,'* and, *'It is never too late to be what you might have been.'* As I watched our teacher, with an ever-increasing sense of dread, I even started thinking, *What would Violet do?*

Violet, incidentally, has begun a new art project. By day, she's taking care of a hard boiled egg dressed in a nappy and, by night, she walks her neighbour's dog. She wants to know which is harder: caring for a baby or caring for a dog. The project is flawed for a number of reasons, the main one being that the egg stinks and she keeps it in her locker during lessons.

I wondered if we could adapt Violet's project in some way. Maybe we could skip the egg bit and find a local dog to look after.

"What are your favourite animals?" I considered that if we did our presentation on animals then I might be able to slip in a few of my impressions.[40]

Ruby squirmed. "I kind of like crocodiles. They have a nice smile."

"Oh... I don't really like them. What about koala bears?"

She shook her head.

"Penguins?"

She wrinkled up her nose.

As I puffed out my cheeks, Bangbo came to mind. "Lizards? Or... Dinosaurs?"

---

[40] I have been practising my *Thoughtful Rabbit*.

Ruby gave a little hum before whispering, "I don't think dinosaurs went extinct."

I blinked at her. "Pardon?"

She shrugged. "I just don't think there was anything so special about them. I saw a documentary once and the presenter said that the word *'dinosaur'* wasn't invented until the 1840s so really they were just animals and, okay, *some* of them went extinct but I doubt they *all* did. And I don't believe they lived millions of years before mankind. And..." She took a deep breath. "There have been many sightings of a massive reptile in the Congo which match the description of a sauropod type of dinosaur."

My jaw almost hit the table. Ruby was usually so placid and, well, *boring*. It startled me that she had such a strong opinion on something. Especially about something as commonly accepted as the extinction of the dinosaurs. "What's a sauropod?" I asked.

"Long necks and tails, tiny heads and massive bodies... The diplodocus would be one of them." Ruby blushed and started chewing her nails.

I thought for a while. I couldn't do any dinosaur impressions but maybe I could learn. "Do you want to do our presentation on dinosaurs?"

"I don't know. Do you?"

"I don't know."

At that point, Ms Sorenson came over. "How are you getting on?" she asked.

We both shrugged.

I expected her to say something else but she just kept staring at us.

"We thought we could do it on dinosaurs," I said finally. "Ruby doesn't think they went extinct."

Ruby looked at me in horror and shook a little, but Ms Sorenson smiled and said, "Fantastic! That sounds like a great project idea." She gave a curt nod and moved on.

I turned to Ruby. "Shall we do it on dinosaurs then?"

"If you want."

I giggled as I wrote *'Bangbo lives!'* at the top of a piece of paper. "Right then!" I said. "Tell me everything you know about dinosaurs in the Congo."

That evening, I sidled up to Jill as she sat doing some work in the living room.

"Do you remember Bangbo?" I asked.

"What's Bangbo?"

"You know! The dinosaur in the story Dad used to read me." When she didn't reply, I added, "Ruby doesn't think dinosaurs went extinct."

Jill snorted and carried on working.

"I wish I still had that book... Do you think Dad's got it?" I decided that would be my first question when he called.

Jill gave an absent sigh.

As if on cue, the phone rang.

My sister threw her work down with a moan and went to answer it. Even though all she said was, *"Hello. Oh..."* I knew straight away it was him.

I wobbled into the hallway, my heart pounding as Jill held the phone out to me. I kind of hoped she would stay with me through the call but, as soon as I had the phone, she marched back into the living room.

I gulped and put the phone to my ear. "Hello?"

"Hi Livi." It made my stomach squirm to hear him say my name.

"Hi... Dad." And again to say his.

"What are you up to?"

"Writing a story," I said.[41]

"A story?"

"Yes..."

"Oh, you're still into that then?"[42]

"Yes."

"What's it about?"

"Erm... It's hard to explain." My chest tightened as I slid down the wall and sat on the floor.

Dad gave a soft hum before asking, "How was school today?"

"Okay," I squeaked. I was about to ask whether he still had my Bangbo book but my throat dried up and I lost my nerve. It suddenly crossed my mind that perhaps Ms Sorenson would find a project on long lost fathers far more interesting than one on dinosaurs. The very thought almost made me throw up.

There was silence for a bit and then Dad asked, "Do you want to come to dinner with me tonight?"

---

[41] Actually, I hadn't done any writing that day. But it sounded more exciting than admitting that I'd spent much of the afternoon digging a splinter out of my foot. Anyway, I wanted to see if he remembered...

[42] ...That will do.

This made me giggle because he sounded like an embarrassed schoolboy asking me on a date. Not that any schoolboys have ever asked me on a date and, if they did, I certainly wouldn't giggle.

"Livi?" His anxious voice brought me back to reality.

"Dinner?" I repeated awkwardly.

Jill, who until then had been doing a good impression of not listening, came out of the living room and shook her head, performing an elaborate mime which I took to mean that something was already planned for that evening.

"I can't," I said.

"Oh." He sounded hurt.

"Maybe tomorrow?" This was more to Jill than to Dad but it was Dad who replied. Jill had gone back to not listening.

"Tomorrow will be great! I'll pick you up at seven."

"Can I bring a friend?" I don't know why I said that. It was one of those idiotic moments, like lying about your age or insulting a dead person. It just slipped out.

"A friend?"

"Yes. I'd like to bring a friend." My brain was being temporarily held up in a traffic jam and a crazed maniac was holding me at gunpoint and forcing me to make ridiculous requests.

"Well, I suppose you could..."

"Yes please. Okay, see you tomorrow." I hung up and let out a shriek.

A friend? A FRIEND?! Why would I want to bring a friend to meet my dad who I barely knew but who was supposed to be an actor playing Hamlet in London? And it wasn't like I had the choice of a whole host of bubbly and awe-inspiring friends to impress him with. I imagined dinner with me and Dad and Ruby-the-timid-carrot and growled at my stupidity. But, now that I'd made such a point of wanting to bring someone, I could hardly change my mind and go alone. He'd think that none of my friends liked me enough to come.

"What's wrong?" Jill reappeared in the living room doorway.

"Nothing. I'm going to dinner with my dad tomorrow."

"Okay." She turned to leave.

"And I'm going to bring Ruby."

Jill looked at me in confusion. "Why?"

"Because I want to!" I turned on my heels as I stomped up the stairs.

~ 9 ~

Dinner with an actor

Ruby arrived at half six in her very best dress.

Belinda came with her, grinning from ear to ear. Every few moments she checked inside her purse to make sure the tissue she'd brought for my dad to sign was still there. "Violet sends her love," she said cheerily. "She's sorry she couldn't come."

"I didn't invite her," I mumbled.[43]

Belinda chuckled and checked her reflection in the living room mirror. "I've never met anyone famous before!"

"He's not famous," said Jill.

But Belinda was enjoying her own voice too much to notice. "We met a few actors when we went to Disneyland, didn't we, Ruby?"

"Did we?" Ruby squirmed as Belinda leant over and smoothed down her hair.[44]

"Of course! Mickey, Minnie, and who was that one you liked... Friar Tuck!"

Ruby blushed.

"Although, I don't mean to imply that your father's craft is as simple as theirs," Belinda rabbitted on. "Ooh, I do hope he'll be kind to us *little* people! Will he perform a small soliloquy for us, do you reckon, if I ask him nicely?"

"That won't be appropriate, Belinda," my sister muttered.

I sat in the corner of the room, tearing the TV guide into tiny shreds. A wave of panic flooded through me as Belinda tested the batteries in her camera. Why had I said my father was an actor? Why had he reappeared at a time when the only thing he was good

---

43 *'Or you!'* I screamed silently.
44 For the record, I was wearing my smart blue jumper and jeans. Later, in the restaurant, I was so hot but couldn't take the jumper off because I still had my school shirt on underneath.

for was being illusive? And *why* had I invited Ruby to come for dinner? I debated setting fire to the rug. I debated turning my dad away at the door. I debated telling Belinda that he'd died and wouldn't be coming after all. I didn't have any matches so I opened my mouth to announce his sudden demise from stage fright when there was a loud knock at the door.

"Ooh!" Belinda jumped up. "Allow me!"

Perhaps I should've got up and beat her to it but, with the morbid curiosity usually afforded to car crashes and deformed animals, I leant against the wall and waited.

We heard Belinda exclaiming, *"To be or not to be? That is the question!"* followed by my dad enquiring nervously, "Have I got the wrong house? I'm looking for Livi Starling..."

"O! What a rogue and peasant slave am I!" Belinda continued.

"Excuse me?"

In the depths of my heart, I hoped that my dad would make his apologies and leave. I would phone him later and apologise for our 'eccentric cleaner.'

"There are more things in Heaven and Earth, Horatio, than are dreamt of in your philosophy..."

"I'm afraid I don't understand... Who's Horatio?"

At this, Jill nudged me and hissed, "Get up, Livi!"

But, before I could do anything, my dad wandered in. "Livi!" he said in relief.

"Hello," I said shyly. Then, as an afterthought, I added, "This is Ruby... and Belinda."

"Nice to meet you." Dad nodded at them before turning to my sister. "What a lovely house!"

Jill gave him a steely stare.

In the silence that followed, Belinda whipped out her camera. "May I?"

"Oh! What a great idea!" Dad exclaimed. I wriggled uncomfortably as he came and put his arm around me, striking the pose of *'Loving Father.'*

Belinda took a couple of shots before handing the camera to Ruby. "My turn!" she trilled, dragging me out of the way by the elbow as she slotted in next to my dad.

He looked rather confused but smiled politely nonetheless.

"I always fancied myself as an actor!" Belinda said, striking a pose.

Dad nodded. "Oh?"

"Yes! Do you think I have what it takes?"

He looked her up and down. "Er... Yes?"

Belinda gave a little squeal and flung her tissue in his face. "Please?"

Dad gave her a puzzled look. He took the tissue from her and was about to blow his nose on it when Jill said loudly, "You should go now or you'll be late for your reservation."

"Yes. Come on, Dad!" I grabbed his arm and ushered him out of the house.

Ruby followed, but not till after Belinda had given her a fresh tissue with the words, "Ask after dessert, that's polite. And remember your manners."

Belinda came onto the pavement to wave us off. I don't know anything about cars but I was pretty sure that a real actor wouldn't drive the noisy old banger my dad owned. I hoped Belinda wouldn't notice that it took him several attempts to get the engine started. For one awful moment, I thought she was going to start trotting along beside us but, instead, she turned to go back into our house. Jill had already closed the door.

"How's school?" Dad asked as we left our estate.

I nodded quickly. "Fine." *Should I expand on that?* I wondered. *Should I tell him about how I'd carved a shrunken head out of my apple core that lunchtime? Or about how I was worried that I'd broken my little toe in P.E? Or about getting into trouble in Maths again? If I told him that Parents' Evening is in a few weeks, would he want to come? Should I confess that I only have a small part in the Christmas show?* In the end, I said nothing.

"How about you, Ruby?" my dad continued. "Is school fine for you too?"

"Yes," she said meekly.

"Good. That's good."

After a few minutes of silence, Dad turned the radio on and started to hum.

He hates me, I thought. *He wishes he was anywhere but here.*

Eventually, we pulled up in the car park of some Italian restaurant. It looked nice; the sort of place an actor might eat. I stole a glance at Ruby but I couldn't work out her expression.

"You can have anything you want!" Dad announced when we'd been seated.

I turned to the menu. I knew he'd said we could have *anything,* but I thought it was probably good manners not to pick something from the most expensive part of the menu, so I missed that bit out. I was tempted by the spaghetti bolognaise but then I had visions of myself splattering it everywhere and looking most ungraceful in the process. I had no idea what *calzone* and *farfalle* were and tonight didn't feel like the night for taste challenges. I flicked to the pizzas.

"Well, I think I'm going to have the *bistecca dolcelatte!*" Dad said enthusiastically.

I had no idea what that was. I flicked back through the menu. It was some kind of steak and it was incredibly expensive. *Good*, I thought. I gave Ruby a smile which I hoped said, *'My dad doesn't worry about money because he's an actor.'*

She stared at me and whispered, "What are you having?"

"I don't know," I whispered back. "Maybe a pizza."

"I was thinking that but they look quite big." She pointed to a nearby table. The pizzas looked as huge as pillows.

"Oh." I frowned. It would be awful to order something and not be able to finish it. What if he made some comment about starving children in Africa? I would seem like a horribly ungrateful child. I turned back to the *calzones*.

Ruby nudged me. "Do you want to share one?"

"Er..." *Was that allowed?*

I looked at my dad and he smiled.

"Can we share a pizza?" I asked weakly.

"If you want!" Dad chuckled. "But don't you want one each?"

"No..." I forced a cough. "We're not that hungry because... because it was a Jewish day at school so we all had a Passover meal." I avoided Ruby's gaze.

Dad looked a bit confused. "Right... Which pizza do you want then?"

Ruby and I consulted the menu for a further nine minutes before finally agreeing on the *margherita* with extra cheese.

Dad motioned for the waitress to come over and we gave our order. I couldn't decide what to drink but went for orange juice as I thought it might make me look healthy. As it happened, Dad and Ruby both asked for lemonade and I wished I'd done so too, but I didn't want to look indecisive by asking the waitress if I could change my mind.

"Orange juice! Very healthy!" Dad said after the waitress left.

"Yeah." I gave a stupid shrug.

"You'd think I'd be sick of lemonade by now. I drink it all the time at work. It's free, you see."

"That's nice," I said quickly. "It's good that you can have whatever you want."

Dad laughed. "I wouldn't go that far! It's just lemonade and cola that are free. We have to pay if we want one of those *Ice Slurps—*"

"But you probably *could* have one, if you really wanted to. They would probably arrange it for you." Dad was about to reply when I skilfully changed the subject with, "Ruby collects banana stickers!"

"Oh really?" Dad looked a little bewildered.

Ruby went bright red. "Sort of," she muttered.

"She's got over 700, haven't you?"

She went even redder.

"Did you bring them with you?" I elbowed her.

She shook her head fiercely and looked away.[45]

Dad gave a thoughtful smile before saying, "There was a funny old man in the cinema today! He thought the popcorn was cotton wool and I said to him—"

"There was a weirdo in the park the other day!" I said rapidly. "Wasn't there, Ruby? Wasn't there?"

Ruby blinked at me. "Who?"

"You know! That man who kept whistling to himself."

"I don't think he was a weirdo. I think he was just walking his dog."

"No, not him! There was another one."

"Was there?"

"Yeah, he was dressed all funny and everything."

"Oh... Okay then."

During the awkward silence that followed, Ruby excused herself and went to find the toilet.

"She seems nice," said Dad.

I nodded quickly. I didn't have much time. "Dad... Please don't say you work at the cinema."

"Why not?" He looked at me, possibly in concern but I couldn't work it out.

"Just don't."

"Are you ashamed of me?"

"No!" *Ashamed? Why should I be ashamed? Ashamed of someone I barely even know?*

"Then, why—?"

"Please will you not mention it?"

Dad frowned. "What should I say then?"

---

[45] With hindsight, I feel bad about using her crazy hobby as a way of changing the subject. I just panicked, that's all.

I took a deep breath. This was going to sound so ridiculous. "Don't laugh but I told them you were an actor. I didn't realise I'd ever see you again." I looked away.

Dad said nothing. I wondered if he was going to tell me off but, when I glanced back, he looked kind of sad.

Ruby was coming back. I shot my dad an imploring stare. To my relief, he smiled and said, "Actor, hey? I can do that!"

"Thanks," I whispered as Ruby sat back down.

"So, Ruby," Dad said with a grin. "What is your all time favourite film?"

"Erm, probably, '*The Adventures of Pipsqueak McCully.*'"

"Oh really?" He gave a nervous cough. He had clearly never heard of it.

"It's about a mouse in the apocalypse," I informed him. I only know because Violet keeps threatening to lend it to me.

Dad raised his eyebrows.

"Or maybe, '*On Borrowed Time.*'" Ruby added.

"Also about the end of the world," I chipped in.

Dad gave another cough before continuing smoothly, "Well, speaking of things being *borrowed,* I was doing a film recently with a friend of the new Doctor Who. One day, The Doctor popped in to give us some tips and, would you believe it, he let me *borrow* his coat." He patted his jacket.

I glanced at Ruby. *Did she believe him?*

"That's right!" my dad continued loudly. "This is no ordinary coat! Now, what do you think of that, Ruby?"

I tried not to giggle as she gave him a shy smile.

Now that I'd ensured Dad wasn't going to blow his cover as a popcorn assistant I was able to relax a bit. I even started to have fun. I ate as slowly as I dared in order to make the treat of having dinner with my dad last as long as possible. I couldn't believe he was actually there. Every now and then I almost had to pinch myself. He seemed to take great pleasure in dropping in as many famous films and faces as he could and somehow managed to turn every conversation into a chance to boast about his various acting exploits. I have to say, he hammed it up slightly, but I hoped that would make him seem even more dramatic. At one point, he almost slipped up by accidentally saying something about there not being enough parking at the cinema, but I don't think Ruby noticed. She seemed too occupied with the dessert menu.

On the way home we told Dad about our Personal and Social Development project and how we were going to prove that dinosaurs had never gone extinct.

"There have been lots of sightings of strange animals in the Congo," I said. "We're going to be... What's it called, Ruby?"

"Cryptozoologists."

"Cryptozoologists," I repeated. "It means people who look for proof of animals that are thought to be extinct or non-existent."

"How exciting," said Dad. "Do you mean like Bigfoot?"

"Yeah! And the Loch Ness Monster and things like that."

"Fantastic!" He looked suitably impressed.

I beamed. "Oh, Dad, do you know what happened to my Bangbo book?"

"What's Bangbo?"

"You know! Bangbo the stegosaurus!"

He looked confused for a moment and then chuckled to himself. "The dinosaur story?"

"Yeah!"

"You were obsessed with it. I think I threw it away."

"Oh." I felt a little stung.

Dad reached for my arm. "Don't worry," he said. "I know a guy who worked on *'Jurassic Park.'* I can get you a real life dinosaur foot if you like!"

He sounded so convincing. I wondered if he remembered he was only *pretending* to be an actor. I didn't say anything.

"Well, ladies, thank you for a wonderful evening." Dad pulled up outside my house and grinned.

"Thanks... er... Livi's dad," Ruby said as she opened the car door.

Dad laughed. "Fancy us spending a whole evening together and you not knowing my name! I'm Charlie. Charlie Teeson, BAFTA award winner— Google me."

"Dad!" I hissed, shooting him a sharp look.

He gave a sheepish grin. "No need to Google me, Ruby. Just take my word for it."

Ruby looked from me to my father. "Thanks... Charlie." She got out of the car and waited for me on the pavement.

"Thanks," I whispered, opening my own door.

Dad leant over. "I'm sorry about the dinosaur book, Livi. I'll make it up to you."

I looked at him and he smiled. Something in me melted and, for some stupid reason, I was scared that I might cry. I quickly got out without saying anything else. It had been such a lovely evening and I didn't want to ruin it. Ruby and I waved as my dad tooted his horn and drove away.

"Well, that was my dad!" I said proudly.

Ruby gave me a curious look. "Don't worry," she said. "I won't tell my mum."

"Tell your mum what?"

"That your dad serves popcorn at the cinema."

"No he doesn't!" I spluttered. I gulped before begging, "Seriously, don't tell her."

Ruby cocked her head to one side. "How come you said he was an actor?"

"He *used* to be an actor. He's just taking a break." When Ruby didn't look convinced, I blushed and added, "I haven't seen him since I was seven."

Ruby looked at me in surprise. I thought she must think I was really weird but she said, "I'm sorry, Livi."

"Don't be sorry! It's not your fault!"

She gave a gentle smile and patted me on the shoulder.

"Anyway," I said awkwardly. "Thanks for coming with me."

We said goodbye and I watched as Ruby crossed the street to her house, then I let myself into mine. Jill was watching some programme about the rise in parents suing schools over playground accidents.

"Flipping ridiculous," she moaned as I came in. "He tripped over his own shoelaces!" Nevertheless, she seemed to be taking notes and I saw her write down, *Employers responsible for blisters obtained at work.*

I perched on the arm of the sofa.

Eventually Jill turned to me. "How was it?"

I gave a coy shrug. "It was alright."

"What did you eat?"

"Pizza."

She nodded. "Well, you'd better get to bed. It's late now."

"Okay..." I lingered for a moment. Jill had been rather uptight since we bumped into my father. I wanted to assure her that I was alright, that I didn't expect too much from him, and that I wasn't going to forget his sudden abandonment in a hurry. I also wanted her to know that I appreciated what a good job she'd done of raising me over the years and that even if my dad asked me to live with him I would, at the very most, only want to stay with him once a fortnight. I didn't know how to put all of this into words so I started to chew my fingernails instead.

"Livi! Go to bed now."

I sucked in my cheeks and edged towards the door. "It's weird my dad being around, isn't it?"

"Hmmm." She avoided my gaze.

"What do you think our mum would make of it?"

"I don't know." Jill turned the volume up on the television. She never likes talking about our mother.

"Do you think she's looking down on us— like from Heaven, or something?"

"I don't know," she repeated tersely.

"If she was still alive, do you think our mum would be friends with Belinda?"

"Livi! Stop asking silly questions and go to bed."

I wrinkled up my nose and went upstairs. When I got to my room, I paused for a moment before pulling out a photo album from the back of my wardrobe. It contained a selection of pictures of me, Jill and my dad from before he left. I had flicked through the album from time to time over the years, always feeling empty when I did so. Tonight, for the first time in years, this emptiness was peppered with hope.

I let out a long sigh as a particular picture caught my eye. I was about six years old and was sitting on my dad's shoulders, wearing face paint and waving a sandwich. I looked utterly enthralled, blissfully unaware that I was riding on such a fleeting moment.

I thought about my dad at the restaurant that evening and felt almost embarrassed at the idea of ever sitting on his shoulders. I shook my head and turned back to the photo, marvelling at how tall my father had seemed back then. His arms were so wide that every hug seemed to go on forever and, when he put me on his shoulders, I'd felt like I was on top of the world— such is the magic of tall people.

~ 10 ~

Free as a bird

Dad rang at quarter past six the next morning.

"I wasn't sure if you'd have left for school yet," he said as I took the phone from Jill who was fuming.[46]

"No, not yet." I cleared my throat and tried to make it sound as if I'd been up for hours.

"I didn't wake you, did I?"

"Of course you didn't wake us!"

Jill scowled and stomped upstairs to have a shower.

"Good." I heard my dad sigh. He paused before adding, "It was nice to see you last night."

"You too!" I said this a little quickly.

"Maybe we'll do it again some time."

"Okay."

There was a long silence.

"Well, I'd better let you get to school," Dad said finally.

"Okay..."

"And, Livi?"

"Yes?" I squeaked.

"Come and see me at the cinema any time you want. I'll get you free tickets to all the films."

Although he couldn't see me, I nodded so hard that I almost cracked my head open on the wall. "I will!"

"Bye then."

"Bye."

I was so excited at the prospect of seeing my dad whenever I wanted to that, for the first week, I panicked and didn't go at all.

---

[46] She had fallen out of bed after mistaking the ringing for the smoke alarm and then tripped over her slippers as she sprinted down the stairs screaming, "Fire, Livi! Fire! Run for your life!"

How often was *any time?* What if I overdid it and looked desperate? What if he thought I was only there for the free tickets?

I confessed to Ruby that I wasn't sure what to do.

"It's alright to be scared," she said.

"I'm not scared!" I protested. "I just don't want to *bother* him."

She gave me a curious look. "Is he married? Does he have any other children?"

My heart leapt. I hadn't even thought of that. "I hope not." It made me ache to think of all the possible people in his life that were far more important than me.

"He looked very young," Ruby continued. "How old is he?"

"How should *I* know? Do you know how old *your* parents are?"

From the look on her face, it was clearly a daft question. She probably knew her parents' birth weights, blood types and national insurance numbers.

"Thirty something?" I guessed wildly. "I know he was a lot younger than my mum because Jill's thirty one so, if Mum was still alive, she would have been at least..." I did some maths on my fingers. "Forty seven."

Ruby raised an eyebrow. "So... Your mum had Jill when she was sixteen?"

"Yeah... I think Jill was a mistake. That's why she never knew her dad."

Ruby chewed her bottom lip. "How old were your parents when they got married?"

I shifted awkwardly. "They weren't married."

"Ohhh." She gave a satisfied nod. "We were wondering why you had a different surname. That explains it."

"Who's *'we'?*"

"Me and Violet."

I felt my cheeks burn as I looked away. I didn't like to think about Ruby and her sister speculating about my family. "His surname is my middle name," I said tersely. "Starling was my mum's surname."

"Why did he leave?"

Her question was like a dart to my heart. "I don't know," I muttered.

"It must've been hard."

"Hmmm."

She gave a sheepish smile. "Maybe you don't want to talk about it?"

"Maybe."

"Sorry." She stayed silent for a while before asking, "Do you want me to come with you to the cinema?"

I shook my head. "I need to do this myself. Thanks, though."

"Do you want me to walk with you to the entrance?"

I was about to say no. Instead, I said, "Yes please. Can we go today after school?"

"Of course."

For the rest of the school day, I was consumed with anxious excitement. Listening to Fester waffle on about triangles is a particularly absurd way to spend a morning when you're about to see your father for only the third time in many years, and learning how to say, *'Where is the cinema?'* in French made me feel just a little bit queasy.

I spent the whole of Ms Sorenson's lesson drawing a giant picture of a diplodocus. Beside me, Ruby was writing an ardent account of possible dinosaur sightings in the Congo. One creature in particular bears striking resemblance to a diplodocus. It is known by the locals as *'Mokele-mbembe'*[47] and, whenever they draw him, their picture looks like a sauropod dinosaur.

"Wouldn't it be cool if we could go to the Congo and actually see one of these creatures?" Ruby whispered.

"Definitely!" I agreed. "Do you reckon our school would pay for us to go? Like on a research trip or something?"

"I don't know..."

I reached for some colouring pencils and started shading in the dinosaur's tail. "I wonder what other things are real that we have no idea about?"

Ruby grinned. "Probably loads of things at the bottom of the ocean."

I nodded. "Or up in space."

"Yeah!"

"People shouldn't be too quick to believe what they're told. They should look into things themselves."

Ruby kept grinning.

I finished colouring in the diplodocus and wrote in big letters across the paper, *'Did they REALLY die out?'* Then I added, *'Don't believe everything you're told!'* in red ink.

At one point Ms Sorenson came over and asked how we were getting on.

"Fine," we sang shyly.

---

[47] Meaning either *'One who stops the flow of rivers'* or *'Monstrous animal.'*

Ruby handed her notes across and started chewing her fingers. Ms Sorenson skimmed over the work and raised her eyebrows. "Girls, this is great. I'm very impressed with your initiative."

"If we could," I began carefully. "We'd go to the Congo and try to find proof for ourselves."

Ms Sorenson chuckled. "It's wonderful to see how much work you're putting into this. I can't wait to hear your presentation." She beamed as she left our table.

Ruby and I exchanged excited glances. I decided that Ms Sorenson was officially my favourite teacher.

All too soon, the bell rang and my stomach lurched. I folded up the diplodocus and took a deep breath.

Ruby caught my eye. "Ready?"

"Yeah."

True to her word, Ruby walked me all the way to the cinema entrance. We barely spoke the whole time. When we arrived, she turned and said simply, "Take heart, Livi."

I gave her an odd look and murmured, "Thanks." Then I walked through the door, fearing for a perverse moment that my dad might not recognise me.

To begin with, I couldn't see him and thought it was just my luck to turn up on his day off. But then I spotted him. He was carrying a stack of paper cups and wearing a badge which read, *"This Overrated Life'— Now in 3D.'*

I lingered by the ticket desk, unsure whether to approach him or not. People were queuing round me and I had to keep shuffling out of the way.

"Are you going to buy a ticket?" one of the cinema staff snapped at me.

"No..."

"Then would you mind moving?"

"Sorry. I'm waiting for someone."

At that moment Dad looked up and caught my eye. "Livi!" He seemed pleased to see me, which instantly made me feel better. "I'm just about to have a break. Wait there."

I nodded and waved, my jaw aching from grinning so hard.

I waited for fifteen minutes while Dad stacked the paper cups, reloaded the popcorn machine and disposed of old paper napkins. The whole time, the attendant behind the ticket desk kept glancing at me and tutting, but I didn't want to move too far. Dad had explicitly said to wait *there*.

Eventually he came over. "Hi Livi."

"Hi Dad."

"How are you?"

"Fine."

"Let's go and sit down somewhere…"

I followed him through the cinema and into one of the empty movie rooms where we sat and made awkward conversation for about twenty minutes. Dad asked about school and I said it was fine. I asked about his job and he said it was fine too. We sat in silence for a bit. Then I asked whether he'd ever danced around the cinema after it was closed. He said no. I gave a sheepish smile and wished I hadn't come. This was a lot harder than dinner.

At the end of it all, however, Dad said quietly, "I'm sorry, Livi. You must think I'm really boring."

I was taken aback. "You're not boring…"

He sighed. "I just want you to like me."

My heart leapt. "I do like you!" I wanted to add, *'I want you to like me too,'* but a lump caught in my throat.

"You'll come again, won't you?"

"Of course!" I wondered if I could skip school the next day and go to the cinema instead.

Dad tentatively reached over and hugged me. I wanted to bury my face in his chest and ask him to come and live with me and Jill.

When we parted I gave a shy smile and said, "Same time tomorrow?"

He beamed. "I can't wait."

~*~

Within a couple of weeks, I knew Dad's rota off by heart and made sure to turn up when he was about to have a break. I gave myself strict orders not to go more than three times a week because, after all, *he* abandoned *me* and I wanted to play it cool. Whenever he saw me coming Dad would wave and grab us both a chocolate milkshake. I didn't have the heart to tell him I would rather have strawberry.

As it turned out, my father didn't have a wife or a girlfriend or any other children. I'd finally plucked up the courage to find out by saying nonchalantly, "So, are you going to introduce me to your family at some point?"

Dad had laughed and said, "There's nobody but me. I'm free as a bird!"

Part of me felt relieved because I didn't know how I would handle hearing other children call him *'Dad,'* but another part of me felt rather lost at the apparent lack of *substance* to his life. I asked about hobbies but he said he didn't really have any except films and watching football. I asked about pets but, before I could impress him with my compilation of animal noises, he said he didn't like animals. He lived alone and did very little other than work. I asked about friends but he said, "Oh, nobody particularly special. A few guys at the pub." I asked what kind of jobs he'd done before the cinema but he replied, "This and that, nothing exciting." I even asked how he had ended up living in Leeds of all places but he just shrugged and muttered something about cheap housing.

I was left feeling totally dumbfounded. He seemed to have exchanged his old life for... *nothing at all.* It's like he walked out of my heart one day and has been drifting around in a void ever since.

Fish and guests smell

When Aunt Claudia found out that my father was back in our lives she let out a shriek and announced she would be on the next train up. She had telephoned to ask if her latest batch of lamb had reached us yet and I casually mentioned that I couldn't chat for long because I was off to the cinema to see my father.

"Your father?" she spluttered. "You don't mean your *father?*"

"Yes, Aunt Claudia. My father. He lives in Leeds. Didn't Jill say?"

Down the hall, my sister swore. It seemed Jill had intended to keep my father a secret. She yanked the phone off me and tried to appease our aunt. "Honestly, Aunt Claudia. We're fine... You don't need to come up."

I heard some muffled squawking.

"Tell her I'm glad he's here," I whispered.

Jill ignored me and batted me away with her hand. "Yes, I know," she continued to our aunt. There was some more squawking and then Jill snapped, "Of course I've thought of that, Aunt Claudia!"

"Thought of what?" I hissed, trying to squeeze my ear up to the phone.

Jill pushed me away. "Livi! Give me one minute, please."

I frowned and flounced out, making a point of slamming the door as I left.

I arrived at the cinema in time to watch Dad finish his shift. I watched from the pillar as he joked with customers and juggled popcorn scoopers. He balanced a paper cup on the end of his nose and said something that must have been funny because it caused a little girl to start laughing. He looked over at me and waved.

As I waved back I felt a queasiness in my gut, the reason for which I could not fully identify. I wanted to laugh and cry both at the same time. "Stop it! Stop it! Stop it!" I turned away as I scolded the butterflies in my stomach.

Dad came over. "Livi? Are you alright?"

I looked up sheepishly. "Just practising lines for our school show," I said in a whisper.

"Oh wonderful! What's the show?"

"Romeo and Juliet." Without thinking, I added, "I'm Juliet."

"Wow!" He looked impressed. "So, you're a bit of a performer then?"

"Sort of."

Dad handed me a chocolate milkshake. "Let's sit outside. I've been cooped up in here all day."

I didn't want to say that it had started to drizzle and that I hadn't brought a warm enough coat so I nodded dumbly and followed him out, trying not to shiver as we perched on a damp bench.

Dad smiled. "How are you?"

"Good. You?"

"Fine, thanks."

I wondered what to say next. "Do you remember my Aunt Claudia?"

Dad grimaced.

I grinned. "Well, she screamed when she heard you were around."

"Screamed?" He looked alarmed.

"Yup." I blew bubbles in my milkshake.

Dad looked away and let out a sigh.

"Did you not get on?" I asked with another grin.

"What?"

"You and Aunt Claudia. Didn't she like you?"

Dad waved a hand. "Oh, I don't think that miserable cow likes anybody." He gave half a smile and I sniggered.

After clearing his throat, Dad began to tell me about one of the new releases at the cinema. It was a film about three men on a desert island who want to play football but haven't got a ball. It sounded really boring but I didn't want to interrupt him so I tried to look interested. All the while, a mountain of questions were pounding round my brain.

By now I have a big mental list of things that I want to ask my father. Top of the list is, *'Why did you leave?'* shortly followed by,

'*What would make you stay this time?*' but I'm yet to pluck up the courage to ask such weighty questions so, every time I see him, I leave with even more.

Eventually Dad finished talking. To fill the gap before he began again I quickly said, "Dad..?"

"Yes?"

My throat grew tight as I wondered what to say. I had the sudden urge to ask, '*Would my mum have liked me?*' But that felt too deep and too desperate. Jill has told me many times that she would've done, but I just wanted to hear it from somebody else. Finally I asked, "What do you remember about my mum?"

Dad scratched his chin and thought for a long while. "She was always giggling," he said at last.

I pictured a jolly woman cracking jokes and roasting chicken. "That's nice."

"She always had a joke to tell," Dad continued. "About the neighbours, Jill, me... She had a wicked sense of humour."

Jokes about other people sounded a bit odd. I raised my eyebrows. "Was she good at cooking?"

"No! She used to say only weak women sit around the house cooking and cleaning. She hated things like that. *Too boring* for her."

"Oh," I said, my illusion shattered.

"I remember, oh, hahaha!" Dad started laughing.

I looked at him expectantly. "What?"

"She used to— hahaha!"

"What? Tell me!"

Dad composed himself and said, "When she was pregnant with you she used to stop policemen and ask if she could pee in their hats!"

I gaped at him. "Why did she do that?"

"She thought it was funny, I suppose. She was just like that."

I frowned. Just like what? *Confusing? Reckless? Audacious?* I didn't imagine my mother to be any of those things. I imagined her being sensible and calm. Although I knew she looked nothing like her, it was hard to imagine my mother without imagining her dressed in Belinda's dresses and baking shoo-fly pie.[48] But it seemed my mother was not the kind of woman who would wear floral dresses or bake tasty treats. I felt a tug at my heart. If my mother was here, would she be proud of me? Would she find me

---

[48] Which, by the way, I still have not tasted.

smart or pretty or funny? Or would she make a joke out of me? I gulped down some milkshake too quickly and started coughing.

"You alright?" Dad asked.

I nodded and spluttered a little. My many questions begged to be asked but I had a burning sensation behind my eyes and I didn't want him to see me cry. "Thanks for the milkshake," I said. "I'd better go. I'm meeting Ruby in the library."

"Ah, how's the dinosaur project coming along?"

"Yeah, good." I forced a smile, grateful that he'd remembered and yet aching for so much more. "Shall I come again tomorrow?"

Dad frowned. "I'm doing a bit of overtime because we've got a few people away."

"Oh?"

"It means I can't take as many breaks."

I sucked in my cheeks. "Okay. When are you free next?"

He chewed his lip as he mulled it over. "Can I call you?" When I nodded, he grinned and added, "We'll have to go out for dinner again!"

"Okay!" I gave him a quick hug and said goodbye. I decided that next time I would try the *bistecca dolcelatte*.

~*~

Aunt Claudia's arrival was like a gush of fresh water. By this, I do not mean that her presence was remotely refreshing but, rather, that she readily and greedily filled every conceivable space that she entered. Within an hour of her arrival, the kitchen smelt of lavender, three pairs of her shoes lined the stairs, her toothbrush was sitting on top of mine, the door of the spare room bore a large *'Do Not Disturb'* sign and the sofa was covered in cat hair. Jill had explicitly said that Aunt Claudia wasn't allowed to bring any of her cats but Aunt Claudia had brought Dora (the furriest one) anyway, believing her to be the exception to the rule because she had an eye infection and needed to have ointment dripped into her eyes every four hours.

The first administering of this ointment was hugely unsuccessful and resulted in half of the bottle being kicked onto the living room floor.

Jill grimaced and ran to get a cloth.

Aunt Claudia cooed over Dora and said, "You poor cat, you."

The silly creature screeched and ran behind the television.

Jill returned with two cloths and threw one to me. "Help me, Livi," she ordered.

I wrinkled up my nose but knew better than to refuse.

"These things happen," said Aunt Claudia, nestling herself in the sofa as Jill and I frantically patted the carpet.

"Yes, it's fine," Jill snapped, her cheeks matching the deep pink stain.

Then, supposedly feeling it was an appropriate time to raise the matter, Aunt Claudia said, "Now then. What's all this about Charlie?"

Jill scowled. "We really don't need to talk about him."

"Don't be daft!" Aunt Claudia exclaimed. "That's why I've come all this way!"

"Nobody asked you to," I muttered under my breath.

Aunt Claudia looked a little affronted but ploughed on regardless. "Well, what is he doing in Leeds?"

"He lives here." Jill scrubbed the carpet with extra vigour. "He works at the cinema."

"Huh!" Aunt Claudia scoffed.

I narrowed my eyes at her. *It's better than rearing sheep,* I thought.

Aunt Claudia gave Jill a stern look. "Is he married?"

"How should I know?"

"He isn't married," I informed them. "Not that it's any of your business."

"Livi!" Jill shot me a warning look.

"Still a bachelor, hey?" Aunt Claudia gave a wry smile. "Can't say I'm surprised."

"What's wrong with that?" I demanded, feeling my cheeks grow hot. "You never got married and you're *years* older than him!"

"Don't be rude, Livi," Jill scolded.

I glared at her. If she had just been firm enough to forbid Aunt Claudia from coming then we could've been spared this ordeal!

Aunt Claudia looked at me thoughtfully. "Oh, I could never love a man." She said this as though she was very proud of herself.

I sniffed. "I'd get lonely if I were you."

Aunt Claudia laughed. "You lack will power."

"It's not wrong to fall in love!"

"It depends who it's with."

"Yes. But it's still not wrong."

"You're young," Aunt Claudia said with a patronising smile. "You'll change your mind."

I rolled my eyes and looked over at Jill, hoping for some encouragement. But Jill was still busy with the stain and avoided my gaze. At that moment, Dora emerged from behind the television and Aunt Claudia scooped her up and blew a raspberry on her tummy.

"You love your cats," I said.

"Of course I do!" Aunt Claudia exclaimed, cat hair hanging off her lip.

"But you've never loved a man?"

"Like I said, I have will power." Aunt Claudia shot me a smug beam. "Unlike your mother," she added slyly.

"What's that meant to mean?" I asked, narrowing my eyes.

She gave an airy sigh. "Jill knows what I mean. Don't you, love?"

Jill gave her a funny look and replied, "Shall I get the dinner on?"

I raised my eyebrows. It wasn't uncommon for Aunt Claudia to make funny remarks about my mother and I'd certainly never been under the illusion that they were the best of friends, but I had the unnerving feeling that something was being kept from me. I followed Jill into the kitchen.

"What did Aunt Claudia mean?" I demanded.

"How should I know?" Jill said irritably, burying her head in the freezer as she dug out some microwavable chips.

"She said our mum lacked will power. Why would she say that?"

Jill didn't reply.

"Does she mean she rushed into things with my dad? Is that why they never got married?" An awful thought struck me. "Was I an accident?"

Jill dug deeper into the freezer.

I tapped her on the arm. "Jill!"

Jill turned to face me. She gave me what I think was supposed to be a kind smile. *Or was it pity?* "Aunt Claudia says all sorts of stupid things," she said, brushing some hair out of my eyes. "Don't worry about it."

"Why didn't Mum and Aunt Claudia get on?"

"That's none of your business."

Notice that she didn't say she didn't know; only that she was unwilling to share any information with me.

I opened my mouth to continue but Jill snapped, "Can you go and keep Aunt Claudia company? I'm trying to cook." She poured some chips onto a plate and opened the microwave.

"Fine," I muttered.

I went back into the living room. Aunt Claudia was having another go with Dora's eye medicine and the cat was screeching wildly as my crazy aunt sang her a lullaby.

Suddenly the telephone rang. My heart leapt at the thought that it could be my father. But it was just Ruby asking if I wanted to hang out.

"We've got our aunt round," I whispered, hoping for a little sympathy.

"Oh that's nice," Ruby said, totally missing the misery in my voice.

I grunted.

"Well, when you're free, we've got this new game. It's a bit like *Monopoly* except you have rabbits instead of money and you don't collect properties—"

I heard Jill calling from the kitchen and cut Ruby off. "I'd better go. Dinner's ready."

"Okay. We're having roast duck tonight. What have you got?"

"Sweet and sour chicken," I lied.

"Nice!"

I hung up and went to eat my chips.

The weekend of Aunt Claudia's visit was the longest, wettest, dullest weekend since records began. Being a countryside snob, our aunt refused to leave the house, stating that cities are full of *'rats, brats and businessmen.'* All she wanted to do was sit in our living room and drink tea and occasionally say something snide about my father.

Jill is a heavy tea drinker at the best of times but she must have drunk at least fifty cups during Aunt Claudia's stay. It wouldn't have been so bad had she not insisted on using a fresh mug every time.[49]

I've decided that tea drinking is a somewhat mindless pastime. It gives the illusion of time well spent, but all it really means is incessant gossip and increased trips to the lavatory.

I sat glumly between the two of them as they chatted and sipped their tea. I couldn't help noticing how very much alike they

---

[49] "Bacteria is a very serious thing, Livi!"

were. They both have a habit of chewing their lip when they're deep in thought and they laugh at the same stupid jokes. I could imagine Jill turning out like Aunt Claudia when she's older.

"Charlie was never the sporty type, was he, love?" Aunt Claudia asked on Sunday afternoon, dipping a chunky biscuit into her current cup of tea.

Jill shrugged. "Not particularly."

Aunt Claudia sniffed and added, "I bet he's put on quite a bit of weight since I last saw him."

Jill rolled her eyes. "Does it matter?"

"I'm just saying. He's probably going grey too."

"I could invite him round if you like," I suggested. "Then you could see for yourself."

Aunt Claudia gave a loud slurp of her tea. "No, thank you."

"But you've come all this way. It would be a shame not to even *see* him!"

She ignored me.

I took a deep breath and looked her in the eye. "Why don't you like my dad?"

"What do you mean?" she asked innocently.

"You know what I mean!" I snapped, shaking a little but determined to look as though I meant business.

Aunt Claudia avoided my gaze. "Well, he abandoned you, didn't he?"

My stomach lurched. "It's more than that. You never liked him, did you?"

Aunt Claudia sighed and stroked Dora, making a great show of considering her words. Finally she said, "I can't answer that."

"Why not?"

When she didn't reply, I tried to catch Jill's eye but she was concentrating hard on her fingernails.

Eventually Aunt Claudia shrugged and said, "You know what they say... A little knowledge is a dangerous thing."

I glared at her. "They also say fish and guests smell after three days!"

I thought this was pretty witty but Jill slapped me on the arm and hissed, "Livi!"

Aunt Claudia laughed. "You should watch that attitude of yours. You'll turn out like your mother."

This was the nicest thing she'd said all weekend. "Good!" I yelled as I stormed out of the room.

I marched straight upstairs where I slammed my bedroom door and threw myself onto the bed. I hated pompous Aunt Claudia and I was angry with Jill for not sticking up for me. Part of me debated calling my dad and asking him to come over. That would give our stupid aunt a shock. But another part of me felt rather protective of him. I didn't want anybody to see him except for me. I didn't want anybody pointing at him, saying he'd got fat or gone grey, or accusing him of being unreliable.

I shut my eyes and imagined my mum sitting with me on my bed. *'Don't worry about Claudia!'* she would say with a grin. *'My sister was always a miserable cow!'*

I gave a sob as I reached down my top and pulled out my mother's locket. "Thanks for the locket, Mum," I whispered.

I raised the silver bird to my cheek and imagined her stroking my hair. *'You're welcome, my darling.'*

A lump caught in my throat. I desperately wanted a hug. Instead, I had to make do with squeezing my favourite teddy.[50]

After moping about for a while, I grabbed some paper and made a list.

Five things my mother would like about me
1. I'm nothing like Aunt Claudia.
2. I would be a very loving daughter.
3. I have a good imagination.
4. I have neat handwriting.
5. I'm destined for something great. I just don't know what it is yet.

---

[50] A fluffy dog dressed in dungarees. His name is Sausage-Legs on account of his long floppy limbs.

~ 12 ~

The meaning of life

I awoke in a good mood for the simple reason that Aunt Claudia would be gone by the time I got home from school. I whistled noisily as I prepared my peanut butter sandwiches for lunch, layering them doubly thick because we had badminton that morning and I knew I'd be extra hungry. Aunt Claudia groaned at my whistling and rubbed her head but I pretended not to notice and did it all the more loudly.

"I guess you'll be gone by the time I get home?" I asked, feigning sorrow.

"I'm afraid so."

I nodded as if disappointed— although not too much in case she reconsidered and stayed an extra day. Then I gave her a hug, thanked her for coming and gingerly patted Dora's tail. "Bye then."

"Bye love," she said. "Don't forget you can always ring me."

"I won't."[51]

I sauntered out of the house, *'Goodbye and good riddance!'* dancing wickedly through my mind. However, my jolly mood was ruined by Violet meeting me on the pavement with the announcement that Ruby was unwell and wasn't coming to school.

"Oh no!" I exclaimed.

"Don't worry," she said, swinging Paul the paper mâché lion over her shoulder. "You can walk with me."

"But we have badminton today!" I felt a little irritated with Ruby. It was understandable that she might occasionally get ill, but entirely unreasonable on a day when we had badminton! Now I would have to pair up with Wayne Purdy who has a really sweaty face.

Violet shrugged.

---

[51] By this I meant I won't *ring,* not I won't *forget.*

I looked up at their bedroom window but the curtains were still drawn. I debated saying I felt sick too and going back home but I didn't want to face Aunt Claudia again.

"Fine," I said with a sigh. "Let's go."

Our school is a thirty minute walk away. Ruby and I counted it once and it takes about three thousand steps, although we may have lost count slightly. I was about to take three thousand steps with Violet Rico by my side.

We'd barely reached the end of our street when she said, "So, Livi..."

"Yes?"

"What's going on with you?"

I looked at her in alarm. *Had she found out my dad wasn't really an actor?* "What do you mean?"

"Oh, you know," Violet said airily. "How do you feel your life is progressing?"

"How my life is progressing?" I repeated in confusion. "It's going fine, I guess. I mean, I'm doing alright at school... What else is there?"

Violet cocked her head to one side. "What would you say is the meaning of life, Livi?"

I gave a little splutter but she was deadly serious. "I don't know. To be happy?"

She gave me a long disappointed stare.

"And, uh, to be as good as you can?"

At this, Violet gave me what I *think* was supposed to be a kind smile but which manifested as more of a belittling grimace. "And who will judge whether you've been good or not?"

I gave a careless shrug. "No idea."

"Do you believe in God, Livi?"

I felt myself blush. "I guess there's something out there. Some grand force or something. I don't really think about it." Violet opened her mouth but I quickly cut her off. "You can believe whatever you want, Violet. Just don't push it on me."

She sniffed and starting fiddling with her paper mâché lion.

Neither of us spoke after that and, three thousand steps later, we reached the school gates.

"Well, it was nice to walk with you," I said curtly.

Violet gave me another of her belittling grimaces but I walked off before she could reply.

I spent the morning pretending not to notice that I was all alone.

During registration, Miss Fairway looked over and said, "Oh, Livi. You're on your own!"

I feigned surprise. "Oh yeah. Ruby must be ill."

Then, throughout French, I pretended to be fine by burying my head in my textbook.

"Eez Ruby away?" Madame Maurel asked.

I gave a casual glance to my side. "Looks like it." Then I shrugged and turned confidently back to my book.

Of course, I couldn't do this in English as Mrs Tilly thinks I'm unable to read. She gave me a sympathetic smile and asked if I wanted to sit at her desk.

"No, I'm fine," I said.

"But Ruby isn't here to help you!" She said this a little too loudly for my liking and came and sat beside me.

"I'm actually getting better at reading," I insisted.

Mrs Tilly ignored me and sat with me for the entire lesson.

By the time it got to badminton I felt like I'd said the words, *"I'm fine, really!"* a hundred times. I dragged my heels as I walked to the P.E block and changed as slowly as possible, tying my laces in triple knots and then reconsidering and leaving them loose instead. Perhaps if I fell over on my way into the Sports hall I would be exempt from playing. I pulled my hair into a ponytail and followed the rest of the girls into the gym. The boys were already there and were being told off by one of the teachers for some inappropriate behaviour in the changing rooms. I was about to approach Wayne Purdy and succumb to an hour of sweaty doom, but then I noticed Kitty Warrington standing alone and looking somewhat peeved. Molly was absent too! I'd been so consumed with pretending not to notice Ruby's absence that it had slipped my attention. My heart gave a flutter of hope as Kitty caught my eye.

She seemed to consider for a moment before jerking her head at me. "Come and be my partner, Livi."

I'm ashamed to say it but I felt close to euphoric as I strode towards her. "Molly away?" I asked as I attempted a smile.

Kitty gave me a funny look. "Obviously."

"Yeah, so is Ruby."

Kitty handed me a racket. "I hope you can play," she said snootily.

I hoped I could too.

We began a doubles match against Wayne Purdy and his partner, a boy called Fran.

None of us were very good and the shuttlecock spent more time on the floor than in the air. At one point, Kitty walloped it a little too hard and it went flying over the back line.

"Out!" Wayne cried triumphantly.

"It was not!" Kitty protested.

"It was totally out!" Wayne exclaimed.

"Way over," added Fran.

Kitty turned to me. "It was in, wasn't it, Livi?"

"Er, it might have been," I said. "I didn't really see."

Wayne gave a growl as Fran said, "Fine. Your point then."

A few minutes later, it happened again.

"In!" yelled Kitty.

"Yeah, I think it was," I muttered.

"Oh, come on!" Wayne threw down his racket in frustration, beads of sweat dripping from his nose.

Fran shrugged. "Just let them have it."

Kitty smirked at me and whispered, "That one *was* out, but whatever!"

I giggled, enjoying the fact that we were sharing a joke.

After a few more minutes and another dubious shot, Kitty declared that we had won. She raised her hand and I gave her a high five. Wayne and Fran looked suitably defeated and demanded a rematch.

I'm pretty sure they won the rematch but none of us were keeping score. Kitty's foul shots got worse and worse and Wayne got sweatier and sweatier and, all the while, I savoured being partners with the coolest girl in school. As the lesson ended, we flung our rackets into the corner and ran to get changed. I wondered if I ought to thank Kitty for being my partner but I didn't think it would be appropriate to try and have a conversation with her while she was getting undressed. I hastily got changed and grabbed my bag, debating whether I would prefer to eat lunch alone or with Violet. Remembering our conversation on the way to school, I decided alone was best. But, as I entered the busy canteen, I felt somebody put their arm through mine.

It was Kitty. "Where shall we sit?" she asked.

I stared at her.

"For lunch." She rolled her eyes. "Let's sit over there."

"Alright..." I followed her through the canteen.

Kitty grabbed an empty table and pointed to the seat opposite her. I sat down very tentatively, looking around to see if anybody was watching. Kitty had a lacy cream lunch bag which looked more like a wash bag. It was emblazoned with garish pink buttons and the words, '*I am Tizzi Berry,*' which made it both an eyesore and an immediate object of envy. I watched as Kitty took her food out and lined everything up in size order. I felt ashamed of my clunky plastic lunchbox and my haphazardly cut peanut butter sandwiches. Kitty had rice cakes. Jill likes rice cakes. If only I'd known I'd be eating lunch with Kitty Warrington I'd have brought rice cakes too! I wished I had some buns or something fancy to share.

"I like your lunch bag," I said.

"Thanks." Kitty eyed my box but said nothing.

We sat in silence for a while. I took great care over every bite of my sandwich as I racked my brain for something interesting to say. The peanut butter stuck to the roof of my mouth. *I put way too much in*, I scolded myself, tilting them away from Kitty so that she wouldn't see and think I was a freak.

"Check this out." Kitty held up her bright pink phone.

On the screen was a photo of what can only be described as a cross between a rat and a half-plucked chicken. I wasn't sure whether I was supposed to be repulsed or excited.

"What is it?" I asked.

"She's not a *what!*" Kitty snapped. "She's a *who*. Her name is Angelica and she's a Chinese Crested."

"A dog?"

"Obviously." Kitty rolled her eyes before looking at me expectantly. "Do you have any pets?"

I pondered whether to say that I had a lamb in Suffolk called Stanley but I figured Aunt Claudia had probably killed it and posted it to someone by now. "My sister said I could have a dog for Christmas," I lied. "I'll probably get a King Charles Spaniel."

Kitty scrunched up her nose. "They have weird faces." She gave me a curious look. "You don't live with your parents, do you?"

I shook my head in what I hoped was a carefree manner.

"Why?"

I gave an airy sigh. "My mum died when I was a baby and my dad's an actor."

"Cool! About your dad, I mean. Sorry about your mum."

"It's alright. It was years ago. I don't even remember her." I tried to smile.

Kitty nodded. "My horse died a few years ago."

"You had a horse?"

"Yeah."

"Cool."

"It was really sad when she died," Kitty continued dramatically. "She got struck by lightning."

"Like that man on the news?"

"What man?"

"There was a man from Harrogate who got struck by lightning." Kitty gave me a funny look so I quickly added, "Never mind, it was a bit weird."

We lapsed back into silence and my brain went into overdrive as I fumbled for some smart topic of conversation.

"Ugh," I said finally. "We've got Maths this afternoon."

Kitty sniffed. "I hate Maths. Fester is such a *pig.*"

"I know! He's like—" I gave my best *Grumpy Pig* impression.

Kitty looked at me in astonishment. "Oh my goodness, do that again!"

I hesitated and gave another grunt.

"Do it again!"

Kitty roared with laughter as I sat there grunting my heart out. I debated throwing in a horse impression but the pig seemed to be going down well and I didn't want to ruin it.

When I stopped, I felt a little giddy.

Kitty patted me on the arm and said, "You're so funny, Livi!"

I felt my cheeks go red. In that moment, I hoped Ruby would be ill all week.

~*~

Despite having a slightly husky voice, Ruby was better the next day and apologised profusely for not being able to be my partner in badminton.

"That's alright," I said slowly. I wondered if I ought to mention that Kitty had been my partner and that we were *sort of* friends now. "Um... There wasn't anyone else to partner with so I went with Kitty."

"Oh right. Was Molly away then?"

"Yeah... We kind of had lunch together as well." I didn't add that I'd sat in Molly's seat in Maths and that Kitty had copied all my answers.

Ruby nodded.

"She's actually alright once you get to know her."

Ruby looked at me oddly.

"Anyway," I said quickly. "Are you feeling better now?"

"Yeah," she croaked.

As we approached the school gates, I saw Kitty loitering with Molly.

"Hi Kitty!" I called, waving nervously.

She gave me half a glance and looked away, laughing as Molly whispered something to her.

My cheeks burned as I forced a smile. "She's really rude, isn't she?" I said to Ruby. "I'm *so* glad you're back."

Our first lesson was double Science but, since our Science teacher was still absent, we ignored the worksheet on mutation handed out by the clueless supply teacher and did some of our dinosaur project instead. After that, we had French. We were supposed to be watching a programme about a superhero called 'Le Grenouille'[52] but, instead, we spent the lesson passing notes backwards and forwards as we discussed which existing animals could be dinosaurs in disguise. By the time we got to lunch, we'd drawn up a list.

Five animals that could be dinosaurs, alive and well today

1. *Komodo Dragons*
2. *Giant Tortoises*
3. *Armadillos*
4. *Lobsters*
5. *Emus*[53]

As we started eating, I caught sight of Kitty and Molly a few tables away. I tried to catch Kitty's eye but she ignored me so I sighed and turned back to Ruby. "Did you know, Kitty does this weird thing where she lines up her food in size order."

"Oh?" Ruby pointed to my lunch. "Have you got rice cakes?"

I blushed. "Yeah... Jill made me have them because we ran out of bread." I took a bite. It was disgusting.

---

[52] Or 'The Frog.' Later, Ruby and I had a competition to come up with the best superhero. I won with 'Infinity-plus-one Man' who is just that bit better than everybody else.

[53] We weren't too sure about emus but I've been getting good at my *Impatient Emu* impression so we thought we could allow for some artistic license.

Ruby gave a sympathetic smile. Then she rooted around in her lunchbox and pulled out a little tub which contained something yellow and slimy-looking.

"What's that?" I asked, wrinkling up my nose.

"Homemade yoghurt!"

I raised an eyebrow. "Yoghurt?"

"Me and Mum made it at the weekend. Want to try some?"

I dipped my finger in. It was surprisingly nice.

Ruby grinned. She started telling me about how Violet had mistaken the yoghurt for cheese spread and poured it over her toast. I pretended to find her story funny but, in reality, I was only half listening. Kitty and Molly were getting up from their table and were laughing really loudly— probably at something far more sophisticated than yoghurt. I forced myself not to watch as they sauntered out.

That evening, Jill and I were invited to the Ricos' for dinner again. We were due at seven but, at half past, my sister was still occupied with searching for fancy glasses online.[54]

"Jill," I scolded. "We're late!"

She turned the computer off with a sniff. "It's only the Ricos."

"That's not very nice," I muttered as she pulled on her boots.

"Says who?"

I couldn't answer that. It's not like we followed any kind of rulebook commanding us to love our neighbours.

As we crossed the street I asked, "Jill, what's the meaning of life?"

My sister gave me a funny look. "Whatever you want it to be," she said carelessly. Then she reconsidered and said, "The meaning of life is to make life as meaningful as you can."

I went over that a few times in my head. It sounded kind of sweet. I grinned as Jill knocked on the Ricos' front door.

Moments later, Violet answered and I said triumphantly, "The meaning of life is to make life as meaningful as you can!"

---

[54] She's convinced that she's developed *Computer Vision Syndrome* from prolonged computer use at work.

Violet looked us up and down and frowned. "You're late. Dinner's been ready for ages."

We followed her down the hall and into the dining room where Jill apologised for being *'a little delayed.'*

"I had a minor emergency," she lied as Belinda swooped in to greet us.

I rolled my eyes and sat down next to Ruby.

"Oh dear!" Belinda simpered. "What kind of emergency?"

"It's fine," Jill insisted. "I've got it sorted."[55] She picked up her cutlery and started eating but a loud, *"Ahem!"* from Oscar caused her to throw her fork back down. "Oh—![56] I forgot."

There was an awkward pause as everyone held hands. I bowed my head and squeezed my eyes shut.

Eventually Stanley said solemnly, "Thank you, gracious Lord, for our food and for your rich and abundant blessings."

I pretended to mumble along as the rest of the family said, "Amen."

While the others started to eat I paused and considered Stanley's prayer. It had sounded rather flamboyant. I wondered how many other people around the world began their meals with an address to someone who might not exist. I regarded the Ricos one by one. Violet and Oscar had begun to discuss the age of the earth and Ruby was accidentally mashing her hair into her potato while she listened. Stanley was humming to himself and Belinda was talking to Jill about mushrooms. I decided that they were all weird and, if God was real, then he must be weird too for liking them. I yawned and glanced casually round the room but then I caught sight of my dad's 'autograph' on the wall and turned quickly back to my food.

Something Violet said caught my attention. She'd been talking about the days of creation and said, "...God made land animals and man and woman on the sixth day—"

"Wait a minute," I interrupted. "Do you mean you believe God made them on the *same* day?"

"Yes," said Violet.

"And do you mean one *day*, like twenty four hours?"

"Yes."

---

[55] By this, she meant she had decided on oval-shaped copper frames with light sensitive lenses. Not that it mattered— a visit to the opticians two days later confirmed that her eyesight was fine.

[56] I have edited out the swearing.

"That's impossible."

"Is it?" She gave an annoying smile.

"Yes," I said irritably. "So you must mean a *length of time*, not a day exactly."

Violet gave a tut and started to reply but, at this point, Stanley got involved.[57] "There are different opinions on this," he said. "Some say the earth is very old; others say it is very young. Of course, this is not withstanding the possibility that there was a gap between the creation of the universe and the filling of it which could make it both ancient and new at the same time..."

I blinked at him and tried to pretend that I knew what he was talking about.

Stanley cleared his throat and continued, "The Old Earth doctrine states that each day of creation was periods of time rather than twenty four hours. So, in this theory, animals may well have roamed the earth for millions of years before mankind were created—"

Beside him, Violet was huffing and puffing as she said, "But obviously that's dumb."

Stanley gave her a firm look. "Others, however, believe that the earth is actually very young— maybe only as old as six thousand years or so, which could mean, yes, that man and woman were created in the same twenty four hour day as the land animals."

I raised an eyebrow. "So... Which opinion is right?"

Violet went to say something but Stanley replied, "I don't think it matters. Both could be wrong for all we know. The important thing is not how old the earth is but simply that God created it."

Jill rolled her eyes at this but she didn't say anything. She just pretended to be listening to Belinda who was still waffling on about mushrooms.

I chewed my lip as I considered the options. "Each day must have been millions of years," I said finally. "Otherwise people would have been surrounded by dinosaurs."

---

[57] A note about Stanley Rico: I didn't like him to begin with because he seemed too dull. But I have since concluded that he is actually a rather decent man. He does sweet things like slip notes into Ruby's lunchbox that say, *'I'm proud of you,'* or, *'Have a nice day!'* and he always waves when I walk past their house. He's not exactly brimming with enthusiasm and I can't imagine him with road rage or anything exciting like that. But he's dependable. And he seems to care.

Violet pretty much spat on me as she whipped out her Bible. "They *were* surrounded by dinosaurs!" she yelled. "Nothing died until after the fall!"

I snorted and turned to Ruby. "Do you believe that? People lived around dinosaurs and nobody batted an eyelid?"

Ruby gave me a long look and slowly nodded.

I was about to laugh when Stanley spoke again. "Is that too hard to believe, Livi? I thought that's what your school project was all about?"

I opened my mouth. "Oh..."

Stanley rubbed his chin. "I think it was in the book of Job that the Lord spoke about a creature named the *behemoth,* a tremendous beast with a tail like a cedar tree—"

Oscar interrupted Stanley's musings with a shriek. "Who would win in a fight between Jesus and a dinosaur?"

Ruby nudged me and whispered, "We should put that in our project."

I gave her a weak smile. I wasn't sure I wanted to put Jesus into our presentation. I doubted it would go down well. I coughed and tried to sound intelligent as I remarked, "It would've been a very busy day for God if he made all the people in one day."

"He didn't make *all* the people in one day," Violet interjected. "Just Adam and Eve. And it wouldn't be tiring for God because he's God."

I shrugged. "How do you know Adam and Eve really existed?"

"Mankind had to start *somewhere.*"

At this point, Jill spoke up. "What about evolution?" I understood from her tone that she was not seeking wisdom from the Ricos. It was the voice she uses when her irritation outweighs the pressure to be socially appropriate.

Unfortunately, Violet is neither gracious nor sensitive when it comes to matters of controversy. "Only an idiot would believe we came from monkeys," she said with a smirk.

"I believe in evolution," Jill said hotly. "Are you calling me an idiot?"

"Are you calling me a monkey?" Violet retorted.

Jill glared at her and was, no doubt, about to say something snide, so I quickly interrupted with, "What does God look like? Does he have a belly button?"

Violet gave a spectacular sigh. "Oh you unbelieving and perverse generation!"

"Excuse me?" Jill looked furious.

"Oh dear," Belinda said, wobbling slightly. "Let's not argue."

"No!" Oscar exclaimed. "God wouldn't like that at all!"

Jill gave one final harrumph and then everybody fell silent and attended to their food.

I caught Ruby's eye and stifled a giggle. I'm not sure we were sharing a joke. I think I just felt embarrassed. I wondered whether God was really out there, *somewhere,* watching our dinner time debate. Did he think Jill was an idiot for believing in evolution? Did he think Violet the zealot was wonderful? Or didn't he find her a little bit annoying? Did he mind that I wanted to look up the behemoth beast that Stanley had mentioned but couldn't because I'd given my Bible away to Ruby? And would he still keep watching me even after I left the Ricos' holy abode? The more I thought about it, the more God seemed like some kind of inexpressible wild animal who may or may not exist. I wondered if there was evidence of him in Leeds museum or sightings of him in the Congo.

I thought about it that night as I got ready for bed and wondered whether Violet was right about God making Adam and Eve.

"How do you make a person?" I muttered as I brushed my teeth. "Out of the dust? Out of nothing? Surely mankind had to grow from something small... like a bug or an egg?" *But then, where did that come from? An even smaller egg?*

I wrinkled up my nose as I suddenly remembered Violet's hard boiled egg, sitting in her locker with a face drawn on it. I realised it must be seriously stinking by now. *Is that what God thinks of us— that we're a rotten mess masquerading as art; a well-intended experiment gone wrong?* I glanced up at the mould on the ceiling. It's been growing recently and doesn't look like Jesus anymore. In fact, it's grown so much that it looks more like an evil alien. It no longer seems worth talking to. I spat in the sink and concluded that I didn't want Violet's God to exist. I was pretty sure he wouldn't like me if he did.

~ **13** ~

Who do you Fink you are?

When I first meet someone I usually ask, *'What are your hobbies?'* or, *'What's your favourite animal?'* or, *'Can you get your leg round your neck?'* and these questions tell me a lot about the person I am talking to. I've noticed, however, that whenever Jill meets somebody, the main question asked is, *'What do you do?'* This can be roughly translated as, *'Define yourself but only mention work...'* Jill is very articulate about the ins and outs of the corporate world and the many perks and irks of her job, but it seems to me that all this question really does is avoid the complicated business of actually getting to *know* someone. *'Who are you?'* would be far more interesting.

I tried it on Timothy Fink who Jill dated for a grand total of eight and a half days.[58]

I said, "Timothy Fink, who are you?"

He replied, "What do you mean? You know who I am. I'm Timothy."

I stared at him. "There's a boy at my school called Timothy. What makes you different from him?"

"Well, I'm not at school for a start," he said pompously. "I'm a managing director—"

And that's how quickly the question becomes about what you do.

I shook my head at his foolishness. "That still isn't *who* you are! Who is Timothy Fink? WHO?" And then, believing I was being incredibly witty, I said with a chuckle, "Who do you *Fink* you are?"

He looked at me blankly.

---

[58] I count the extra half a day because that's how long Jill was waiting for him before he sent a text to say that he wasn't coming over but could he still get that free subscription to *'Busty Week.'*

I felt like a genius. Perhaps I would write a self-help book, or become a psychotherapist, or start a religion. I was about to press on and ask about his deepest fears and childhood secrets but then I caught sight of Jill and she was fuming.

"Why don't you go and watch television?" she suggested.

"But I'm getting to know Timothy Fink!" I protested, aghast that she couldn't see how much I was helping.

"No. *I'm* getting to know Timothy Fink," she snapped. "You're just asking stupid questions."

I gave a huffy sigh and left them to it.

As I shut the kitchen door, I heard Timothy Fink say, "I recently hired a new secretary."

And Jill replied, "I once had a summer job as a secretary."

So I re-opened the door and yelled, "That's not who you are!" before slamming it shut behind me.

I decided that if I was going to write a self-help book, or become a psychotherapist, or start a religion, then I would need to thoroughly understand the human condition. The next day, I went to the school library and took out twelve psychology books. I told Ruby about my plans.[59]

"You can be my first patient," I said.

She looked apprehensive. "Okay..."

"So..." I pretended to skim through a book entitled *'Cognitive Therapy for Beginners'* and propped it open on a photo of a lady looking stressed. "Who are you, Ruby Rico?"

I expected her to get nervous and maybe cry and say she didn't know. But, instead, she looked at me very seriously and said, "Why? Who are *you*, Livi Starling?"

"I'm..." I stopped and shook my head. *"I'm* asking the questions! Come on! Who are you?"

Ruby shrugged. "Same as you, I guess."

"What do you mean *same as me?*" I said, astounded. "We're completely different!"

"Are we?"

"Yes! You like crocodiles and collecting banana stickers. You bite your nails and wear baggy clothes—"

---

[59] I missed out the bit about starting my own religion because I was pretty sure she wouldn't approve. She might even threaten to pray for me and I didn't want those well-meaning yet deadly vibes interfering with my new found genius.

"Okay. That's me then."

"No! That's not you. That's just facts. Who are you under all that?"

"What? Under my baggy clothes?" Ruby grinned. "Under my clothes, I'm naked. Same as you."

"Oh shut up!" I made a big show of slamming shut *'Cognitive Therapy for Beginners'* and huffily gathered up the rest of the books. "If you're going to be stupid then I'll ask somebody else!"

I hoped I looked like a serious academic and I hoped she felt like a fool but, to my utter annoyance, Ruby just giggled.

I didn't want to admit it, but Ruby sitting there all smug and self-assured left me feeling rather unsettled. I'm not sure how I expected her to answer the *'Who are you?'* question and I was forced to admit that I couldn't answer it for myself either.

I'm Livi Starling. *But that's just my name.*

I'm a fourteen year old girl. *Like millions of others.*

I like writing and making animal noises. *But those are just things that I DO.*

What makes me special? What makes me different? What makes me *ME?*

The only great thing I have going for me is that my dad is an actor— and that isn't even true. I started to feel sorry for myself as the familiar pang of wanting my mother welled up inside. I don't even know what her favourite colour was. I hope it was yellow, like mine.[60]

At lunchtime, I overheard Kitty and Molly discussing their *'Almost-Name'*— the name they would've been given if they'd been a boy. Kitty's would've been *'Derek.'* I imagined her as a boy named Derek and wondered whether I would fancy him.

I sent a text to my dad to ask what mine was.

He replied, *'What do you mean almost name? LOL.'*

I sighed and wrote, *'What you'd have called me if I was a boy.'*

Five seconds later, *'No idea. LOL.'*

I couldn't work out if he was laughing at me or just trying to be cool.

When I got home, I went on the internet and typed, *'Who am I?'* into Google. I discovered that my entire DNA sequence would fill two hundred 1,000-page books. I exhaled slowly as I realised that

---

[60] Specifically, *'Lollipop Yellow,'* the colour of an old crayon under my bed.

was a pretty big life story, but then I panicked and wondered whether it was possible for any of that DNA to *fall off* somehow and leave me mutated. I clicked on some links but got distracted by a game called *'Genome Attack'* where you use pieces of DNA to attack pesky garden gnomes. After that, I read a few articles about the Law of Identity,[61] before stumbling upon a site waffling on about how we are born with a *'God-shaped hole'* which only intensifies as we seek to know ourselves better. As if to taunt me further, a flashing piece of text at the side of the page read, *'There is nothing more powerful than a person who knows who they are.'*

~*~

By the weekend, I had a startling pile of neglected homework. I'd spent the whole week looking for clues to my identity but, other than reaching level thirty on *'Genome Attack,'* I had very little to show for it.

I scolded myself for wasting so much time as I spread my homework out on the kitchen table. Our English assignment featured another morbid piece of literature in the form of a poem entitled, *'Goodbye Forever.'* I bit my lip as I started thinking about my dad. I know he'd said he had a bit of overtime coming up, but I had expected him to call by now. It had been two weeks and, other than our brief text exchange regarding my Almost-Name, I'd heard nothing.

After a few more minutes of pretending to work, I drifted down the hall and picked up the phone. I felt strangely nervous as I waited on the end of the line. By the fifth ring, my imagination went a little wild and I found myself fearing that he'd run away in the dead of night, or been transferred to a cinema in the Congo, or spontaneously combusted.

Finally, just as I was about to hang up and try his mobile, he answered with a curt, "Yes?"

"Dad, it's me!" I said breathlessly.

"Hi Livi! How's tricks?"

"Tricks?"

He laughed. "What have you been up to?"

---

[61] Namely, that a thing is the same as itself. Therefore, contrary to the Double theory, the only person I am identical to is me.

"Just school and stuff. How about you?"

"Oh, not much. We've had some all-night showings of 'Dream of the Platypus.'"

I made a noise which I hoped sounded sympathetic. Then I said, "Hey Dad, can I go round your house?"

His reply wasn't the keen response I'd been hoping for. "My house?"

"Yeah. It would be nice to see where you live." I tugged at my socks.

"You could, but it's only a small flat. And it's not very tidy."

"I don't mind! Someone died in ours."

"What?"

"Before we moved in."

"Oh!" Dad chuckled. "Well, if you don't mind a bit of mess then you're welcome any time."

"Thanks!" I paused. "How about today?"

"Today?"

"Yeah," I crossed my fingers and wished I could see his face. "Or are you working?"

"No, I'm not working," Dad said finally. "I'll come and pick you up in half an hour."

"Okay!" I hung up with excitement and hummed to myself as I went back to the kitchen to pack my homework away.

Jill, who had obviously been eavesdropping from the living room, came into the hallway and asked, "Have you done all your homework?"

"Pretty much," I lied. "Dad's coming to take me to his flat."

Jill pursed her lips but didn't say anything.

"He's had a lot of overtime," I said, as if I needed to explain.

She sighed. "Livi... I don't want you to get hurt."

"Why should I get hurt?"

She took my hand. "If things don't work out."

"What do you mean?"

"I mean... if your dad leaves again."

I pulled my hand away. "Why would he leave again?"

Jill looked at me and said nothing.

"He won't leave again," I insisted, my chest aching a little.

"I just want you to be alright."

"I'm fine!" I snapped, feeling peeved at her for ruining my good mood. Jill kept staring at me so I gave a spectacular sigh and added, "I've got stuff to do."

I ran up the stairs two at a time. Then I went to my room and put my shoes in order. After that, I cleared some clutter from my desk, straightened up my teddies and put away a pile of laundry that Jill had left on my bed. Dad was a little longer than half an hour and, with hindsight, I could've done *some* homework in that time, but at least I now had a tidy room. I paused and sat on my bed, swinging Sausage-Legs by the ear as I wondered what to do next.

Finally Dad arrived. He tooted his horn before knocking out a rhythm on the front door.

I was in the middle of putting my books in reverse alphabetical order so I yelled at Jill to let him in. When I didn't hear any movement from the living room, I tossed the rest of my books onto the floor and trotted down the stairs.

"I told you to get the door," I said irritably to Jill.

She ignored me.

I tutted and yanked the door open.

Dad greeted me with a purple flower. "Ta da!"

"Oh! Thanks!" I wondered what I should do with it. "I'll er... go and put it in some water." I ran to the kitchen.

Dad chuckled as he poked his head round the living room door. "Hello Jill! How are you?"

I heard her snap, "Fine."

I threw the flower in the sink and returned to the hallway. "The flower in the sink is mine," I told Jill as I hurried my dad out of the house. "So don't steal it."

Jill scowled and said nothing.

My dad's flat was almost twenty minutes away. I'd had no idea Leeds was so huge. We could've driven around Little Milking thirty times in the time it took to cross the city. As Dad drove I peered out of the window, taking in the various sights. I saw a sign to a medical museum and asked if we could go there some time.

"Sure," he replied.

"Have you ever been?" I wondered if they had real live brains.

"Nope."

"Why not?"

"Never thought of it."

I bit my lip and wondered what to say next. "What's your favourite thing about Leeds?"

"Dunno."

I sighed, breathed on the window, and drew a heart.

In the silence that followed I had a sudden irrational fear that perhaps my dad wasn't driving me to his house after all. Perhaps he was kidnapping me. That sort of thing is on the news all the time. How could I be sure my dad wasn't a murderer in disguise? I shot him a quick glance, wishing I had a personalised handkerchief that I could spit in and toss out of the window as a clue for the police.

He caught my eye and grinned. "It's great to see you, Livi."

I blushed and scolded myself for being so daft.

Eventually, we arrived at a large block of flats called *The Grumbles*. I thought this was quite a funny name for a tower block. I imagined a load of miniature people called *The Grumblings of Grumble Towers*. They would be so tiny that they can't climb the stairs and have to tunnel through the wiring. It's their job to maintain everybody's lighting and there are seventy Grumblings in Dad's flat alone. I smiled to myself and decided I would make it into a story for Dad some day.

We had to go up six flights of stairs to get to Dad's flat[62] and, when he unlocked his front door, he had to push it really hard to get it open.[63] I followed him in and tried not to screw up my nose as the smell of leftover curry filled my nostrils.

"Well, this is it!" Dad said, waving an arm around.

The room was very small, with a living area on one side and a little kitchen surface at the other. By the sink was a hallway leading to two rooms.

"It's nice..." I wandered over to the window. The view was of a crane doing something painful to a nearby building.

"Have a seat." Dad gestured to a faded blue sofa.

"I need the toilet," I replied stupidly.

Dad pointed to the archway by the sink. "It's through there. Oh, but be careful because the toilet seat's broken."

I nodded and padded down the hallway. I assumed he meant that the toilet seat was cracked or slightly hanging off its hinges. But he meant *actually* broken. It lay in three shattered pieces next to the bath. I stared at the toilet in confusion. Was I meant to sit on the rim or would it be better to squat? What if I fell in or wet myself? I stood in bewilderment for about five minutes before deciding it was safer not to go at all.

---

[62] This would take two hours for a Grumbling.
[63] Grumblings in the way.

Dad smiled as I returned to the living area. "I've put the kettle on."

"I don't like tea."

"Oh! Would you like some juice?" He opened his fridge and shook half a carton at me.

If Jill ever gets juice it's for a special occasion and we can't drink it all at once. I wondered if Dad prized his juice as highly. If so, I didn't want to waste it.

"Water is fine."

"Alright." Dad turned to the sink.

I perched awkwardly on the sofa. There was a banana on the floor and I sneakily peeled the sticker off for Ruby, sticking it to the inside of my sleeve for safekeeping. Beside the sofa stood a bookshelf crammed with DVDs. He only had two books: 'The Idiot's Guide to Cooking with Ham,' and, '100 Films to Watch Before you Die.' I peered inside the cover of the second one. Dad had ticked off most of the films. I shuddered and wondered if that meant he would die soon.

Dad poured himself a cup of tea and then joined me on the sofa. "How's school?" He handed me half a glass of water.

I took a quick sip. "Good..." I was about to tell him about mine and Ruby's progress on our project but my water went down the wrong way and I started coughing.

Dad chuckled. "I saw a programme about ants the other day."

I tried to look interested.

"Apparently there are more than 22,000 species of ant. Isn't that incredible?"

"That's a lot. Do they all get on with each other?"

"They didn't say."

"Oh." I tried to think if I'd seen anything good on television recently. "Did you see that programme about cloud spotting?"

"No."

"There was a cloud that looked like a man walking his dog."

Dad nodded and asked if I wanted to watch a film.

"Okay," I said, glancing idly at his collection. They were mainly action movies with dark covers and stupid taglines like, 'You can run, you can hide, but you'll never play golf again,' and, 'He sold his own brain. He can't remember why.'

In the end, we watched a film about a man who ate a car. It was the most tedious thing I've ever watched. It was even worse than the three part series on limestone that we watched in Geography. I kept stealing glances at my dad and, every time I did so, I felt my chest ache. I wondered if he was pleased to have me over or whether he'd rather be doing something else.

As the end credits came up, I said, "Thanks for inviting me round your house, Dad."

He nodded and flicked over to the special features of the film.

I let out a sigh and picked at a scab on my arm. I pretended to be interested as we watched twenty minutes of deleted scenes—scenes so boring that they had been deemed too boring to feature in the original boring film.

Finally they came to an end and Dad turned the television off. He grinned at me and I forced a smile.

"Oh!" Dad jumped up suddenly and ran over to the kitchen area. He pulled something off his fridge. "Look what I found the other day!"

I felt a tug at my heart as Dad handed me a small faded photo. It was of me, Dad and Jill at a fair. I was about six and had ice cream down my dress. Dad had one arm round my shoulder and the other round Jill's. We all looked happy. As I gazed at the three of us, memories from that day came flooding back. I remembered clinging onto Dad's hand on the ghost train. I remembered Jill being harassed by an over-friendly dog. I remembered crying because I wanted Dad to win a gigantic cuddly unicorn on the hoopla but all he managed was an inflatable hammer.

I wondered whether my dad had been looking for old photos or whether he'd found it by mistake. Did it make him feel sad? Did he wish he'd never left? Did he wonder what he'd missed? Did he feel the same gaping hole as me?

As I looked up at his cheery grin, I had a sudden burning desire to ask him the same question that had tormented me all week: 'Who are you?' But I didn't dare. I gulped and looked away.

"I'd better drive you home now," Dad said. "I told some friends I'd meet them at the pub to watch the football."

I blinked and gave a quick nod. "Here you go." I held the photo towards him.

"You can keep it if you like."

"No, it's yours," I insisted. "You should keep it." By this I meant, 'You want to keep it, right?'

Dad smiled and took it from me. "Okay."

I sat in silence as Dad drove me home. I had enjoyed seeing him but, for some reason, I felt kind of sad. It was like I wanted something from him but I couldn't put my finger on what it was.

"Thanks for having me," I said as we reached my house.

"You're welcome! Come any time!"

I forced a smile, ignoring the painful ache that had sprung up in my chest. Then I hurriedly let myself into my house and ran upstairs. I was bursting for the toilet.

That night, I had a bad dream. I can't remember all the details but, at one point, my mother was there and she couldn't remember me. I awoke in a cold sweat and gave a small whimper of self-pity. I often dream about my mother, although she never seems to have a clear face.

I couldn't get back to sleep so I got up to get a drink of water. Lying at the bottom of the stairs was a crumpled heap. It looked like a man in a dressing gown and I screamed because I thought it was the ghost of Mr Denby, the man who lived in our house before us.

Jill came running out of her bedroom. "Livi, what was that for?"

"I thought I saw a ghost," I whispered.

"It's four in the morning!"

"Well, ghosts come out at night, don't they?" I peered over the banister. "I think it's just my coat. Sorry."

"Go back to bed," Jill snapped.

I gave her a long look. I wanted to ask if we could get up early and make homemade yoghurt, like Ruby and Belinda. But she started moaning about how it would be my fault if she was tired at work. So I glared at her, slouched back to my room, and lay daydreaming about my mother and how great my life would've been if she'd lived. My dad would never have left, for a start. He and my mother would be happily married. We'd have a farm, like Aunt Claudia, except we wouldn't eat our sheep. Jill would live down the road— close enough to visit but not near enough to boss me about. Maybe I'd even have some younger brothers and sisters who would look up to me and think I was cool. We'd be one big happy family. And, should anybody ask me who I was, I would tell them, *'I know exactly who I am. I'm one of them.'*

~ 14 ~

A hideous loophole

Just when I was starting to get used to life in Leeds, something happened which made me want to buy a nuclear bomb and wipe it off the map completely.

It all began when Fester sprung a surprise maths test on us.

Our class protested and a few people started pinging rubber bands across the room.

Fester gave a foul sneer. "Don't forget that it's Parents' Evening tonight," he said menacingly.

The rest of the class lapsed into silence. But I didn't. I hummed under my breath to show that I couldn't care less for Fester's threats. Parents' Evening was of little concern to me due to the happy fact that Jill was invited to a charity event through work. I'd reasoned that since she was already busy, there was no need to bother her with invitations to other trivial events. I'd debated asking my father but then I remembered he was supposed to be an actor in London. Ruby was still the only one who knew the truth.

"Silence, Libby Starling!" Fester warned, as my rendition of 'Bohemian Rhapsody' grew in fervour.

"It helps me concentrate," I replied smugly. I reached for a bright red colouring pencil as I designed a cape for 'Infinity-plus-one Man.' I felt invincible.

That night, as Jill was getting dressed into her fanciest outfit, I settled myself happily in front of the television. A new reality show was about to begin, featuring animal lovers competing to win their very own customised zoo, and I didn't want to miss it.

Jill came down at about five to seven and said, "There's leftover pasta in the fridge. You can heat that up when you want your dinner."

"Okay," I said, eyes glued to the television. The opening credits had begun.

At that moment, there was a soft tapping on the window. I looked up to see Belinda's face scrunched up to the glass.

"Hello!" she warbled. "Only me!"

My stomach lurched as Jill, forcing a smile, leant over and opened the window.

"I thought we could go together," Belinda said as she poked her head through the open gap.

"Excuse me?" Jill clearly didn't recall inviting Belinda to the fundraiser.

"Parents' Evening!" Belinda said in a sing-song voice. Then, noticing Jill's confusion she added, "Don't say you haven't read the newsletter!"

Jill's eyes flashed with fury before she composed herself. "Of course I read it. Livi, get your shoes on."

I tried to protest. "But your charity event! You can't let the charity down!"

Jill gave me an icy glare and switched the television off.

Heart sinking, I pulled on my shoes and followed my furious sister out of the house.

Ruby was waving nervously in the back seat of their car. As I got in beside her she whispered, "I tried to tell my mum you weren't coming but she didn't listen."

"It's fine," I said coolly. "How bad can it be?"

"Oh, Jill!" Belinda said, cooing over Jill's shiny black cocktail dress. "You're looking mighty sophisticated. Very grown up indeed."

Jill turned a deep shade of red and scowled at me. She didn't say a single word throughout the drive. Beside her, Belinda jabbered non-stop about Violet's reports the day before which had been mainly good apart from a somewhat *'perplexing'* report from her Art teacher who said Violet's work lacked structure.

As our school came into view, lit up in the dark like a beacon of doom, I sank deeper into my seat and wondered how credible it would be to feign falling unconscious.

Before we got out of the car, Jill turned in her seat and said, "Ruby, could you write me a full list of all your teachers, please?"

I shot Ruby a warning glance but, of course, Ruby's a good girl so she dutifully did as she was told.

When we'd piled out of the car, Belinda put her arm around Ruby and said, "Right then, my little carrot. Where are we going first?"

Ruby consulted the organised list in her planner. "We're seeing Miss Dalton at quarter past seven." She smiled at me. "See you later, Livi."

"See you," I replied, turning uneasily to Jill who was pulling down the bottom of her dress. She looked rather uncomfortable as we made our way into the school building.

Unlike Ruby, who had booked appointments with all our teachers and had a carefully planned route to take her mother on, all Jill and I could do was wander round and hope to fill empty slots. The first classroom we came to was Madame Maurel's. A French CD was playing lightly in the background.

I gave a tentative knock. "We don't have an appointment, but can we come in?"

"Of course! Of course!" Madame Maurel smiled. "Good evening, Ms Starling! How ees the baby?"

Jill looked startled. "Baby?"

My teacher raised her eyebrows. "I'm sorry. Maybe it is too soon to tell, yes?"

Jill gaped at her but, to my relief, Madame Maurel didn't appear to notice. She was too busy hunting for my exercise book in the pile in front of her.

"Ah, yes!" she said when she found it. She flicked through my work and tutted. "Livi haz a very good imagination," she said. "But she does very leetle work." She held up a page which was covered in doodles and the words, *'Ruby est un singe. Elle aime bananes.'*[64]

Jill shot me a disapproving look.

"I'll try harder," I said.

Madame Maurel peered at me over her spectacles. "Zat will be good."

"Well, thank you for your time," Jill said, rising from her seat.

"Goodbye!" Madame Maurel sang. "And by zee way, zat dress is perfect. You can hardly see your bump at all!"

As we left the classroom, Jill took me aside and hissed, "Why did she think I was pregnant?"

"I said you were," I said sheepishly.

"Why?"

---

[64] *'Ruby is a monkey. She likes bananas.'*

"It's French... It's like talking in code. No one expects you to tell the truth."

Jill rolled her eyes. "Where next?"

"History?" I pointed to a nearby classroom. "Unless you don't want to wait?" I indicated the small queue at the door.

"We'll wait," she snapped.

When it was our turn, Mr Holborn greeted us with a beam and said, "Ah, Livi! Take a seat. And this must be your mother?"

"Yes," I said quickly.

Jill looked at me in bewilderment as Mr Holborn shook her hand and enquired, "How are the bees?"

"Bees?"

"It must be a great deal trickier keeping them in the city!"

"I don't keep bees."

"Oh!" Mr Holborn shot me a puzzled glance before saying briskly, "Well, Livi is progressing marvellously in History." I hoped he would stop there, but he continued with, "Although she keeps forgetting to bring in the watch that we're all so excited to see!"

"Watch?"

"Yes, given to Churchill by the Indian prime minister."

Jill snorted but said nothing.

I gave a wry smile and gestured to the queue at the door. "We should probably let you see someone else now."

Mr Holborn nodded and, as we got up to leave, finished with, "It was nice to meet you, Mrs Starling. I hope you find a job soon."

"It's *Ms* Starling and I already have a job. That's why we moved to Leeds."

"I thought Livi said you moved because your village was inbred..."

Jill gave him a baffled frown and left the room.

I followed her out and tried to explain than Mr Holborn was just a little eccentric.

Jill said nothing as she marched down the corridor. Her little heels clicked noisily on the vinyl floor and, in her black dress, she looked like a very glamorous (although very angry) magician's assistant. It crossed my mind that that would've been a superior lie to *'bee keeper.'*

I wanted to go and see Ms Sorenson next. I was pretty sure she would give me a good report and I hadn't told a single lie in her class so there would be nothing to infuriate Jill, but there was a big queue outside her classroom and Jill said she couldn't be bothered to wait.

"It's just *Personal and Social Development*. I don't even know what that is."

"It's really good! I told you about mine and Ruby's project—"

Jill shook her head and looked down my list of teachers. "I want to hear your English report. Where's Mrs Tilly's classroom?"

I shuddered. Jill definitely wouldn't like this one.

Mrs Tilly's room was on the second floor. We weaved in and out of students and their parents, catching snippets of praise and criticism all around. Some lucky kid was getting twenty quid. We passed a wall displaying some of our recent Art work and I pointed out my picture of Ruby which was drawn in the style of Giuseppe Arcimboldo.[65]

Jill wrinkled up her nose. "How is that Ruby?"

"Look!" I pointed out her grape eyes with tiny banana pupils. "Those are her eyes... And these grapes are her nostrils and the carrots are her hair..."

"Couldn't you draw her properly instead of messing about?"

"That's what we were meant to do!"

But she just said, "Hmmm," and marched on.

There was a pretty sizable queue waiting to see Mrs Tilly so I suggested that perhaps we could see if Ms Sorenson's classroom was less busy yet, but Jill said firmly that this one was important. I spotted Kitty Warrington with a lady who must have been her mother. At any rate, she had the same stuck-up nose. Kitty's mother was talking to a woman who turned out to be Molly's mother. From my eavesdropping I learnt that Mrs Masterson had just left Molly's father due to years of suspected infidelity and Molly was spending the evening packing her bags and deciding who she wanted to live with.

Kitty looked mildly amused as she said, "She could come and live with us."

But Mrs Warrington scolded her, "Don't be daft, Kitty!"

Then the two ladies got their diaries out and arranged a date to meet up so that Mrs Masterson could *'tell all the juicy details and have a good cry.'*

I thought it must be nice to have a mother who is best friends with your best friend's mother. I wondered if the four of them went

---

[65] He was a painter who painted fruit and fish and other things in such a way as to look like faces. I was particularly proud of my picture of Ruby in which I had captured her whole likeness by drawing only grapes, bananas and carrots.

on shopping trips together. I felt a pang of envy. The last time I went shopping with Jill she started haggling in a charity shop.

Wayne Purdy emerged from Mrs Tilly's classroom, looking miserable as a woman muttered furiously in his ear.

Mrs Masterson nodded to Kitty's mother and said, "My turn."

Mrs Warrington grinned. "Good luck!"

Without the two ladies nattering away it became very quiet in the hallway. My stomach ached with hunger and I hoped it wouldn't start to rumble. I sneaked a peek at some of the people around us and debated over which students looked most like their parents. I decided Ritchie Jones looked like an exact clone of his father, right down to his big ears and the annoying way that he scratched his throat. There were twelve parents waiting and eight students. I figured Connie Harper's father would be the first to die because he looked really old and kept coughing.

At one point somebody moaned, "How much longer? It's the same every year. They're never on time!"

A few people murmured in agreement.

"It's because people push in," Mrs Warrington chipped in. "All the ones who haven't bothered to make appointments."

There was more disgruntled mumbling and I tried to look as though I agreed, catching eyes with a girl from my class and exchanging friendly smiles. Jill looked rather peeved.

In the silence that followed Mrs Warrington pulled out a comb and started combing Kitty's hair.

Kitty scowled. "Stop it, Mum!"

Mrs Warrington sniffed and threw the comb back into her bag. She glanced at Jill and said, "They think they're so grown up at this age, don't they!"

Jill chuckled politely. "They think they know everything."

"Yes, quite!" said Mrs Warrington. "Kitty can't even boil an egg."

Kitty caught my eye and glowered. I wrinkled up my nose as if to say, *'Only losers can't boil eggs!'*

But Jill replied, "Neither can Livi," much to my annoyance.

I glared at her and pretended to be interested in the display of war poetry behind us.

Eventually, we reached the front of the queue. Mrs Tilly invited us in and apologised for our wait. Then she realised we didn't have an appointment in the first place and said, "Ah! So you're one of those troublemakers that keep everybody waiting!"

Jill went red and a few parents tutted. We followed Mrs Tilly into the classroom and, as we sat down, she gave me one of her usual sympathetic smiles.

"Well, Livi hasn't had a great start," she said to Jill. "But we can forgive her because of, you know, her situation."

Jill gave her a sharp look. "Situation?"

"Yes, you know..." When it became clear that Jill didn't know, Mrs Tilly continued, "Her severe alexia." *As if my made up condition had a real name!*

"Her what?"

I sank deeper into my seat and avoided Jill's gaze.

Jill sat in stunned silence as Mrs Tilly explained I would need to spend more time practising my reading at home and that perhaps if Jill could spare an hour a week that would help me improve more rapidly.

"People often underestimate how beneficial it can be for a struggling child to have a supportive parent or guardian taking an active interest in their progress," Mrs Tilly said, giving Jill a meaningful look.

Jill opened her mouth in fury but said nothing.

"But, other than that, I'm very pleased with Livi's work," Mrs Tilly concluded. "She has such a good imagination."

I glanced optimistically at Jill but she was still not smiling. She thanked Mrs Tilly for her time and stormed out of the room.

As we left, a few parents shot us impatient scowls and I heard someone mutter, "Downright inconsiderate... pushing in without an appointment!"

This made Jill march even faster and I almost had to run to catch up.

"She said I have a good imagination," I said, trotting along beside her. "Madame Maurel said that too. That's good, isn't it?"

Jill ignored me. "You told your English teacher that you can't read! Why would you say such a stupid thing? You *love* reading!"

I shrugged. With hindsight, it did seem a little daft. "I felt nervous," I said lamely. "It's hard being new."

Jill snorted and grabbed my arm. "We're leaving."

"Aren't we going to wait for Belinda and Ruby?"

"We'll walk."

"You're kind of hurting my arm..."

"I know."

As Jill dragged me through the foyer, I caught sight of Miss Waddle and had the vain hope that she might think Jill was a film star. I tried to fix a happy grin on my face but a familiar voice caught me off guard.

"Libby!"

I turned and shuddered.

Fester gave a smarmy smile. "I thought you weren't coming tonight." He looked Jill up and down and put his hand out. "I'm James[66] Lester," he said smoothly. "You must be Libby's sister?"

"We're about to leave," I said. If she thought the other reports were bad, she really didn't need to hear this one.

Fester looked disappointed. "I have a spare slot now if you'd like to quickly discuss Libby's Maths work?"

Clearly perceiving Fester's continual incompetence with my name to be my own doing, Jill scowled at me and hissed, "Seriously, Livi, how bad does this get?"

Before I could reply, I saw Fester gulp and go a little red. "I beg your pardon. I meant to say 'Livi,' of course..." He gave me a curious look, as though discovering me for the very first time, before repeating his offer to Jill. "As I said, we could discuss Livi's Maths work now, if you'd like?"

Jill sniffed. "It's quite alright, thank you. I don't think I can bear to hear another ridiculous report. I'd prefer to take her home and kill her sooner rather than later."

Fester forced a laugh. "What makes you think her Maths report will be ridiculous?" he said in a sickly sweet voice that made me want to vomit.

"Well, will it?" Jill snapped.

Without a moment's pause, Fester replied, "Of course not! Lib— Livi's fantastic at maths!"

"What?" I nearly died of shock.

"Really?" Jill's grip on my arm loosened slightly.

"Yes. Why don't you come and sit down?" He gestured towards an empty classroom.

Jill paused for a moment and then followed him in, throwing me a warning glance.

I shrugged and nervously sat beside her.

What followed next was perhaps the most traumatic three minutes of my life.

Fester told Jill that I was wonderful at maths and then complimented her on her dress.

---

[66] As if Fester has a normal name like 'James!' I figured he'd be called 'Adolf' or something.

Jill giggled and said she liked his tie.[67]

Fester asked whether I got my maths skills from Jill.

Jill said certainly not because she was horrendous at maths.

Fester said he was sure she would be good at it with the right teacher.

I sat gaping at them, pinching myself in the hope that I was only dreaming.

As we got up to leave, Fester said to Jill, "I'm not really meant to do this, but would you fancy going for a coffee some time?"

I froze and tried to send Jill a telepathic message warning her that this man was my absolute nemesis but, to my utter dismay, she said, "I'd love to go for coffee some time!"[68]

"Fantastic!" With a sickening grin, Fester got his phone out. "What's your number?"

Jill gave a coy smile and recited her number. She forgot a couple of digits and there was much flustered giggling as she tried to recall it. Words cannot describe the utter mortification I felt as we stood in the doorway— parents and students pressing in around us— with my sister, my *stupid* sister, going soppy over the most hated teacher in school.

"Great," said Fester. "I'll just drop-call you so that you'll have my number too..."

Then there was the excruciatingly loud sound of Jill's ring tone, *'Wake me up before you go go,'* and more pathetic giggling as she hunted in her bag to turn the wretched thing off.

Fester grinned and said, "Great," again.

I exhaled loudly. "Can we leave now, please?"

Jill turned in surprise. I think she'd forgotten I was there. "Well, it was nice to meet you, James," she said.

"You too, Jill." Then Fester looked at me and said in an annoying drawl, "See you in my class tomorrow, Livi."

I opened my mouth to make some smart remark but nothing came. In the end, I just stood there gaping like a goldfish.

As we re-entered the foyer, Ruby and Belinda emerged from a nearby classroom.

"Ah, hello girls!" Belinda cooed.

Jill turned to her and positively smiled.

I knew things must be bad if Jill was genuinely smiling at Belinda.

---

[67] It was a dumb tie covered in fluorescent numbers.
[68] She doesn't even *like* coffee!

I locked eyes with Ruby and tried to convey through my facial expression the horror of what had taken place but she just looked at me in confusion.

"Are you ready to go?" asked Belinda.

Jill let out a sigh and said, "Wonderful."

I wanted to remind her that she was supposed to be angry with me for all my bad reports. She could glare at me, yell at me, pin me to the notice board— *anything* other than smile like a dope. *Meeting Fester for coffee! Was she crazy?* An awful thought came to mind: *What if they kiss?* I gave a moan and said loudly, "How were your reports, Ruby?" Then, before she could reply, I added, "Mine were awful. Jill's gonna kill me when we get home."

Belinda gasped.

Ruby gave me an odd look.

Jill tittered and said, "Don't exaggerate, Livi. You're at a new school. It will take time for you to settle in."

"But I lied!" I exclaimed as we headed to the car. "I said you were pregnant. I said you were my mother. I said I couldn't read. And you didn't even meet my Religious Studies teacher— she thinks we're Jewish and that you're training to be a rabbi!"

Ruby and Belinda looked at me as though I was insane but Jill sighed and said, "Get in the car, Livi." She held the door open for me and cocked her head sideways.

I gave a growl as I clambered in beside Ruby. Ruby gave me a quizzical look but I just shook my head.

I sat in stunned silence the whole way home, my head spinning as I re-lived the ordeal of Jill and Fester flirting. I'm sure it's prohibited for teachers to ask parents out on dates and yet Fester seemed to have found a hideous loophole.

In the front of the car Belinda was gushing about how nice all our teachers were and my sister was nodding ardently.

I glared at the back of Jill's head. I felt it was incredibly reckless of her to agree to go on a date with a man she'd only just met. He could be a murderer for all she knew. I recalled Aunt Claudia's recent words about having the will power not to love a man. At the time I'd thought these were just the musings of a bitter old woman. But now I badly wished Jill would show a little of that will power. If she was this irresponsible, what else might she do? I felt sick as I considered the possibilities. By the time we got home, my imagination had run ahead of me and I was convinced that I would be walking my sister down the aisle by the end of the year.

~ 15 ~

Monkeys in the rain

When I saw Fester the next day I was expecting him to acknowledge me in some way, perhaps with a sly wink or a knowing nod. But, as he took the register and began a boring discourse on triangles, he barely looked at me at all. I wondered, with a vain surge of hope, if he had completely forgotten about meeting my sister. Perhaps he'd taken the numbers of several ladies the night before and Jill was just one of many. I rested my head on my hands and eyed him over my pencil case as he paraded in front of the class.

"All three sides of an equilateral triangle are the same length," he drawled, pointing to a bunch of triangles on the board.

I yawned. "Like how your width with outstretched arms is the same length as your height." I didn't even bother to raise my hand.

Fester turned. "Is that true?"

"Yes. I saw it on 'Freaky Human' and Ruby and I checked it."

Some of the class nodded in agreement. They'd obviously seen the same programme.

Fester gave an annoying smile. "Well, I'll have to try that one day." He turned back to the board.

"Do it now," I challenged.

A few people giggled at my audacity.

Fester chuckled. "I don't think so."

"Go on, Sir," I said. "Don't be boring."

Wayne Purdy guffawed. "Yeah, go on, Sir!"

Fester gave me a very long look. Then he smiled, shrugged and lay down on the floor.

The class burst into astonished laughter.

Ruby gaped at me.

"I'll measure him!" Kitty yelled.

She and Molly ran forward with rulers and laid them end to end by his side. After they'd done his height, he stretched his arms out and they measured his width. The class watched and discovered to our amusement that his width was three inches longer than his height.

I gave a cry of delight and shrieked, "You're a monkey!"

The rest of the class stared at me and Fester looked a little surprised. But I narrowed my eyes at him, as if daring him to tell me off.

Finally, Fester gave a small smile, got up off the floor, and said, "Yes. I suppose I am." Then he told us all to settle down and do some work. "Equilateral triangles! Pages 60 to 66 in your workbooks."

I kept laughing, perhaps a bit too much, until Ruby dug me in the ribs and whispered, "It's not *that* funny, Livi."

When I got home Jill was in the kitchen, humming in a rather disconcerting way.

I watched her warily. "You're not seriously considering going on a date with Fester, are you?"

"Who's Fester?"

I rolled my eyes. "My Maths teacher, Mr Lester."

She shot me a disapproving look. "Don't be rude. Call him by his proper name."

"*Everybody* calls him Fester. And *nobody* likes him. He's also a monkey."

"Livi!"

"Well, he is. It's scientifically proven." When Jill didn't reply, I added dramatically, "He'll probably break your heart into a million little pieces."

Jill laughed. "Don't be stupid."

"Well?" I demanded. "You didn't answer my question."

"As a matter of fact, James called me this afternoon. We're having dinner tonight."

"*Dinner!* Last night it was just going to be coffee and now it's full-blown *dinner?*"

She laughed again. "I can leave you some money for a takeaway if you want?"

"Don't bother!"

I ran straight to my room where I yanked my Maths book out of my bag and stabbed it several times with my scissors. I imagined everybody at school finding out that my sister had gone on a date with Fester. As if my hopes for greatness weren't being dented enough already, did Jill really have to trample on them further?

I stayed upstairs until I heard Jill leave a good two hours later, then I stomped round the house in a rage before making myself some toast. I'd debated asking Ruby if I could go to hers for dinner but I didn't want to have to tell her why.

Perhaps it won't be so bad, I told myself as I plastered my toast with peanut butter. Jill had dated several men before. In fact, she'd already seen at least two guys since moving to Leeds.[69] As far as I could remember, Jill had never had a serious boyfriend. That's not to say she hadn't tried. Given half a chance she would throw herself headfirst at the feet of any available suitor, but any love affair would invariably end with lots of tears and the proclamation that she was *'done with men.'* There was no reason to jump to any conclusions about this one. Perhaps, given an hour with Fester, Jill would realise how dull he was and run home screaming.

After watching some television and eating half the tub of peanut butter I stomped back to my room and tried to focus on some homework. I must have read the same passage in my Geography textbook at least thirteen times before I eventually gave up. The minutes went by and, as my clock ticked past ten, I started to feel anxious. Jill clearly hadn't run home early.

Finally, I heard a vehicle pull up outside. I peeked out of my window and saw Jill emerge from a dark blue car. She ducked momentarily back into the car and my stomach lurched as I hoped beyond hope that they weren't kissing.

Jill came into the house, humming as she bounced up the stairs. She knocked on my bedroom door. "You still up, Livi?"

I pretended I was asleep but she pushed the door open and started to tell me about the steak she had eaten and how delicious the sauce was. I tried to listen but all I could think about was how a passionate kiss can suck the pressure out of your ear and cause you to go deaf.

Eventually I cut her off. "It's kind of past my bedtime."

She chuckled. "Goodnight then."

~*~

---

[69] Timothy Fink and a guy from her office who I didn't even meet.

I've heard that when you fall in love it sticks horribly to your face. For a whole week Jill wore a ghastly grin. The days passed like a slow and painful bout of flu except Jill's face was the headache and Fester was the phlegm that kept getting up my nose.

They went on another date and, this time, Jill came back with flowers. The pathetic note on the side read, *'If you were an angle, you'd be acute.'* Then he phoned her three nights in a row and Jill spent the whole time giggling and twirling her hair.

Even when I shut myself in my room and turned the music up I couldn't concentrate on anything other than the thought of Fester's smarmy face. It made seeing him in the flesh even worse. He didn't treat me any differently, didn't address me in any fancy way, or do anything to let on that he now had this unbearable claim over my life, but it was like there was some unspeakable bond between us and I hated it. The sole perk was that he was finally calling me by the correct name— although I'd have gladly changed my name to *'Libby'* if it could have meant never seeing him ever again.

I couldn't wait for the weekend. Dad had said I could go round his flat again and I was desperate to have a bit of respite from Jill's glee. But, while I was waiting for Dad to come and pick me up, he rang to say that the car was in the garage having a service.

"Can we reschedule for next week, Livi?"

"Next week?" I echoed, my heart sinking into my stomach. "But that's so long away..."

"I'm sorry. I'd offer to meet you in town but I need to stay at home in case the garage rings."

I gave a heavy sigh. Then I had an idea. "I could come on the bus!"

Dad didn't answer for a moment. "Would you be alright coming on your own?"

"Of course! I know how a bus works."

"Well, alright then. That'd be great."

Since Dad lived on the other side of Leeds, I needed to get a bus into the city centre and then another one out again. I hadn't wanted to question Dad on which bus to take in case he told me not to bother, so I just guessed and hoped for the best. I spent the whole journey feeling sweaty and anxious and wishing I'd brought Ruby with me. Eventually I recognised the bright blue rooftops of *The Grumbles* and pressed the bell with a sigh of relief.

Dad was watching television when I arrived. He ushered me in and said, "Just watching this programme about ambulance drivers. Is it alright if we watch the end?"

I nodded and sat beside him.

Dad put his arm around me and I leant against his shoulder, watching as a driver named Clint explained the adrenaline he felt when responding to an emergency call.

I've always been fascinated with ambulances. In primary school, a girl called Becky Barrett broke her arm. I tried to peer inside the ambulance when it came for her but the dinner lady told me to go away and stop staring at poor Becky. Becky returned a few days later with a smug smile and a neon pink cast and, when I asked her about the ambulance, all she said was, "It was amazing, Livi! You'd have loved it!" For a while I ran a little clumsily in the hope that I too would fall and break a bone, but I never did.

I sat up straight and concentrated on the programme. Clint was arriving at a disco where an old man had had a heart attack. Clint checked for a pulse and shook his head at his colleagues. Then they lifted the man onto a stretcher and carried him across the dance floor to the exit. The oblivious party carried on dancing, shuffling slightly out of the way as the dead man drifted past. That must be the worst possible way to die— in the middle of a crowded room with nobody noticing.

"There was nothing we could do for him," Clint said sadly to the camera. "When it's your time to go, that's it."

My stomach lurched. Ambulances suddenly didn't seem so special. Whenever the time comes for *me* to go, I want everybody to notice and be sad. I want it to be a very grave occasion, on account of how *great* I am. But this ridiculous longing made me feel incredibly small.

"Dad," I whispered as the credits came up. "How do you want to die?"

He gave a snort. "I don't care, as long as I'm not too old when it happens."

I wasn't sure if he was joking or not.

"I'd like to be cryogenically frozen," he continued with a chuckle. "Then some robot can defrost me in the future."

"You'd better die sensibly then," I cautioned. "You can't land on your head or die mysteriously otherwise they can't freeze you."

Dad laughed. "Do you want a drink?"

I nodded and then remembered his toilet seat was broken. "Actually, I'm not thirsty."

"Alright." Dad leant against the sofa and yawned.

"Dad, do you believe in God?"

"Don't know. I never think about it."

I looked at him curiously. I hoped that by the time I got to his age I would *know*. "What about Heaven?"

He stuck out his lip. "Doesn't matter to me."

I was aghast. "Don't you care what's going to happen to you after you die?"

"Why should I care? Can't be much worse than this life!"

As he grinned, I felt a little stung. *Was his life really all that bad? Was having me over really such a chore?*

"I believe in Heaven," I said. "I think it will be nice— with rides and stuff."

Dad chuckled. "Good for you! If I die first, I'll save you a seat on the Teacups."

I giggled before asking casually, "Did the garage ring yet?"

He shook his head. "It probably won't be ready till Monday. They'll have to order in a new brake disc." He started rooting around under his sofa. "Do you want to play a game? I've got *Scrabble* somewhere under here."

"Okay."

Dad retrieved a tatty box and plonked the board onto his coffee table. Before we began, he warned me that some of the letters might be missing. That was true. We only had about fifteen vowels in total. It made for a somewhat arduous game and we resorted to frequent peeking in the letter bag. Dad took about ten minutes on each turn and, although it was his own fault for suggesting we play such a boring game, I couldn't help but feel guilty that he was spending his precious day off on something that was clearly so taxing. He also kept spelling words wrong but I thought it would be rude to correct him.

We were about to finish (and I'd won by a clear mile) when the phone rang.

"The garage?" I suggested.

Dad shrugged and ran to answer it. As the person on the other end spoke, Dad's face broke into a grin. "Hey Phil! Watch the game, did you?" He laughed and began a lengthy analysis of some football match from the night before. At one point, I heard him say, "No, no. Just playing *Scrabble* with my daughter."

My heart throbbed at the offhand way in which he'd spoken about me. It was strange to be referred to as his daughter. It felt too personal, as though he hadn't quite earned that right yet. There ought to be a word for somebody who is biologically related to you but emotionally still something of a stranger. Perhaps he ought to call me his '*Almost-Daughter*.'

135

I leant over and peered at Dad's letters. He had four 'N's, two 'H's and a 'J.' I tipped all the *Scrabble* tiles onto the floor and tried to make the longest word possible. I almost made *'cryptozoologist'* but Dad only had three 'O's. I settled for *'dinosaurfinder'* instead. Then I yawned and started flicking spare tiles across the floor. I wished Dad would hurry up and tell Phil to go away. I watched the clock as the time ticked by and wondered if he would even notice if I got up and left.

Eventually Dad ended his call and returned to the sofa. "Have we finished then?" he asked.

"Yeah," I replied cheerily, trying to pretend that his phone call had been a fleeting few seconds instead of a painful twenty five minutes.

Dad leant over and read aloud, *"Dinosaurfinder."*

"I was going to make *'cryptozoologist'* but you don't have enough 'O's."

"Ah, yes. *Crypto-dino-gist...* You're still into that?"

"Yeah. I might want to be a cryptozoologist when I'm older. That's if I don't become a famous writer."

Dad nodded and smiled.

"I wondered about being a spy. But they need to be boring and forgettable."

"You can't do that then. You're totally unforgettable!"

My chest tightened as I asked desperately, "Do you believe in me, Dad?"

He chuckled. "Course I do. You're real aren't you?"

"I mean, do you believe I could be a writer or a cryptozoologist one day?"

"Sure! You can be anything you want."

My heart leapt. "Thanks."

Dad knelt beside me and started to pack the *Scrabble* tiles away. I retrieved the ones that I'd flicked across the room and tossed them into the letter bag. We didn't speak for a while and the clicking of the *Scrabble* tiles sounded so heavy in the silence.

After shoving the box back under the sofa, Dad asked whether I wanted a drink yet. I said no. I was starting to need the toilet.

Dad sank back into his seat with a sigh. I couldn't work out if he was bored or just deep in thought. It made me want to cry but, when he looked at me, I fixed a polite smile on my face and sifted absentmindedly through a pile of dull-looking films by my foot.

"Want to watch one?" Dad asked.

I gave a little cough. "Can we do something else?"

"What else?"

I felt my cheeks grow red. "The medical museum?"

Dad shook his head as though I was being ridiculous. "My car's in the garage."

"We could get the bus?"

"I need to stay here in case they ring."

"But I thought you said it wouldn't be ready till Monday?"

Dad gave an irritated sigh and I blushed. I wished I could think of something bold to say. Perhaps I could give him an ultimatum: *'If you really love me, take me to the medical museum.'* My chest knotted with fury as I opened and closed my mouth. "We can watch a film," I muttered, kicking myself for being such a loser.

~*~

That afternoon, Jill breezed uninvited into my room and asked, "Do you want to come to the fair with me and James?"

I shot her an indignant look. Three days earlier, when I'd drawn Jill's attention to the flyer on our doorstep, she had replied, *"I hate fairs."* Suddenly, it was all she could talk about!

Jill blinked at me. "Well?"

"I hate fairs!"

She gave me a funny look. "Suit yourself."

Half an hour later, Fester pulled up outside our house. Jill ran out to meet him and the two of them walked off towards the park.

I swore round the empty house before wandering across the street to Ruby's.

"There's a fair in the park," she said when I arrived. "Shall we go?"

"No!" I yelled, stomping quickly up to her room.

Ruby followed me up and gave me a quizzical look. "Why not?"

"I know someone who lost a leg on a carousel," I lied. Ruby gasped so I added hastily, "Anyway, it's started to rain." I pointed to the window where a few drops had begun to fall.

"Alright. Want to play a game?"

"Not *Scrabble.*"

Ruby opened a drawer and pulled out a battered edition of *Guess Who.* We played about twenty rounds before growing bored. Then we renamed all the characters according to who they most looked like in our class and asked new questions like, *'Are they good at art?'* or, *'Are they friends with Kitty Warrington?'* Our favourite character was a copper-haired lady with a dazzling smile and dimples. We named her *'Ms Sorenson.'*

As we played, I kept peering out of Ruby's window. The rain got heavier and heavier and I hoped that Jill and Fester were getting utterly soaked.

Eventually I looked out and happened to see them rushing round the corner. They were holding hands and scampering like two monkeys in the rain. Half a rainbow hung haphazardly above them. It would've been so perfect, had he not been such an ape.

"As if Fester has monkey arms!" I said, breathing a quiet sigh of relief that Ruby hadn't seen the two of them together.

She laughed at me. "Are you *still* going on about that?"

I shrugged. "It's funny... I bet Fester's the missing link between animals and humans."

Ruby gave me a dubious look but said nothing.

"We share 98% of our DNA with monkeys," I told her.

I expected Ruby to stay quiet but she sprang to her feet. "Don't you realise how much DNA we *have?*" she grabbed a book off her shelf. "If each letter was a bit of DNA, the DNA in us would fill..." She waved her arms around before saying, *"Loads* of books."

"Two hundred 1,000-page books," I said haughtily.

"Exactly! So, even if two sets of books were 98% identical, that different 2% would tell a *completely* different story."

I flipped open the nearest book. It happened to be Violet's censored storybook. As a result of her artistic censoring, *'The Golden Goose'* was now entitled simply, *'The old Goo.'* I closed it again. "They're clever though."

"Only compared to other animals," Ruby retorted. "Not *really* clever. I mean, nobody would marry one."

"I hope not," I muttered. I wondered what the sentence would be for killing a monkey.

~ 16 ~

Ruby's ego

Ruby and I were innocently drawing dinosaurs at break when Violet came over with a very determined look on her face. "I've asked thirty people," she said.

Ruby looked a little stunned and said, "Okay."

"How about you?" Violet demanded. "Who did you ask?"

Ruby shifted uncomfortably. "Can we talk about it later?"

"Did you invite Livi?"

Ruby shot me a quick glance before hissing, "Violet, go away."

"You haven't invited her, have you?" Violet put her hands on her hips.

"Invited me to what?" I asked.

"Nothing," Ruby whispered.

"*Nothing?*" Violet shrieked. "Only a massive *party!*"

I looked at Ruby in bewilderment. "What party?"

"We're having a party tomorrow night," Ruby muttered. "It's no big deal. You can come if you want but you don't have to."

I felt a little wounded. Why was Ruby having a party and not inviting me? "Tomorrow night?" I glanced at the date on my school planner. *October 31st.* "A Halloween party?" I ventured.

Ruby winced as her sister let out a loud snort.

"God hates Halloween!" Violet scolded. "We're having a Light party."

"What's a Light party?"

"It's a silly thing my mum made up," Ruby said quickly. "We just turn all the lights on and hang out."

"And we *pray,*" Violet added. "You forgot that, Ruby. We pray against the devil." She shook her head. "I can't believe you didn't invite Livi."

"It's alright," I said. "It doesn't sound like my kind of thing."

Violet stared at me. I tried to smile but felt rather creeped out. Eventually she walked away.

"Wow." I looked at Ruby. "Your sister's crazy."

Ruby was bright red. "I'm sorry I didn't invite you."

"Don't worry about it! I think I'm busy anyway."

"But I still should have asked you."

"Honestly, it's fine!"

Ruby fell silent.

I felt a bit awkward and tried to break the silence. "Did you hear Fester this morning when his voice went all squeaky?"

But it seemed Ruby wasn't done. "I should be more like Violet," she whispered.

"Don't be stupid!" I cried a little loudly. "Violet's really..." I waved my hand dramatically.

"I know. But at least she's not afraid to say things."

"But sometimes she says *silly* things."

"That's better than not saying *anything*." Ruby looked utterly depressed. "I didn't invite you to the Light party because I was too ashamed to mention it."

"Well, that's... understandable."

She shook her head. "I shouldn't be ashamed. I should just *say* things! I'm awful!" She sounded rather choked up.

"You're not awful, Ruby."

"I am!" She reached for a tissue and blew her nose noisily before continuing, "I'm too self-obsessed. I avoid awkward situations. I never smile at people on the bus. There's a tramp in town who always asks for 37p and I never give him anything. My ego gets in the way."

"Don't be silly!" I nudged her playfully. "You've got the smallest ego of anybody I've ever met."

"Well, it must be pretty big," Ruby said sadly, "if you've known me this long and I've never once told you that Jesus is my best friend."

I bit my lip and glanced around. People were walking past and it was rather embarrassing. Usually, if your best friend is someone that nobody else can see, then the best place for you is a padded cell. Of course, I didn't repeat this to Ruby.

"Forget about it," I said. "I don't mind."

"But I do!" Ruby cried, her eyes wide. "I really, really *do!*"

I patted her tentatively on the back before hoisting her up by the arm. "We're going to be late for Art."

She gave a snuffle. "Thanks for not judging me, Livi."

I couldn't reply honestly to that so I just shrugged and said, "Let's go."

As if to make things better with her best friend, Jesus, Ruby spent the rest of the day talking about him as much as possible.

"Jesus once fed 5,000 people with five loaves of bread and two fish," she said over lunch. "He also called himself the bread of life."

I nodded politely.

"He didn't mean he was made of bread or anything."

"I get it."

"Jesus often spoke with stories, you see..."

She even invited Kitty Warrington to her Light party. I was mortified for her.

"You're such a loser!" Kitty sneered. "What do you do? Sit around the house with the lights on? Are you afraid of the dark or something? I'm surprised you don't like Halloween; you don't even need a mask with your ugly face."

Kitty and Molly laughed all the way down the corridor, leaving Ruby gazing mournfully after them.

"It's okay," Ruby told me shakily. "Jesus said to love our enemies."

That afternoon, we had Religious Studies. I know there are some people who look like their pets, but our teacher, Miss Dalton, is the kind of person who looks like a vegetable— something that's a cross between a turnip and a cabbage. I once overheard her offering Miss Fairway some lettuce from her garden so I suppose the likeness makes some sense. We rarely discuss religion in her lessons. We just dance around hazy moral issues like fox hunting and capital punishment. Occasionally, Miss Dalton will say, "Well, isn't this very interesting?" but she doesn't seem to have any opinions of her own. Today, we were discussing leadership.

"Who can think of somebody who was a good leader?" Miss Dalton asked in her most condescending voice.

As if playing straight into Ruby's hands, somebody said Jesus.

Ruby gulped and raised her hand. "He was more than a good leader," she whispered. "He was God."

A few people snickered.

"Well, he was," Ruby insisted, much to my embarrassment. "Otherwise, he must have been evil or a madman!"

I thought this was an odd thing to say about her pin-up hero. I shot her a sideways glance and silently begged her to stop.

141

"Only somebody who was really evil or really mad would claim to be God if they weren't," Ruby said, shaking a little.

"Yeah, whatever!" Molly Masterson scoffed.

"It says in the Bible—" Ruby began.

For *her* sanity as much as for mine, I threw my hand in the air. "Hitler was a good leader," I said loudly.

The class gasped.

Miss Dalton looked at me strangely. "Hitler?"

"I'm not saying he was a good *person,*" I said quickly. "I'm just saying he must have been a good *leader* to get so many people to follow him."

I heard someone behind me mutter, *"Nazi."*

"I'm not! I just mean Hitler must have successfully convinced all those people to go along with him. Do you think his followers realised they were the bad guys?"

When nobody answered, Miss Dalton said, "I expect most of them thought they were doing the right thing."

"Exactly!" I rose to my feet. "So, Hitler was a *successful* leader who got hundreds of people to follow him. Hundreds of *normal* people— just like you and me." There was an uncomfortable silence but I ploughed on. "How do you know someone like Hitler won't rise up in *our* lifetime with leadership skills that convince us to follow them? How do you know *you're* not capable of being a Nazi? Or *you*? Or *you?*" I pointed wildly at my classmates.

They were gaping at me as though I was about to pull out a gun and shoot them all.

Miss Dalton cleared her throat. "That's quite enough, Livi."

I shut my mouth and slid red-faced into my chair.

The rest of the lesson was punctuated by odd whispers of *"Nazi!"* and everybody sniggering.

I pretended not to notice and focused on trying to draw the perfect circle. Apparently, if you can draw a perfect circle then you are either psychotic or a genius. I have a vain hope that I will achieve it one day.

The lesson came to an end and Miss Dalton set the homework assignment: *'What makes a good leader?'*

"And let's try to think of leaders who *didn't* cause the murder of millions of innocent people." Miss Dalton looked at me.

The class laughed.

I got out of that lesson as quickly as possible, vowing never to speak in class again. I'd thought I was making perfect sense. But, as it happened, I think I came off even worse than Ruby.

Our final lesson was Drama. The original Romeo had pulled out with a note from his mum explaining that he needed to devote more time to the rest of his schoolwork[70] so Miss Waddle spent most of the lesson working with Kitty and the new Romeo, a boy called Freddie Singh who is about a foot smaller than Kitty and pronounces Juliet *'Dooliet.'* The rest of us were supposed to be choreographing fight scenes but were actually hanging out in the props cupboard discussing who fancied who and whether Miss Waddle was older than thirty.

After a half-hearted attempt at plotting a series of fake punches with Ruby, I explored the props cupboard. This led to me having a *genius* idea involving Ruby, a wooden sword, some red paint and the head of a mannequin: After ducking a few of my punches, Ruby would dive for cover behind the audience. I would then thrust the wooden sword into a gap in the audience and Ruby would scream and toss the mannequin's head through the gap, red paint dripping poignantly from the neck. Believing that my idea was so good that it barely needed rehearsing, we spent the next ten minutes sawing off the head of the most Ruby-looking mannequin and filling it with red paint. When Miss Waddle called us through to perform our scenes I could hardly contain my excitement and, much to Ruby's dismay, eagerly volunteered us to go first.

But what seemed like such a great idea turned out to be a complete disaster. My fake punches were so clumsy that I almost hit Ruby in the face and Ruby stood there for so long that I eventually had to whisper to her, "Run into the audience now!"

Ruby gave me a terrified look and then wobbled towards our classmates, tripping over someone's foot as she ran. She even stopped and stammered, "Whoops, sorry. Erm... Is this right, Livi?"

Caught off guard, I paused before digging the wooden sword into the audience and did not factor for Molly's fat arm being in the way or her responding with mild hysteria when the mannequin's head came whizzing past her nose.

"There's blood all over me!" Molly shrieked, pointing a chubby finger at me as if I was a witch.

"A plague on both your houses!" I said valiantly, feeling a little bit of improvisation at this point couldn't go amiss.

---

[70] The truth was he was petrified of the kiss scene and was rumoured to have said, "I'd rather die than have Kitty find out I'm bad at kissing."

Miss Waddle stopped our performance with a loud shout and demanded to know what I was playing at. I soon realised that this was a rhetorical question.

"It's not a real head, it's just—"

"Get out. NOW!"

In my props cupboard fantasy, Miss Waddle had applauded my creativity and promoted me to the role of a small speaking part. Instead I found myself outside the Drama studio, sitting amongst everybody's smelly shoes and debating the consequences of tying all their laces together.

Eventually, Miss Waddle came out and said, "Livi, are you ready to be sensible?"

I didn't know whether or not this was another rhetorical question so I waited for a moment before giving a cautious nod.

"Okay then." She held the door open and ushered me in, gesturing to be silent as Freddie and Kitty were in the middle of rehearsing Romeo and Juliet's suicide scene.

The rest of the class turned to stare as I came in. Molly scowled at me. Kitty smirked. The mannequin's head was lying upside down on Miss Waddle's desk. It crossed my mind that it would make a useful pen holder. I sucked in my cheeks and went to sit beside Ruby.

"Are you alright?" she whispered.

"Yeah," I muttered.

Miss Waddle resumed directing Kitty and Freddie, giving them useless advice such as, *"Be more sad,"* and, *"Sigh a bit,"* which led to a forced and contrived love scene in which Kitty bit her lip in an attempt to produce real tears. I mouthed her lines along with her and wished I was cool enough to play Juliet.

At the end of the lesson, Miss Waddle called me over and asked if I would put the mannequin's head back. "This is rather morbid, Livi," she said with eyebrows raised.

"But did you see what we were trying to do?" I asked desperately.

She didn't reply.

Kitty sauntered past. "Be careful, Miss," she said. "Livi's role model is Hitler!"

I glared at her and turned back to our teacher. "That's not true, Miss."

Miss Waddle didn't look convinced. I went to pick up the mannequin's head but she stopped me. "Actually, I'll put it back, Livi. You can go now."

"Okay..." I felt her gaze on the back of my head as I shuffled out of the room and located my shoes.

Kitty and Molly had just finished tying my laces together. They flung my shoes down with shrieks of "Nazi!" and went running down the corridor.

On the way home from school I turned down an invitation from Ruby to help her and Violet prepare for their Light party.

"I'd love to," I lied. "But I said I'd help Jill choose a budgie."

"You're getting a budgie?"

"Yeah." *Stupid lie. I would have to sort that out later.*

"Well, have fun!"

"You too..."

"Thanks! We're going to make streamers of all the references of light in the Bible!"

I nodded.

"I know you probably won't come tomorrow," Ruby said as we reached our street. "But I'm really glad I told you about it."

I forced a smile.

"I feel much better now that I've decided not to be ashamed of Jesus!"

"Good, good," I said dumbly. I forced another smile and let myself into my house, hurriedly shutting the door before Ruby could speak again.

I rubbed my head as I trudged up the stairs. Ruby becoming a mini version of Violet was just the start of my worries. The disgrace in Miss Dalton's class coupled with the humiliation of the Drama rehearsal was almost too much to bear and, every time I thought about Kitty's smug face, I felt a surge of anger. I gave a growl as I looked at myself in the mirror. My nose is poky, my hair is a boring shade of brown[71] and my teeth are ever so slightly wonky. Aunt Claudia once said that I have an *'unimposing'* face. By that, I think she meant I'm nothing special.

I stared at my dull brown eyes and longed for Kitty's bright blue ones. "She's not *that* pretty," I said out loud. "And she's definitely not *nice*. So why do people like her?" I scrunched up my face as I whispered, *"My dear Romeo, do you find me lovely?"*

I spent the next hour in front of the mirror, reciting Kitty's lines and thinking of as many sad things as I could. To squeeze one tear out— just one tear— would've been euphoria.

---

[71] Do NOT say *'mousy.'*

Five things to feel sad about
1. *Miss Waddle yelling at me.*
2. *Not being allowed a pet dog.*
3. *The eleven million people killed by the Nazis.*
4. *Not being able to see my mother. Ever.*
5. *The fact that I'm yet to discover a way to be great.*

At far as I could tell from my careful curtain twitching, the Ricos' Light party was surprisingly successful. I peeked out at about half seven and saw a few cars roll up. A handful of chattering youths were dropped off and greeted by an excited Violet who was dressed head to toe in glow sticks. From behind my curtain she looked like some kind of ethereal glow worm. I kept vigilant watch, expecting the guests to run out screaming when they found out it wasn't a Halloween party after all but, after a couple of hours, the party was still in full swing. Through one window I could see a handful of people dancing. I wondered if that meant they'd finished praying against the devil. Or perhaps it was some kind of prayer dance. I didn't recognise any of the guests and wondered where they'd all come from.

At one point Jill came up and asked, "Are the Ricos having a Halloween party?"

I pretended to look nonchalantly out of the window. "Oh, that?" I said, as if it was nothing. "It's a Light party."

"What does that mean?"

"I guess it's sort of an *anti*-Halloween party."

"And Ruby didn't invite you?"

"She did! It just sounded a bit silly. I didn't want to go."

"So why have you spent the entire evening watching it from the window?" Jill smirked.

"I haven't!"

She gave an annoying laugh and turned to go. "By the way, James is coming over for a bit."

My stomach lurched. "Fester's coming over?"

"Don't call him that!"

"Don't let him come over," I begged.

"I was telling you, not asking you."

I glared at her. "I don't want to see him. I'm staying in my room."

"Suit yourself." Jill shrugged and walked out.

I let out a screech and threw my pillow at the door.

Fester turned up about ten minutes later, bearing a massive bucket of chicken. I heard him complimenting Jill on her hair as he shook off his coat and laid his car keys on our side table. Then he called up the stairs, "Would you like some chicken, Livi?"

I desperately wanted to ignore him but the aroma wafted up the stairs and under my door and it smelt *so* good. I opened my mouth to refuse his dirty chicken but began to salivate instead. I pulled myself away from the window with a groan, annoyed at my lack of self control, and trudged down the stairs.

"Good evening!" Fester said cheerily as I entered the living room. He was wearing a shirt bearing the words, *'I don't suffer from insanity, I enjoy every minute of it.'*

"Nice top," I said sarcastically.

He grinned. "Thanks."

I wanted to grab a couple of pieces of chicken and take them back to my room but Jill wouldn't let me. So I wolfed the food down as fast as I could, doing my best to ignore Fester's irritating voice and Jill's even more irritating laugh every time he spoke.

"This is a nice house," Fester said, glancing round the room.

"It's alright," Jill replied, waving a dismissive hand. "The wallpaper is a bit odd[72] and there's some mould in the bathroom... And a mouse in the kitchen... But we like it here, don't we, Livi?"

I yawned and shoved a handful of chips into my mouth.

Jill leant behind the sofa and reached for her handbag. "How much was the food?" she asked Fester.

He chuckled. "It's my treat."

I rolled my eyes as Jill blushed and said, "That's very kind of you, James."

Fester gave a smarmy smile, kicking his shoes off as he made himself at home. "What have you been up to today, Livi?"

I shrugged. "Just stuff."

---

[72] It's covered with grey bears. That Mr Denby must've been a strange old man. I really hope the afterlife offers him better things to do than to visit his old home. Sometimes I get scared that he might pop back to see the neighbours— particularly Solomon and Helen Tagda, the elderly couple on our left. Although, having said that, the Tagdas frequently keep us awake with their bitter squabbling so I wouldn't blame Mr Denby if he's relieved to be shot of them.

"Ah, *stuff!* Interesting indeed!"

"Loads of stuff actually. But nothing I want to tell *you.*"

"Livi..." Jill shot me a warning look.

I pushed my plate away. The chicken wasn't worth it. "Thanks for the food," I said coolly before running back up the stairs.

I closed my door and barricaded myself in with a pile of dirty laundry. It didn't seem likely that Jill would give Fester a tour, but I wanted to be on the safe side.

I peeked out of the window. Ruby's party was still going strong. With a sigh, I grabbed some paper and started doodling. It began as a picture of Fester but then I added horns and a tail. I drew some people dancing round him and sniggered to myself as I thought about the devil for a bit. I wondered whether he existed and, if so, whether he was remotely frightened by the Ricos' Light party.

A sudden noise outside made me jump and I stopped doodling and looked anxiously out of the window.

It was just a cat.

Even so, I pulled my curtains tightly shut as I whispered, "Go away, devil. I don't believe in you." Then I scribbled over my drawing and made a mental note to accept Ruby's invitation next year.

~*~

"Did you enjoy your party?" I asked Ruby casually during registration on Monday morning.

"Yeah!" she exclaimed. "You should have come."

"I was really busy," I lied. "My dad took me to a film premiere." I instantly remembered that Ruby knew the truth about my dad and blushed. "I mean... a preview at the cinema."

Ruby gave me an odd look but said nothing.

"Did you have a lot of guests?" I continued, desperate to know where all the people had come from.

"Yeah. Quite a lot of people from church came."

"Ohh..." I said slowly. *"Church* friends."

Ruby nodded and dug around in her bag for her phone. "I took some photos."

I pretended to be interested in the abundance of blurry photos of people decorated in glow sticks and other non-spooky attire.

There was a shot of Belinda wearing a white bed sheet with eye holes. For a moment, I thought she had entered into the fun of it and dressed up as a ghost. But it turned out she was the Holy Spirit.

"Nice," I said politely, desperate for Miss Fairway to look up and tell Ruby to put her phone away.

The whole day was a pain, with Ruby making another determined effort to be more like Violet. I was hugely relieved when she confessed on the way home that she'd had enough.

"I was praying about it and it's just not me," she said, picking chewing gum off her face.[73]

Wary of saying anything to cause her to change her mind, I said simply, "Whatever makes you happy."

Ruby gave me a funny look. "I'm definitely going to stop being ashamed of what I believe," she insisted. "I just realised I need to be who God made me to be, and I'm not Violet."

I nodded.

"And, Livi... If you ever have any questions about God or Jesus or church or anything, I want you to know you can ask me."

I forced a smile. "Thanks. But I don't have any."

"But if you ever do."

"Okay!" I said quickly. A few people from our class were nearby. "I will."

---

[73] Ruby had mentioned Jesus to a sixth form boy after hearing him blaspheme. The sixth former had threatened to spit his gum at her. Ruby had frozen for a moment and then turned the other cheek. Literally.

~ 17 ~

The biggest slice

'*Livi, I'm running a little late. LOL.*'

I stared at my phone. For the past couple of weeks, Dad had been promising to take me to the museum to see a new exhibition on Yorkshire writers. Now that the day had arrived, I feared he had changed his mind at the last minute.

I paused before replying, '*OK. See you soon.*'

While I waited, I watched a squirrel run feverishly through the branches of a nearby tree. I kind of wanted it to fall. I thought it would make a good addition to my dead animal photo collection and took a moment to attempt a *Startled Squirrel* impression.

A lady looked over and chuckled. "That was good."

I tried to look humble. "Thanks."

I carried on watching the squirrel as it darted higher up the tree. It moved with so much skill and precision for such a trivial little creature. As I marvelled at how cool it would be to be able to climb like that, a sudden thought struck me: if we really evolved from animals, why can't we climb like a squirrel, fly like a bird, or run like a cheetah? We can't even breathe underwater like a common sponge. I scrunched up my eyes and looked up at the sky. I hoped to see some sort of sign— perhaps a cloud that looked like Jesus. But I didn't.

I checked my watch and frowned. Dad was now more than '*a little*' late. I had half a mind to get up and go home but the thought of missing him made me ache. For a second, I yearned to call Jill. But I knew that was stupid. She would just tell me that my dad was useless. I took a deep breath and decided that, when he came, I would sulk and demand to know what had taken him so long.

I had prepared a good *Pouting Pony* impression when Dad finally arrived. But, before I could unleash it, he swept me into the air with a massive hug. "Sorry I'm late, Livi. Let's skip the museum and go straight to lunch."

The hug caught me off guard so I just said, "Okay. Where shall we go?"

Dad decided on a cheap café nearby but, as we entered, I saw Kitty Warrington, Molly Masterson and a couple of other girls from our class sitting at one of the tables.

"It looks busy in here," I said. "Let's go somewhere else."

"It's fine. There's space over there." Dad pointed to a table near Kitty and her gang.

"I feel a bit sick. I don't think I'm very hungry."

"Nah, you'll be alright after you've had some sausages. Quick, before anyone else grabs the table!" Dad started to weave through the café so I ducked my head and followed him, crossing my fingers as we passed Kitty's table.

"Chips have hardly any calories," Molly was saying.

"Only, like, a *million,*" Kitty replied mockingly.

It looked like somebody else was going to reach the table before us and, in his haste, my dad tripped on the back of Kitty's chair. She turned and scowled.

"Oh sorry!" Dad said, before lunging at the empty table.

"Hi Kitty." I attempted a friendly wave.

She turned her nose up and ignored me.

I hoped Dad wouldn't notice and think I was unpopular. "Are they friends from school?" he asked as I joined him at the table.

"Yeah, sort of," I said, looking back to make sure Kitty and Molly weren't listening.

Fortunately, they were too busy throwing chips at one another.

"That's nice." Dad smiled. "Do you have a lot of friends?"

"Obviously." I rolled my eyes like Kitty Warrington.

"Good. I'll go and grab us some food."

I nodded and shot a glance at Kitty's table. I suddenly felt ridiculously geeky going out for lunch with my dad instead of with a group of friends. I expected that if Kitty was ever spotted in public with her father it would be whilst doing something sophisticated, like sailing.

Kitty and the others were talking about the Christmas show[74] and I caught a whiff of Kitty bragging about her acting skills.

---

[74] Incidentally, I have finally been given a line in the show: '*A tragedy of love cut short.*' I've been practising it non-stop all week. Every time I pass a mirror, I repeat it. I think I've pretty much nailed it.

"Vicky, I mean *Miss Waddle*, said I'm a natural."

Molly sneered. "Yeah! A natural show off!"

Kitty gave a melodramatic yawn. "You're just jealous."

"Yeah, right," said Melody Vickers, one of the other girls. "Jealous because you have as much talent as a performing monkey!"

The girl beside her, Annie Button, put her hands under her armpits and screeched like a baboon.

The rest of the group started laughing.

"That was rubbish!" Kitty roared.

Annie giggled with embarrassment. "You do better!"

Kitty shook her head. "No thanks."

Then Molly threw her head back and gave the most ludicrous attempt at a monkey impression I have ever heard.

A few people turned to stare.

Kitty looked utterly mortified. "Shut up, you idiot!" she hissed.

I looked up and caught Kitty's eye. She smirked and I blushed and looked away. I wondered if she remembered how good my pig impression was.

My dad returned with a tray of food and said loudly, "They had a deal on so I got us two hotdogs each."

I forced a smile and wondered how many calories were in a hotdog. Dad grinned as he tucked into his food. I tried to enjoy mine but was painfully aware of Kitty and the others nearby. I fought to think of something that would be worth overhearing.

"Have you done any films recently?" I shot my dad a meaningful look.

"Do you mean have I *watched* any films recently? Obviously I've seen all the current releases."

"No! I mean have you done any *acting* recently. You know, as an *actor?*" I cast a quick glance at Kitty's table but I don't think any of them were even listening.

Dad looked baffled. "Sure. I've done hundreds."

I sniffed and forced down some chips.

By now, Kitty and her friends had grown bored and I watched out of the corner of my eye as they left the café. Kitty had snuck half a sausage into Annie's hood and Molly was teasing Melody about her shoes. I wondered if a sausage in the hood was a sign of Kitty's approval. Is that what *cool* friendships are all about: throwing chips and insulting one another? It looked like quite a lot of hard work. I wondered if they were off to Miss Waddle's house for brownies and felt a pang of envy. I had a sudden reckless idea that Dad and I should follow them and find out where she lived. I could pretend I was walking past and desperate for the toilet. Then she would have to let me in.

The moment we finished eating, Dad looked at his watch and said, "Well, I'd better get you home now."

My heart sank. I was sure there was still time for the museum.

"I need to get some new shelves for my living room," Dad explained. "And you won't want to come trudging round hardware stores with me!"

I very much wanted to go trudging round hardware stores with him but I just shrugged and said, "Okay."

As we drove back to mine, Dad switched the radio on to hear the latest football scores. I felt sick from the sausages and wound down my window to let some air in. I leant over, closed my eyes, and pretended I was a dog.

"Do you mind closing the window?" Dad asked suddenly. "I can't hear the radio."

I blushed and wound it up again.

"Thanks." Dad grinned.

I tried to smile back but was still feeling queasy.

Eventually, Dad switched the radio off and muttered, "Flipping clowns, the whole lot of them."

"Did you lose?" I asked.

"It's just half time. But the linesman flagged for offside over a perfectly good ball; otherwise we'd have drawn level."

I had no idea what he was taking about but it sounded important. I tried to nod seriously.

"Here we are!" Dad sang, pulling into my street.

I racked my brain for some way to stall him. "Do you want to see a poster I made for Religious Studies?"

He raised his eyebrows. "I'll have a quick look."

"I'll just get it!"

I ran indoors and grabbed my poster off the kitchen table. It was a collage of Jewish traditions which I'd been working on all morning. In the middle was a sketch of a bearded man wearing a hat. I ran back outside and held it up.

Dad chuckled. "Very good."

"Thanks. I made one about Muslims too. We're not studying them or anything; I just thought it would be good to keep my options open. Shall I go and get it?"

"Er... Maybe next time." Dad glanced at his watch. "I really need to go and get these shelves."

A lump formed in my throat. "Okay."

At that moment, Fester's car pulled up. Jill was sitting in the passenger seat looking a little irritated but, as soon as she saw us, she grinned and waved.

Dad looked at me. "Who's that?"

"Stupid nobody," I muttered.

Jill gave Fester a quick hug before getting out of the car. Then Fester tooted his horn and drove off.

"You're not dating *him*, are you?" my father asked as Jill came towards us.

"What's it to you?" she snapped.

"Nothing. It's your life. You can do better, that's all."

"That's what I keep telling her!" I chipped in.

Jill rolled her eyes and flounced indoors, slamming the door behind her.

I shrugged. "She always dates weirdos."

Dad gave a funny laugh. "I'd better go. It was nice to see you."

I felt my insides churning. I wished he could stay longer but I knew Jill would be angry if I offered him the shelves off our wall. "Nice to see you too," I whispered as he got back into his car.

He gave a cheery wave and I waved back, feeling quite sad once he'd driven away.

"Hi Livi!"

I turned and saw Ruby and Violet coming towards me. Violet was carrying a cardboard box full of ripped material and Ruby was grinning inanely.

"Guess who we just saw driving out of the estate?" she exclaimed.

My stomach lurched but I tried to stay cool. "No idea."

"Fester!"

"Mr Lester," Violet scolded, sounding a little like Jill.

I tried to look surprised. "Oh? How weird."

"Yeah! Imagine if he lives round here?"

"Hmmm." I quickly changed the subject by turning to the contents of Violet's box. "Are you moving house?" I joked, poking a ragged t-shirt.

Violet didn't bat an eyelid. "It's a new art project. *'Coats for goats.'*"

"Goats would probably eat the coats," I said. "Goats eat everything."

"That's the point." Violet gave me a withering look and stomped off.

Ruby grinned before pointing to my poster. "What are you doing with that?"

"Oh. I was just showing it to my dad." I forced a smile.

"How come?"

To have said, *'I was desperate for him to stay longer,'* would have sounded far too pathetic. Much more sensible was to reply, "He's Jewish."

Ruby raised an eyebrow. *"Actually* Jewish? Or *'Jewish'* like you and Jill?" She smirked.

I gulped as I felt my cheeks go red. "Okay fine, he's *half* Jewish."

Ruby gave me a long look. "Well, I'd better go. I told Mum I'd help her tidy the attic."

I wrinkled up my nose. "Poor you!"

"I want to! Mum reckons she's got some old jewellery up there."

"Oh." I wished *we* had an attic full of treasures.

Ruby turned to go but I called her back. "Wait!"

"What?"

I took a deep breath. "Please don't judge me... Jill's dating Fester."

Ruby looked at me in surprise. She thought for a moment before saying, "Why would I judge you?" Then, before I could answer, she continued, "Ooh! What's his real name?"

"James."

"Really?" Ruby giggled. "That's such a normal name."

I rolled my eyes. "Please don't tell anyone."

"Alright." She stood staring at me for a while and I felt rather awkward.

"Well... have a nice afternoon." I fumbled for my door key.

"You too."

I went indoors where I kicked my shoes off and threw my stupid poster on the stairs. Jill had spread some of her work out on the kitchen table.

I poured myself a drink before enquiring, "Did you go round Fester's house?"

She glared at me. "His name is *James.*"

I shrugged and repeated, "Did you go round his house?"

"Yes."

"What's it like?"

155

Jill sighed. "It's a nice house. Fairly tidy, big garden, three cats."

"Ha! I knew he had cats! And did you look inside his wardrobe? Does he only have two shirts?"

She gave me a funny look. "Of course I didn't look inside his wardrobe."

I forced a yawn and watched glumly as she carried on working. Her brow was furrowed and she looked rather stressed. Every time I made a sound, she turned and frowned. I started to feel irritated. Ever since we moved to Leeds, my sister has seemed more bothered about her dumb job than about me. Sometimes I wish we could go home to Little Milking where everything was simple and you could feel important just by having a haircut.

"Can you do this sum for me?" Jill asked suddenly.

"No."

"Come on, Livi. You're good at maths."

"I'm rubbish at maths! Fester lied to you."

Jill frowned but said nothing.

I tipped the rest of my drink into my mouth and gargled it at the back of my throat.

"Don't do that!" Jill yelled.

"Can we go to a hardware store?" I asked gingerly.

"What for?"

"Just to browse."

She let out an exasperated sigh. "Livi, please!"

"How long will you be?" I traced a line down the table. "We could go to a hardware store afterwards. Or make brownies... Like Vicky."

"Who's Vicky?"

"My Drama teacher, Miss Waddle."

"Don't be rude. Call her by her real name."

"That *is* her real name!"

"Oh." Jill turned back to her work. "Not today."

A bubble of rage erupted inside me. I threw Jill a perfect *Pouting Pony* impression before galloping up the stairs.

~*~

Four hours later, Fester arrived uninvited because he *'just happened to be passing.'* I made the mistake of thinking he was the pizza delivery guy and almost tripped over the rug as I ran to open the door.

"Oh, it's you," I sneered.

He gave an annoying smile. "Is Jill in?"

Jill came out of the kitchen. "James! Were we meant to be meeting..." She paused before adding, "Again?"

"No, no!" he said. "I just thought I'd say hello."

"Oh! That's nice." Jill looked a bit ruffled. She'd been struggling through her mountain of work all afternoon. "We've just ordered a pizza."

"There won't be enough for you," I added.

Jill was about to scold me but Fester said, "That's fine. I've already eaten." He took his coat off and hung it over the banister.[75] Then he retrieved a paper bag from his pocket and gave it to Jill. "I've got a present for you."

Jill looked flattered. "Oh, James, you shouldn't have!" She tore open the bag and pulled out a fridge magnet. Her face fell as she looked at it.

I peered over her shoulder. The magnet read, *'Your village called. They want their idiot back.'*

"No *really,*" I said with a snigger. "You *shouldn't* have."

Fester was looking at Jill expectantly. "Funny, isn't it?"

"Yeah." She forced a smile. "Hilarious."

I went back into the living room where I'd been watching a game show in which people compete to win their weight in crisps. To my annoyance, they followed me in. I turned my back on them and tried to concentrate on the television.

Fester asked Jill how she was getting on with her work and she replied, "Fine."

"Busy afternoon?"

"Well, yes. I was with you for most of it, remember?"

Before Fester could respond, the pizza came and he jumped up to answer the door. "Let me get that!"

"There's a tenner on the side table," Jill called after him.

"It's fine," he replied. "I'll pay."

"Cool!" I said to Jill. "Free dinner!"

But she looked a little annoyed. "There's money right there, James."

He ignored her and paid for the pizza himself. "My pleasure!" he said as he brought the pizza through to us.

---

[75] Today's awful shirt read, *'I Love Pi.'*

Jill sighed and reached for the box.

Even though he'd said he'd already eaten, Fester reached in and grabbed the biggest slice.

Jill went red. "James, that's the biggest piece! If it were me I'd have offered that one to *you!*" She forced a smile as if to imply that she was only joking, but I knew she was deadly serious.

"Well, that's good." Fester grinned. "Because I've got it!"

For the briefest moment, I thought Jill was going to shove his face into the pizza. But she composed herself and said, "Fine."

"Now, here's an interesting maths puzzle," Fester said suddenly. "How do you cut a pizza into eleven slices by making only four cuts?"

"James, you know I can't do maths," Jill said stiffly.

"It's simple. I'll talk it through with you." He retrieved a pen from his pocket and scrawled on the lid of the pizza box.

I yawned loudly and turned up the volume on the television. Jill didn't even tell me off.

I saw her eyeing the clock a few times and knew she would be itching to get on with her work, so I tried to come to her rescue by saying, "You're behind on your work, aren't you, Jill?"

But she just looked at me awkwardly and said, "No."

Eventually, it got to half ten and Fester said, "Fancy that! Doesn't time fly when you're having fun?"

Jill stifled a yawn. "Yeah. Well, thanks for coming." She got up and walked him to the door.

As he was leaving, Fester said to my sister, "By the way, I've booked us a table for *Hurry Curry* tomorrow night. It's only fifteen pounds a head for an all-you-can-eat Indian buffet."

"I don't like spicy food," she replied.

"Then this will be a fabulous chance to stretch your taste buds!" I couldn't see but was sure he was pulling a stupid face.

"I'm not wasting fifteen pounds on something I know I'll hate!"

Fester chuckled. "I'll pay."

"I don't want you to."

"Why not?"

"I don't need you to pay for me." She sounded peeved.

Fester laughed. "Come on, Jill. I'm happy to pay."

I heard Jill swear. "Why don't you come right out and say it? You're richer than me."

Fester gave a splutter. "Don't be daft! Just think about it. I'll call you tomorrow."

"Fine." Jill gave him a quick hug before closing the door. Then she came back into the living room and sighed.

I pretended I hadn't been listening. "Shall we watch a film?"

"I can't! I'm so behind on my work."

I rolled my eyes. "Then why didn't you say so when I asked? I gave you a perfect opportunity to get rid of Fester." I paused. "I mean *James.*"

She just growled, muttering something under her breath as she left the room.

On the other side of the wall, our neighbours started up their usual loud bickering. I picked up the TV remote, turned the volume up to the max and flicked through the channels. There was nothing worth watching and I felt a surge of self-pity, certain that Kitty Warrington's Saturday evenings weren't as pathetic as mine.

I wondered whether my dad had found some shelves. Perhaps he was putting them up right now. Did he wish I was there to help hold them straight or was he enjoying the challenge of doing it alone? I wondered, fleetingly, what it would be like to live with him. But then I remembered that his toilet seat was broken. Plus he lives miles away from my school. He probably wouldn't want me living with him, anyway, otherwise he surely would've asked by now.

I stared hard at the television, willing myself not to cry as the newest '*Mr Tooth*' commercial filled the screen. '*He cares for you, now that's the truth! So give a grin to Mr Tooth!*'

I let out a long sigh. Part of me wanted to hate my father for being busy and complex and so downright *unavailable*. But another part of me longed to do whatever it took to gain his approval.

It's strange that we often chase the love that evades us. Jill has always been here for me, so I would rather see my dad; a compliment from Kitty Warrington is more thrilling than Ruby's genuine friendship; and, despite the fact that she's never given me so much as a smile, every weekend I wish I was round Miss Waddle's house eating brownies.

~ 18 ~

A very private letter

I awoke on Wednesday morning to some fantastic news.

"I've split up with James," Jill said vacantly over breakfast.

A colossal cheer erupted in my chest but I tried to look sympathetic as I said, "Oh! Why?"

Jill sighed and caressed her head. "It just didn't work out." She grabbed a handful of vitamin supplements, her way of compensating for never learning how to cook.

I nodded kindly. "You mean he isn't *'The One'?*"

Jill snorted. "I don't think there is a *'One.'* Life's not like that. It's messy and complicated and rubbish. Take your vitamins." She waved the bottle at me.

"Life isn't rubbish!" I scolded. "Life is about... making as much meaning as possible, remember?"

"It's not that simple, Livi."

"Of course it is. You can do whatever you want." I paused before adding, "But please don't date Fester again."

She growled and looked away. "I can't do whatever I want."

"Yes you can."

Jill looked at me as though I was being stupid. "Do you really think I enjoy selling advertising space for sleazy magazines?"

I shrugged. "Why do you do it then?"

"Because!" Her nostrils flared up like an angry mule. "There are bills to pay... We need food, clothes, money for rent!"

I shrugged again. "I'm going to be a famous writer when I'm older. And a part-time cryptozoologist."

"Hmmm."

"I wondered about being a spy but they have to be forgettable." When Jill didn't reply, I added, "Dad says I'm totally unforgettable."

"What?" Jill squinted at me, distraction etched across her face.

"Never mind."

I couldn't wait to tell Ruby the good news. I met her on the doorstep and whispered, "Jill's split up with Fester!"

"Oh! Is she alright?"

"Of course. Isn't it great?"

"I guess so." Ruby peered into our house and said, "Hi Jill."

"Hi Ruby," Jill replied. "How are you?"

"Fine, thanks. I'm sorry to hear about you and Fes— I mean, Mr Lester."

"Thanks."

I rolled my eyes and pushed Ruby out of the house. "We'll be late for school."

We had Maths that morning. I shot Fester a big grin. He gave me a rather terse smile in return and looked away. I wondered whether he'd been up all night crying over my sister. I hoped *she* wasn't crying too much over *him*. I decided that if I ever fall in love, I will only do it once and I'll make sure it sticks; not just to our faces but to both our hearts. I thought about Jill, hating every moment at work and dating every loser that came her way. Her problem, I decided, was that she aimed too low. Perhaps she'd never set herself reasonable goals. I ignored whatever work we were meant to be doing and made a list instead.

Five things I will do before I die

1. Discover a dinosaur alive and well and name it 'The Ruby Raptor' or 'Livi-Saurus.'

2. Do something really spontaneous like show up at the airport with a bag and my passport and take the next available flight.

3. Have a building or zoo named after me.

4. Write down all the good ideas I have ever had.

5. Fall in love and live happily ever after.

I slipped my list across to Ruby. She was thrilled at the idea of having a dinosaur named after her.

"My uncle did that," she added, pointing to number 2. "He ended up in Coventry."

I raised my eyebrows. "Well, I'd plan it better than that..."

"Ooh, you could ask Miss Waddle to name the new Drama studio after you!" she continued eagerly.

I bit my lip. "Maybe..."

"When you fall in love, can I come to your wedding?"

I took the list off her. It suddenly seemed very stupid. "Ruby, do you ever wish you were destined for something great?"

She shrugged. "I think I am."

I rolled my eyes. "Yeah, I think I am too. But we're not really, are we? We haven't even got good parts in the Christmas show."

Ruby turned and faced me. "My mum says that it doesn't matter if I mean nothing to the whole world because I mean the whole world to God. That means I'm pretty great." She shot me a bashful smile.

I breathed sharply out of my nose. I wished *my* mum was alive to tell me nice things like that.

That afternoon, we had Ms Sorenson's lesson, also known as *Favourite Class*. Ruby and I now have a full folder of articles relating to the existence of dinosaurs. When Ms Sorenson came to see how we were getting on, we lapsed into our usual shy mode as we told her about a story we'd found on the internet about a gigantic snake whose fossilised remains had recently been found. According to the article, the monster (named Titanoboa) was so massive that its diet consisted of crocodiles and giant turtles.

"He would eat them whole," I said, pointing to our drawing of a crocodile being swallowed by the snake.

"And he weighed more than a ton," Ruby added.

Ms Sorenson beamed the whole time. It made me ache a little.

"Oh, before I forget, I saw something that might interest you..." She began to root around in her bag.

Ruby and I exchanged curious glances and I felt a shiver of excitement. Ms Sorenson had brought something for us!

She pulled out a filofax and I saw that it was labelled *'Audrey Sorenson.'* I'd never liked the name *'Audrey'* but suddenly it was the most wonderful name in the entire universe. As she licked her fingers and thumbed through the filofax, I wondered what it would be like if she was my mother. The very thought made me feel hugely idiotic and deeply forlorn. For one stupid moment, I thought I was going to cry.

I have only ever called one teacher *'Mum.'* Her name was Miss Allendale and she taught English at my old school. She liked my stories and always gave me a good mark and a sticker. One spring, some of the older students started a lunchtime Poetry club and Miss Allendale put up a notice about it in our form room. I didn't go for the first two weeks but, on the third week, I lingered in the doorway, watching as a hoard of sixth form girls entered clutching furry pink journals.

Miss Allendale came up behind me and said, "Are you coming in, Livi?"

I asked, "Do you think I should?"

And she replied, "Absolutely!"

So I did.

I sat near the back and tried to look attentive as the sixth form girls got up one by one and read their long eloquent tales of woe. I didn't read anything but, every now and then, Miss Allendale caught my eye and smiled. When everybody had finished, a debate broke out over who was the best poet of all time. A particularly loud girl said we should all go round and give our opinion. I was terrified. I didn't think I could name any poets except for *The Cat in the Hat*. That was the moment I thought I would *never* be a writer.

But, when the meeting ended, Miss Allendale came over to me and said, "I'm glad you came today, Livi. Will you come next week?"

And, although I didn't intend to, I said, "Yes," because I didn't want her to be insulted.

"Great! I hope next time you'll read something?"

"I don't know..."

"You should. You write beautifully!"

"Really?" Apparently, when people lie they look to their right so I studied Miss Allendale's expression but she was staring straight at me. I blushed and added, "I like *The Cat in the Hat*."

She laughed and said, "Me too!"

And that was the moment I decided I would *definitely* be a writer. So I whispered, "Thanks, Mum," accidentally-on-purpose, just to try it out.

She laughed again and told me I was sweet.

"Ah, here it is," Ms Sorenson said, retrieving a piece of folded up paper. "I saw it in a library book about cave paintings..." She unfolded the piece of paper and spread it out in front of us. It was a picture of a dragon-like beast carved into a rock.

I wasn't sure which I was most happy about: the fact that this would be great for our project or the fact that Ms Sorenson had seen the picture and cared enough to spend time and money photocopying it for us.

"Thanks, Miss!" we sang.

She beamed and stood up.

I wished I could think of something to make her stay with us a bit longer. "Is our project alright?" I asked pathetically.

"It's more than alright! I'm so proud of you both." She gave us another smile.

I felt a lump in my throat as she walked away. I wondered whether she would have children one day and what she would name them when she did.

That evening, I asked Jill, "What's my Almost-Name?"

"Your what?"

"The name I would've had if I'd been a boy."

She gave me an exasperated look. "How should I know?"

I sighed. "What was yours?" Maybe it would be the same.

"I have no idea."

"Why didn't you ask Mum?"

"Because I didn't care!"

I glared at her. Sometimes I don't think she realises how selfish she is. She had our mother all to herself and doesn't seem the slightest bit interested in sharing her.

I stormed out of the room and stomped loudly up the stairs. I was going to go to my bedroom but the open door of the spare room caught my eye. Since moving in, that room had been piled high with all the useless things that don't have a home anywhere else, together with years of junk that Jill had never brought herself to throw away. Today, however, the patch of carpet that was visible from the landing was clear. Jill had tidied. Feeling curious, I went in and closed the door. A hat-stand in the corner held some old scarves and there was a pile of chipped ornaments, dusty books, and strange paintings under the windowsill. The camp bed, slightly dented from Aunt Claudia's stay, was leaning against one wall. Everything else had been filed into neat boxes. Jill had even assembled a little wooden shelving unit to house it all. I marvelled at her handiwork as I ran a finger across the many boxes. 'House...' 'Bank Statements...' 'Receipts & Warranties...' Boring. I was about to leave when a box in the bottom corner caught my eye. It was simply labelled, 'Jill.' My heart started to pound. I took that as a sign that the box was both totally none of my business and exactly what I hadn't realised I was looking for. I paused for a moment and put my ear to the door. If Jill caught me, she would go absolutely berserk.

I shook my head. *I can't go through her things... Can I?*

Without thinking, I carefully lifted the box off the shelf.

There could be things about our mother in here, I reasoned. *And, if there are, Jill has no right to keep them from me.*

I sat with my back against the door and put the box beside me. If Jill came up, I would say I was doing some Art homework. I unfolded a scrap of paper from my pocket and drew a quick sketch of the hat stand. That should be convincing enough.

Then I reached into the box.

I pulled out an old photo album and flicked through it. The pictures were mainly poor quality shots from what looked like Jill's teenage escapades with friends: a trip to London, a trip to the beach, Jill with nameless girls making peace signs at the camera, and way too many party shots of people looking sweaty and getting far too close to the camera (and each other). There were plenty of gaps where photos had been taken out and there were very few of our mother.

Stuffed into the back of the album was a faded pink envelope containing a handful of shots of me as a newborn baby. My heart throbbed as I pulled them out and peered closely at each one. I had seen them before and even had a copy of the top one in a frame in my wardrobe but this time, for some reason, I felt like I was seeing them for the very first time. A sudden urgency arose inside me; a deep and unquenchable need for an answer to a wordless question.

I went through the photos slowly. My mum was in four of them, looking bright and alive, as though she had never contemplated dying. Tears filled my eyes as I ran a finger across her face. In one shot she was gazing at me with great fondness as I slept in her arms. It hurt to have no memory of that gaze. I sniffed and turned to a shot of me and my father. Dad looked tired and awkward as he held me up like a floppy monkey. I came to the end of the photos and went through them again, frowning at how few there were. There weren't even any of me and Jill.

Taking a deep breath, I shoved the photos back into the envelope and sifted through the box, hoping for another album that would fill in the gaps. I didn't find one. Instead, I uncovered a pile of countless place-settings bearing the name *'Jill Starling'* gathered from what must have been over a decade of weddings. I turned some over in my hands marvelling at the different fonts and the absurdity of keeping such a collection. Then I brushed them aside and unearthed a small velvet green book marked *'Private.'* My heart skipped a beat. Jill kept a diary? This was a revelation to me. I'd thought she was far too unfeeling for that kind of thing. I picked the book up and turned it over in my hands. Snooping around was bad enough, but reading Jill's diary... Surely that would be crossing some dark unforgivable line. What would my mother say? I hesitated and closed my eyes.

"God, if you're real," I muttered. "Please forgive me." I bit my lip before adding as an afterthought, "And don't let Jill find out."

I carefully opened the diary. To my disappointment, the first entry was rather boring.

'I asked Mrs Jennings if she thought I could make it as a psychologist. She said yes but I'll need to work hard for my exams.'

I glanced at the date and did some calculations. Jill would've been sixteen. As if she wanted to be a psychologist! I suppressed a smirk as I flicked through the book. The dates darted around, sometimes skipping several weeks or even months. Like the photo album, several pages of the diary had been ripped out and I couldn't help but feel slightly unnerved— what could Jill possibly be hiding from herself?

Several pages on, I read,

'I don't think she understands me at all. What kind of mother tells her daughter to wear more make-up?[76] I hate the way she jokes about my ankles and I hate how she embarrasses me in front of Charlie. If he laughs at her jokes again, I'll punch him.'

I felt a sort of indignation at Jill's words. Here she was insulting both my parents, utterly ungrateful as to how lucky she was to have them.

A few pages later, there was a page full of scribbles and just one word: *'Gutted.'*

I carried on flicking in the hopes of discovering what was so gutting, but the next few pages had been torn out. I started to feel frustrated. It was almost as if Jill had known I would one day be looking for clues and had thwarted my efforts in advance. I shook the book in irritation and, as I did so, a letter fell out.

---

[76] I was baffled by this. Perhaps Jill was a very ugly teenager.

'Dear Jill,
Your mother told me about the baby. I have to say, I wish
you'd talked it over with me first but what's done is done. It
will be alright. You're a good girl, Jill.
Love from Aunt Claudia.'

My blood ran cold. Baby? What baby? *Was it me?* And why
was Aunt Claudia saying, *'You're a good girl, Jill,'* as if really she
was a bad one? I flicked frantically through the pages, desperate for
revelation, but I found no more clues. Fear and anger rose up
inside me. *Why had she torn the truth out?*

"Livi?" It was Jill.

I swallowed and tried to sound normal. "Yeah?"

"Are you in there?" She knocked on the door.

"Just doing my Art homework!" I yelled. "Hold on..." I shoved
Aunt Claudia's letter into my pocket, tossed everything else back
into the box and thrust it onto the shelf. Then I fixed a smile onto
my face and opened the door. "Drawing a still life," I said, holding
up my hasty sketch of the hat stand.

Jill raised an eyebrow. "It's not very good."

In that moment, I hated her.

I thought about the letter all week. I'd stashed it safely in the
starling box from Ruby and got it out whenever I dared, growing
more bewildered and afraid as I tried to figure it out. It wasn't
dated but presumably it was written around the same time as Jill's
diary. So, who was the baby and where was it now? And why were
there so few photos from when I was born and none of me and Jill?
I played scenarios through in my mind, each one growing more
and more perverse.

1. Jill is my real mother. She persuaded her mum to pretend to
be my mother so she could continue in her studies as a
psychologist. She's not in any of the photos as her saggy
tummy would have given too much away.

2. Jill found me in the park on her way home from school and
kidnapped me. Her mum went along with it and pretended I
was hers to stop Jill being arrested but my real mother is out

there looking for me. Jill destroyed any photos that may have linked herself to the crime in a moment of paranoia.

3. My whole family is part of a secret government initiative. My mother has been living undercover since I was a baby and, all these years, my father has been with her. Aunt Claudia thought it was a bad idea for Jill to look after me as she wanted me to live with her and her cats, but Jill refused. There are hardly any photos of me because my parents insisted on taking them all. It was their only consolation for having to be apart from me. My father sent the word to Jill to move to Leeds because I'm almost ready to find out the truth. Any day now, we'll all be reunited.

By Saturday, I was feeling desperate. I went to the living room and eyed Jill as she sat surrounded by work on the sofa.

She looked up. "Do you want something?"

"I'm doing a project about families for History," I lied. "Can you tell me about when I was a baby?"

Jill tutted, as if I'd interrupted something important. "What do you mean?"

"I don't know... Interesting stories, important events, top-secret information..."

Jill thought for a moment. "Hold on." She went upstairs and emerged a few minutes later with the envelope of photos from her secret album. "You can have these."

I frowned as I turned them over. "Have you got any more?"

Jill looked just as frustrated. "There are loads in there."

I pulled them out. "There are six."

"How many do you need?"

"I need *loads!* I need all the photos that have ever been taken!"

Jill rolled her eyes. "It's just a school project."

"No, it's—" I stopped and took a deep breath. "There must be more photos than these."

Jill shook her head. "Sorry."

"I don't even have any of *you and me* from when I was born."

"I must have been taking the pictures."

"But you're not in *any* of them."

Jill didn't answer for a moment. "Maybe I had to work."

"Don't you remember?"

"I'm sorry, Livi. I've never been a photo person."

I resisted the urge to scream. "But there isn't a single photo of you with me as a newborn baby. Don't you find that strange?"

Jill began to look uncomfortable.

Like a seasoned detective, I ploughed on. "Did there *used* to be some and you lost them? Or have there never been any?"

"What? I'm sorry, Livi. I wish there were more, but there aren't." She got up.

"Wait!" My heart was pounding as I went over the possibilities I had explored a few nights before.

3. My whole family is part of a secret government initiative. My mother has been living undercover since I was a baby...

"What, Livi?" Jill gave a heavy sigh. I wasn't sure if she was irritated or concerned.

I took a deep breath and blurted out, "Did Mum really die?"

"Don't be silly."

I went up close to Jill and studied her eyes. They were looking down. I couldn't work out what that meant on the lying scale so I tried again. "Are you sure she died?"

Jill gave me a pitying stare. "What are you asking that for, Livi? You've been to her grave, for goodness sake."

I sucked in my breath and turned away. That was true. I've been to her grave plenty of times.

*'In Loving Memory of Livi Jean Starling
Devoted Mother to Jilliana and Livi.'*

I've always found the wording strange. Surely a devoted mother shouldn't die.

A sudden thought occurred to me. I may have been to the graveyard and seen a tombstone with my mother's name on, but how do I know for certain that my mother is actually *under* it? According to *'Freaky Human,'* every year in England more than three thousand people are buried with nobody at their funeral. There must be plenty of unmarked graves lying around. How hard could it be to claim one and buy a false tombstone for it?

My voice shook as I said, "Can I see her death certificate?"

I think I had hit a nerve because Jill grimaced and snapped, "Please, Livi! Can you just drop it?" She got up and started dusting the mantelpiece.

My sister never dusts anything.

I stared at her and realised how little I knew her.

~ 19 ~

Totally stuffed

At about three in the afternoon, there was a knock at the door. I peered out of my bedroom window and saw Dad's car on the pavement. My heart leapt as I ran down the stairs two at a time and yanked the door open.

"Hi Dad! What are you doing here?"

"Thought I'd surprise you."

I felt a surge of joy. "Thanks!"

Jill emerged from the living room looking frosty.

"I'm going out," I told her.

"Aren't you meant to be seeing Ruby this afternoon?"

"Nah," I lied. "She's ill."

At that moment, Ruby appeared on the doorstep. "Ready for the ice rink, Livi?"

Jill shot me a sharp look.

"Uh, Ruby, I can't come skating after all. Our Aunt Claudia has Mad Cow's Disease and we're off to visit her." I avoided my sister's gaze and threw Ruby my very best apologetic face. "What are you doing tomorrow?"

"Just church." Ruby shrugged. "You can come if you want?"

"She would be delighted to," Jill said loudly. "Wouldn't you, Livi?" She clearly thought me attending church with the Ricos was suitable penance for letting Ruby down.

"Er, sure," I muttered.

"Great!" Ruby looked jubilant. "I'll see you tomorrow."

I frowned at my sister as Ruby skipped across the street. "Let's go, Dad," I said, marching out of the house.

"Don't ruin your appetite!" Jill yelled after me. "We're having lasagne tonight."

"Ooh, lasagne!" Dad said with a grin. "My favourite."

Jill slammed the door.

Dad gave me an awkward smile as we got into his car. "She doesn't seem very happy."

"She's probably on her period."

"Oh."

"Anyway... Enough about her. Where are we going?"

He perked up and turned to face me.

Let it be Disneyland, thought a small irrational part of me. *Or, at the very least, bowling.*

"There's an important game on today. I thought we could go down to The Bell and Whistle and cheer the Mighty Whites on!" He gave an expectant grin.

"Bell and what? Mighty who?"

Dad's grin disappeared. "Football?" he said limply.

"Oh." My heart sank.

"Oh dear. I thought you'd be excited."

"I don't mind..." I said, trying to inject the right balance of humility and disappointment so that he might change his mind and say, *'Actually Livi, you deserve better than football. Let's go bowling.'*

Dad said nothing for a moment. I hit him hard with the silent distant eyes.

Eventually he said, "You really don't mind?"

I felt a lump in my throat. "I don't mind."

"Thanks, Livi! It's a very important game, that's all."

I nodded.

"I'm glad to be able to share it with you."

I nodded again. Maybe I was just being selfish. After all, it's not like we'd arranged to see each other. He had driven all this way so that he could share an important game with me. I shot him a smile to let him know I wasn't being ungrateful. "It sounds great."

The pub was full of chanting men who were either drunk or very strange. There weren't any tables free so we found a couple of stools and perched at the bar.

Dad bought some lemonade for me and a beer for himself. "It's about to start!" he said eagerly.

I forced a smile. "So, what are the rules? They just have to kick the ball into the net?"

He chuckled. "Just watch. You'll soon pick it up."

I glanced at the screen. Twenty thousand tiny people were doing a Mexican wave.

The referee blew a whistle and the game began. Within five minutes, I was bored.

Half an hour into the game, Dad's team scored a goal and the whole pub erupted in crazed cheering. Dad even grabbed a nearby barmaid and swung her in the air. Someone else shook my shoulders and knocked over my drink. It was a little startling. I wanted to cover my ears and hide. It happened again five minutes later and I hoped beyond hope that that would be it.

After what felt like *forever,* the referee blew his whistle again and the players ran inside.

I breathed a sigh of relief and pretended to look happy. "We won, right?"

Dad laughed. "It's half time. Plenty of time left to muck it up."

My heart sank lower. "Half time?"

Dad nodded and asked if I wanted another drink.

I shook my head. It was bound to get spilt like the first one.

The second half passed as slowly as the first. Dad's team got two more goals and their opponents had a man sent off. I alternated between wondering whether my dad really cared about me and distracting myself with more and more ludicrous explanations for Aunt Claudia's letter to Jill and was close to tears by the time the match finally ended.

I rather hoped Dad would take me straight home but he spent a good twenty minutes locking arms with a bunch of other men and joining them in some senseless chant. I wondered whether he was drunk or just very, very happy. It felt strange watching him; this man who was my father. If Jill and I had not moved to Leeds, we may never have met again. Did he ever think about that? Did he feel any guilt *at all?* I blinked hard as my mountain of unanswered questions rose up like a flood, begging to be released. Not once, since that first day at the cinema, had Dad ever mentioned his departure. Not once had he offered an explanation. Not once had he said sorry. I had avoided the question, fearing it would be almost rude to draw attention to his shortcomings. But I couldn't bear it any longer.

Dad winked as he came and sat down. "Wasn't that brilliant!"

"Yeah..." My chest grew tight. I wondered whether this was the best time to ask. I didn't want to ruin his good mood but I feared that if I didn't ask now then I never would. I took a deep breath and, without looking him in the eye, whispered, "Dad, when I was little... Why did you leave?"

His soppy grin evaporated. "Maybe you should ask your sister."

"I have. Loads of times. She just says it's because you're an idiot. Well, she calls you worse than that..."

Dad looked hurt.

"Sorry," I added.

"She really hates me, doesn't she?"

"Yes."

"She's so..." He looked away and shook his head. I couldn't tell whether he was wounded or angry.

"What's wrong?"

Dad didn't answer for a while. He looked like he was fighting with himself. Finally he said, "I wanted to stay, I really did. But Jill made it impossible for me."

"How?" I sat bolt upright. *Was I about to find out the truth?*

Dad put his head in his hands and sighed. He kept opening and closing his mouth and seemed to be considering his words very carefully. I did my best to fix an expectant but nonchalant expression on my face. He needed to know that I was interested, but not desperate. I didn't want to scare him off.

"We had a row. Jill told me to leave and never come back."

My jaw fell open. *"Jill made you leave?"*

Dad looked away. "Yeah."

"Why?" I spluttered.

"Well..." Dad cleared his throat. "Jill got it into her head that the three of us could be a family. She had always been rather... besotted with me. I said it would never work and she got angry."

I was astounded. So Jill hadn't always hated my dad. In fact, she'd— "What do you mean she'd been *'besotted'* with you?"

Dad blushed. "I mean... She fancied me."

I stared at him. *"Seriously?"*

He avoided my stare. "Yes."

I stopped to think about it. In a way, it *kind of* made sense. Dad was several years younger than my mum and only a few years older than Jill. I had always imagined that their closeness in age had caused her to reject him as a potential stepfather, but clearly things were much more complicated.

"But *why...?*" I felt like I was struggling to breathe. "Couldn't she just get her own boyfriend?"

Dad stopped to think. "I guess I was far too dashing!" He grinned.

I shook my head. I wasn't in the mood for jokes. "How serious was Jill? I mean, was it just a little crush or did she try to steal you from Mum?"

Dad pursed his lips. "Maybe we shouldn't be talking about this."

"We have to!" I shrieked. "I need to know!"

Dad flinched and glanced around. "Well, keep your voice down."

"Sorry." I gulped and tried to compose myself. "So, Jill wanted you for herself... Carry on."

Dad sniffed. "That's about it."

I looked at him in dismay. "But I don't understand! Why..? What..?" I stopped to think. "Did Jill fancy you right from the beginning?"

"I don't know." Dad stroked his chin before reconsidering. "I mean, no." He paused. "Did you know about the engagement?"

"What?"

"Oh, you didn't know." Dad winced and put a hand over his eyes. "Never mind— Jill was engaged once but it doesn't matter."

"Who was he? What was his name?"

Dad took a while to answer. "Ricky..."

Jill had a fiancé called Ricky? Why had I never known this?

I continued to gape at my father. "What was he like?"

"Nice enough. They were going to get married after Jill finished college. She was too young really..." He fell silent.

"What happened?"

Dad puffed out his cheeks. "Oh... Jill wasn't very nice to him. They soon broke up. I suppose that's when she started to pay more attention to me..."

I sucked in my cheeks. "Did Mum know?"

He exhaled slowly. "Yes. They weren't that close at the best of times so all the fuss about me caused quite a bit of friction." He gave an awkward smile. "When your mum fell pregnant, Jill moved out and went to live with your Aunt Claudia. They didn't speak for nearly a year— until your mother got ill. I'm sure Jill regrets that now. She was only young, remember. People do daft things when they're young..."

My head spun as I tried to piece it all together. "Jill left when Mum got pregnant with me? Then where was Jill when I was born?"

"At Claudia's. She didn't see you until your mum got ill."

I was aghast. "So, if Mum hadn't died, Jill might never have bothered to meet me?" My heart shattered as my *'Secret government initiative'* option fell to pieces. "That's why there are no photos of Jill with me as a newborn baby..." I swallowed hard.

My dad paused. "I don't know if I should be telling you this."

"I want to know!"

Dad gave another sigh. "Of course, nobody expected your mother's health to fail as rapidly as it did. She got ill and died within weeks. There just wasn't the time to *sort it all out*, if you know what I mean. It was a tough time for Jill. I expect that's why she never told you."

"And, the moment Mum died, Jill pursued you *again?*" I was horrified. *Was my sister a lunatic?*

"Well..." Dad paused. "Not right away. For several years she kept things strictly platonic for your sake. But..." He swallowed. "I suppose it got hard for her."

"I can't believe this..." I shook my head with such force that the locket Jill gave me for my birthday swung forward and nearly whacked me in the eye. I imagined my sister plundering it from our mother's dead body and wondered what else she might have taken. "Jill never tells me anything!"

Dad looked at me suddenly and said, "Livi, you mustn't mention any of this to Jill."

"Why not?" I exclaimed. The first thing I wanted to do was go home and scream at her.

"You just mustn't. I wouldn't have told you unless I thought I could trust you."

I opened my mouth and then shut it again. "You *can* trust me."

Dad didn't look convinced.

I felt my heart pounding. "You *can* trust me," I repeated.

"Promise you won't say anything?"

"I promise." I was trembling a little.

Dad smiled and took my hand. "Good. Are you hungry?"

I thought about Jill warning me not to ruin my appetite. Then I thought about her stalking my poor father and causing such misery to my dying mother. I thought about her sending my dad away and forbidding him from seeing me just because she couldn't have him.

"Starving," I said.

By the time I got home, I was positively shaking. I was furious with Jill. How could she have kept this from me? She had been *besotted* with my father... She had wanted him all to herself... All this time, she'd been treating my father horrendously, making out that he was the bad guy when *she* was the reason he'd never been around.

I heard Jill say hello as I came through the door but I ignored her and ran up to my room.

175

Once I'd closed my door, I pulled Aunt Claudia's letter out of my starling box and stared at it. As I went over my list of possibilities, a new crazy idea came to mind:

4. Jill killed our mother because she thought she and my dad and me could be a family together.

I shuddered and warned myself not be so stupid. Jill wouldn't do that. *Would she?*

I climbed into bed without even taking off my shoes and pulled the covers tightly over my head. As I thought about everything my dad had told me, a painful thought kept nagging away at me. It made some perverse sense that Jill might try to send my father away if she couldn't have him for herself, but he still made the choice to actually leave. Why didn't he insist on taking me with him? I was his *daughter* after all. Didn't he fight for me? Didn't he *want* me? Or did Jill hold me at ransom? I felt tears stinging the backs of my eyes and buried my face desperately into Sausage-Legs' outstretched arms.

There was a sudden distant ping of the microwave followed by Jill calling, "Lasagne's ready!"

"Not hungry!" I yelled.

I heard Jill thundering up the stairs. I wiped my eyes and hastily shoved the letter out of sight.

"I told you not to ruin your appetite!" she exclaimed as she stormed into my room.

"Don't you knock?" I snapped.

"He bought you dinner, didn't he?"

"Yup," I said cheerily. "We had burgers, chips and apple pie. We even stopped off for a milkshake on the way home. I'm totally stuffed."

Jill stared at me. "I can't believe you did that." She looked like she was about to cry.

I felt guilt rising in my chest but I curled my hands into fists and dug my nails into my skin. *No mercy.* I gave a careless shrug. "Oh well."

Jill gave a whimper, brought a hand to her mouth and left, slamming my door behind her. I buried myself deeper into my bed and cried.

~ 20 ~

Dancing to God

The next morning, I was awoken by a text from Ruby letting me know that she would come and get me in ten minutes. I was momentarily confused and then let out a groan as I remembered I'd promised to go to church with her. I jumped out of bed and yanked open my wardrobe. *What do people wear to church in this day and age? Did I need a hat?* I pulled out my nicest dress— a scarlet frock decorated with green butterflies. I'd spent more time begging Jill to buy it for me than I had ever actually wearing it. Was this the day for its big outing? As I held it up against myself and looked in the mirror, a peculiar temptation crossed my mind: *If I start going to church, Jill will have to buy me pretty dresses.*

I smiled despite myself and pulled the dress over my head. I did a little twirl and combed my hair. Then I went to brush my teeth and poked around in Jill's toiletries looking for something that would smell nice. *Heaven Scent.* That sounded appropriate for church. I wasn't quite sure what to do with it and hastily dabbed some on my wrists, neck and behind my ears. Then I gazed at my face in the mirror and wondered if I should put on some make-up. I rooted around in more of Jill's stuff and picked up some lipstick. I stood poised over the mirror unsure of how to apply it but, before I could attempt to paint my face, I was interrupted by a knock at the front door followed by Jill shouting, "Livi! Are you ready?"

I ran back to my bedroom and peered out of the window. Ruby and Violet were waiting for me. They were wearing *jeans and baggy jumpers.* I gave a cry of confusion as I ripped off my dress and reached for yesterday's sweater.

"Livi!" Jill sounded impatient.

"I'm coming!" I yelled back, pulling my clothes on as quickly as possible.

I galloped down the stairs and tried to sound cool as I said, "Here I am! Ready for church!"

Ruby grinned as Violet said, "You smell nice!"

"Thanks." I gave a shy smile and glanced at Jill.

She didn't meet my eyes. A pang of anger hit me but, for the benefit of Ruby and Violet, I pretended everything was normal.

There was a sudden toot of a car horn and my heart juddered as I looked across the street. Belinda was waving cheerfully from the passenger seat of the Ricos' large estate car. Stanley had turned around and was trying to settle Oscar who was swinging a toy cat by its tail.

Belinda wound down her window and called out, "Would you like to come, Jill?"

"No, thank you!" Jill yelled back.

Belinda gave a sad smile. "Maybe next week?"

Jill ignored her and asked me, "Have you got everything?"

I gulped and looked at Ruby. "What do I need?"

"Nothing!" said Ruby. "Just come as you are."

I suddenly realised that I had no idea what their church was like. What if people asked annoying questions about my family or what I believed? What if they made me stand at the front and introduce myself? What if the church was an hour's drive away and I was stuck with the Ricos all day? Was there *any* way I could get out of this?

"Let's go," Ruby continued.

I turned to Jill. "See you later," I said cautiously.

"See you," she muttered, closing the door behind me.

I was expecting an old decaying chapel so was hugely surprised when, ten minutes later, we pulled into the car park of a local high school.

"This is your church?" I asked in confusion.

"No," said Violet. "This is just where we meet. The church is the people inside."

I raised an eyebrow. "How... post-modern."

"Not at all!" she retorted. "It's how Jesus intended it."

I shrugged and followed them into the school hall. It looked like *our* school hall except the walls were blue instead of peach and the room was crammed full of people with expectant faces. We grabbed some seats near the side and I pretended to be interested in the bulletin that some smiling lady had handed me on the way in. There were notices about upcoming events which included a walk in the Dales and some conference in Brighton. Under a heading entitled 'Family News,' there was a photo of a couple who had recently got married as well as prayer requests for people who were ill. I studied the photo and looked around the room to see if the couple were there. I spotted them a few rows in front of us. They were jabbering away with some friends, looking tanned and excited.

A few minutes later, something resembling a rock band (complete with guitars and noisy drums) appeared on the stage and began playing music. The congregation got to their feet and started to sing. I got up and stared at the words that were being projected onto a screen. I was expecting some slow, dreary hymn about morning breaking or something, but this song was loud and energetic and people were clapping their hands as they sang at the tops of their lungs.

> *'I am loved by the King, by the King of Kings*
> *Jesus who died for me*
> *I am my Lord's and my Lord is mine*
> *Who died to set me free...'*

A few people had their hands raised in the air. I wondered if I should do it too but, to my relief, Ruby leant over and whispered, "Do whatever you want. You don't have to sing or stand unless you want to. It's okay."

"Thanks," I whispered. I stood for a bit longer and then sat down and watched.

As they sang about Jesus being raised from the dead, I found myself wondering whether God was *really* real, *really* there, *really* listening. Did these people truly know him or were they deluded? And, if he *was* real, what could God possibly think of *me*? Did he pity me for my mother dying? Or had he wanted her for himself? Was he there when Jill sent my father away? And was he watching to see what would happen now that I knew the truth? I bit my lip and reconsidered. *Well, not the whole truth.* I thought about the secret letter hidden in my starling box. What did God think about *that?*

I swallowed hard and forced a carefree smile. I didn't want people to wonder what somebody like me was doing in church. Then I glanced across and saw to my absolute shock that Stanley Rico was dancing in the aisle. *Dancing.*

I nudged Ruby. "Look at your dad!"

She smiled at me.

I wondered why she wasn't utterly mortified. "He's dancing!" I whispered, in case she'd missed it.

"I know," she whispered back. "He likes dancing to God."

I opened my mouth and closed it again. Then I turned back to watch Stanley, feeling a combination of embarrassment, pity and perplexity as he hopped from foot to foot and waved his arms around. I'm pretty sure Stanley knew he was a poor dancer. And I'm pretty sure he didn't care. He looked so happy to be making an utter fool of himself. I couldn't imagine my own father dancing in public.

'Unless it was a really good football match,' a little voice prompted.

I thought back to my dad in the pub the day before. He had danced, sort of, every time his team scored a goal. Which was sillier: Stanley Rico dancing to God or my own father dancing because of a ball being kicked into a net?

After the singing, a man got up to preach.

He began by reading a passage from the Bible. *"...So do not worry, saying, 'What shall we eat?' or 'What shall we drink?' or 'What shall we wear?' For the pagans run after all these things, and your heavenly Father knows that you need them. But seek first his kingdom and his righteousness, and all these things will be given to you as well."*

Then he talked about how nothing we pursue on Earth will fully satisfy unless we first seek God.

"We all live for something," he said. "We all have one top priority. Perhaps it's your job, or your friends, or your health, or your next holiday. But all of these things can let us down. All of these things are fleeting. Jesus tells us that we need to make *him* our top priority because he alone will *never* let us down." He paused before adding, "The fact of the matter is: if you live for stuff, then you will be *stuffed!*"

Everybody laughed.

I looked round in astonishment. I didn't think you were allowed to tell jokes in church.

After that, I lost concentration. Beside me, Violet was taking ardent notes and Stanley was nodding thoughtfully. I kept thinking about really inappropriate things, like how funny it would be if the fire alarm went off.

As the talk drew to an end, the preacher said, "Perhaps this is new to you and you're wondering what the singing was all about and how you can get to know God better?"

My stomach lurched. I hoped Ruby hadn't told him I was coming.

"If that's you," he continued, "and you know you need to make things right with God, I'm going to ask everybody to close their eyes now so that you can respond."

Everyone closed their eyes and bowed their heads. I pretended to close my eyes but secretly I peeked at the people around me. It all looked rather solemn, like a serious game of *Sleeping Lions*.

The preacher went on, "If you want to meet Jesus today, I'd like to ask you to be brave and raise your hand. A few of us would love to pray with you after the service."

I opened my eyes a crack further and swivelled round carefully in my seat. A lady a few rows behind us raised her hand. I turned back to face the preacher. He nodded kindly at the lady and then seemed to look straight at me. I shut my eyes and willed myself to be invisible.

"Wonderful," he said. "Let's praise God for what he's done today."

There was another song. And then it was over.

I stood up with a mighty sigh, grateful to have survived and assuming that we would be leaving, but Ruby just grinned and said, "Shall we get a drink?"

"I thought it was finished."

"It is. But everyone likes to stay and catch up with one another for a while."

This struck me as incredibly odd. I thought people only went to church because they *had* to. Nobody here seemed in a hurry to leave.

Stanley and Belinda were talking to an older couple in the drinks queue, Oscar was playing tag with a group of young children and Violet had gone over to congratulate the newly-married couple. I assumed Ruby and I would just sit quietly and wait as the more sociable members of her family caught up with their friends but, suddenly, two teenage boys eating biscuits appeared beside us.

"Hey Ruby!" they sang.

"Hi!" said Ruby. "This is my friend, Livi." She turned to me. "This is Mark, and that's Joey."

I was taken aback. Ruby was friends with *boys*. And rather nice-looking boys at that. She began talking and joking with them without even the faintest whiff of social awkwardness.

"How was your week?" Mark asked.

"Good," she replied. "How was yours?"

"Great, thanks!" Then he turned to me and asked, "Were you the girl who got baptised in the river?"

Ruby shot me an anxious glance as she said to her friend, "Livi's not a Christian."

Mark stopped whatever he was about to say and said, "Oh."

"That's alright," Joey piped up. "Hey, what did you think of today?"

"Er..." I felt myself blushing. "It was interesting."

"Will you come again?"

"I don't know... We're quite busy on Sundays."

"Oh right. What do you do?"

"Uh..." I shrugged and said quickly, "Gardening and stuff."

Joey looked confused[77] but didn't say anything.

"Livi can do animal noises," Ruby said suddenly.

I shook my head. "Don't be silly!"

Her friends stared at me.

"I'm going to get a biscuit," I muttered, wandering off before they could ask me to do any impressions.

I weaved in and out of the crowd, feeling restless and out of place. I hoped nobody would have a radar for non-Christians. The hall was still so full; it didn't look like anybody had left yet. They were all just standing around, talking and joking and drinking tea. I was expecting to see a lot more *weird* people but everyone seemed kind of normal apart from the whole Jesus thing.

By the tea and coffee table, I spotted a girl from the year above. She always seems to be surrounded by lots of friends at school. I wondered if they knew she went to church.

As I reached for a biscuit, she caught my eye and smiled. "Are you new?"

I didn't want her to ask me what I thought so I said, "No. I come a lot."

"Oh cool! How long have you been coming?"

"Er... A few months."

"Do you know many people?"

---

[77] Although not as confused as Ruby who knew full well that we don't have a garden.

I debated saying I knew Mark and Joey but, at the last moment, I said, "Just Ruby Rico." I gave an apologetic smile as I anticipated her mocking.

"Oh, Ruby's lovely!" she said to my utter surprise.

Lovely? She was odd, kind of geeky; at a push, *quirky.* But lovely? I was perhaps her closest friend yet I never thought of her as *lovely.* I gave an awkward shrug and walked back to Ruby and the boys.

"Hey, did Ruby tell you about our band?" Joey asked eagerly.

"Band?"

"Oh, it's nothing!" Ruby said with a giggle. "We just make music for fun sometimes."

"Not just fun," Joey insisted. "We did a charity concert in the summer. Ruby's our lead singer."

"Seriously?" I tried to imagine Ruby as a hardcore rock chick belting out tunes to millions of screaming fans. I wondered if Stanley danced to their songs.

"Did you tell Livi what we're called?" Mark asked.

Ruby shook her head.

Joey gave a big grin before exclaiming, *"The Glory Seekers!"*

The three of them laughed. I didn't get the joke.

"Sounds good," I said weakly.

Ruby beamed. "Anyway, we'd better go." She pointed to Belinda who was beckoning us from the other side of the room.

The boys nodded at Ruby before turning to me. Joey smiled and Mark shook my hand. "Nice to meet you," they said.

"Yeah," I whispered, feeling like Ruby was the coolest girl in the entire world and I was nothing more than her pathetically ignorant friend.

As we were leaving, I caught sight of the lady who had raised her hand in response to meeting Jesus. She was talking to the preacher's wife and looked happy. I wanted to go up to her and ask if she'd *really* met Jesus and, if so, where was he now? Did he have to rush off to another meeting?

I felt anxious all the way home. I hoped none of the Ricos would ask me what I'd thought of their church. I had no idea what I would say. Thankfully, Oscar had banged his head by walking into a door[78] so everyone was preoccupied with making sure he was alright.

---

[78] I sometimes wonder just how gifted that child really is.

When we got back to our street I slid out of the car and thanked Ruby's parents for taking me.

"You're so welcome, Livi!" Belinda trilled. "Please come any time."

Stanley nodded as he carried a whinging Oscar through their front door. "It was great to see you."

Violet remained in the car, writing in her journal.

Ruby stood with me on the pavement for a while.

"So..." she said. "What did you think?"

I rolled my eyes. "It was alright."

"Did you like it?"

"I don't know."

"What did you think of the preach?"

I wrinkled up my nose. "I got a bit bored."

"That's okay... What did you think about the idea of seeking after God?"

I shrugged.

Ruby paused for a moment. "If God was real, what would you ask him?"

"I don't know."

"Think about it."

I shrugged again and pretended I wasn't interested. As Ruby smiled, I sighed and looked away. I already knew what I would ask God and I didn't want to think about it. I would ask, *'What have you done with my mother and when can I have her back?'*

~ 21 ~

Dogs made of fog

For the whole of the next week Jill was in a strange mood. One moment she would be reasonably jolly; the next, I would hear her moaning and groaning as she crashed round the house in a frenzy.

One evening I was struggling with some homework in the living room when I thought I heard her whimpering on the phone. I threw my work down, yanked the door open and burst into the hallway, afraid that she was about to get back together with Fester.

Jill looked at me in surprise and quickly hung up. "Just Aunt Claudia," she said.

"Oh." I stared at her for a while before saying casually, "You and Aunt Claudia are really close, aren't you? Would you trust her with a secret?"

She gave me a funny look. "What do you mean?"

"I don't know. You tell me."

"What?" Jill frowned and trotted up the stairs.

I went back into the living room and sighed. Our aunt's letter was still a total mystery and was constantly on my mind. As was the revelation that it had been Jill who had made my dad leave. I hadn't told Ruby about any of it. I was afraid that she might say something unhelpful. Or, worse, just stare at me.

I decided to abandon my homework and watch television instead. There was a programme about people being surprised by long lost family. One man was found by a brother that he didn't even know existed. Somebody else had spent ten futile years looking for their birth mother and had been reunited after only a week's effort by the production team. I found myself getting a little choked up as the reunited mother and daughter held one another and sobbed.

I imagined the presenter knocking on our door and asking, *'Is Livi Starling in?'*

I would look at her in surprise. *'I'm Livi Starling.'*

'Do you know where your mother is?' She would give me a dazzling smile.

'Oh,' I'd answer sadly. *'She's dead.'*

'No, Livi...' The presenter would wipe a tear from her eye. *'We found her.'*

I would gasp at the sight of my mother running towards me. She'd be wearing a yellow ball gown and her face would be radiant. She'd take me in her arms and weep and confess that she'd thought about me every day, ever since I was wrenched from her arms by masked intruders.

Jill came in and I hastily wiped my eyes. "Have you done your homework?"

"Most of it."

"Most of it? Go and finish *all* of it." She sat down, snatched the remote control off me and started flicking through the channels.

"I was watching that!" I cried.

"I'm not in the mood to argue." Jill flicked all the way through the channels until she came back to the programme about long lost families. The presenter was speaking to another woman looking for her mother.

"I miss Mum," I blurted out.

Jill looked at me oddly. "How can you miss somebody you've never known?"

I glared at her. Of all the inconsiderate things she could've said. I wanted to pull her hair out. "Don't you miss her?"

"Sometimes," Jill muttered, flicking through the channels once more.

A ball of fury erupted in my chest. "You never talk about her."

She shrugged.

I pressed on. I wanted to make her cry. "Do you remember her last words? Did you see her die?"

Jill turned in outrage.

"Was it scary?" I persisted.

"Shut up!"

I opened my mouth to continue but a lump had caught in my throat. Instead I ran to my room, throwing myself onto my bed as I imagined my mother with the face of Audrey Hepburn and the disposition of Audrey Sorenson. I curled up into a ball, crying and aching as I lay there missing her. I knew it was stupid. As stupid as missing my great great great grandmother who was just as dead and unknown.

I clutched Sausage-Legs to my heart as I thought angrily of Jill, sitting there all smug because she'd had our mother to herself. She knew what her voice sounded like, how it felt to hug her and whether she sang in the shower. I wondered what my mother's final thoughts were. Did she worry about what would happen to me? Did she beg Jill to take good care of me and warn her never to yell at me? Maybe she had dreams for me and maybe I've not done them yet. Maybe Jill even knows what they were but is too selfish to bother sharing them with me.

As soon as I heard Jill go to bed, I crept into the spare room and took out her box of secrets.

This time, I went through it all very carefully, determined not to miss a thing. I scrutinised every photo and read each diary entry word for word. The photos were as dull as before and most of what remained in the half-mutilated diary was pretty devoid of any emotion. But, now that I was looking so attentively, I did discover a couple of entries relating to her fiancé, Ricky,[79] although they didn't specifically say his name. I expected he comprised much of what had been torn out and censored. I shook the diary a few times, hoping a few more secrets would fall out, but nothing did.

After putting the diary down, I pulled out all the wedding place-settings and counted them. There were thirty one. *Jill's age*, I thought ironically as I tossed them aside.

My hand brushed against something shiny and I lifted out a small photo of Jill looking smitten with a tanned, brown-haired man. On the back was written, *'Me and Ricky Martin.'* So this was Ricky. This was the man Jill might have married, had she not been besotted with my father. He looked nice enough. If only Jill had had the sense to stick with him! I narrowed my eyes at her infatuated grin and wondered where poor Ricky was now.

Next, I pulled out a piece of blue paper covered in writing.

'I have a huge black dog made of fog.
He follows me around and nibbles my toes.
The faster I run, the more he grows.
The more he grows, the darker the fog.
The darker the fog, the less I see.
The less I see, the less of me.'

---

[79] One read, *'I hate him and love him both at the same time,'* and the other said simply, *'I'm calling it off.'*

At first, I was rather peeved that Jill had once had a dog and never told me. But then I read it again and realised this was Jill's attempt at a poem. And not a happy poem at that.

I felt sick as a wave of guilt washed over me. There was nothing happy in this box at all. I had one last half-hearted dig around the bottom but I no longer felt like a deserving wronged detective. I felt like a rotten snooping sneak. I gave a growl of annoyance and hurriedly put it all back.

~*~

Jill's mood reached a crescendo on Saturday afternoon. Ruby and I had spent the day at the library, compiling evidence for our project. We had exhausted pretty much every book on dinosaurs, fossils and reptiles, and were finally ready to put it all together. The two of us entered my house, jabbering with excitement as we discussed which creatures to include. We burst into the living room before stopping in shock. Jill was on the sofa in tears. Her make-up was streaked across her face, her hair was a mess and there were tissues everywhere. Even more unexpectedly, Belinda sat beside her, rubbing her back.

"My poor dear..." she cooed, shooting us a friendly nod as she offered Jill another tissue.

Jill looked up and wiped her face. "Oh, hello girls," she said in a strained voice.

My hands grew clammy. I feared she had discovered her letter hidden in my starling box and tried to play it cool as I asked, "What happened?"

"Nothing, nothing," my sister babbled. "I'm fine."

Belinda gave me a kind smile and whispered, "I was just walking past when I saw through the window that Jill was crying." She squeezed Jill. "I think it's the stress of everything. Is that right, Jill? The stress of a new job? Being in a new city?"

Jill whimpered, "I think I'm just tired."

"Get an early night," Belinda said. "Livi can come to ours for dinner."

Jill nodded blankly.

"That's alright, isn't it, Livi?" Belinda leant over and patted me.

"Yeah," I said dumbly.

Belinda forced a chuckle. "Look at all this mess!" She started picking up the wet tissues.

"Leave that, Belinda," my sister stammered.

Belinda waved a hand. "Go and run yourself a bath. Let me sort things out."

Jill looked like she was about to burst into tears again. She wiped her eyes and said, "Thanks." Then she shot me a sorry smile and went upstairs.

As we followed Belinda out of the house, Ruby looked towards the stairs and said, "I hope Jill's alright."

"She'll be fine." I forced a shrug. "It's just hormones or something."

Belinda put a hand on my head. "Your sister has a lot on her shoulders."

I shifted uncomfortably. I know it sounds unkind, but I was a little annoyed with Jill for causing a scene.

Belinda made roast beef, complete with a rainbow of vegetables, homemade Yorkshire puddings, cauliflower cheese and two types of potato. After a week of microwave meals, it looked divine.

I tried not to salivate as Violet began a lengthy prayer, thanking God for peas, carrots, cauliflowers, gravy granules, farmers, shopkeepers and beef.[80]

As soon as she finished, I piled my fork up high, trying not to look too ungraceful as I wolfed it down. It tasted amazing.

"On a score of one to ten," Oscar said with his mouth full, "this is eleven."

"Thank you, darling!" Belinda simpered.

"It's better than the chicken from last week," Oscar continued. "We should have beef *every* week."

"I like it when we have duck," Violet chipped in.

Ruby nodded and added, "Do you remember the time Oscar got some duck stuck up his nose?"

As they all laughed merrily I was struck by the painful awareness that I was not a part of this family. I was a gatecrasher at their special weekend roast. I wondered whether Jill was out of the bath yet and whether she'd found anything to eat.

"I have a riddle," Stanley said suddenly.

The rest of the family turned to him and he grinned. "You are at a crossroads and you don't know which way leads to the castle.

---

[80] Her stint as a vegetarian has officially ended.

There are two men at the crossroads: one always lies and the other always tells the truth. How do you work out which way to go?"

"Ooh, very good..." Belinda sat back and scratched her chin.

"Why do you want to go to the castle?" Oscar demanded.

"To meet the king."

"Goody!" Oscar rubbed his hands together before suggesting, "You could ask them which one is lying?"

"They'll both accuse each other."

"Oh yeah..." Oscar put a hand over his mouth and smirked.

"I know," Violet piped up. "Ask them a simple question first and trust the one who gets it right."

Stanley chuckled. "You can only ask *one* question."

"Oh..." Violet and the others lapsed into silence as they tried to crack Stanley's riddle.

Stanley beamed at me but I shrugged and looked away. In actual fact, I'd heard it before. The answer is you ask one of the men which way the *other* man would tell you to go and then you do the opposite. I chopped up my food as small as possible and concentrated on not looking at anybody.

Once or twice Ruby dug me in the ribs and said, "What do you think, Livi? What would you ask?"

But I just grunted and said, "Dunno."

After a while Ruby started to look a little wounded but I pretended not to notice. I pretended that I couldn't care less for her father's stupid riddle or her mother's stupid roast beef. But, if I was completely honest, I envied Ruby. I envied her neat, clean, respectable family. I envied her for having parents who were both alive and very loving, an older sister who *wasn't* the boss and a gifted younger brother who was *dare-I-say-it* rather cute. I envied them having dinner together around a fancy table and making homemade yoghurt in their mouse-free kitchen. I envied the simplicity of their lives and all the things they took for granted.

I swallowed hard and wiped my eyes, bitterly ashamed at the tears that kept forming at the edges. For one absurd moment I wondered what life would be like if Belinda was my mother. I wondered how it would feel to be greeted every morning with her beaming smile and the words, *'How's my clever little carrot today?'* Except she couldn't call me a carrot because my hair isn't orange like Ruby's. She'd have to call me her sweet potato, or mouldy apple, or some other brown thing.

"Oh, I know!" Violet said triumphantly. "You ask one of the men which way the other man would tell you to go and then do the opposite!"

"Wrong!" Stanley sang.

I looked up. Surely that was right?

Violet gaped at her father. "That does work, Dad."

Stanley shook his head. "Do you give up?"

"I give up," Oscar said, blowing a raspberry.

Violet wrinkled her brow. "Fine."

"Go on, tell us!" Belinda pleaded.

Ruby and I nodded in agreement.

Once he had everybody's attention, Stanley leant in and whispered, "You read the signpost!" He threw back his head and roared with laughter while the rest of his family protested that he was being stupid.

Violet leant over and gave him a playful shove.

"That's just silly," Oscar said, shoving a pea up his nose.

"Oh, Stanley," Belinda gushed. "You funny man!"

I stuffed the rest of my food into my mouth and stood up. "I'm going to go now."

"Oh! You're welcome to stay a bit longer!" said Belinda. "We could play a game or bake some cakes?"

"I feel tired," I lied. "I probably have the same hormone thing as Jill. I think I'll just get an early night too."

Belinda cocked her head sideways. "Bless you, Livi."

I gave Ruby a half-hearted wave and turned to go.

She followed me to the door. "Are you alright?"

"Yeah! I'm completely fine."

She didn't look convinced.

"Goodnight!" I forced a grin and turned away, blinking hard to keep from crying.

Across the street, I fumbled for my house key and hastily let myself in. Then I kicked off my shoes and trotted up the stairs, pausing for a moment outside Jill's closed bedroom door before heading miserably to mine.

~ 22 ~

What are you trying to save us from?

The next morning I found Jill in the living room, staring into space. The curtains were firmly shut which I assumed was to prevent Belinda from spying.

"Are you alright?" I asked, wondering whether to hug her but slightly afraid that she might start crying again if I did.

She gave a feeble smile. "I'm fine."

"Do you want to talk about anything?"

She shook her head. "I was just tired. To be honest, I'm more upset about the fact that Belinda saw me crying."

I giggled. *"Poor, dear Jill! What a mess!"* I mimicked in my best Belinda voice.

Jill laughed and then fell silent.

I wasn't sure what to do next. "Can I put the telly on?"

She nodded.

I picked up the remote and flicked through the channels. I eventually settled on *'Hair's a Surprise,'* a reality TV show about a blind hairdresser. Jill hates the show and usually insists that I change it but today she said nothing.

Suddenly, there was a knock at the door.

I looked at Jill but she was staring vacantly at the television.

"I'll get it then," I said, leaping expertly from the sofa into the hallway. I groaned at the sight of Belinda looking fuzzy through the frosted glass. "It's Belinda," I hissed.

Jill didn't reply.

"Should I let her in?"

She shrugged.

Belinda knocked again and pressed her face against the glass. "Is that you, Livi?"

I whimpered and fixed a grin on my face as I opened the door.

Belinda was in her slippers and clutched a mug of steaming tea. She gave me a concerned smile. It was almost as good as the ones Mrs Tilly gives me.

"Hello," I said in the most cheery voice I could muster.

"How are you both today?" Belinda asked softly.

"Great!"

"Is Jill up?" Belinda poked her head in and tried to see round the open living room door. "Hello Jill, dear!" she cooed.

Jill gave a pathetic smile. "Morning Belinda."

Belinda held out her mug of tea. "I thought you might like this."

Jill looked at her for a moment before taking it and awkwardly placing it on the floor next to her existing cup of tea.

Belinda cleared her throat. "I'd like to ask you something, Jill. Would you like to come to church with us this morning?"

My sister snorted and explained for the hundredth time that we don't go to church.

Belinda cocked her head to one side. "What is church, Jill?"

Jill eyed her strangely. "Church is a place where—"

"Wrong!" Belinda trilled. "Church is a group of people."

"I knew that," I said proudly.

Jill frowned at me before turning back to Belinda. "I appreciate the invitation but I'm not religious."

"It's about family..." Belinda went on as if Jill hadn't spoken. "And you and Livi really *need* family."

"I think I ought to know what we need and your stupid church isn't it!"

Belinda paused for a moment. "Would Livi like to come?"

Jill turned to me and snapped, "Well?"

I shook my head. "No, thank you."

Belinda looked disappointed. "Alright," she whispered. "I'll be praying for you."

I hope I shut the door fast enough for Belinda to miss Jill cursing her.

"Why does she always have to try and save everyone?" my sister yelled. "What exactly does she think she's saving us *from?*"

I shrugged and turned back to the television but I found I couldn't concentrate. Jill's question went round and round my head and I couldn't help but feel a little curious about what I might be missing that day in church. Perhaps Jesus would be there again with another chance to meet him.

That afternoon, I did something I thought I'd never do. I went across the street and asked if Belinda was in.

It was Stanley who answered the door. "Hello Livi! I'm afraid Ruby's out at the moment."

"I want to see Belinda," I replied.

Stanley raised his eyebrows before inviting me into the sitting room where Belinda sat knitting a garish orange jumper for Oscar.

"Oh! It's lovely Livi!" she cooed when I walked in.

I forced a smile and perched awkwardly beside her on the sofa.

Stanley asked if I wanted a drink.

"No, it's okay. I, er, I've got your mug." I handed him the one Belinda had brought round that morning.

"How marvellous!" Belinda beamed as though I was returning a prized pet. "Did Jill like the tea?"

I didn't feel it would be appropriate to say that Jill had poured it straight down the sink so I nodded ardently and said, "She said it was delicious. The best tea ever."

Belinda sighed and looked at her husband.

Stanley smiled and disappeared with the mug. Then, despite the fact that I'd said I didn't want a drink, he reappeared moments later and handed the mug back to me. It had been filled to the brim with fresh tea. Then he excused himself and went upstairs.

I offered the tea to Belinda. "Do you want this?"

She chuckled and pointed to a half-drunk cup beside her. "I have one, thank you! You enjoy that."

I forced a smile and took a nervous sip. It was too hot and I burned my tongue. Then, in my haste, I spilt it on my lap and burned my thigh.

Belinda watched as I grimaced and put the mug down. "Is everything alright?" she asked.

"Yes. I just don't drink tea so I didn't realise how hot—"

"I mean, what's going on, Livi? You don't usually come to see me."

I blushed and looked up at Belinda's concerned face. I meant to articulate things a little more sophisticatedly but, in the moment, I got tongue-tied and just blurted out, "What are you trying to save us from?"

Belinda paused before setting her knitting down. "The eternal fires of Hell!" she exclaimed.

I took a deep breath. "What if you're wrong?"

She looked at me for a very long time before replying. "Livi, if I am wrong, it doesn't really matter... What if *you're* wrong?"

I was taken aback. "Wrong about what?"

"The way you live your life. As if none of this has any relevance to you." She picked up a Bible from the side table.

I shrugged. "Well, it doesn't. I'm not religious."

Belinda gave a hum as she flicked through the Bible. She cleared her throat before reading, *"Turn to me and be saved, all you ends of the earth; for I am God, and there is no other."* She looked at me. "Are you on the earth?"

I rolled my eyes. "Yeah, but the Bible's just—" I was about to say, *'Just a load of stories,'* but caught myself in time. "I don't have any faith," I said instead.

"Oh, you have some faith, I'm sure. You just don't know where to put it." When I didn't answer, Belinda added, "If you were ill and doctors told you to take a pill, you'd trust them, wouldn't you?"

"I guess so."

"Would you demand all the proof first?"

"No..."

"Why not?"

"I don't know. Because doctors should know what they're doing..."

"Well, that's faith, isn't it?"

I screwed up my nose. "I suppose."

"And you believe your teachers at school, don't you? You accept what they tell you."

"Yeah... They should know what they're talking about."

"But how do you know that they *do?*"

I thought about this. "I suppose they don't always," I admitted. "I'd always believed that dinosaurs had gone extinct because that's what we were taught in school. But, now I've done some research for myself, I'm not so sure."

"Exactly. You'd put your faith in it without even realising!"

"Alright..." I was reluctant to agree with her but I could see that she had a point. "But, still..." I waved a hand at her Bible. "I can't believe in the Bible just because *you* tell me to."

"Of course not." Belinda gave a soft smile. "But perhaps you should ask the Lord to reveal himself to you."

"Hmmm..." I fiddled with a cushion. God ought to be a lot simpler than this. If he's real, you should be able to look into the sky and see his face. Not dig around like a cryptozoologist searching for clues.

As if reading my mind Belinda beamed and said, "The proof is *everywhere*, Livi. In every sunset, every flower, every newborn baby, every twilight stroll, every beating heart..."

I forced a smile. Her life was clearly more romantic than mine.

Before I could think of a reply, Belinda said, "Your sister doesn't like me, does she?"

I squirmed and tried to say, *'Yes she does!'* but the words got stuck in my throat. "What do you mean?"

"I can see it in her face. She *abhors* me."

"I don't know... If you think she doesn't like you then why do you keep trying so hard?"

Belinda sighed and poked her knitting. "If you believed you knew something that would save Jill from a great danger, you'd want to tell her, wouldn't you? Even if it meant she might not like you anymore, you'd risk everything for the chance to save her. That's how I feel about Heaven and Hell. That's why I invite you to church. Your souls are worth more than you realise."

I was stunned. This was the most astonishing thing I'd ever heard Belinda say. Perhaps it was the most astonishing thing she had *ever* said and there was no one there to witness it but me. I felt like a solitary explorer alone in the jungle witnessing the birth of a rare exotic bird. For all her faults and annoying quirks, I figured that if Belinda was that willing to save us then she must be a much better person than me. I doubt I would ever try to save *her* so badly. I didn't even tell her when her shoo-fly pie was burning. I recalled all of mine and Jill's dark conversations and suddenly felt very sheepish.

"But, if we don't *want* to go to church or find out about God or any of those things..." I mumbled.

Belinda gave a sad smile. "Then I'm sorry for pushing you."

I felt a lump in my throat. "I'd better go." I jumped up from the sofa.

Belinda followed me to the door. "Thanks for coming to see me, Livi. I know I'm a bit silly sometimes but I really care about you and Jill."

I gave her an awkward smile and began to walk away, feeling extremely unsure of myself.

Then, just as I was beginning to think I had wildly underestimated Belinda, she called loudly, "Oh, Livi, perhaps you should pray that God sends you a dinosaur!"

I let out a bemused splutter as I sprinted to my door.

It's alright to be angry

"There's Jill!"

I looked to see where Ruby was pointing. "Where?"

"There. With your dad."

My heart stopped as I followed her gaze. Jill and my dad were sitting together in a nearby café, a plate of nachos between them.

"What...?" I gaped at them. Up till this point, I'd barely even seen Jill share a *conversation* with my father, let alone a plate of food.

"Shall we see if they want to come ice skating with us?" Before I could protest, Ruby wandered over to the café and tapped on the window.

They turned at the same time and their smiles turned to surprise. Jill waved awkwardly and Dad beckoned for us to come in. I felt my heart racing as Ruby and I walked through the door and weaved through the busy café to their table.

"Hi girls!" Dad said when we reached them. "Jill and I bumped into each other in the queue. We thought it made sense to share since we were both waiting."

Jill pointed to their plate. "Do you want some nachos?"

I said nothing.

Dad held out two menus. "Sit down. Do you want a drink?"

I eyed Jill carefully as I sank into a seat. She hated my dad. Why the sudden change of mood?

Jill caught my eye and looked away. "I suppose I should go?" She said this as though she wasn't entirely sure.

Dad nodded. "It was nice to bump into you."

"You too." She looked almost shy as she patted my dad on the shoulder. "Have a nice afternoon," she said to me.

"Bye then," I said, keen for her to hurry up and leave.

She adjusted her bag and left.

Dad turned to me and Ruby. "Have you decided what you want?"

Ruby looked at me. "What are you having, Livi?"

I shook my head and slid my phone out of my bag, shielding it under the table as I wrote my dad a text. *'Don't read this out loud— What was that all about?'*

My dad jumped as his pocket vibrated. "I've got a text." He pulled his phone out. "Oh! It's from you... *'Don't read this out loud—'"*

"Dad!"

Ruby gave me a quick look as my dad whispered, "Oops!" He paused for a moment before texting back, *'People will share a table with anyone when they're hungry!'*

I frowned. *'But she hates you.'*

Dad chuckled. *'Maybe I'm winning her over. LOL.'*

As he grinned at me, I felt a surge of anger. What was he doing? After telling me how besotted Jill used to be with him, was he now trying to entice her?

I was about to text a fierce reply when Ruby gave a cough. "Er... Livi? What are you having to drink?"

I swallowed hard, feeling like I might pass out. "Nothing."

"Oh. Shall we go ice skating then?"

"Actually, I feel a bit ill. Can we do it another day?"

Ruby's face fell. "If you want..."

"Would you like a lift home?" Dad offered.

"No." I jumped up from my seat. "We'll walk."

I marched out of the café as fast as I could, not even stopping to give my dad a farewell hug. I was positively fuming inside.

Ruby followed at a trot, shooting me an anxious glance as we got outside. "What were you texting your dad about?" She looked a little self-conscious.

"Nothing," I muttered. I glanced back and saw my dad fiddling with his phone. A sudden panic took hold of me. What if he was texting Jill to tell her that the coast was clear and that she could now return? "Wait here," I commanded before marching back into the café.

Dad looked up in surprise. "Hello—"

I shot him my most perfect *Ominous Owl* face. "You do realise that if you ever married Jill, then that would make my sister my stepmother and that kind of thing would seriously mess a child up. You don't want me to end up in jail or rehab or on a daytime chat show, do you?"

Dad let out a splutter. "We just bumped into each other, Livi! I was only being friendly."

I breathed sharply out of my nose. "Promise?"

"Of course!" Dad looked at me as though I was crazy. "Trust me."

I started to feel a little unsure of myself. "Okay. Bye then."

I barely said a word as we walked home. All I could think about was Jill and my dad eating nachos together and the stunned look on Jill's face when we caught them. Perhaps my dad thought it was innocent enough but, after hating him for so long, it was totally out of character for Jill to suddenly be willing to sit with him. Ruby looked at me once or twice and asked if I was alright but I fobbed her off by saying I had a stomach ache.

We reached my house and Ruby tried to follow me in but I pretended not to notice and put an arm across the door as I said, "Well, it was nice to see you. See you again soon!"

Ruby looked hurt as she stepped back. "Okay... See you."

I closed the door and kicked my shoes off, ready to confront my sister.

Jill was in the living room with the curtains drawn and a blanket over her shoulders. She looked like she'd been crying again. I hoped this wasn't going to become a regular Saturday afternoon feature.

"Hi Livi," she said, forcing a smile. "How was the ice rink?"

"We didn't go," I snapped.

"Oh? Why not?"

"Didn't feel like it."

"Oh." Jill sniffed and blew her nose.

She looked so pathetic huddled under her blanket that I just lingered in the doorway, unsure of what to say. "So... You don't hate my dad anymore?" I asked finally.

She gave a funny smile. *"Hate'* is a strong word. I suppose he's alright."

I wanted to shake her and demand she tell the truth— that she wasn't just a hungry person sharing a table with someone who was *alright*, but a besotted person looking for love in all the wrong places. As if it wasn't bad enough when she hated my dad, did I really have to contend with her *loving* him now? *'This isn't a game!'* I wanted to shriek at her. *'This is my life. You can have your meaningless relationships and endless heartbreaks, but not with my dad!'* I didn't know how to say this in a way that didn't involve lots of screaming and tears so I just flicked the door frame and muttered, "So... You just randomly bumped into each other?"

"Yeah." Jill gave a loud snuffle and looked away.

I stood and stared at her, imagining her as a soppy teenager besotted with my father and then as a stubborn young woman sending him away when he refused her advances. "Hey, Jill," I said coolly. "You know when I was little? Why did my dad leave?"

Jill frowned. "You know why he left. Because he's an idiot."

"But why? Did he give a reason? Or..." I paused. "Did something happen?"

Jill wouldn't meet my gaze. "I don't know."

I felt a surge of anger as she sighed and picked her fingernails. I had to take several deep breaths to compose myself. Dad had made me promise not to tell Jill that I knew the truth. Why he was so keen to protect her was beyond me. But I hated the idea of letting him down.

Jill turned and forced a smile. "Oh, Livi... Is it alright if you go to the Ricos' for dinner tonight? I think I need an early night."

"Again?"

"Yeah. I could do with some time on my own."

I let out a snort.

"Are you okay?"

"Fine!" I yelled, turning on my heels.

"Are you sure?" Jill called weakly as I ran up the stairs.

I let out a growl and sprinted to my room, slamming the door behind me. Didn't Jill realise how useless she had been recently? Didn't she know that eating dinner at the Ricos' made me feel totally out of place and inadequate? Didn't she care that I wanted my mum so badly with a longing that only intensified whenever *she* went to bed early? It was quite selfish of her, I thought, to be more consumed in her own sorrow than in mine.

When I arrived at the Ricos' for my charity dinner, they were busy putting together a jigsaw. They'd only managed the edges so far but, from the thousand pieces that were strewn across the living room floor, it looked like it was going to be heavily grey and rather boring.

"Come and help us, Livi!" Oscar patted the floor beside him.

I shuffled over and picked up the box. It bore a picture of an eagle flying through a storm. There was lots of rain and lots of clouds and, as I'd suspected, lots of grey.

"Interesting," I muttered.

"Here you go." Violet plonked a handful of pieces onto my lap.

"It's okay," I said, brushing them off. "I'll just watch."

Ruby caught my eye and beckoned me to follow her to her room. "Are you okay?" she asked once she'd closed the door behind us.

"Yeah." I wandered mindlessly over to her and Violet's bookshelf, keeping my back to her as I pretended to examine their books.

"Are you sure?"

"Yeah," I said again, pulling out a random book. "Is this good?"

Ruby leant over to check the title: *'Pipsqueak McCully and the Girl on the Edge.'* "It's really good. Want to borrow it?"

"Uh, one day." I shoved it back before plonking myself onto a beanbag. I picked up an orange cuddly moose from the floor and tried to smile but Ruby kept looking at me, all concerned. "What?" I snapped.

She bit her lip. "You're not angry with *me,* are you?"

"Of course not! Why would I be angry with you?"

Ruby brightened a little. "Phew."

"I'm not angry with *anyone,"* I insisted, giving the moose's face a squeeze.

Ruby watched me for a moment. "You seem angry."

"I'm not!"

"Are you sure? Not even a little bit?"

"Why should I be angry?"

"You don't seem to be getting on very well with Jill."

"It's just hormones," I said, my voice cracking slightly.

"It's alright to be angry, you know."

I didn't answer. I was scared I would cry if I said anything else.

Ruby sat there staring at me.

Eventually, I sniffed and said, "She annoys me sometimes. She gets depressed and does silly things— like dating Fester and eating nachos with my dad... She's so stupid." A rogue tear slid down my face and I hastily brushed it away.

Ruby came and put an arm around me. "She must get lonely."

I opened my mouth to reply and then closed it again. I hadn't thought about it like that. I'd thought Jill was just stupid. But I supposed Ruby was right. She must get lonely. "I guess..."

Ruby chewed her lip before asking, "Can I pray for you?"

I shook my head. "I don't even know if I believe in God."

"Can I pray for you anyway?"

"No! If God isn't real then it's just a waste."

Ruby sighed. "Alright."

I leant back against her wall and rubbed my eyes. "What's for dinner?" I asked indifferently.

"Roast beef again, I think." Ruby wrinkled up her nose.

"Don't you like it?"

"Yeah! But we had it last week. It's nice to have something different."

I sucked in my cheeks and said nothing. If only roast beef two weeks in a row was the greatest of *my* worries.

The lights were off when I got home. Jill's blanket was draped over the banister and the kitchen tap was dripping. From next door came the faint murmurings of Mr and Mrs Tagda having one of their usual arguments.

I kicked my shoes off and stormed up the stairs. I tried to stamp really loudly, hoping Jill might wake up and come and tell me off. Then I could yell at her for going to bed early and I would feel better. I stood outside her bedroom door, unsure whether I wanted to bang rudely on the door or sneak into her bed for a hug.

In the end, I stood on the empty landing and burst into tears. Then I went to the bathroom to splash cold water on my face before running to my room and flinging myself on the bed, tears obscuring my vision as I buried my head in my pillow.

Ruby was right. I *was* angry. So angry. I wanted to shout and scream and break things. Now that I'd started crying I couldn't stop and the tears came heavily with gasps and grunts and lots of snot. It was like a bomb had exploded in my chest and I writhed on my bed, contorting wildly as I surrendered to the torrent of despair.

I desperately wanted some comfort and I was angry with Jill for not being available. I wanted to push her out of her bed and demand that she pay me more attention. I wanted to drag her into the spare room and force her to watch as I shred the contents of her box of secrets into tiny little pieces. I wanted to slap her until she answered all my questions about my mum and the past and Aunt Claudia's letter.

But it was more than Jill. It was my dad too. I was angry with him for being physically absent for most of my life and so *emotionally* absent now. I wanted to yell at him and ask why he'd never bothered to fight for me. I wanted to throw a tantrum or give him the silent treatment until he broke down. The suspicion that this would just cause him to walk away overwhelmed me with grief.

Most of all, I was angry at not having my mother. I wanted her more than I've ever wanted anything and it hurt so badly. I was jealous of everybody in the world who had a loving mother and so fiercely angry that mine had to die. How could that be fair or right?

"Why?" I cried into the nothingness. "Why did you have to let her die?"

I lay on my bed sobbing and shaking and unable to think clearly. Then I thought about Ruby offering to pray for me and almost shrieked at the idiocy of it all. What would I even ask for? For my mother to be alive and happily married to my father? Or, if that was too far-fetched, maybe I could ask for my dad to fall in love with Ms Sorenson and for her to marry him and adopt me?

I wailed at my stupidity. "I'm so rubbish. Everything is rubbish. Why won't you *do* something?"

I suddenly realised that I was angry with God. I was angry with him for the stupid mess of a family he had given me. I was angry with him for not coming in that moment to console me. Then I remembered I didn't even believe in him and I started to get really angry with him for not existing. I gave a howl and beat my fists into my bed. I hated God and yet I didn't even believe in him. I didn't believe in him yet I couldn't stop blaming him. I began to cry deep, heavy tears, whacking my hands against the side of my head in frustration. I wondered if God was up in Heaven, watching me and wondering what all the fuss was about.

I squeezed my eyes shut as I growled, *"God, if you're real, I want you to go away and leave me alone."*

~ 24 ~

Good like Livi

Hitler was in the news twice this week. Once because the features of a house in Wales had a rather striking resemblance to his face; and then again because a celebrity couple had come under ridicule for naming their son *'Adolf.'*

Everyone was talking about it in Ms Sorenson's class and, of course, Kitty took the opportunity to say loudly, "Livi likes Hitler, remember?"

And everybody laughed at me.

"No I don't!" I protested.

"You said he was a good leader," Kitty sneered.

"I didn't mean it like that!" I exclaimed, looking up to make sure Ms Sorenson didn't think I was a Nazi.

Ms Sorenson just looked at me and said sharply to Kitty, "That's enough, Miss Warrington." Then she informed the whole class that since we couldn't work sensibly we would now have to work in silence.

Everybody groaned and a few people begged for a second chance.

"Ten minutes of silence," Ms Sorenson said firmly. "And then we'll see."

The muttering died down and we all went back to our projects.

I glared at Kitty and she caught my eye and stuck her finger under her nose like a moustache.

"Ignore her," Ruby whispered. "She's so... catty."

I grinned despite myself and drew a picture of a hideous-looking cat. Then I smirked at Kitty as if I'd just found out some ugly truth about her.

She raised her eyebrows and demanded, "What?"

I gave a coy shrug and hissed back, "Wouldn't you like to know?"

"Miss Warrington and Miss Starling!" Ms Sorenson barked suddenly. "I said silence! If I have to tell you again, you'll both be in detention."

I was mortified. Ms Sorenson was angry with *me*.

"Sorry, Miss," I muttered.

Her expression remained stern as she gave a quick nod.

I bowed my head and went back to my work, my cheeks burning with the shame of being told off by the wonderful Audrey Sorenson. I drew spirals over my notes, rapidly blinking back the tears that were threatening to spill out of my eyes.

Ruby kept poking me and asking me to check her work but I could barely think straight. I felt utterly miserable. What if Ms Sorenson never forgave me? What if previously she'd liked me but now considered me a bit of a troublemaker?

As the lesson came to an end, I wondered whether I ought to go over to her and apologise for talking. I also wanted to fully explain that I did not like Hitler, in case she wasn't sure. I packed up my bag really slowly and cast a cautious glance in her direction. She was busy telling off Melody Vickers and Annie Button who have written less than a page between them for their project on horses. I dragged my heels across the room and loitered in the doorway but it didn't look like she'd be finished any time soon.

"Are you coming, Livi?" Ruby nudged me.

"Yeah..." I cast one last glance at Ms Sorenson before following Ruby out.

We'd barely left the building when Melody and Annie came running out behind us. I bit my lip and wondered whether to head back and try to catch Ms Sorenson.

"Get out of the way!" Melody yelled as she swerved round me.

I turned in annoyance and almost swung my bag into Kitty Warrington.

She tutted before saying coldly, "Watch it, Nazi."

Beside her, Molly let out a loud snort as she roared, "Yeah! Watch it, Nazi!"

I tried to ignore them as we crossed the playground. Molly, Melody and Annie were in hysterics as Kitty marched beside me with her legs stiff and one arm in the air.

"How can I be a Nazi?" I exclaimed as the four of them followed me and Ruby out of the school gates. "I've never killed anybody."

"You look like a Nazi," Molly said snidely.

"That's stupid. Nazis don't look like anything special."

Kitty smirked. "Exactly."

I rolled my eyes.

"You should check your family tree," Melody suggested. "Perhaps you're related to Hitler."

"You actually *could* be," Annie said, looking at me in horror. "What if you *are?*"

"I'm not!" I snapped. "For your information, my mum was half Welsh and my dad is half Jewish."

"And half Nazi," Kitty muttered under her breath.

The whole gang burst into hysterics again.

I scowled at them and stormed off, Ruby trotting dutifully beside me.

"Don't listen to them," she whispered once we'd crossed the road. "They're just being mean."

"I know!" I cried. Even so, my stomach churned as I feared they could be right. I knew very little about my family history. How many leaps away from Hitler might I be?

"I wonder if that celebrity couple actually wanted to name their baby after Hitler..." Ruby said thoughtfully. "Or do you think they just liked the name *'Adolf?'*"

I shrugged and looked behind me. "I don't know."

"Isn't it strange that because of one man the name *'Adolf'* is doomed forever?" Ruby pressed on. "I mean, there are probably murderers named *'Bob,'* or, *'Brian,'* or, *'George,'* and yet people call their babies those names freely and without judgement."

"That's because Hitler was the worst," I said.

Ruby went to reply but I stopped her. Kitty's gang were still within earshot. "Can we change the subject?"

"Oh okay." Ruby started rooting around in her bag. "Do you want to see my new banana stickers?"

"Yeah, alright."

Despite feigning interest in Ruby's stickers and her long-winded story of how she'd acquired them, I found myself thinking about Ms Sorenson's lesson. I wished I could go back in time and do the class again. I'd refuse to rise to Kitty's taunts and would say instead, *'You seem far more fascinated by Hitler than I do.'*

And Ms Sorenson would exclaim, *'Well said, Livi! Now get on with your work, Miss Warrington, otherwise you'll be in detention!'*

By the time we reached our street, I had just about managed to convince myself that Ms Sorenson probably didn't think I was a

Nazi, when Ruby turned and said, "What if you *are* related to Hitler?"

I was outraged. "I'm not!"

"But, if you were, would it matter?"

"Of course! I don't want the DNA of a murderer inside me."

"But there have been heaps of murderers throughout human history. You must be related to *some* of them."

"Then so are you!"

She didn't bat an eyelid. "Yeah, probably."

"So you have the DNA of a murderer too."

Ruby didn't reply.

I frowned and said, "I'm *not* related to Hitler."

She smiled. "Okay. Bye."

I watched as Ruby crossed the street and let herself into her house. I couldn't believe her nerve. How dare she suggest I could be related to Hitler! I stormed inside and threw my school bag on the floor. Then I marched straight to the computer. I wondered if there was any way to verify that I was of no relation to Hitler— or *any* murderer, for that matter. Unfortunately, Google didn't provide an online DNA test, but I did end up with a disturbing list.

Five facts about an evil man

1. For a short time, he advocated a sinister faith called 'Positive Christianity' which featured an Aryan Jesus Christ who hated the Jews.

2. His half-niece died in suspicious circumstances.

3. When serving in the army during the First World War, his fellow soldiers described him as 'odd' and 'peculiar.'

4. Under his control, the Nazi party murdered approximately eleven million people during World War II, including six million Jews.

5. When it became clear that he wouldn't win the war, Hitler committed suicide with his wife Eva Braun.

I sat back and sucked in my cheeks. *Now, that's evil.* If mankind were to stand in a line from *'Good'* to *'Bad,'* I was certain Hitler would be on the very far edge. I wondered who would be standing next to him. Was it simply a matter of how many people you've killed? Would average murderers be classed as *'OK'* compared to Hitler? And, as long as you've never killed anybody, are you *'Good'*? I screwed up my nose as I considered it. Maybe, when you die, God— or some other cosmic force— puts you on a scale and decides how good you've been: *'Perfect,' 'Good enough,' 'Hitler-Evil...' and a million shades of grey in between.*

I paused. *Where would I be on the scale?*

I fetched a notebook from my bag and began to compile a list of all the bad things I've ever done. I started with big obvious crimes like swearing and lying. Then I moved on to smaller misdemeanours like thinking I'm better than someone else, avoiding eye contact with the tramp who asks for 37p and judging people who wear clogs. To my surprise I filled six pages. There were at least thirteen accounts of being rude to Jill in the last week alone— and those were just the ones I remembered.

I exhaled as I read my list through. I pondered handing it to some holy judge and watching them read it. *'I'm good really!'* I would insist. *'I haven't killed anyone so I'm good enough for Heaven, right?'*

I quickly made another list; this time of *good* things I've done. But I didn't get very far as this mainly consisted of bad things I *haven't* done. *I've never killed anybody. I've never punched anybody. I've never vandalised a bus stop.* It was distinctly unsatisfying. Are people only *'Good'* because they avoid doing bad things? What if a person does all the right things just so they can make it into Heaven but lives with evil thoughts in their heart?

Right on cue, I heard Helen Tagda yelling on the other side of the wall, "You filthy skunk, Solomon!"

Mrs Tagda is always calling her husband a skunk or a toad or some other foul beast. Sometimes she even yells, "I'll kill you, you old warthog!" I had assumed she must be right in her estimations since Solomon Tagda is a rather smelly man who hardly ever smiles.

Mr Tagda attempted a grovelling apology as Helen yelled, "Go and get the pies!"

Every afternoon, Mrs Tagda fills her granny trolley with pies to deliver to homeless people at a shelter in town. The people at the shelter must think she's a saint; but they don't hear the way she fights with her husband. Where would they be on the goodness scale?

A moment later, their front door opened and I saw Solomon shuffling past our window. Jill had arrived home and I peered from behind the curtain as the two of them engaged in small talk.

"Just upset the missus," I heard Mr Tagda say.

"Oh dear," Jill said politely. "I hope you sort things out soon."

Mr Tagda nodded before saying cryptically, "I'm *'A Good Man Lost,'* I am."

"Pardon?"

"My name," he replied, as though that explained everything. "It's an anagram."

Jill gave him a funny look and made her excuses but, as Solomon Tagda shuffled away, I watched him with new-found fascination.

I ran back to my notebook and turned to a fresh page. After a lot of work, I discovered that *'Helen Tagda'* is an anagram of *'Death Angel.'* That changes everything. He's not a filthy skunk, after all. And she's more frightful than I'd imagined. People aren't always who we think they are.

Five facts about a tragic man
1. He lost both his parents as a teenager.

2. He wanted to be an artist and sold a few amateur paintings but was denied entry into Art school because he wasn't good enough.

3. Whilst serving in the First World War, he saw many of his colleagues die and was presented with prestigious awards for his bravery.

4. He was against smoking and offered a gold watch as an incentive for his close friends to quit the habit.

5. He and his wife were found dead the day after their wedding.

With those facts in isolation, Mr Hitler really doesn't sound so evil.[81] In fact, he sounds terrifyingly *normal.* What if Hitler's favourite colour was the same as mine? What if we would cry at the same films? Or laugh at the same jokes? What would it take for me to be as wicked as him? I've never killed anybody but, in small ways, I am very selfish. I get impatient at people for walking slowly, I sulk if Jill makes me wash up and I make every effort to ignore the people in town raising money for the local donkey sanctuary. If I'm completely honest, I care more about myself and my petty worries than I do about the other seven billion people in this world— a hundred of which will have died by the time I've written this sentence.[82] *Am I closer to Hitler than I am to perfection?*

---

[81] Not that I would EVER say this within earshot of Kitty Warrington.

[82] According to *'Freaky Human.'*

I took a deep breath and tore my good and bad lists out of my notebook. Then I scrunched them up before turning to a new page. I stared long and hard at the clean white sheet. Maybe— now that I'd caught myself early— I would be able to change and become a better person. I made a vow to be as good as possible from now on and wrote in big letters, *'Being Good. The New Improved Livi Starling,'* leaving lots of space so that I could write down all the good things I would soon do.

I sat back with a satisfied sigh before wincing as I realised this meant being nicer to Jill. I could hear her plodding around upstairs and wondered whether I should buy her some flowers to cheer her up. But then I looked out of the window and saw that it was raining so I decided to begin by vacuuming the house instead.

As I left the living room, I caught sight of some dust on the hall mirror and wiped it with my sleeve. Then I went into the kitchen where the vacuum cleaner had sat unused for weeks. The kitchen was a mess, with unwashed plates everywhere and a hundred empty mouse traps lining the windowsill. Perhaps I would clean it after I did the vacuuming. I dragged the clunky vacuum cleaner over to a plug socket and switched it on. Then I lugged it haphazardly across the kitchen, humming to myself over the noise.

Jill came running in. "Did you spill something?"

"Nope! I just thought I would do something nice for you."

She blinked at me. "Oh!"

"Afterwards, I'm going to clean the kitchen," I added nobly.

"Really?" Jill looked stunned. "Thanks so much, Livi!"

I grinned. This *Being-Good* thing felt *great!*

~*~

For the next week, I kept an account of all my good and bad deeds. It began easily enough but got harder when I realised that I *thought* a lot of mean things, even if I didn't say them. Also, sometimes I did a good thing just to get that nice feeling. For example, in Thursday's Maths class, I politely said, "I'll hand the worksheets out, Mr Lester."

I revelled in the stunned look on Fester's face and, as soon as I sat back down, I added to my lists: *'Good: I was nice to my enemy.'*

I felt pretty proud of myself until I realised that that kind of carefully-orchestrated goodness probably doesn't count. In fact, the more I thought about it, the more I realised how few of my good deeds had been totally genuine after all.

When I was little we had a teacher who let us play board games every Friday. Everybody got rather high-spirited about winning and there were frequent tears and tantrums, culminating in our teacher yelling that if we couldn't play nicely she would ban games altogether.

I was a bad loser like the worst of them until, one day, I discovered a private game that I could always win: I simply *tried* to lose. Then I would fix a brave smile onto my face and say, "Look, Miss! I lost again, but I'm not a bad loser, am I?"

And our teacher would get the attention of the whole class and proclaim to my delight, "Look at Livi, being a good sport even though she lost again! Why can't you all be good like Livi?"

I'd felt smug at the time. But surely I was only kidding myself. Were my present good deeds just as artificial? Like Helen Tagda handing out pies, just because someone thinks you're good it doesn't mean you truly are— *even if that someone is you.*

~ 25 ~

The past is the past

For my seventh birthday, my dad bought me a pair of yellow trainers with flashing red lights. They were the most amazing shoes I had ever owned and I wore them everywhere, feeling very special every time they lit up. My dad said I looked like a spaceman. I felt more like a princess. I thought nothing could hurt me when I wore them; I was valiant, brilliant, invincible. But, in reality, I fell many times in those trainers. And I was wearing them on the day he left.

It was a sunny day and I had spent the morning kicking my shoes against every available surface, delighting in the flashing lights as I waited for my dad to come and take me to the park.

Jill appeared, looking rather serious, so I quickly hid my feet and said, "I'm not doing anything."

She just shook her head and asked if I wanted to go to the playground.

I said, "We can ask Daddy when he comes."

Jill put her arms around me and said, "I'm sorry, Livi. Your dad isn't coming anymore."

I thought she meant he'd got stuck in a traffic jam or forgotten his way to our house. So I shrugged and said, "Okay then."

But then she hugged me so tightly that I realised something awful must be happening and, although I had no idea what it was, I grew terribly scared and started crying.

Jill cried too and promised, "It will be alright."

The following week, I asked, "Is Daddy coming this week?"

But she said, "No."

That's when I realised he wouldn't be coming *ever*. This revelation hit me in various ways. There was the initial heart-wrenching pain of abandonment which came in great suffocating waves as I waited in vain by the front door. And then there were the smaller losses, like realising he wouldn't see my new haircut, or wondering who would eat the pickle from my Big Mac.

I told everybody at school that my dad was a pirate and had to go away on business. For several weeks I brought in shiny pebbles and pretended it was treasure that my dad had sent from Asia.

I think some of the parents complained because one day Jill said, "Don't tell people your dad is a pirate, Livi."

So I was forced to reconsider. I decided that my dad was the true heir of a foreign dynasty and had gone to fight the evil impostor king so he could take his rightful place on the throne. He couldn't tell me otherwise my life would be in danger, but he'd come and get me soon and take me to his castle. After a while I convinced myself that it was true. Whenever I found myself feeling sad, I would entertain myself with wild daydreams of my future as a princess until the wait became slightly more bearable.

Jill, however, knew nothing of my father's royal heritage and was miserable for a long time. On one occasion I came out of school and saw her sobbing her eyes out at the school gates. Parents were eyeing her with distaste as they hurriedly collected their children and ushered them away.

A girl called Alice Moody saw Jill and said loudly, "Isn't that your sister, Livi?"

Without batting an eyelid, I replied, "No. I don't know her."

The next day, a game was created in the playground called 'The crazy woman at the gate.' Kids would take turns to be my sister wailing hysterically as they tried to capture anyone who got close.

When she saw me, Alice Moody smirked and said, "Want to go next, Livi?"

I glared at her and said, "If you don't stop this stupid game, I'm going to tell on you."

Alice laughed and ran round the playground yelling, "Livi loves her sister! Livi loves her sister!"

And, even though it was true that I did love Jill, everybody was laughing so much that I jumped onto the nearest bench and shouted, "No I don't! I HATE my sister!"

The whole playground fell silent and everybody stared at me as one of the dinner ladies came running over to tell me to 'stop being stupid and get off the bench.'

After that, I was wracked with guilt, afraid that Jill might leave too and it would be my fault.

For Christmas that year, Jill offered to buy me some new trainers but I insisted that the ones from my dad still fit fine. I was convinced that if I wore them for a whole year then my dad would reappear at the end. So I wore them everywhere and, every time they flashed, I stopped and made a wish. Unfortunately, the soles wore out pretty quickly and my feet grew so fast that it wasn't long before my toes poked out of the ends. They barely lasted six months. By my eighth birthday, the lights had gone out completely.

~*~

After ten whole days of trying to be good, I reviewed my lists. They were quite a disappointment. I'd thought a lot of mean things about Kitty, Molly and Fester, and there were loads of occasions when I could have done something kind for Jill but decided not to. The nicest thing I'd done was help Ms Sorenson with the register—except I'm not sure that counts as I'd been dying to do that for weeks. If God is out there, I really don't think he'd be that impressed with me. Even when I try *extra, extra hard*, I can't go *one day* without doing or thinking something bad.

I lay on my bed, feeling sorry for myself. Perhaps I ought to blame my parents, or lack of them, for my inability to be truly good. I wondered what kind of person I'd have been if my mother had lived or if my father had never left. Perhaps I'd still be wearing shoes with lights.

As old memories came bubbling to the surface, I hugged my knees to my chest and let a couple of tears fall. Then I gazed absentmindedly out of my window where I caught sight of Violet directing Ruby and Oscar in a photo shoot. Oscar was dressed as a dog and was taking the role very seriously, yapping and rolling around and ignoring Violet's command to sit still. Ruby was wrapped in bubble wrap and looked hugely unimpressed. I sniggered despite myself and made a mental note to tease her about it later.

Violet propped up a sign between them which read, *'If I ruled the world, less animals would die from swallowing plastic.'* I rolled my eyes and decided that if Violet ever ruled the world I would become a hermit and go and live in a cave. I watched as Violet fiddled with her camera and yelled for Stanley to come and help. "Daddy! I need you!" I had never heard her call Stanley *'Daddy'* before. She looked rather pathetic as she flapped her arms about and waited for him.

As I continued to spy on her, it suddenly dawned on me that Violet was seventeen— the same age Jill was when she started looking after me. I couldn't imagine Violet raising a baby. She couldn't even look after a hard boiled egg.

"Wow," I said out loud. "Jill was *her* age..." *Jill was young and immature, with a baby to take care of and nobody to help her...*

I thought about Ruby's speculation that Jill must be lonely. Had she *always* been lonely? Throughout my entire childhood? I'd never noticed. I had assumed, as children do in their self-absorbed way, that Jill was in a whole different realm to me; a grown-up realm where everything was ordered and sensible. I'd never understood why she was crying. I'd never thought to ask her whether she was lonely.

I was hit by a pang of guilt. Jill had done a lot for me over the years, most of which I'd never understood or appreciated. It made me feel bad to think of her trying to be brave and strong and having nobody to talk to about it. If she had been as daft and hapless as Violet then it was no wonder she'd done something as stupid as sending my dad away. Perhaps she'd regretted it soon afterwards but hadn't known how to make it better. Maybe the combination of guilt and loneliness had caused her to spiral into an ever-increasing neurosis leaving her incapable of finding true love.

I bit my lip. Poor Jill. *What a mess.*

I watched through the window as Stanley came to Violet's rescue and helped her turn the camera on. She took a couple of selfies before grinning and aiming the camera at her siblings.

I sighed and wondered what I could do to help Jill. Perhaps I could borrow the Ricos' camera and offer to give her a makeover and photo shoot? I could make her look really beautiful and set her up with a profile for an online dating site. *'Smart, pretty and lonely. Desperate for love.'* I'd vet the responses to make sure she only met the good ones. Or perhaps I could hold auditions and pick her somebody special like a contortionist or a mime artist.

After mulling it over, I went downstairs and sat beside Jill on the sofa. She was poring over a heavy folder of notes.

"Hi Jill!" I said.

She shot me a quick smile before turning back to her work.

"What would your perfect man be like?"

Jill gave me a funny look. "What?"

"Do you like tall men? Brown-haired or blond? Do you like men with special skills like cooking or juggling—?"

She frowned. "I don't want *any* man right now. I think Aunt Claudia's right."

"What do you mean?"

"It's a waste of time." She ruffled her papers a little roughly.

I paused. "Have you ever been in love?"

Jill breathed heavily through her nose. "No."

"*Ever?*" I pushed, longing for her to break the façade and pour out her heart. I wouldn't even mind if she cried if she would just be honest with me. I debated asking if she'd ever dated anyone called Ricky, but I thought better of it. "Not even when you were young, like before I was born?"

She gave me another funny look. "No. I have never been in love."

I sighed. "Fine. But if you *could* fall in love, what kind of man would you like?"

"Seriously, Livi," she said, with a hint of irritation. "I'm not interested right now."

I watched her for a while, wishing I could read her mind. I wanted to know why she'd never told me about her old fiancé or about being besotted with my father. Dad said he'd told me all that stuff because he trusted me. So did that mean Jill hadn't told me because she *didn't* trust me? Did she think I wouldn't understand? Because I was pretty sure I *would*, if she'd just tell me. I wondered how I could ask her about everything without breaking my promise to Dad. Perhaps I could say that I knew and then beg her not to tell him. But what if she got angry and blew my cover? What if Dad decided to leave again on account of the fact that I was untrustworthy? My insides knotted with fear.

Jill was looking at me strangely. "Are you alright?"

I forced a smile. "I'm fine."

She didn't look convinced and put her pen down. "Livi, I'm sorry I've been so busy lately. If I can just hit these targets, they'll ease off and I'll have more time."

"I know."

Jill gave a sad sigh. Then she grinned and proclaimed, "That's it! I've done enough for today. How about we do something fun this afternoon?"

"I can't. I'm seeing my dad."

Her face fell.

"Sorry."

"That's alright. Maybe next week?"

I nodded. "Maybe."

I went back to my room. Perhaps the dating site wasn't such a good idea. I sighed and wondered where the mysterious Ricky was now and whether Jill ever thought about him. Did she wonder what might have happened if they'd got married? Maybe they'd have had several children and Ricky would be a stay-at-home dad so that she could pursue her dream of being a psychologist instead of working at a job she hated. They would be a normal family and Jill would be happy. Of course, I don't know where that would have left me, the stray sister. I pushed that thought out of my mind and gave another sigh. If Jill had Ricky, would life get better? Would she stop crying on Saturday nights and learn to cook roasts? Maybe I could track him down and see if he was still single.

~*~

I met Dad at the cinema where he was waiting with two chocolate milkshakes and half a box of popcorn.

"Just seen a trailer for the new *'President Robot'* movie!" he exclaimed as we made our way to some empty chairs in the foyer.

"That's nice."

"How have you been?"

"Fine, thanks."

"Good. How's Jill?"

I gave half a shrug. "I think she's lonely."

"Oh?" He looked concerned.

I thought about my plan to reunite Jill with Ricky and realised Dad might be able to help. "You know Ricky?" I said.

"Who's Ricky?"

"Jill's old fiancé."

He gave me an odd look. "What about him?"

"Do you know where he is now?"

"No idea."

"Oh." I pouted.

"Why?"

"I don't know," I said cagily. "I thought I could see whether he still likes Jill and maybe he could come and surprise her or something."

Dad almost choked on his milkshake. "Don't do that!"

"Why not? It might make her feel better."

Dad shook his head. "It won't. Trust me, Livi. Don't even mention his name to her. It will just upset her."

"Why? Maybe he was her one true love!"

"No. He wasn't."

"How do you know?"

"I just know."

I opened my mouth to protest but he put up a hand and said, "Promise me you won't start meddling."

I frowned. "I'm not *meddling*. I'm trying to help."

"It's meddling, Livi. The past is the past."

I took a deep breath but didn't say anything else. I didn't want to make him mad.

Dad cleared his throat and changed the subject. "How's your project going with Ruby?"

"Yeah, fine," I said quickly. I felt a little uneasy about our almost-argument and was keen not to dwell on it. "We've found an article about a clam that's over four hundred years old."

"Wow! Sounds amazing."

"Yeah." I smiled and leant over to blow bubbles in my milkshake. Some of the chocolate splashed up my nose and made me splutter. "Oh, Dad?"

"Yes?"

"It's not a big deal but, next time, could I have strawberry?"

"Don't you like chocolate?"

"It's alright. I just like strawberry better."

"I've been getting you chocolate milkshakes for months," Dad said incredulously. "And it's only now you tell me that you'd rather have strawberry!" He tipped his head back and roared with laughter, like it was the best joke he'd heard all year.

I gave a shrug and forced a laugh too.

After we'd finished our milkshakes Dad said he had a few things to get in town. I nodded and followed him round the post office, the pound shop and a couple of games stores. The city centre was pretty packed and, as we weaved our way through the crowds, we passed some kids busking with violins, a pushy market researcher and three stalls selling scarves.

"Sorry, Livi," Dad said suddenly. "This must be really boring for you."

"It's alright."

He glanced around and pointed to a nearby clothes shop. "Let's have a look in there!"

I stared at him. "That's *Tizzi Berry!*"

218

"Is that bad?"

"It's just expensive."

"Let's look anyway."

"Okay..."

I had often peered through the window of *Tizzi Berry* and imagined myself as one of their mannequins but I'd never been inside. As we crossed the doorway, I looked around and breathed an awed sigh. The displays were immaculate. The sales assistants were stunning. The clothes themselves were like tiny pieces of Heaven. I caught sight of a range of bags covered in felt bananas and thought of Ruby. Then I gravitated towards a rail marked *'Sale'* where I spotted the most amazing coat *ever*. It was bright red with big black buttons shaped like horses. It looked like the sort of coat a film star would wear. Or a famous writer. Or Kitty Warrington. I went over to it and ran my hand across the fur lining of the collar.

"Want it?" Dad asked, catching my eye.

"Oh!" I blushed. "I don't know."

"You can have it if you like."

I turned the sleeve over. "It's a hundred quid," I said, pushing it aside.

"That's fine." Dad pulled it off the rail. "Try it on."

"Really?"

"Yeah!"

Feeling oddly guilty, I took the coat from him and tried it on. I checked myself out in the mirror and gave Dad a sheepish shrug.

"Do you like it?" he asked.

"Yeah, but..."

"But what?"

"It's a hundred quid."

"So?"

I shrugged again and shook the coat off. Dad took it from me and strode towards the till.

As the sales assistant greeted my dad and scanned the price tag I lingered with trepidation, afraid that she might think I was incredibly spoilt. She asked me if I wanted to wear it right away and I gave a careful nod. Then I watched as she hunted for scissors and slowly cut the tags off the sleeve. She handed me the coat and, as I put it on, Dad tapped his credit card against the till and whistled. I know I ought to have felt grateful but I couldn't shake off the strange guilty feeling.

"Thanks, Dad," I whispered as we left.

"You're welcome!"

I tilted my head to the side and let the furry collar tickle my ear, feeling like a supermodel as I strode down the high street in the greatest coat in the world.

Dad popped into a couple more games stores but they didn't seem to have what he was looking for so eventually he said, "Stuff it. Let's go."

On the way to his car, however, we passed one of the stalls selling scarves. Dad rubbed his chin, stopped, and started to look. I wondered if he was about to offer me one and rehearsed what I ought to say. *'Wow, Dad, are you sure? I really don't expect you to spoil me like this!'*

Hopefully, he would reply, *'It's the least I can do. You're worth it!'*

After some browsing, Dad held up a pink and blue tartan scarf. "Do you think I should get this for Jill?"

I looked at him in shock. "What for?"

"For winter. To wear round her neck."

"I mean *why?*" I said irritably.

"She might like it."

I gaped at him. What could be more stupid and confusing than buying my sister a present? Didn't he realise how that could give her totally the wrong idea? I wanted to push the point further but he'd just spent a hundred pounds on a brand new coat for me. The scarf was only a fiver and it wasn't even very nice. I didn't want to seem ungrateful. "It's *your* money," I muttered.

Dad smiled and pulled out his wallet.

I sniffed and looked away.

As we hurried towards the car, it started to rain. I prayed Dad would drop the scarf in a puddle but he didn't.

"Will you hold it while I drive?" he asked, tossing the stupid thing onto my lap.

I dug my nails into it. *What would he do if I threw it out of the window?* I wondered. *Would he make me get out and walk?* I comforted myself by stealing glances of my new coat in the mirror.

Every now and then Dad caught my eye and grinned. "You look great," he said at one point.

I gave a quick smile and fiddled with the buttons.

When we reached my house I got out of the car as quickly as possible, hoping Dad had forgotten about the scarf. I would tell Jill it was from me. But he took it from me and said, "I'll just pop in and give this to Jill."

I suppressed a frown as I unlocked the door.

Jill was emerging from the kitchen. "Oh, hi," she said.

"Check out Livi's new coat," said Dad.

I gave an awkward spin.

"Looks lovely." Jill raised her eyebrows.

I wanted to add, *'It was a hundred quid,'* but I didn't.

Dad handed her the scarf. "This is for you."

Jill looked at him in surprise. I clenched my fists as she whimpered like a lovesick puppy.[83] "Oh, Charlie! That's so kind."

Dad shrugged. "The winters are cold up north."

Jill giggled. "Thanks."

"Well, I'd better go." Dad gave me a hug and threw Jill a careless wave.

It was only then that I realised I'd been holding my breath. "Bye," I muttered. "Thanks again for the coat."

He winked and left.

I turned to Jill. She had a very disconcerting look on her face. I saw her run her hand across the scarf.

"It was a fiver," I said.

She gave an indifferent smile. "It's nice, isn't it?"

I scowled at her. "It was just from some person in the street. It's probably stolen."

Jill blinked at me as I stormed up the stairs.

On my way up, I caught sight of my angry expression in the mirror and moaned. I was supposed to be being nice to her but she made it so difficult! I sighed as I realised, *I will just have to try even harder to be good.*

---

[83] A fairly convincing lovesick puppy at that. I ought to know; I've been perfecting that impression for weeks.

~ 26 ~

Drifting in space

For our English homework we had to write a newspaper article about a fictional event. In typical Mrs Tilly style, the more tragic the better. For inspiration, I watched the ten o' clock news and took ardent notes on a convicted killer on the run in London. I wondered whether to write an article about a convention of mass murderers annihilating one another. Or perhaps a speculative account of a murderer dying and finding himself next to Hitler on the way to Hell.

Before I could make up my mind, the news moved on to a feature about a man running on a pool of custard. I figured being pushed into a vat of custard would be quite an original way to die so I grabbed some paper and wrote in big letters, 'A Very Sweet Death.' Then I began to draw a jar of custard.

The next story was a report about some bank changing its logo. I wasn't sure this was particularly newsworthy and wondered if they'd run out of things to say. I imagined what it would be like if there was no news one day. The newspaper headlines would all be blank and newsreaders would declare, 'Breaking News! There is nothing to report! Nothing has happened. Nobody has killed anybody, the weather is calm all over the globe and none of the world leaders have said anything stupid.'

I was about to grab some fresh paper and write an article about 'The Day Nothing Happened,' but then the programme concluded with the news that the sun might die earlier than expected. I dropped my pen and turned up the volume.

"Every second, the sun burns up at least four hundred million tons of hydrogen," a scientist with bushy white eyebrows was explaining to the camera. "Well, there is not an endless supply of hydrogen and when it runs out: BOOM!" He clapped his hands. "No more planet Earth!"

I was aghast that he could talk about it so calmly and wondered when this supreme devastation was going to take place. I sat open-mouthed as the scientist went into detail about 'helium' and 'nebula' and other made-up words.

"But *when?*" I begged. "When will everything explode?"

Finally Professor Bushy-Brows concluded that this wouldn't occur for another few billion years. "Of course," he said with a chuckle, "mankind will inhabit the rest of the solar system by then and will be able to watch the destruction of the earth from the safety of Neptune."

I breathed a sigh of relief but, as I went to turn the television off, I wondered how the scientists could be so sure. Didn't they once think Pluto was a planet? Well, they got that wrong. What if they've got the sun stuff wrong too? What if a billion years is just a trick of the light? What if the sun is going to burn out in our lifetime? What if it happens without warning? I glanced around the room as if, at any moment, the earth might collapse in on itself. A sudden tap on my shoulder made me scream.

Jill gave me a funny look as I stumbled backwards. "Livi, it's late. You should go to bed now."

"Can't I stay up a bit longer? What if the world ends tonight?"

"Don't be silly."

I stared at my sister and sighed. She was just a highly evolved monkey destined for oblivion. I knew there was no point in arguing so I gathered up my work and went upstairs.

When I got to my room I leapt onto my bed and gazed out of the window. The moon was full and the stars were plenty. I wondered how many babies were being born at that very moment and whether any of them were being named 'Livi.' Then I thought about all the people who were dying and wondered where in the universe they would be going next. I wondered if God was really out there and whether he knew about the confusion with the sun. Did he have his almighty finger on a big red button, ready to press it and send the world into extinction? I crossed my fingers and hoped that the end of the world would at least wait until I'd achieved some form of greatness. I saw a shooting star and, without thinking, I whispered, *"I wish the world wouldn't end yet."* I let out a moan as I realised how dumb it was to make a wish upon a lump of lifeless rock. As if the night sky has the power to make my dreams come true.

Although Jill had said it was late, I felt she didn't quite grasp the severity of the situation. So, as soon as I heard her going to bed,

I crept back down to the living room and turned the computer on. I typed, *'How big is the universe?'* into the search engine and found a video which showed how small Earth is compared to the sun, other bodies in the solar system, the galaxy and the universe itself. I found myself growing alarmed as the video zoomed further and further out, whizzing past billions *(zillions)* of stars as Earth faded into nothing. I learnt that even if you were travelling at the speed of light, it would take 100,000 years to get to the edge of the Milky Way, and it is estimated that the Milky Way is only one of at least 125 billion galaxies in the universe— no doubt all as complex and intricate as ours. Earth is minutely *tiny*. Infinitely insignificant. I watched the video eleven times, growing more and more overwhelmed. I know absolutely *nothing* about the ends of the universe. I can't even find my way around *Leeds*.

I clicked on another link and listened to half a lecture by some man who declared that there are two things mankind cannot fathom: infinite space and eternal life.

"'Everything' is a very mighty word," he said. "To combine *all* that exists— every star and atom, thought and number— in one place, is beyond the scope of our finite minds."

I shivered and hugged my knees to my chest. I tried to imagine everything in the universe (not to mention whatever is *beyond* the universe) and soon felt my head throbbing from the strain.

I hoped the man would say something to ease my confusion but he just concluded, "Perhaps the bigger question is: how is it that *anything* exists at all?"

I turned the computer off and ran upstairs where I lay in bed, frozen with terror. I am tiny. I am nothing. I live for a moment in the vastness of the universe and then die, never to be seen again.

I felt small all week. Things like what to watch on telly or where to sit for lunch fade into insignificance when you realise how tiny you are. Even my brand new red coat felt meaningless against the backdrop of eternity.

The day came for us to hand in our English homework. Mine consisted solely of the headline and the jar of custard. I'd been so consumed with researching the universe that I'd forgotten to finish it.

Thankfully, Mrs Tilly just gave me a pitying smile and said, "You coloured that in very neatly, Livi."

"Thanks." I shot her my best *humble low-achiever* nod.

After collecting our homework, Mrs Tilly made us watch a film about punctuation. It was excessively dull and such a waste of my precious finite existence. The lights were slightly dimmed and Mrs Tilly was transfixed by the television so I grabbed some paper and started doodling. I drew a picture of a stegosaurus chasing a sparrow.[84] Then I wrote my name over and over again until it looked like a meaningless mess. *Livi Teeson Starling, Livi Teeson Starling, Livi Teeson Starling...*

Next, I made some anagrams of my name and came up with my top five:

1. *'Tis Everlasting Lion'*
2. *'Listing Revelations'*
3. *'Naiveties Strolling'*
4. *'Attiring Loveliness'*
5. *'Telling Vain Stories'*

And then I wrote this, which I think makes me a semi-genius:

> *'I forget I **A**m alive*
> *Won't be**L**ieve the world is free*
> *But **I** know I will survive*
> *And li**V**e out this life for*
> *M**E**...*
>
> > *...An**D** I forget I won't survive*
> > *B**E**lieve this: I am free*
> > *But I know life is **A**live*
> > *For the worl**D** will outlive me.'*

I wanted to put my hand up and ask Mrs Tilly if I could share it. I would call it *'Realising You Are Very Small in a Massive Unknown Universe.'* But I was supposed to be slow with my reading and writing so I passed it to Ruby instead.

"It's an anagram," I whispered.

She raised her eyebrows and muttered, "Cool," which I don't think quite captured my brilliance.

I pointed to the anagrams of my name. "Want me to do one for you?"

"Okay!"

---

[84] *Hungry Sparrow* being my current favourite animal noise. Not that it matters; I'm just going to die.

"What's your middle name?"

Ruby blushed and picked up a pen. She wrote in tiny letters, *'Ethel.'*

I smirked and wrote, *'Seriously??!!'*

Ruby shot me a wounded look and turned away.

A surge of guilt rippled through me as a nagging voice said, *'Well, that wasn't very GOOD, was it?'*

I bit my lip and drew some mindless squiggles over my sparrow. Then I concentrated on making the best possible anagram for Ruby.

As the lesson came to an end, Mrs Tilly switched the lights back on and said, "I hope you all enjoyed that!"

I caught Ruby's eye and shot her a hopeful smile as I slipped her my favourite anagram of her name: *'Be Truly Heroic.'*

Thankfully, she smiled back.

Later, I added to my lists: *'Bad: I insulted Ruby's middle name. Good: I made Ruby a nice anagram.'* I hoped they would cancel one another out.

~*~

That weekend, Ruby and I finally made it to the ice rink. We shuffled around the side like little old ladies, squealing and giggling and clutching one another in terror while children half our size whizzed past. We fell over at least thirty times between us before we stopped counting.

"He's like a *zillion* times better than us!" Ruby said in awe, pointing at a child the size of Oscar.

"Yeah!" I grinned. "Hey, do you know how big the universe is?"

"Pretty massive." Ruby shrugged.

"Billions and billions of light years across. Billions of stars and billions of galaxies." I paused before adding dramatically, "And the sun could explode at any moment."

Ruby nodded.

I looked at her, aghast. "Doesn't that frighten you?"

She shook her head. "God made it all."

"And he could destroy it all, just like that!" I clapped my hands together and almost fell over.

"Well... he *will* one day."

"What?"

"The Bible says one day all the stars will be dissolved and the moon will turn to blood and the sun will never rise again."

This time I really did fall over.

"Are you alright?" Ruby giggled as she bent down to help me up.

I gaped at her. "You're joking, right?"

She shook her head.

"But that's..." I searched for the right word. "*Horrible.* I thought God was meant to be nice."

"He *is* nice," Ruby insisted. "He's gonna make a new Heaven and a new Earth."

"Oh... So we'll just go and live there instead?"

Ruby looked at me. "Well, kind of," she began. Then she sort of shook herself and said rapidly, "I mean, no. I mean, if you love Jesus then you get to live with him forever and, if you don't... then you won't."

I sniffed. "You mean Hell?"

Ruby blushed.

I narrowed my eyes at her. "You can't tell me I'm going to Hell just because I don't believe the same thing as you."

We'd stopped moving and stood clumsily at the side, shivering as a cold wind blew across the ice.

Ruby didn't say anything for a while. Eventually she muttered, "I didn't mean to offend you."

"You didn't," I snapped. I wished I was an expert skater so I could skate away but all I could do was cling to the side and try not to fall over again.

"I don't want you to go to Hell," she whispered.

"How would you feel if I said you were going to Hell if you didn't like guinea pigs?"[85] I demanded.

"Well, I would probably think you were crazy... Or, if I was pretty sure you weren't crazy, I'd ask you more about them."

I gave a grunt. "People are allowed to believe different things."

Ruby blinked at me.

"I don't have to believe in God."

She said nothing.

"I tried church, remember? I didn't like it."

When Ruby still didn't respond, I rolled my eyes and finished with, "I'm a good person. And it's not nice to tell good people that they're going to Hell."

---

[85] I knew for a fact that she hates them.

I thought that was the end of the matter but, before I could change the subject, Ruby piped up, "It's not about being good. Nobody can be good enough. It's about being forgiven."

I screwed up my nose. "What's that meant to mean?"

Ruby chewed her bottom lip for a long time. Then she kind of straightened up as she blurted out, "Everybody messes up and everybody hurts God and it causes a big rift if it doesn't get fixed!"

I frowned and looked around, hoping nobody was listening.

Ruby swallowed hard. "It's like... One time, Violet painted a self-portrait and, when she wasn't looking, I drew a banana on her head. She was really upset and wouldn't let me stand in her side of the room for days, which was hard because the door is in her half..." She blushed and thought for a moment. "On our own, we're doomed because our sins make us dirty and nothing dirty can be with God."

I opened my mouth to interrupt but Ruby continued quickly, "But it doesn't have to be that way! God wants to be with us so much that he sent Jesus to die for the sins of everybody in the world so that *anybody* who comes to him can be made clean. All you have to do is believe. I was wrong to ruin Violet's painting but God won't hold it against me because Jesus has paid for it. In fact, God won't hold *any* of my sins against me because when he looks at me he no longer sees me dirty. He sees me clean. It's like dressing up... I'm kind of wearing Jesus. I can have *his* DNA." She paused before adding, "I'm not better than you, Livi. I've just been forgiven. And you can be too, if you just accept him!" She gulped and shook a little, as though she had been holding back for a long time and finally thrown up.

I stared at her, my head reeling as I tried to process her words. "I'm sure Violet has forgiven you," I said irritably. "So why should *God* care if you ruined her painting?"

Ruby took a deep breath before launching into another tirade. "All our sins are offences against God! He wants us to love him and love each other and, when we don't, it hurts him. If our sins aren't dealt with then our relationship with God is broken and you can't go to Heaven if you don't make up with God."

"That's not fair."

"It's more than fair! It's free!" Ruby paused before adding, "Free for *us*. It cost him everything."

I narrowed my eyes. "You're telling me that Jesus died for my sins and all I have to do is believe in him?"

"Yes!"

"If that were true then I could be as horrible as I liked and just ask God to forgive me."

"You could..." she said slowly. "But, when you love somebody, you don't really want to hurt them."

"So, you actually *love* Jesus?" I sneered.

"Yeah."

"Well *I* don't. How can I love somebody I've never known?" I instantly thought of Jill asking me something very similar about our mother. This irritated me and I glared at Ruby as though it were her fault.

She pulled her hat tighter over her ears and shrugged. "Let him love you first."

"What?"

She blushed and said nothing, shrinking back into the timid old Ruby I had come with.

I sighed. "Let's not talk about it. My Aunt Claudia says you should never talk about religion or politics. It just gets messy."

Ruby shot me a sad smile. "Okay. Sorry, Livi."

"I'm sorry too." I forced a smile and linked my arm in hers.

We carried on skating, or rather shuffling, round the ice and didn't mention God again. I tried to focus on other things, like skating in a straight line or counting the number of people who were wearing bobble hats, but Ruby's words kept going round and round in my head. Her love of Jesus and her sorrow at my unbelief unsettled me. Unlike Violet, who expressed her faith with lots of shouting and persuasion, Ruby just seemed to *know* that God loved her and she expressed this with a quiet certainty. I found it incredibly disconcerting. I wondered whether she was crazy (although, admittedly, the most sensible crazy person I'd ever met) or whether she had something that I didn't have. And if she *did* have something that I didn't have, would I want it, could I trust it, and would it be worth it?

~ **27** ~

Any other mother

The last couple of weeks of term arrived without warning and with them came the day of our presentations. Ruby and I had spent two hours the night before practising in front of Ruby's family.[86] But now that the time had come to do it for real we were both petrified.

As we waited with the rest of our class outside Ms Sorenson's classroom, fretting over whether our presentation would be good enough, a curious idea struck me.

"Hey, Ruby," I said. "Will you ask God to send us a dinosaur?"

Ruby looked at me incredulously. "You want me to pray?"

"Yup."

"Does that mean you believe in God now?" She gave a slight smile.

"No! It's just worth a try."

"Alright." Ruby took a deep breath and said into the air, "Father God, I pray you'll send us a dinosaur." She beamed at me. "There you go!"

I was amazed at how simple it was. "That's it? He's definitely heard you?"

"Yeah."

"So..." I looked around. "When will we get it?"

Ruby giggled. "God isn't a vending machine, Livi."

"Alright... So, we just wait and see what happens?"

"Yeah. But trust that he's heard and that he cares and that he'll do what's right."

"But we might not get a dinosaur?" I frowned.

"You might get something better."

---

[86] Belinda told us we were stars and Stanley filmed us for Ruby's grandparents. Upon their advice, I decided not to include any of my animal impressions, especially after Oscar started crying at my *Ravishing Raptor*.

I screwed up my nose. "But I want a dinosaur."

"I used to pray for curly blonde hair," Ruby said with a grin. "But I'm kind of glad God never said yes to that prayer. And, once, I prayed for an extra set of arms!"

I laughed. "Do you think God thought you were silly?"

"Nope. He's my Father. He likes it when I talk to him."

The word 'Father' jarred with me. If I asked *my* father for different coloured hair or a dinosaur he'd definitely think I was silly.

We sat there staring at each other for a moment.

"If I *did* start believing in God," I began carefully. "Would I have to be... I don't know..." I shrugged and looked away. I was about to ask whether I would have to become *weird* but stopped myself in time.

"Have to be what?" Ruby pressed.

"Don't know..."

She smiled. "Are you scared you'd get really weird?"

"No!" I blushed. "Don't be silly! I just mean, like, would I have to change?"

She gave me a funny look. "Would you *want* to change?"

I shook my head firmly. "No."

"You're happy the way you are?"

I opened my mouth to say, 'Yes,' and then reconsidered. "Well, not *exactly* the way I am..." I thought about the events of the last few weeks. "Sometimes I get upset about silly things or I think mean things when I don't want to..." In my head, I added, *I want to be good but I keep being bad, I've snooped through Jill's belongings and stolen a private letter, I'm rude to her and don't express myself properly and I can't shake this angry feeling whenever I think about my mother.*

"Well," said Ruby. "Don't you think God would want to help you change those things?"

"Wouldn't he just make me feel guilty? He's *perfect* after all."

"No. He wouldn't. He loves you, Livi."

I didn't know what to say. Part of me felt like standing up and jeering, *'I can't believe you're such a weirdo!'* but another huge part of me longed for her words to be true. A lump caught in my throat. "I'll think about it," I muttered.

Ms Sorenson came out at that moment and ushered us all into the classroom. She had moved the tables to the back and arranged the chairs into rows facing the front. Ruby and I grabbed two seats at the side and cast one another nervous smiles.

When everybody had settled down, Ms Sorenson said, "Good afternoon, 9.1. You've had several weeks to put together a presentation on something that interests you. Today you will share the fruit of all your hard work."

I heard Kitty whisper, "Yawn, what a bore."

Ms Sorenson threw her a warning glance and said, "I want to remind you to be respectful of one another. Anybody who cannot be sensible will go straight outside."

I sat up straight and tried to look sensible.

"Who wants to go first?"

Everybody looked away.

Ms Sorenson smiled wryly. "Alright. Who wants to go second?"

A few people shuffled but nobody volunteered.

"Who wants to go third?" she continued.

I looked at Ruby and shrugged. It might be alright to go third. At least then we'd get it out of the way. "We'll go third," I offered.

Ms Sorenson grinned. "Fantastic! Off you go then."

I gaped at her. *"Third,"* I said desperately. "Not *first.*"

"Well, nobody went first. Then nobody went second. And I can tell you now that they were the worst presentations I have never seen. Now it's your turn."

A few of our classmates giggled.

Ruby went bright red. I felt like I was going to throw up. We wobbled to the front of the class and propped our pile of posters up against the wall.

I cast one last look at Ruby and took a deep breath. "We're going to talk to you about dinosaurs," I told our classmates.

Most of them looked unimpressed. Kitty wrinkled up her nose.

Ruby coughed and added, "We don't think they went extinct."

At this, a few people sniggered. Others raised their eyebrows or looked at each other in confusion.

Feeling a surge of courage, I proclaimed, "During our research, we've investigated many claims of living animals that resemble dinosaurs. We've also looked at possible dinosaur sightings and evidence that dinosaurs may have lived alongside man." I went into detail about some of the things we'd discovered and, as I spoke, Ruby held up posters and gestured to the appropriate details. Ms Sorenson's picture of the dragon cave painting went down particularly well. We also had a collage of a diplodocus which Violet had created for us out of vegetable peelings. As Ruby held it up, I said, "In the Bible, there is a creature called a behemoth which is written about like this: *'What strength he has in his loins, what power in the muscles of his belly! His tail sways like a cedar; the sinews of his thighs are close-knit.'* Some people think this creature refers to a hippo. I don't know about you, but Ruby and I have never heard of a hippo with a tail as big as a cedar tree."

I saw Ms Sorenson smile when I said this.

"Before we began this project, I took it for granted that the dinosaurs died out millions of years ago. But I've learnt that there are many layers of truth and you cannot know something for sure until you've done thorough research for yourself." I paused and looked hopefully towards the back of the room. This would be the perfect time for God to send a velociraptor through the window. Nothing came so I sighed and concluded, "When it comes down to it, it's really all about faith. Maybe the dinosaurs lived millions of years ago and maybe none of them are left. But the 'proof' isn't as infallible as we might think."

"We're finished," Ruby added.

The class applauded politely as we went to sit down.

"Thank you, girls!" said Ms Sorenson. "That was wonderful."

Ruby and I grinned at each other.

We put our work under our chairs and relaxed as Kitty and Molly began their presentation on chocolate. As a little gimmick, they handed out chocolate coins.

They spent so long handing them out that Ms Sorenson said, "Alright, girls. Let's get on with it."

Kitty blushed and said, "Basically, we're doing our presentation on chocolate and whether it makes you feel happy. Put your hand up if you were happy when we gave you a chocolate coin?"

Most of the class raised their hand. I glanced at Ms Sorenson. She didn't have her hand up so I felt it was alright not to raise mine.

Molly made a great show of counting how many hands were up. Then she and Kitty waffled on about the various ingredients in a bar of chocolate. At one point, Molly said the words, 'the *breast* chocolate,' instead of, 'the *best* chocolate.' She looked utterly mortified as the class roared with laughter and I almost felt sorry for her.

When they had finished, I looked over at Ms Sorenson. She smiled and said, "Thank you, girls." But I'm sure she didn't sound as pleased as she had with ours.

The next couple of presentations were about rainforests and shoes. Then there were three in a row about football. I tried to look interested but, to be perfectly frank, ours was the best. The rest were mainly dull, although I did learn a few things from Wayne and Fran's presentation on how to draw robots.

When everybody had finished, Ms Sorenson arose and said, "Thank you, 9.1. With a few exceptions,[87] this was a terrific time of sharing. Now, if you would kindly put the room back in order, you will be free to go."

While we jumped up and dragged tables back to their proper places, Ms Sorenson went and sat behind her desk. She pursed her lips as she wrote in her filofax. I wondered whether she was ranking us in order and prayed to God that I could be her favourite. My chest ached as I pondered for the umpteenth time how different life could have been with a mother like Audrey Sorenson.

After school, we had our final dress rehearsal for the Christmas show. Miss Waddle gave us a grand telling off because several people still didn't know the words to the opening song. She also told us off because a total of six people were absent.[88]

"We have not had a single rehearsal with the whole class present!" she bellowed, banging her register against the desk.

We tried to look apologetic but it seemed a little daft that she was chastising *us* when the people to blame were absent.

The rehearsal was tediously boring, with Miss Waddle groaning and yelling every time something went wrong. Even though it was a dress rehearsal (which means *no stopping)* she made Kitty and Freddie perform the balcony scene at least five times. There were eleven more pages of script between that scene and my next one. I started daydreaming about what Romeo and Juliet might have been like had they lived.

I imagined a forty year old Juliet saying to her beer-bellied Romeo, *'You used to be so romantic.'*

'And you used to be beautiful,' he would snap back.

By the time it came to the death scene, I was convinced their love had only worked because it had never been properly tested.

Kitty and Freddie were both dead[89] and I arose to deliver my line. I looked over at Freddie whose nose was twitching and began, *"A tragedy of..."*

---

[87] Namely Melody and Annie, whose presentation on horses consisted solely of Annie doing an impression of a donkey. As Ruby nudged me and grinned, I felt mightily relieved that I'd removed all the animal noises from ours.
[88] No doubt they'd been avoiding Ms Sorenson's class.
[89] Well, not *really*, but pretending to be.

"Love cut short," Miss Waddle prompted impatiently.

"I know. I was just wondering... Is it really a tragedy that they died?"

The class gasped.

Miss Waddle looked up from the script and snapped, "Livi, this is a dress rehearsal!"

I tried to explain. "I mean, if they'd lived, there wouldn't be a story to tell, would there? Let's face it, nearly fifty percent of marriages end in divorce and they fell in love so young in what can only be described as a whirlwind romance. They didn't even prove they had an effective strategy for dealing with conflict and, when the going got tough, it's not like their families would've been much use..."

Miss Waddle threw down her script. "Do you want me to give your line to somebody else?"

"No..."

"Then can we carry on?"

I nodded and said meekly, *"A tragedy of love cut short."*

Freddie sneezed and Kitty elbowed him in the ribs.

The rehearsal came to an end and we sat looking sorry as Miss Waddle told us it had been awful. As she berated Kitty and Freddie for the lack of chemistry between them, I closed my eyes and daydreamed about my parents. I expected they'd been hopelessly romantic together and wondered whether their love would have remained just as strong had my mother not died.

'I'll love you forever, Charlie,' my mum would say.

'I'll love you more, Livi,' he'd reply.

I screwed up my nose as I tried to picture it. I've never met anybody with the same name as me. How would it have felt to have known my mother, Livi? Would I have liked having the same name or would I have wanted my own? And then, because it was hard to imagine a grown woman named *'Livi Starling,'* I found myself dreaming once again about a mother named *'Audrey.'*

As if on cue, I overheard Kitty going over one of her lines, *"A rose by any other name would smell just as sweet..."*

That may be true, I thought. *But perhaps a rose by any other name would not have died so young.*

~ 28 ~

Saving Jill

"Who was on the phone?"

"Just Aunt Claudia."

Something about the look in Jill's eyes convinced me that she was lying. She had sounded rather giggly before I'd walked in. And she'd hung up pretty swiftly.

I followed Jill into the kitchen and watched as she put the kettle on. "Is she well?" I asked.

"Who?"

I rolled my eyes. "Aunt Claudia."

"Oh! She's fine." Jill turned away and hunted for the sugar. "Do you want a cup of tea?"

I gave her a long look. "I don't drink tea."

"Of course not." Jill gave a vacant smile and turned to go. My stomach lurched as I noticed she was wearing the scarf from my dad.

"How was your day?" I asked coolly.

Jill blushed and walked out. "It was fine." She wandered up the stairs and into her room where, a few minutes later, I was sure I could hear her on her phone once more.

I had half a mind to burst in and grab the phone off her. I would bet anything I'd find my father on the other end.

I spent the whole night wondering what to do and was still wide awake when my alarm clock rang the next morning. Before going to bed, I had sent my dad a nonchalant text to ask if he'd phoned anybody that afternoon but he hadn't replied. I had debated calling him and commanding him never to speak to Jill again but I was afraid he would just laugh and do it all the more. Was he leading her on? Or was he playing games with *me?* I was convinced that if I didn't act soon, he and Jill might suddenly elope and never return.

I groaned and covered my head with my pillow as I thought about all the cryptic clues I had gathered over the recent weeks: Aunt Claudia's letter, Jill's fiancé Ricky, and the fact that Jill had once been besotted with my father. What did it all mean?

I pulled open my starling box and grabbed the letter. As I read it for the hundredth time, a new possibility came to mind:

> 5. *Jill and Ricky are my real parents. I got taken off them by social services on account of Jill's flighty emotional state but she stole me back after her mother died. She is quite within her rights to date Charlie Teeson since he is of no biological connection to me.*

I scowled at myself in the mirror. This was getting ridiculous. I had to find out the truth once and for all. I bit my lip and held the letter tightly in my hand. Then I went down to the kitchen and, in my most mature voice, said, "Jill, we need to talk."

Jill gave me half a glance. "Now? Can't it wait until tonight?"

"No. It's very important."

She looked a little worried. "Is everything alright?"

I took a deep breath and placed the letter on the table.

Jill jumped up with such force that her chair crashed to the floor. "How dare you go through my things!"

"I didn't. I just found it—"

"You liar!" Jill looked positively livid.

All my maturity evaporated as I exclaimed between splutters, "I promise, it was on the side of the shelf..."

She glared at me and marched out of the room. I followed her, my heart beating wildly as she opened the front door.

"Wait!" I squeaked. "Is the baby me?"

"What?" Jill turned in fury.

"Is it me?"

"Don't be stupid."

"Then who is it?"

Jill said nothing for a moment and then, shaking, she muttered, "I had an abortion."

"What?" My jaw dropped open. "You killed a child?"

Jill gave me an icy glare and stormed out, slamming the front door behind her.

Ruby arrived moments later and, as we walked to school, she jabbered on about something stupid, probably banana stickers.

I nodded and grunted in all the right places but, all the while, my head was spinning. *Jill had an abortion. Jill got pregnant by Ricky and then aborted the child, breaking his heart in her naïve pursuit of my father. Jill was absolutely mental. No, worse than mental— wicked.*

I stopped in the middle of the pavement. "Is my sister going to Hell?"

Ruby went bright red. "Why do you ask that?"

"Never mind."

"Are you okay?"

"Fine."

"Do you want to talk about anything?"

I shook my head. A sob erupted from my chest as I wailed, "I want to go home!"

Ruby put a hand on my shoulder, "Do you feel ill? Do you want me to walk you home?"

"No!" I yelled. "I mean *home*. Back to Little Milking and my old house." *My old life, my old innocence, my old ignorance.* I wiped my eyes on the back of my hand.

Ruby looked alarmed. "Livi, what's wrong?"

"Nothing," I blubbered, marching off ahead of her.

She ran to catch up and trotted in silence beside me for the rest of the journey. I could sense her looking at me but I ignored her.

Our first lesson was Religious Studies. Miss Dalton had prepared a brain-numbing lecture on the ethics of the motor racing industry and its potential impact on the environment. Of all the pointless things we'd studied in her classes, this had to be the worst.

I yawned and looked around the room. I eyed my poster on Jewish traditions. In the weeks since I had created it the poster had been vandalised and my Jewish man was now sporting a somewhat distasteful little moustache. I blinked quickly to stop myself crying and glanced at a different wall. Another class had created a display entitled, *'What is Heaven like?'* Somebody had written, *'The place where every sad thing is made better.'* Somebody else had added, *'The place where God is,'* and someone else, *'Where good people go when they die.'*

I raised my hand. When Miss Dalton failed to notice, I blurted out, "If Heaven is real, how do we get there?"

Miss Dalton stopped and stared at me, as if she'd forgotten she was sharing the room with twenty eight teenagers. "Well..." She adjusted her glasses. "Different people believe different—"

"What do *you* believe?"

"I'm an atheist so—"

Something inside me erupted. This was possibly the most critical lesson in the curriculum and I was being taught by someone who had absolutely no faith in anything. "Then what are you doing teaching us Religious Studies?!" I shrieked.

The class gasped.

Miss Dalton stood up and said, "Livi, that was unacceptable behaviour."

Ruby looked horrified. The rest of the class started whispering. I think Kitty Warrington giggled. *I hate her.*

"I don't feel well," I muttered. "I'm going to the nurse." I arose, packed up my bag, and walked out of the room.

I wandered aimlessly for a while and then, without really thinking about what I was doing, I went to the library and booked out a computer.

I typed, *'Which religion should I choose?'* into Google. A quiz popped up and I quickly filled my answers in but the results were inconclusive due to me saying, *'I don't know,'* to pretty much every question. Next, I tried, *'How do I get to Heaven?'* But the answers just seemed to be people's *opinions* when what I wanted was absolute *fact.*

After some impatient web surfing, I found a website which gave an overview of different belief systems. I tucked my feet under myself and began to read. The bell rang and I crossed my fingers and hoped that nobody from my class would find me in the library. Fortunately nobody did and I spent the whole of break with my eyes glued to the screen, ignoring the bustle around me. The bell rang again and the noise died down as everybody left the library.

My next lesson was Maths but I decided that I would not be going. Instead I spent the next hour highlighting large chunks of text from the internet and copying them into a document which I had titled, *'Theories of Life and Death.'*

Finally, after exhausting a list of all the major religions and philosophies, I narrowed my eyes and pressed *'Print.'*

At that moment, Fester came into the library. I tried to duck out of sight but he caught my eye and came waltzing over. "You missed my class."

I didn't answer.

"Was there a pressing issue that you deemed more important?" Fester continued sarcastically.

I glared at him. "Do you know how to get to Heaven?"

He gave a bemused snort. "No."

"Then, yes, I had something far more pressing than attending your stupid class." I went to retrieve my pile of printouts.

"I hope you're going to pay for those," he said.

"Take them out of Miss Dalton's salary."

Fester raised his eyebrows and changed his tone as he asked, "How's Jill?"

"I don't know yet!" I screamed, flapping fifty five pages of internet theology in his face before storming off to find a more secluded table.

I picked a spot in the far corner, near the tatty old books that nobody looks at. Then I spread everything out and went through it all, circling things that jumped out at me. I thought about what Belinda had said; how it's not about whether or not you *have* faith but what you put your faith *in*. As I pored over all the many theories and ideologies I realised that Belinda was right. To believe in *anything* takes faith. Even believing in *nothing* takes faith to assume it doesn't matter. She was also right when she said that if Jill was in danger I would do anything it took to save her. I truly would— even if that meant converting to some major religion right there and then in the middle of the library. But I had no idea what to put my faith in. Should I tell Jill to pray five times a day? Repent from her sins? Attempt to become one with the universe? Cross her fingers for a healthy reincarnation? And what if I picked the wrong religion?

By the end of the morning, I'd sorted all of the world's religions and philosophies into four main categories.

1. There is no God and no Heaven. Deal with it.

2. If there's a God or a Heaven, we'll find out when we die. Stuff happens regardless of anything we do.

3. There is a God, or even many gods, and the way to Heaven/enlightenment/perfection is through our own efforts, hard work, nice deeds or happy thoughts. Not everyone will go to Heaven but YOU can if you do the right things. Basically: be good enough.

4. There is one God and one way to Heaven: through faith in the only truly good person who ever lived— Jesus.

Was that it? All the theories of eternity reduced to four options, two of which I have no control over and a third which I'm a persistent failure at? I rubbed my head as waves of confusion crashed over me. I wished I'd put my hand up when I was at church with Ruby. I could have met Jesus and found out whether or not he liked me. I could have asked him to come home with me and present his case to Jill.

I stayed in the library throughout the whole of lunchtime feeling sick and angry and numb as I read my list over and over. I knew Ruby would be wondering where I was and I was torn between guilt and indifference when I considered that she might be worried about me.

As I racked my brain for an alternative option, I moaned at how ludicrous it sounded. If *Option Jesus* was correct then the whole of mankind is doomed without him, no matter how good we try to be.

That would make me as lost as Hitler, I thought grimly. I shook my head and scribbled over my notes. *That's just stupid. I deserve to go to Heaven more than Hitler, don't I?*

Just before the bell rang, Ruby found me and came running over with an anxious look on her face. I shoved the internet printouts into my bag and tried to look normal.

"Are you alright, Livi?" she asked, sitting beside me.

"Yeah."

"Do you want to talk about anything?"

I shook my head.

"Okay..." Ruby looked quite sad. "The bell's about to go..."

"Yeah," I repeated, picking up my bag and storming out of the library.

Our next lesson was Design and Technology. Our teacher announced that he had a treat for us. Unless it was a free ticket to Heaven, I wasn't interested.

"We're going to make egg cups!" he said, holding up some ugly wooden thing he'd made earlier.

I exhaled slowly. Sitting in a pokey little classroom and carving out an egg cup did not feel like a productive use of my time. I don't want to be a carpenter and I don't like eggs. So I picked up my bag, walked out of the classroom, and went home.

As I reached my house, I was surprised to hear voices. My first thought was that we had burglars so I clenched my key tightly to attack with if necessary. But, as I stood there listening, it became clear that the voices were Jill and Dad and that they were in the middle of a blazing row.

I opened the front door just in time to hear Jill yell, "I gave up *our* child only to end up bringing up *yours!*"

I walked into the living room. "What's going on?"

Jill stared at me in shock. "You're meant to be at school!"

"You're meant to be at work!"

"Go back to school."

"No." I walked shakily across the room and sat on the sofa. "What did you mean when you said, *'I gave up our child only to end up bringing up yours'?*"

"Nothing." Jill turned away. "I was just angry. Charlie, you'd better go."

"No!" I got to my feet. "Don't make him leave! You always make him leave when you don't get your own way."

"What's that meant to mean?" Jill snapped.

"It was your fault he left!"

"What?"

"I know all about it," I blurted out. "I know you liked him and I know about Ricky."

"Who's Ricky?"

"Don't pretend. Dad told me everything."

"Livi, it's alright—" my dad began.

"Who's Ricky?!" Jill's eyes were like fire.

"Ricky Martin!"

"Ricky Martin?" Jill looked from me to my father. "The singer?"

"Ricky Martin, your fiancé!" I yelled back. "The one you treated like dirt because you wanted Mum's boyfriend to be yours instead!"

Jill's jaw dropped open. "You lying—!"[90] Without warning, she lunged at my dad and punched him in the face. "Charlie *was* mine," she hissed at me. "*We* were engaged. He got me pregnant then said we weren't ready to bring up a child. He made me have an abortion. The whole time, he was sneaking around with Mum. Are you happy now?" She stormed out of the house. Seconds later, I heard the roar of her car as she drove away.

My heart caught in my chest and for a moment I thought I might pass out.

---

[90] I have edited out the swearing.

Dad had stumbled backwards when Jill hit him and now had blood dripping out of his nose. He turned to me and said, "Livi—" He looked like a monster, some foul new breed of animal.

I ran away.

I don't even remember leaving the house. One moment I was close to fainting in our living room; the next I was sprinting through the neighbourhood. Once I started running, I couldn't stop. I wished I could run so fast that I could run right out of this world. I ran past a wall covered in strange graffiti, past the corner shop, past Helen Tagda and her trolley filled with pies and past some girls bunking off from the posh school round the corner. I fixed a determined grin on my face and hoped they would think I was training for a race. Or maybe running away from the police. I wondered how it would feel to have just robbed the post office and now be running away.

I ran until I thought I was going to turn inside out. Then I limped, panting, into a nearby park and dragged myself over to a bench. I don't know how long I sat there, staring into space. Every time someone walked past I forced a smile but, all the while, Jill's words went round and round my brain. *'Are you happy now? Are you happy now? Are you happy now?'*

I couldn't imagine ever being happy again. I wasn't just an accident. I was the worst mistake in the history of the world. My mother, my *wonderful mother*... She was awful. All this time I'd thought that if only my mother hadn't died then the four of us would be one big happy family. But every good idea I've ever had about her is a complete lie. She didn't plan me. She didn't love my dad. She probably didn't even love *me*.

At some point, I started to cry. I let the tears slide down my cheeks and made no effort to wipe them, leaving them to harden on my face like cement. I know this will sound stupid but I began to recite Shakespeare. By now, I knew the entire *'Romeo and Juliet'* script off by heart and I sat on the bench reciting the death scene, feeling the tears roll down my face and savouring a bizarre kind of joy at being able to manufacture real tears, just like Kitty Warrington.

Eventually my phone rang. It was Jill. Seeing her name dance across the screen filled me with joy and sorrow in equal measures. Joy because she'd noticed I was missing. Sorrow because everything hurt inside and I wanted to make her pay.

I pressed the answer button but didn't speak.

"Livi? Are you there?"

I gave half a grunt.

"Where are you?"

"Park."

"Where?"

"Near the golf course."

"Stay there. I'm coming."

I had some twisted desire to get up and start running again. But I didn't. I waited. She took so long that I worried that she'd died or changed her mind along the way. But finally I saw her coming over the hill. I closed my eyes and dug my nails into the palms of my hands as she sat down beside me.

"I'm so sorry," she whispered. "I should have told you sooner... That wasn't how I planned it..."

I looked at her sadly. I didn't know what to say.

"I don't want you to think badly of our mother," she added, her voice cracking slightly. "She'd have been so proud of you."

Tears filled my eyes. "But she..." I spluttered. "She... with your *fiancé*..."

"She did a silly thing, that's all. But she loved you very much." She tried to smile as she went on, "Apparently, when she was pregnant with you, she used to ask policemen if she could pee in their hats."

A sob rolled out of my mouth. "That's just stupid."

Jill took my hand. "I'm sorry."

We sat in silence for a while and, as the *'Romeo and Juliet'* script danced through my mind, I started thinking about my father. I wondered whether he was crying with regret. Or whether he'd gone to the pub to watch some football. For one pathetic moment, I hoped he might be looking for me.

Right on cue, Jill said, "I hope Charlie didn't bleed on the carpet."

I sniffed and wiped my eyes. "Did you really love him?"

When Jill answered, she sounded close to tears. "I thought so." She gazed into the distance and said nothing for a while. "It was never real love... I can see that now. I was just a besotted teenager."

I gulped but said nothing.

"He hasn't changed," Jill continued, more to herself than to me. "His heart was always just out of reach. Charming one minute and then absent the next..." She shook her head. "I wanted to please him so much that I always let him choose for me; even stupid things like what I ate for lunch or what shoes I would wear. But he never wanted to choose. I'd wear the shoes he'd picked and he wouldn't even notice. So I offered him more and more until the thing he chose to take was the thing I didn't really want to give away—" She stopped and sobbed.

I put an arm around her. "You must hate me," I muttered.

Jill turned to look at me. Her cheeks were flushed and mascara was dripping down her face. "Why should I hate *you?*"

"Because I must be a constant reminder of the child you lost. I'm the one who should have been aborted."

Jill shook her head. "No! Never think like that. I hated Charlie for betraying me. I hated our mum when she died and left me to pick up the pieces. And I hated myself the most for—" She let out a moan before whispering, "But not you, Livi. I never hated *you*. The first time I looked into your eyes, I knew I loved you." She rooted around for a tissue but didn't find one and wiped her nose on her sleeve instead.

I felt sick. *Would I do the same? If Jill got pregnant by the man I loved, could I ever bring myself to hold that baby?* Suddenly, my entire world spun around. Jill was the best person in the universe and it was me who needed saving, not her.

"Thanks," I said quietly. I gulped before adding, "I understand why you made him leave."

Jill gave me a sad look. "I never made him leave, Livi. He was just an idiot."

"Oh." A sob erupted in my throat and I shook a little as Jill held me tight.

"I'm such a mess." Jill wiped her nose again. Then she put her head in her hands and cried, "God, save me!"

Although I knew she didn't mean it, because she didn't believe in God, I squeezed my eyes shut and prayed, *And me, God. Save me too.*

~ 29 ~

What I learnt this term

When we got home, Dad had gone. Of course, this wasn't a huge surprise. We were unlikely to have walked in to find him cooking us dinner or reclining by the imaginary fire. Even so, his absence was so potent that I almost couldn't breathe. Jill asked if I was hungry. I said no. She said she wasn't either but that some chocolate might make us feel a bit better. It didn't.

Jill let me have the next day off school. I heard her calling the school secretary to tell them that I had concussion. Then she phoned her work and said she had bird flu. After that, I drifted back to sleep and didn't wake up until the afternoon when Jill came in with some sandwiches.

"How are you feeling?" she asked, pulling out her first aid kit, as if anything in it might make me feel better.

"I'm okay. How are you?"

She gave a sad smile and said nothing.

I took a deep breath. "Jill, will you tell me the truth?"

She blinked at me. "I have."

"I mean..." I bit my lip. "What was Mum *really* like?"

Jill sat beside me and let out a long sigh. "She was funny and charming and kind." She paused. "But she wasn't very sensible. And I never felt like she understood me."

"So... she was a bad mum?" I whispered.

Jill grimaced. "People are complicated, Livi. She did her best."

I swallowed hard. "What was it like when she died?"

I thought Jill was going to say that she didn't want to talk about it but instead she replied, "It was tough." Then she looked out of the window and didn't say anything for a while.

I held her hand and tried to be patient.

Eventually Jill continued, "I was living with Aunt Claudia and I remember her bursting into my room and saying, 'Your mother is dying, you'd better go and make up with her.'"

"Wow. That's a bit tactless."

"That's Aunt Claudia." Jill sighed. "I got a taxi straight to the hospital. By the time I arrived, I was in such a state and Mum started crying when she saw me. She kept saying she was sorry and that she missed me and that she didn't want to die with me angry with her." Jill stopped and cleared her throat. "Then Charlie walked in holding you. You took one look at me and giggled. And Mum said, 'Look, she likes you. That's the first time she's done that.'" A tear slid down her cheek. I reached over and wiped it off. Jill smiled sadly and concluded, "Mum asked if I would look after you and I didn't question it."

I felt a lump in my throat. "Do you ever regret it? It's quite a big duty."

"It's never been my duty. I love you."

She put her arms around me and I let out a sob. "It must have been hard though," I whimpered.

"Loving you wasn't hard. But being *enough* for you was. The worst moment was when you came home from nursery and asked if I was your Mummy." Her voice cracked as she whispered, "I almost said yes." She turned to face me. "I know it's hard without your mother, Livi, and I'm sorry that you'll never have her. And I wish there was something I could do to take that pain away—"

I shook my head. "It's alright," I said through tears. I pulled my duvet round myself.

Jill stroked my hair and the two of us lapsed into silence.

There was a sudden knock at the door.

My sister peered out of my window. "Ruby's here."

I shuffled deep under my duvet and muttered, "I don't want to see her." I had no intention of seeing Ruby Rico ever again. There was no way I could face telling her the awful truth about my awful family. I wondered how much it would cost to pack up our things and move to the Congo.

Jill didn't say anything.

Ruby knocked again and Jill got up and went down to answer the door.

I heard Ruby ask, "Is Livi alright?"

Jill said something to her then closed the door. She came back to my room and put her hand on my back. I wriggled deeper into my bed, out of her reach.

"Ruby's worried about you," Jill whispered.

I ignored her.

"She wanted to let you know that you got an 'A' for your dinosaur project."

I felt a deep pang. *I love Ms Sorenson.*

When I didn't reply, Jill continued, "Belinda came by when you were sleeping."

I grunted.

"I told her what happened."

I threw the duvet off my head. "You *told* her?"

"I told her everything."

A lump caught in my throat. "Do they think we're awful?"

Jill shook her head. "Ruby made you this." She handed me a homemade card. It was covered with banana stickers, paper birds and paint that hadn't even dried yet.

The inside read, *'Dear Livi, We love you. From your crazy Leeds family!'* All of the Ricos had signed it. Ruby had written, *'You're the bestest BESTEST friend I've EVER had.'*

I covered my face with my hands and sobbed.

My dad called that evening. It sounded like he was on a train because the line was funny and we kept getting cut off.

"Livi, I'm sorry about ev... sorry, tunnel... and I hope you under... tunnel..."

"Dad, I can't hear you properly."

"I just... and I thought.... love you Livi."

"I know."

"I'm not...[91] I'm not a villain, Livi."

"I know," I said again.

"I'll call you soon."

"Okay. Bye."

Afterwards, I thought of a million things I should have said and a million more things I should have asked. His words, or at least those I had heard, swam round my head all night and I rehearsed over and over what I wished I'd said instead.

'I'm not a villain, Livi.'

'I wish you were,' I would say.

'What?'

'If you were bad, truly bad, and you hated me, then I could hate you back and not feel guilty. But, because you love me— in

---

[91] This was a real pause, not a tunnel.

your own strange way— you're not all bad which makes everything confusing and all the more painful. So your love, which you thrust upon me as though it's a blessing, is actually a curse.'

'Oh, Livi, I had no idea...'

'I'm going to go now. Jill wants me.'

I rehearsed the speech all week but he didn't call again. I think he's gone to Hollywood to be a magician. He's getting really good at disappearing.

~*~

I wanted to stay off school for the rest of the term but Jill said I had to go in on the last day because I couldn't miss my Drama show.

"I don't mind missing it," I said. "I'm only a rubbish part."

But Jill insisted that it would be good for me. "I'm missing an afternoon of work especially to watch you," she said.

"You hate work!" I snorted. "You'd miss an afternoon of work to watch paint dry if you could!"

Jill laughed before saying seriously, "Even so. You'll feel a lot better if you do it."

I very much doubted that but I got out of bed with a moan and pulled my school uniform off the floor.

Jill must have told Ruby that I was going back to school because, twenty minutes later, she came knocking and asked if I wanted to walk together. I nodded and tried to smile, hoping she would take that as a hint not to ask any annoying questions. Thankfully, she just smiled back and we walked the whole journey side by side in silence.

When we got to the school gates, Ruby took hold of my arm and whispered, "I'm glad you're back, Livi."

I felt my eyes filling with tears as I sniffed and said, "Thanks, Ruby."

The day passed rather uneventfully. I thought everybody would be looking at me strangely and wondering where I'd been all week but my absence appeared to have gone unnoticed and nobody even batted an eyelid when I came through the door for morning registration.

Most of our teachers let us chat and play silly games because it was the last day— except for Fester who tried to get us to do a worksheet on polygons. School would be finishing early to make time for our Drama performance so Fester's class was the last one of the term.

Naturally, nobody did a single bit of work. Ritchie Jones even took the liberty to get out his phone and play some tunes. Some of the girls sang along and Fester tried to silence them by throwing out vain threats like, "I can still give you a detention, you know!" but nobody took any notice.

Ruby and I played hangman over our worksheets and doodled on the polygons to turn them into monsters.

Every now and then I looked over at Fester. I wondered if he was going to tell me off for being rude to him the other day but the lesson passed without him so much as glancing in my direction. He just sat poring over his own polygon sheet, although I doubt he was drawing monsters on his.

As the bell rang, our class cheered and ran for the door.

Ruby grinned at me. "Our doom awaits!"

I gave a melodramatic groan as I packed up my bag and followed her out.

As I passed Fester's desk, he looked up and gave a quick smile.

I gave him half a smile in return. "Happy Christmas, Fes— Mr Lester."

"Happy Christmas, Livi. See you next year."

Miss Waddle was dressed in an elegant two piece suit and looked quite startled (like an alert guinea pig in fancy dress) as she ordered us straight into the changing rooms. When we were all ready, she ushered us into the Drama studio and made us undergo an elaborate warm-up routine before getting incredibly teary about how proud of us she was.[92] Then she gave us one last thumbs-up as she led the way into the theatre.

The audience were chattering excitedly but fell silent when they saw us. We scampered onto the stage and took our positions, me as the back door and Ruby as the window.

The lights came up for the opening song[93] and I sang my heart out, fixing a militant expression on my face, despite facing the back of the stage.

---

[92] I assumed she wasn't really thinking about me and Ruby when she said this but I tried to look pleased with myself regardless.

[93] *'If walls could talk, these ones would weep; and this door would run, if it only had feet.'*

250

As the song ended, the audience chuckled at the sight of Ritchie Jones dressed as Father Christmas.

He grinned cockily before proclaiming, *"Come with me to fair Verona where two houses are torn apart by a feud. If they don't learn to get along, somebody could get seriously hurt..."*

This was followed by a fight scene featuring absolutely none of the moves we had choreographed weeks ago in class.

The first scene ended and Ruby and I went to sit at the side of the stage with the rest of the chorus or, as Miss Waddle calls us, *'the weak actors.'*

Even though I was barely visible to the audience, I tried to stay focused by pretending I was a citizen of Verona, perhaps a lady selling flowers at the side of the road. There were several long scenes where we had nothing to do except sing from the side and, once or twice, I had to stifle a yawn. It came to the scene where Romeo and Juliet first proclaim their love for one another and Ruby and I traipsed back onto the stage to form a piece of the balcony.

Freddie Singh, who I thought was doing a sterling job as Romeo, was hoisted onto the shoulders of Wayne Purdy who was playing a sweaty tree. Freddie's sleeves were a little long so he looked even smaller than usual and a few audience members tittered as he exclaimed, *"It's me, fair Dooliet!"*

Kitty grimaced and began one of her long sections. She got most of the way through it then froze. The colour drained from her face and she stood gaping for a long time as she fumbled for her line.

Someone in the audience coughed.

Ruby caught my eye and raised her eyebrows.

At the side of the stage, Miss Waddle was frantically scouring the script but, in her haste, the script slipped out of her hands and onto the floor. Kitty looked utterly mortified as she stood in the full glare of the lights, looking helplessly at the rest of us.

I sucked in my cheeks before prompting as quietly as possible, *"Deny yourself and take all of me instead."*

Kitty blinked at me. "What?"

At this, the audience laughed.

Kitty went bright red. She chewed her lip and shot me a desperate stare.

"Deny yourself and take all of me instead," I whispered again.

Kitty nodded and turned back to Freddie. *"Deny yourself and take all of me instead!"* she said loudly.

Someone in the audience gave a cheer.

The rest of the show went without a hitch. The audience seemed to enjoy it. At any rate, they laughed at most of the jokes, although somebody's grandma fell asleep on the front row.

As my big line approached, I started to feel a little nervous. Kitty and Freddie were halfway through the death scene and I had a sudden irrational fear that my dad might come in and ask why I wasn't playing the lead. I squinted into the audience and saw Jill and Belinda on the third row. Jill caught my eye and grinned. I gave her a quick smile before looking away.

Kitty gave her last line, contorting her face as she squeezed out one little tear, and then died in spectacular fashion.

Several of us came and stood sombrely over the bodies of Romeo and Juliet, and Molly Masterson squawked out a tune on the flute as we scattered petals across the front of the stage.

I stood in the middle and proclaimed, *"A tragedy of love cut short!"* indicating Kitty and Freddie who lay fidgeting by my feet.

Ritchie Jones, still dressed as Father Christmas, stepped forwards to conclude the action. *"Never was a story of more woe than this of Juliet and her Romeo."*

At this, Kitty and Freddie arose to sing the final song with the rest of the cast. The song was called *'The Dead Roses'* and, like the rest of the music, had been composed by Miss Waddle herself. She stood at the side and mouthed all the words.

When we finished, the audience erupted in applause. Kitty and Freddie stepped forwards to bow, followed by the rest of us. Then, after a moment of lingering, we ran off the stage giddy with excitement.

"You said your line really well, Livi!" Ruby whispered, grabbing my arm as we hurried back to the changing rooms.

"Thanks. You looked good in your *Surprised Priest* bit."

"Thanks!"

We changed out of our costumes and our classmates sang Christmas songs as they celebrated the end of term. I wished I was carefree enough to sing along but, at the mention of *Christmas* and *spending time with family,* I felt rather sad.

On our way out of the changing rooms Ruby nudged me and asked, "What are you doing for Christmas?"

"We're going to Aunt Claudia's." I wrinkled up my nose. "But we'll be home for New Year's Eve."

She looked at me curiously. *"Home* as in *Leeds?"*

I let out a long breath as I realised what I'd said. "Yeah," I said finally, giving her a playful shove.

I rolled my eyes as she grinned.

Leeds is my home, I told myself. *This is my school. And Ruby is my best friend.*

We wandered into the foyer, looking out for Jill and Belinda. Before we could spot them, I saw Ms Sorenson and my heart beat wildly as she waved and came over.

"Well done, girls!" she exclaimed. "You were great."

"We were just rubbish parts," I said shyly.

Ms Sorenson shook her head. "No you weren't. The scene where you reminded Kitty of her line was my favourite bit." She gave me a wink and walked off.

A little packet of joy exploded in my chest. "I'm going to audition for a main part next year!" I told Ruby, much to her amusement.

Then Jill came over, followed by Belinda, and both of them hugged us and said well done.

"Aren't you glad you came in for that?" Jill said with a smile.

I shrugged and said, "Don't know."

We made our way across the foyer and I turned to say goodbye to Ruby.

"It's alright," said Jill. "Ruby and Belinda are coming back with us."

Belinda beamed and added, "Your kind sister gave me a lift here."

I grinned as I linked arms with Ruby and headed for the door. We passed Kitty Warrington who was in tears as her mother told her off for forgetting her line.

"You looked so *foolish* out there, forgetting such a simple line! Somebody from the *chorus* had to help you!" her mother scolded.

Kitty tried to protest then saw me watching and turned away.

I felt a bit bad for her but I also felt rather smug. And then I felt guilty for feeling smug. I wished I was such a good person that I only ever felt good thoughts even for my worst enemies. But I've tried to be good and I officially *cannot do it.*

As we drove out of the car park, Belinda jabbered away about how amazing the show had been. I don't know whether or not Jill agreed but she did a good job at sounding like she did. I smiled to myself and turned back to look at our school one last time.

It was the end of my first term in Leeds and school had taught me that animals that are poorly adapted to their environment are less likely to survive than those that are well adapted, there are three types of averages in maths, some Jews write God's name as 'G-d' for fear of disrespecting him, and Hitler was the worst person who ever lived. However, this term I have also learnt that there is no conclusive proof that the dinosaurs went extinct, *'eleven plus two'* is an anagram of *'twelve plus one,'* everybody wants to be safe but nobody likes to think they need saving, and the worst person who ever lived is me.

~ 30 ~

A greater story still

Before we left for Aunt Claudia's, I went over to the Ricos' to exchange gifts with Ruby.

Jill stopped me at our door and handed me a wrapped package. "Give this to Belinda," she said dismissively.

I raised an eyebrow. "What is it?"

"Tea leaves."

"You bought them a present?"

Jill rolled her eyes. "I'm just being polite."

I giggled as I shook the package and hurried across the street.

Belinda answered the door and (in her own words) was *'touched to pieces'* by Jill's gift. "This is a little something for the two of you," she added, handing me a dish covered in foil.

"What is it?"

"Shoo-fly pie. Just heat it in the oven for thirty minutes."

I smiled and made my way upstairs.

I was incredibly excited about my Christmas present for Ruby. I'd done some research on the internet and discovered that collecting banana stickers isn't so strange after all. In fact, there are plenty of avid collectors. One lady has over 10,000. There are even conventions. After a lot of correspondence I'd managed to acquire six rare banana stickers marked *'Rooby'* from a lady in Canada. All she'd wanted in return was packaging from some British beetroot. I'd stuck the stickers onto some sparkly card and wrapped it carefully in yellow tissue paper.

Ruby's eyes widened when she opened it. "How did you get these? They're amazing!" She threw her arms around me.

"I thought you'd like them," I said proudly.

"I do!" Ruby couldn't stop staring at them. She handed me a small rectangular present. "Okay, open yours now!"

I grinned and tore into the shiny green paper. It was the free red Bible that I'd given Ruby at our joint birthday party.

Ruby beamed. "I thought you might want it some time."

I wasn't sure what to say. I didn't know if she was playing a prank on me; some kind of belated revenge for giving her such an awful birthday present.

"Thanks..." I said.

She kept grinning. "You're welcome."

~*~

We arrived at Aunt Claudia's in time for dinner. She had cooked lamb, of course. Other than a paltry stump of a tree in the corner of the room, you couldn't tell it was Christmas. Aunt Claudia said decorating the house with baubles and fairy lights was far too much effort.

"And it looks ridiculous too!" she added, mint sauce dribbling down her chin. "Who wants some fat old man hanging in the window anyway?"

Jill gave a quick smile and said nothing.

I shoved some lamb into my mouth and eyed Jill carefully. I hoped she was alright. She hadn't said much on the drive down. The next morning we would be going to our mother's grave. She had died around Christmas so visiting her grave on Christmas Day had become a bit of a tradition. I was suddenly aware of how extra painful this time of year must be for my sister. I caught her eye and gave what I hoped was my most loving smile.

She smiled back. "What did Ruby give you for Christmas?"

I made a big deal of chewing my food and flapping my arms around in the hope that Jill would get bored and move on. She just looked at me expectantly.

"A Bible," I said finally.

"A Bible?"

"Yes, a Bible." I didn't add that it was the very same Bible that I had given her three months ago, and a *free* Bible at that.

Aunt Claudia gave a snort. "She's not one of those God Botherers, is she?"

"She's a bit weird," Jill replied.

"She's really nice!" I exclaimed.

"I didn't say she wasn't nice," Jill insisted. "Just that she's a bit weird."

"Well, she's *my* weirdo."

Aunt Claudia chortled at that. "Good for you, Livi."

Later, I retrieved the red Bible from the pocket of my suitcase. I hadn't noticed until now but Ruby had written inside the front cover, *'Dear Livi, I hope you find the answers you're looking for. Love from Ruby.'*

I looked at it for a moment before whispering, "Is my mum in Heaven?" I shut my eyes, flicked through the Bible and jammed my finger into a random page. Heart racing, I peered at what had been chosen.

'Neither circumcision nor uncircumcision means anything; what counts is a new creation.'

What was that supposed to mean? I turned the Bible over in confusion. Maybe I didn't do it right. I tried again. "Will my dad come back?"

'The LORD is gracious and compassionate, slow to anger and rich in love.'

Well, that made slightly more sense but it didn't really answer my question. I shook the book, breathed deeply and tried one last time. "Are you real?"

'Jesus replied, "Feed my sheep."'

Jesus kept sheep? Or was he talking in code? I kicked myself for being so stupid as to try Violet's dumb game. With a yell of fury, I threw the Bible across the room. Then I feared God would be angry with me for throwing his sacred book so I quickly retrieved it as I cried, "Why are you so complicated?"

I'd wanted to give Jill a really special Christmas present to make amends for everything that had happened recently. I spent ages trying to make her name into an anagram but 'J's are pretty awkward. The best I could come up with was *'Jilliana Starling: Lil' Jar, Giant Snail.'* I used it as a stimulus to write a story about a lonely snail trapped in a tiny bottle. It began with the words, *'Dear old snail you may be grown, but still you're lost and far from*

home...' It ended with the snail being rescued by the singing of a bird called *'Sister Starling.'*

Jill started crying when she read it. Aunt Claudia couldn't see what all the fuss was about.

"This is for you," I said with a grin, tossing our aunt a fleecy jumper covered in cats. "I've seen lots of old ladies wearing them in Leeds market."

She loved it and pulled it on immediately. I took a sneaky photo on my phone and sent it to Ruby.

Jill gave me a dress and a notebook covered in hummingbirds.[94] Aunt Claudia gave us a grotesque garden gnome[95] and a music compilation entitled *'Winter Chills.'* We put the CD on in the car on the way to the cemetery. It was the most horrendous excuse for music I've ever heard and mainly consisted of what I imagined to be middle-aged women singing through a sock. I saw Jill wrinkling up her nose and fiddling with the volume control while Aunt Claudia sang her heart out.

As we drew near to the cemetery, Jill switched the music off and said, "Let's save some for later."

"Good idea," said Aunt Claudia. "We don't want to spoil ourselves."

Jill pulled into a parking space and we got out. There was nobody around besides a dog walker who smiled and bid us a merry Christmas.

I gave the dog walker a grim smile. It's hard to know how jolly you should be in a cemetery.

Aunt Claudia shivered and said, "Trust your mother to die in the winter!"

I glared at her. "You can stay in the car if you want!"

"Don't be rude, Livi." Aunt Claudia shook her head and muttered something to Jill about the youth of today.

Jill gave her a polite nod.

We wandered through the graveyard, following the familiar maze of tombstones and ornaments towards our mother's grave. Hers is between a marble angel and a conveniently placed bench. The bench has somebody else's name on it but, in my mind, it's my mother's bench. Whenever I sit on it, I leave a little space for Mum.

---

[94] I had also asked for a personalised handkerchief in case I am ever kidnapped but she didn't get me that.

[95] It was three-foot tall and held a gun. "We don't have a garden," said Jill. "I know. But you should," our aunt replied.

It's the closest thing I have to sitting with her on a sofa. I made myself comfortable and looked over at her cobalt tombstone. It looked rather simple compared to the marble angel beside it.

Jill leant over and laid a wreath then came and sat beside me. Knowing my ritual of pretending our mother is there, she left a space between us. This left little room for Aunt Claudia who perched awkwardly on the arm of the bench. None of us spoke.

I stuck out my tongue as it started to snow.

Beside us, Aunt Claudia was sighing and twitching and muttering under her breath.

Eventually Jill turned and hissed, "Aunt Claudia, go and wait in the car!"

Aunt Claudia shot her an affronted look but grudgingly did as she was told.

I tried to catch Jill's eye to congratulate her but she wouldn't look at me so I went back to staring at our mother's grave. The wreath was fast becoming submerged in snow. I thought about how, if our mother had lived, the rift between her and Jill may have lasted forever. Perhaps I would never have met Jill. Would I rather have had my mother? I started to shiver and it wasn't just because of the snow. Jill put her arm around me as I shuffled across the space between us and leant into her shoulder. As I stared and stared at my mother's grave, life suddenly felt so temporary and fleeting. *Is this really it?* Is the meaning of life really just to be happy for a short time, filling your life with as much meaning as possible before the darkness takes you away? A lump caught in my throat. I want there to be something *more* after I die. And I don't care if it doesn't make sense or isn't mathematical.

I closed my eyes and begged God silently, *I WANT to believe. Help me believe. I want you to be real. I want you to love me, if that's what you're all about. If that's possible...*

I looked back at my mother's grave and wondered for the millionth time how I would like to die. *Happy, laughing, of something sensible, not of something silly like Human Monkeypox... Not that it matters. Once you're gone, you're gone, right? Unless there's some divine castle in the clouds... I want to get to the castle... I want to see the king... I'm at a crossroads and I don't know which way to go...*

As the snow got heavier, I squeezed my eyes shut again and pleaded, *God, if you're real... please give me a sign...*

At that moment, Jill nudged me and pointed. I opened my eyes just in time to see a deer emerge from the trees ahead. It was tall and slender with massive grey antlers and it looked utterly at home amongst the snowy graves. My heart caught in my throat as it looked up. It seemed to gaze straight at us as it sauntered gracefully across our path.

Jill smiled at me but didn't say anything.

"Jill," I whispered urgently. "Do you believe in God?"

She shrugged. "Sometimes."

"Right now," I pushed. "This very second, do you believe in him?"

Jill looked away for a long time. Then she said, "No."

I felt deeply disappointed. I was so sure that if she'd said yes then I'd have believed too.

When we got back to Aunt Claudia's I rang Ruby. I asked about her Christmas and she told me about her mother dropping the roast potatoes, Violet making art out of the Christmas cracker hats and Oscar blowing up the Christmas tree with his new chemistry set. I laughed at all the right bits.

"How about you?" she asked.

I took a deep breath and told her about the deer. "I thought it was God giving me a sign," I admitted. "But Jill clearly didn't think so. So how do I know which one of us is right?"

Ruby thought for a moment. "Maybe you were both right."

"How?"

"God doesn't always talk to everybody in the same way. You asked for a sign so maybe he gave you one. Jill didn't ask for anything so she just saw a deer."

"But what if I'm wrong? What if it was just a deer?"

Ruby sighed. "Then it was just a deer."

~*~

The next day, I went for a walk around Aunt Claudia's field. It was covered in a blanket of untouched snow and I walked as softly as I could, savouring the beautiful crunching sound under my feet. As I crossed the middle I stopped at the sight of a dead mouse. It had probably frozen to death, poor thing. I stared at it and marvelled at the fact that it had probably lived its whole life without knowing what it was. Animals are lucky in that way. They might get startled by predators or loud noises but they don't sit around wondering where they came from or how they're going to die.

I took my phone out to take a picture and then reconsidered and put it away. Instead, I covered the mouse with some snow and placed a holly leaf over the top.

I walked slowly back to my room and lay on my bed. I thought about the mouse's corpse rotting away until its DNA unwound completely. If we are just a bunch of random atoms then why do we *care* about things? Why do we long for love and happiness and meaning?

There was a sudden knock on my door, followed by Aunt Claudia calling, "Do you want a turkey sandwich, Livi?"

"No thanks," I yelled back.

"Okay, love." There was a pause, then she added, "I'll be downstairs if you need me."

I rolled my eyes at the idea that I might need her. Immediately, I felt a pang of guilt. *How awful not to be needed.* I bit my lip as I glanced round the room. The walls were plastered with rosettes from various cat shows and, behind the door, a large poster read, *'Twenty reasons why cats are better than men.'*

I got up to have a closer look.

'1. When they tell you they love you, you know they mean it...'

As I read down the list, I found myself wondering what Aunt Claudia had been like when she was my age. Did she smile more? Did she send other things besides dead lamb in the post? Did she ever lie awake secretly wishing she was great? Had she been bitter and miserable her whole life or did something happen to make her that way? I realised that if my understanding of my sister could be so small then I certainly didn't know Aunt Claudia. She must have a past. She must have reasons for choosing cats over men. She must have some private heartache which caused her to live alone, never daring to love or be loved.

The poster ended with: *'20. They don't notice when you're ugly.'*

I stopped and thought about this. The only way you can know that you're *truly* lovable is if you can find somebody who loves you despite knowing all the ugly things about you. There is a chance that nobody will. Perhaps Aunt Claudia was too scared to find out. Maybe that's why she'd stuck with cats.

My gaze fell on my Bible. I picked it up and whispered, "I don't want to get scared of love and buy a hundred cats."

I flicked carelessly through it and then stopped. On one page, Ruby had highlighted a piece of text. It said simply, *'God is love.'* In the margin, she'd drawn a bird and written in tiny writing, *'Faith is not a leap into the dark. It's a journey towards the light.'*

I stared at it before saying out loud, "But how do I know it's safe?"

I remembered Ruby's suggestion that I should let Jesus love me first.

"But how do I do that?" I muttered. *And does he really love me? Like Jill does, and not just out of duty? What if I get too close and he tells me I'm too ugly after all?*

~*~

The rest of our stay at Aunt Claudia's was boring and uneventful. I saw one of the cats fall off the windowsill but that was about it. During a particularly heavy snowfall I tried to cajole Jill and Aunt Claudia into going outside for a snowball fight, but my paranoid sister said she didn't want to get her feet wet[96] and my miserable aunt warned me that taking the snow off the top of her wheelie bin counted as theft. We were meant to stay until New Year's Eve but, a couple of days early, Jill announced that she needed to get back to do some work.

I knew for a fact that this wasn't true, that actually she was beginning to get irritated with Aunt Claudia's constant fussing and moaning, but I was glad so I added, "I have some homework too."

Jill caught my eye and we shared a smile. Perhaps she won't turn out like Aunt Claudia after all.

Aunt Claudia hugged us, told us to *'be good,'*[97] and sent us away with a kilogram of lamb.

As we drove away it began to snow again. I prayed and prayed that God would send me another deer and kept my eyes peeled the whole way home but I didn't see one. In the end, I pulled out my life story and flicked through it, doodling here and there and wondering which pages I would some day be tearing out. This isn't the story I'd intended to write. I'd thought I was somebody special, destined for greatness, unravelling my grand narrative for a future

---

[96] "Frostbite is a very serious thing, Livi!"
[97] Fat chance.

generation. As I scribbled across the front page, I felt silly and ashamed for thinking that mine is the greatest story ever told. I really am just a drop in the ocean.

The snow was pretty thick when we got back to Leeds. As we came to a stop outside our house we noticed a big creature made of snow by the front door.

"What is that—?" Jill began. Then she stopped because across the street Ruby had emerged from her house.

I waved and grinned. It was good to be home.

"Want to come over, Livi?" Ruby asked, greeting me with a hug.

I looked at Jill. "Is that alright?"

"Of course. Oh and Ruby, is this snowman from you?"

"Yeah," Ruby said shyly. "It's a diplodocus."

"Really?" Jill stared at it for a moment. "It's... lovely. Thanks."

Ruby beamed.

I smiled at Jill as I crossed the street with Ruby.

Her and Violet's floor was covered in a massive nativity scene made from tinsel and tissue paper. I stepped over it and perched next to Ruby on her bed. We talked about snow for a while and about how good it would be if it snowed so much that school got cancelled. Then we talked about Christmas pudding and how nobody we know really likes it.

Finally Ruby said, "It's pretty cool about that deer you saw."

"Yeah," I said quietly. I pretended to look around her room. Violet's painting of Jesus on the cross caught my eye. I sighed as I read the familiar words at the bottom. *'God loved the people of this world so much that he gave his only Son, so that everyone who has faith in him will have eternal life and never really die.'* I read it again. *'...everyone who has faith in him will have eternal life...'* Was it *really* that simple? Just *believe* and you're saved? No hard work, no divine standard, no trying to be good?

"What are you thinking?" asked Ruby.

I blushed. I was about to say that I was thinking we should grab some trays and go sledging in the park. Instead, I blurted out, "I don't know what to believe."

"About God?"

I looked away. "It's like I *want* to believe, but something is stopping me."

Ruby gave an encouraging nod. "You're at a crossroads..."

I groaned but Ruby ignored me and continued, "You sort of believe but you're scared. I suppose you have to choose one path and then walk down it."

"It's not that simple."

"Do you want all the answers first?"

"Yes! I want to be *sure.*"

"Sure of what?"

"Sure that God is really *real!* Sure that Jesus actually *likes* me!"

"How sure?" Ruby asked.

I shrugged before saying bitterly, "I was sure I was destined for something great."

"What if you are?"

I rolled my eyes. "Don't say silly things."

"How sure?" she repeated. "*'There's-going-to-be-a-storm-tonight'* sure? Or, *'Dinosaurs-in-the-Congo'* sure? Or, *'If-I-get-into-this-car-it-probably-won't-crash'* sure?"

"What? I don't know! How sure are *you?*"

Ruby tilted her head to one side. "I'm very sure *now.* But, to begin with, it was just my best bet. It's like any friendship, I suppose. You don't know to begin with how it will work out. Like... When I first met you, I was scared that you didn't like me. But we got to know each other and eventually I felt less shy with you and look at us now!"

I gave a soft hum.

"Jesus is the same. He wants to be your friend and, if you say yes, then that friendship can grow and in time you'll be more sure."

"But I want to be sure *now.*"

"You want to know how much Jesus loves you?" Ruby pointed to Violet's painting, held her arms out wide, and said, "This much."

I looked from Ruby to Jesus, both with their arms outstretched, peace in her eyes and pain in his. It occurred to me for one dangerous moment that perhaps God was holding his breath, loving the world and desperate to be loved in return, waiting to see which path I would choose. Perhaps, when Jesus was hanging on the cross, paying for the sins of mankind, he was dying of a broken heart...

I gave a groan and put my head in my hands. "Fine! Just do it!"

Ruby didn't reply. I looked up to see her smiling at me.

"What?" I demanded.

"You want to ask Jesus into your life?" she whispered.

"Yes, yes, yes. Just stop saying it. It sounds ridiculous."

She smiled again. "Well, go on then."

I was aghast. "What do you mean, *'Go on then'?* Don't you need to sign me up to some course or do something to me or wave your hands over me?"

"No. You just need to tell God that you're sorry for living your life separate from him and that you believe Jesus died for all the things you've ever done wrong and you want him to come into your heart and help you live for *him.*"

"Is that it?"

"Yup."

"That's *it?*"

"Yup."

"And then I'll be one of *you?*"

Ruby giggled before saying seriously, "No, Livi. Then you'll finally be you."

~*~

A note from Ruby...

Dear Reader (that means YOU!)

I just want to tell you that no matter what your earthly family is like, you have a Father in Heaven who loves you and wants to spend time with you. He's not angry or distant and you don't have to be perfect before you come to him. In fact, you can't be. Just tell him you want him and he'll do the rest. He's waiting, arms outstretched, with a greater destiny for you than you could ever imagine. Like my mum always says, it doesn't matter if you mean nothing to the whole world, because you mean the whole world to him!

If you've never thought about God like that before, maybe take some time to ask Jesus to come and be your friend. He's dying to get to know you. I mean, literally, he actually died and then rose again— just for you!

Love and banana stickers,

Ruby E. Rico

Lightning Source UK Ltd.
Milton Keynes UK
UKHW010603090819
347684UK00001B/79/P